INVASION!
The Fury ships were closing.

In the captain's chair of the *U.S.S. Voyager,* Commander Chakotay could think of only one way out. *But do I have the guts to take it?* he asked himself. Chakotay shrugged, feeling his heart begin to race just at the thought; but he had no choice . . . he had to get the Furies off his tail, and that meant they had to think the *Voyager* was dead.

"B'Elanna," he said after a moment, "how long would it take you to reconfigure the shields to metaphasic?"

"About two minutes; but why would I want to . . . Chakotay! You *can't* be thinking of—"

He nodded, lips pressed together either in a grim smile or an amused grimace. "Set a new course," he said, "directly into the sun."

Look for STAR TREK Fiction from Pocket Books

Star Trek: The Original Series

Star Trek: The Next Generation

Star Trek: Deep Space Nine

Star Trek: Voyager

STAR TREK® VOYAGER™
INVASION!

BOOK FOUR

THE FINAL FURY

DAFYDD AB HUGH

INVASION! concept by John J. Ordover and Diane Carey

POCKET BOOKS
New York   London   Toronto   Sydney   Tokyo   Singapore

An *Original* Publication of POCKET BOOKS

POCKET BOOKS, a division of Simon & Schuster Inc.
1230 Avenue of the Americas, New York, NY 10020

A VIACOM COMPANY

This book is published by Pocket Books, a division of Simon & Schuster Inc., under exclusive license from Paramount Pictures.

ISBN: 0-671-54181-1

First Pocket Books printing August 1996

10 9 8 7 6 5 4 3 2 1

POCKET and colophon are registered trademarks of Simon & Schuster Inc.

Printed in the U.S.A.

THE FINAL FURY

PRELUDE

THE WAR RAGED FOR A HUNDRED THOUSAND YEARS.

The Furies once were hosts of heaven; but heaven was all but closed to them now. The Unclean swept across the vast expanse of space, across the 217 million star systems known mapped, and held in heaven by the Furies. The new enemy was unlike all those who had preceeded it: alone among the sentient races of the galaxy, the insectoid Unclean were unaffected by the Terrors unleashed upon the disobedient by the lords of heaven.

Taken by surprise, the host—six hundred and sixty-six separate races bound together into a single people—were driven first from the planets at the rim of the galaxy, whence the Unclean invaded, drinking energy and draining away the life-force of entire armadas of a million ships or more. Perhaps the Unclean were the cursed union of vermin and castaway subjects, fleeing their rightful lord on the Throne of the Autocrat. Perhaps instead they came from *outside,* and were not of this galaxy at all; the latter was the more popular speculation among the war leaders among the Furies—it mattered not, for the Unclean burst upon the righteous hosts like an ocean upon the volcano, washing them away.

A fragment of a story dating from that dark time hinted at a greater darkness: that the subject races cast their lot *with the Unclean,* rebelling against their righteous masters. They stood their ground even when the Furies sent the Terrors. Though the subject races died like bugs beneath the Fury heel, and though the Terror lash was used against them over and over, still they maintained, fighting until the end of the first millennium—when the Furies were forced to retreat from the rim of the galaxy.

The farthest provinces were lost.

For century after century, the Furies retreated. There were battles—many times, the hosts stood against monstrous swarms that flew through the starry void without ships, without life-support. The first great stand engaged 93,109,907 Fury vessels carrying enough warriors to people a hundred planets against Unclean too numerous to count; but the records left by Subcrat Ramszak the Ok'San, who stood four meters tall and sported a hand where one ear should have been, gave the count as more than ten Unclean for every Fury.

The *last* great stand involved a mere fifty thousand ships, give or take, with warriors spread thin among them. Tiin, the Cannibal Whose Bed Would Not Be Shared, commanded the final defense, this time from the Autocrat's chair; Tiin traced his ancestory back through an entirely male line for a thousand generations to Ramszak himself, but he fared no better than his illustrious but defeated ancestor.

A small fleet of a few thousand ships lured the main contingent of the wasplike Unclean by attacking them from out of the black. The attack broke a four-century truce; but the hosts of heaven were not bound by promises made to insect minds.

The Unclean responded to the taunt. The entire remaining *field-unity* of Unclean pursued the marauding fleet; and when the last Fury ships retreated, they numbered twenty-one out of more than four thousand.

The enemy approached them from different vectors; but

when the swarms assembled for attack, and the Furies prepared to die, a blast of light engulfed them. The Furies fell through nonspace, their minds reeling from the passage.

The enemy made to follow the hosts . . . but as they approached, the light changed, their space-born, space-living bodies melted, fused, reduced in seconds to atoms, and then less than atoms, and everything at last, after many steps, over the space of microseconds, transmuting to dead.

The light was so great that scientists among the subject races would be able to detect it even after three or four millennia. The swarms were decimated but not annihilated; the remaining wasps fell upon few remaining Furies as they passed through the swirling, gaseous debris that had once been living members of the Unclean.

Tiin was unprepared for his responsibility; he was, in the end, a poor representative of the line that had begun with Subcrat Ramszak. He lost control of his few ships, and the captains panicked, firing wildly . . . almost as if they were suddenly bathed with their own Terrors—though all Furies were, quite simply, immune to fear themselves.

Against the backdrop of a sky turned negative, black suns silhouetted against a sky yet white from the collapsing stars, a single, small host made the journey along the entirety of the wormhole, a trip that took four years—or no time at all. When they reached the other side, the light faded. Wherever they were, there would be no return to their bright black heaven.

It was not until they found and settled a planet that they realized the enormity of the Unclean victory . . . for the Furies were trapped in a hellish realm of space, so far from heaven that they sickened and began to die from sheer loneliness. The Fury surgeons studied the disease for hundreds of years. The symptoms were always the same: black depression, followed by ennui, then anomie, the loss of all ethical and moral boundaries. They grew their population, even while the best and most promising were struck down in their prime of intellect and will by the Factor, as it was called.

D'Mass, the greatest Autocrat-in-Exile, who was the last to unite all the Furies, himself diagnosed the Factor: they had lost their way, their purpose, their reason for existing. The hosts of heaven were born to *rule* heaven, not watch it from so far away that the light they observed was generated by the stars of heaven at precisely the moment when Ramszak had staked everything on an all-or-nothing bid to destroy the Unclean . . . and had lost.

Under D'Mass, all of the Furies worked together to develop and construct an artificial wormhole to bring them back home. But when D'Mass died, his two sons fell to quarreling between themselves.

In the end, D'Vass sought to leave with nine-tenths of the Furies to found a new world and forget about heaven; while his brother Bin Mass chose to stay and direct all efforts to the artificial wormhole. But Bin Mass could not afford to lose the talent in D'Vass's host; they battled from dawn until dusk, then slept together as brothers, only to wake and do battle again. Millions of Furies died in the war, slain by their brothers out of heaven. At last, D'Vass fled—but with a greatly diminished host, a mere forty thousand.

Bin Mass had conquered the hearts of his people; and by rededicating the Fury hosts to reclaiming heaven, no matter how long it might take, he conquered the Factor as well. No longer were the Furies lost and wandering; now they were focused and driven.

They would eradicate the Unclean from the blessed place, no matter what the cost. The time would be ripe someday; the moment would come. And when it did, the galaxy would tremble once more to the cold, brittle voice of the Autocrat.

CHAPTER

1

Captain Kathryn Janeway of the *U.S.S. Voyager* sat behind the desk in her quarters, swaying gently, trying to avoid actually becoming ill onto the stack of duty rosters littering the desktop. The ship rolled back and forth, causing the fluids in her inner ear to perform acrobatics.

Well, I knew it was going to happen, she thought; this far from the Federation, from the nearest starbase, without any chance for maintenance or repair other than what the crew did themselves, Janeway knew the ship systems would begin to fail, one by one.

Unfortunately, the most recent one to fail was the inertial damper/gravitic stabilizer system. Motion that ordinarily would be damped down to a slight vibration instead became a lurching, rolling gait that was causing terrible havoc with crew health . . . and morale.

Is this the torture that sailors on the old oceangoing ships had to endure? she wondered, swallowing several times. *If it is, I wonder how anyone survived to cross a small lake, let alone an entire ocean!*

She stood, feeling the air clammy against her sweaty skin.

Like most everyone else in Starfleet, Captain Janeway had ridden on sailboats, sloops, four-masters—in the holodeck. Controlled by a friendly computer that understood the unpleasantness of seasickness and minimized the roll, pitch, and especially yaw.

But the present nauseating dance was constant, uncontrolled, interminable . . . and worse, it included the fear, haunting the back of her mind, that if the ship hit a subspace fiber bundle, they would lurch violently—as they already had once, throwing everything, including Captain Janeway herself, to the deck in a heap.

Or into a bulkhead, headfirst; the holographic doctor was already treating one crew member who had fractured one of his vertebrae and suffered a serious concussion; the next time, someone could be killed.

Janeway cleared her throat, swallowing again. "Janeway to Torres," she croaked; her voice was so strained, it took the computer a moment to recognize her.

"T-Torres here," said the equally strangled voice of the *Voyager*'s chief engineer, Lieutenant B'Elanna Torres; Janeway felt an uncaptainlike pleasure when she noted that Torres's vaunted Klingon half did not prevent her from being as spacesick as the rest of the crew.

"Do you have a new time estimate?"

There was no need to specify any further; the only problem on anybody's mind on the ship was the failure of the gravitic stabilizers.

"Estimate . . . excuse me, Captain." The sound cut off momentarily. When it returned, B'Elanna Torres's voice sounded a bit weaker. "Estimate unchanged. Twelve to twenty-four hours, depending on . . ."

"On?"

"On whether we can fix it at all, using these damned bureaucratic, stupid, useless—"

A new voice chimed in, annoyed; Lieutenant Carey rose to defend Federation procedure against unorthodoxy.

"Depending on whether someone who shall remain nameless will just stick to the process, instead of trying a hundred so-called shortcuts!"

Damn, thought the captain; *they've been doing so well!* It must be the nausea, she decided; everyone was edgy, including Janeway herself.

The captain reached into the depths of her soul, bypassing as well as she could the depths of her stomach; she spoke with the Command Tone she had learned at the Academy. *"That is enough,* people. We're in a difficult enough situation without you two bickering. Torres, would it help if I were to reconfigure the stabilizers to run off the replicator-holodeck power grid?"

"Nothing will help," said the half-Klingon engineer, letting her pessimistic human side take over. "We'll never get the ship steady. I'm sick, and I just wish I were back in a nice, safe Maquis ship without all this weird, bioneural circuitry!"

Janeway forced the conversation back to solutions. "I'm going to redirect the power; keep working, stop arguing, and give me a better time estimate in fifteen minutes. Janeway out."

The captain stood; it was hard to maintain balance with the deck rolling beneath her feet, but the nausea was less intense. If the *Voyager* struck another subspace fiber bundle, she would just have to hope she didn't break anything on the way down.

Her stateroom was spacious by Starfleet standards . . . almost as large as any bachelor apartment in a minor city on any insignificant planet in the Federation. But she loved it; it was hers. The entire ship was her stateroom.

A voice full of peeved indignation invaded her space. "Neelix to Captain Janeway!" Neelix, the ship's Talaxian cook, had never quite caught on to the fact that he did not need to bellow when initiating communications; the computer would figure it out at normal speaking volume.

"Janeway here. What's wrong, Neelix?" She was glad not to be in Neelix's kitchen; she could imagine the carnage wreaked upon pots, pans, and vats of food by the failed stabilizers.

"What's wrong is this insufferable turbulence! I'm trying to prepare a bravura meal for the crew, and I can't even keep my ingredients from flying off the counters onto the floor!"

"Neelix, don't you think if we could stop the rolling, we would have already?" *Ouch! Didn't mean to be that harsh.* "We're working on it, Neelix." She leaned against her desk as the ship lurched again; a stack of reports fell to the deck with a loud clatter.

"Well, why don't you simply *stop the ship* until you fix the problem? Surely we can afford one or two days' delay. But we can ill afford a crew too sick to even enjoy the simple, culinary pleasures."

Janeway rolled her eyes, grateful that the comm link was auditory only. She waited a couple of beats until she could speak calmly. "Neelix, if we stop the ship in our present situation, without gravitic stabilizers, the angular velocity of the warp-core reaction itself will cause the ship to start spinning like a top."

"Really? What an odd design decision."

"We're going the speed we're going precisely because it minimizes the roll."

"This is the minimum?"

"This *is* the minimum, Neelix. Now please return to your duties and let me return to mine. Janeway . . . wait, what did you say you were cooking?"

"I didn't say. I'm cooking pate of Denethan blood-bladder, Ocampan cream punch, and a Federation dish whose recipe I found in the computer . . . Three-Cheese Quiche!"

"Oh," said the captain, feeling her stomach begin to roll in the opposite direction from the ship. "Very—very good. Carry on. Janeway out."

Swallowing repeatedly, she shuffled forward through the door and onto the bridge. "Captain on the bridge," chimed the computer protocol program, but as usual nobody paid any attention; Captain Janeway was long on performance but short on ritual.

Everyone on the bridge looked grim-faced but determined; *determined not to disgrace himself by actually succumbing to spacesickness,* she thought. The curved bridge console actually seemed to warp slightly, another trick of the instability. Lieutenant Tom Paris used his elbows to steady himself against the helm; his hands played across the console, making minor adjustments. Janeway didn't know whether they did any good; perhaps it just made Paris feel better to be "doing something."

Ensign Harry Kim hunched over his console, staring at his viewer; he had nothing much to do at the moment, but he continued scanning the sector anyway . . . probably for the same reason Paris made continual course adjustments.

Janeway was surprised to note that even Lieutenant Tuvok, who normally stood at his tactical station, was seated.

She stood at the door to her ready room, preventing it from closing, and surveyed the bridge crew more carefully, assessing their health. Paris looked jovial and full of bonhomie; but he sweated profusely, and his face was white. Tuvok appeared at first glance to be unaffected by the ship's motion, but Janeway knew him well enough to understand that he felt as sick as everyone else; he simply placed the feeling in the same category as an emotion—something to be ignored and suppressed.

Commander Chakotay, sitting in his command chair, looked inquiringly at the captain, his face asking whether he should relinquish command. His face also looked slightly green.

Janeway smiled, gritting her teeth. "I see the ancient nausea remedy of your people worked no better for you than it did for me."

Chakotay tried unsuccessfully to smile. "It only works when the water comes from the Long Woman Mountains, not the replicator."

Of all the crew on the bridge, Kim was the only one completely unaffected by the rocking and rolling of the ship . . . a fact that Captain Janeway found both annoying and perplexing.

She sat heavily in her chair, whence she checked the forward viewer; the computer stabilized the image, but it couldn't stabilize Janeway's head. Thus, she saw the stars as jagged lines, rather than dots; the effect was disconcerting, to say the least.

"Ensign Kim," she called.

Harry Kim eagerly swiveled his chair around. "Yes, Captain?"

"I wrote a—excuse me—I wrote a program that transfers power from the replicator-holodeck power grid to the gravitic stabilizers. Implement it."

"Aye, Captain."

"Activate Emergency Medical Holographic Program."

The doctor's face suddenly appeared on the viewer; Janeway found him much easier to look at than the star jags.

"Please state the nature of the emergency," said the doctor as programmed; but he immediately appended "that is, if it's something different from the emergency I'm already very busy attending to."

"Doctor, *please* tell me you can do something."

If it was possible for a hologram to look pained, the doctor managed it. "Captain, the situation is unchanged. As I've told you, all my remedies lose efficacy over time. I presume that the ship will at some point, actually stop rolling. If you insist upon allowing the ship to continue rolling indefinitely, there is nothing I can do.

"The situation is unchanged here as well," said Janeway, softly.

"Correction," said Lieutenant Tuvok from his station; "the situation has changed rather dramatically."

The captain held up her hand to the doctor and turned to her science officer.

"Captain," continued Tuvok; "I am picking up a distress call."

"From whom?" asked Janeway, simultaneously grateful for the distraction and irked at the poor timing. "Is it any race we're familiar with?"

"Yes," said Tuvok, "we are quite familiar with the signal. The distress call is coming from a Starfleet shuttlecraft."

In the shocked silence, Captain Janeway asked, "Another wormhole? Is the signal current?" Once before, they had been fooled by a communication that came through a freak wormhole; but that transmission from a Romulan ship turned out to have come from decades in the past.

"The signal is of the type currently in use by Starfleet," said Tuvok; "it comes from a Galaxy-class starship shuttle-craft, the *Lewis,* which Starfleet records indicate is attached to the *U.S.S. Enterprise.*"

"Does its stardate match ours?"

"Yes, Captain. I do not believe the signal is coming to us through a wormhole. The indications are that the shuttle-craft is, indeed, in this quadrant, approximately two-point-one-five light-years distant."

Tuvok stood; Janeway noted that even the Vulcan had to grip his console to steady himself. "Captain, it is reasonable to assume that we are not the only representatives of the Federation in this quadrant. Despite the distance, which ordinarily is far beyond our capacity to scan in any detail, I picked up a single life-form aboard . . . a human male. He is not moving but is alive."

"How is this possible, Tuvok? That you could scan him, I mean."

"I can only conclude that something is boosting both transmissions, our scan and the shuttlecraft's distress call."

Janeway sat back, nonplussed. A *Federation* ship and pilot? She had dreamed of such a break for so many months; and now, maybe . . . maybe . . .

She dismissed the daydream. As captain, she had a job to do; she had a ship to protect. She could not allow her reason to be overwhelmed by what she *wanted* to be true.

"Shall I lay in the course, Captain?" asked Paris.

Captain Janeway hesitated. Under ordinary circum-stances, she would have assented even before Paris finished the question. But the circumstances were not ordinary.

She looked at Lieutenant Paris, who still wore his frozen smile, holding down his nausea by a great act of will. He sat poised over the helm console, ready to engage the course he had already computed.

Everyone stared at Janeway. *Oh well,* she thought, *I guess this is why they let me wear the four pips.*

"Stand by, Lieutenant Paris." She raised her voice. "Janeway to Torres. Lieutenant, have you been monitoring the distress call?"

"I just picked it up," came the engineer's voice, stronger now. "Captain, it might be a trap! We're being lured closer. . . . There couldn't possibly be a Federation ship out here."

"I might point out," said Tuvok, with impeccable, Vulcan logic, "that there *is* a Federation ship out here: the *U.S.S. Voyager.*"

"Tuvok's right," said Janeway; "if we can be sucked here by an unknown force, so can someone else."

"I can feel in my gut that there's something wrong with this entire setup," insisted B'Elanna.

Again, Tuvok spoke up. "Captain, Starfleet protocols require that we—"

"I am well aware of Starfleet protocols," sighed Janeway.

The question was, did the safety of her ship take precedence over a shuttlecraft distress call? And so far away from the Federation, was there even a Starfleet, let alone protocols?

As soon as she asked herself the question, she knew the answer. Wherever there was a Starfleet ship, there was Starfleet. "Lieutenant Paris, lay in a course and engage. If the door opens in one direction, perhaps it will open in the other direction as well."

"Everyone hold tight," warned Paris; "without the stabilizers, this is going to be a rough turn."

The captain braced, but she wasn't prepared for what she felt: the *Voyager* felt as though it suddenly accelerated *backward* at several g's. It was a trick of perspective; all the rolling was ultimately an illusion. *Under classic subspace theory,* she recalled, *the ship doesn't really exist at all at warp speed;* as near as Janeway could judge from watching the crew sway, no two members of the crew reacted to precisely the same motion.

They all reacted to a horrific forward force when they turned, however. Janeway felt as though she were dangled upside down by her feet with a kilogram weight attached to each eyeball; but when Paris completed the turn, the ship returned to the familiar enemy of stomach-churning rolls.

"En route to intercept the shuttlecraft," gasped Paris, swallowing hard.

"En route to intercept the shuttlecraft," gasped Paris, swallowing hard.

We had better have a plan of action long before we arrive, she decided. "In my ready room," said the captain, rising as smartly as possible under the circumstances.

The senior staff assembled around the discussion table— or the "peace rock," as Chakotay jokingly thought of it. Chakotay looked around the room, trying to gauge reactions: B'Elanna looked suspicious, Paris excited, Kim nervous, and Janeway worried.

The captain turned to her helmsman. "Mr. Paris, how long to reach the shuttlecraft?"

"I'd give it a good two days to be sure."

Chakotay spoke up. "We might be able to shave that down to twenty-four hours by accelerating to warp seven, but at that speed, we might lose some crew members to sudden gravitic neutralization."

"I'm not willing to risk killing my own crew," said Janeway. "The castaway will have to wait the extra day."

She looks haggard, thought Chakotay; *she's lost track of her spirit guide. Of course, so have we all,* he mentally appended; when mind and body were out of balance, mistakes became more likely.

"Mr. Tuvok," asked the commander, "how did you first pick up the signal?"

Tuvok still controlled the spacesickness that had laid low everyone else except Harry Kim. "Commander, the signal appeared mysteriously, already activated. I cannot be certain, but I believe I caught a faint echo from the wormhole itself. I was only able to scan at such a long distance by using the distress beacon as a carrier wave."

Janeway typed at her console, possibly playing with some equations. "People," she said, "I've modeled every variation for power-boosting I could think of, and I simply cannot come up with a scenario by which a shuttlecraft could project a distress beacon two light-years. A starship, maybe . . . but the power is simply not present on that shuttlecraft."

"The signal must be boosted somehow," said Tuvok.

B'Elanna Torres, sitting next to Chakotay, called up the schematics of the shuttlecraft; the commander watched over her shoulder. "You're right," said B'Elanna to the captain. "I *knew* there was something wrong with this entire scenario! It *is* a trap, and this proves it. We should get as far away from here as possible, Captain."

Ensign Kim sat on Chakotay's other side; the young man appeared to want to say something but was worried about interrupting his elders. Chakotay knew how he felt. "Mr. Kim, you have a comment?"

"Sir," said Kim, "when I was a kid, my best friend and I had a pair of communicators his mother gave us. We used to talk late at night, when we were supposed to be asleep, comparing interpretations of Paganini and Bizet."

B'Elanna stared at Kim for a moment, seemingly embarrassed. She opened her mouth to speak, but Chakotay put his hand on her arm.

Kim continued. "Then Alex moved to Singapore, far outside the range of the hand communicators we had. But we were still able to communicate: at prearranged times, we each got near the local comm-sat repeater, and it picked up the weak communicator signal and bounced it off the satellite. We sort of piggybacked the signal."

Tuvok had been quietly typing on a terminal from the moment Kim mentioned a repeater. "Captain," he said, "the signal does show evidence of having been boosted by a repeater, similar to Ensign Kim's scenario; the records indicate a faint subspace echo in the original signal, which our computer filtered out before we heard the message."

"Lieutenant Torres," said Janeway, "are you satisfied with this explanation? Does it seem reasonable?"

B'Elanna hesitated a long time, her rational, human side arguing with the warrior mentality of her Klingon side. She gave a questioning glance at Chakotay, who reassured her with a smile; *you are taken seriously,* he tried to convey. "Well . . . it *is* possible, I guess," she said. "I—I withdraw my recommendation that we ignore the signal, Captain."

"Good; I don't like to buck my senior crew. I much prefer we all sign on to a particular course of action."

Chakotay blinked. "Say, does anybody else notice anything different?"

B'Elanna was the first to speak. "Yes; the ship isn't rolling anymore!"

"To be precise," corrected Tuvok, "it is still rolling at approximately twelve-point-three percent of the former range of motion."

"I can live with that," mumbled Paris, his face slowly returning to a more normal shade. His smile did not look quite so strained to the commander.

"So," said Torres, "it seems I was wrong about your power-shunting trick as well, Captain. I seem to have been wrong about everything. Not the best quality in a ship's engineer."

Uh-oh . . . Lately, Chakotay had noticed B'Elanna's self-confidence dropping. He knew her better than anyone; *this is more serious than a momentary phase,* he realized. He would definitely have to talk to Janeway about it.

The captain tried to reassure her engineering officer. "B'Elanna, it was just an idea I remembered from an systems problem set back at the Academy."

"Maybe I should have stuck it out at the Academy."

"You're a good engineer, B'Elanna. Just because you didn't take the full course at Starfleet doesn't mean—"

"Captain, may I return to my station? I want to fully incorporate your innovation to eliminate the final twelve percent of roll."

Worse, thought Chakotay. B'Elanna's Klingon half would never allow her to admit her insecurity; she would not be able to turn to anyone, not Harry Kim—not even Chakotay himself.

"Certainly, B'Elanna," said Janeway. "Let me know when you think you'll regain full control of the stabilizers."

Chakotay winced as he heard the captain emphasize *you'll* in the order; B'Elanna picked up the emphasis in a heartbeat, and she took it as patronizing. He had known B'Elanna for a long time, and that was definitely the wrong approach. Chakotay could see her stiffen visibly.

"I think we've discussed about all that we usefully can

before arriving at the signal," said Janeway. "Now, let's get back to work."

B'Elanna Torres left the ready room and returned to the engineering deck and quickly brought up a visual representation of the wave equation the captain had uploaded. Torres told herself the slight tremble in her hands was a lingering effect of spacesickness.

Spacesickness also accounted for why she had not seen before what was so clear now: that Janeway's casual idea was the nucleus of a damping field that could entirely replace the gravitic stabilizers. *Of course; the stabilizers are basically redundant using the new system. All the time I spent repairing them was just wasted time, now that the captain has solved the problem by waving a magic techno-wand.*

You failed, whispered the tiny voice in B'Elanna's ear; *failed failed failed failed—and here comes Carey to gloat.*

Lieutenant Carey sat down beside his division officer, obviously very upset. "Sir, I'm really sorry I undercut you like that in front of the captain. I was very queasy, but that's no excuse."

"Thank you, Carey. But you were right about Starfleet procedures, and I was wrong."

"Well, I didn't figure it out either! It's the captain; she's just so—well, if she weren't a captain, she'd be the best chief engineer in Starfleet. Let's forget about the argument and just get on with the job. Deal?"

"You're right," said Torres without emotion. Without *audible* emotion; even she did not know which statement she was agreeing to, what Carey said out loud or what B'Elanna was convinced he really meant.

Within thirty minutes, building on the brainstorm of her friend and commanding officer, Torres fully controlled the ship's roll. She went through the remainder of her duties hollowly, wondering when the axe would fall, when Janeway would realize that Torres was really just an impostor in a Starfleet monkey suit.

CHAPTER
2

JANEWAY CHEERFULLY GAVE THE ORDER TO INCREASE TO MAXI-
mum sustainable speed; the jury-rigged stabilizers held, and
the *Voyager* shaved the travel time from two days to just
under one day; but the distress signal ceased transmission
only three hours into the journey.

When the signal died, so too died the sidebanded scan by
which Tuvok could still report a living but immobile human
being. The captain sailed into inky blackness, unable even
to tell whether any sort of reception committee awaited
them.

She lay on the couch in her quarters, staring up at the
ceiling. Her door chirped; it was Tuvok and Chakotay,
arrived at last. The Vulcan had detected an anomalous
reading regarding the star nearest the distress signal, and
Janeway's executive officer had thought it important enough
to bring to her attention. Tuvok's first words, however, were
"I suggest we not discuss this matter with the crew."

"Why not?" asked Commander Chakotay.

*For a former Maquis, you have an odd antipathy toward
secrets,* thought Janeway.

"I fear the data may spark more fears of trickery."

"What's the reading?" asked Janeway.

"Captain, the spectral signature of the star indicates that it should be emitting a great deal more radiant energy than I detect. The light is redshifted far more than it should be, considering the distance, indicating some force drawing energy from the system."

"What could suck energy out of a star like that?"

"I would suggest a very high gravitational field, except the star's gravity appears to be normal for its position on the main sequence. The planets orbit at their proper distances and speeds."

Janeway thought for a long time. It was not that she did not trust B'Elanna Torres; it was just that . . .

"Why throw gasoline onto the fire?" muttered Chakotay.

"Gasoline?"

"Yes, Captain," said Tuvok; "the highly inflammable liquid used—"

"Yes, yes, I remember," said Janeway; "but what do you mean, throw it on the fire, Chakotay?"

"Why encourage further controversy?" explained the commander.

"All right. If both of you think we should keep it quiet, I'll have to agree. But slow our approach as we near the system; keep us out of sensor range—assuming there's anyone to scan us. And assuming they have sensors roughly equivalent to ours."

For the next eighteen hours, Janeway and B'Elanna between them tweaked the gravitic stabilizer into holding; at last, Janeway gave the order to match velocities with the star.

"Put it on visual," she said, standing in front of her command chair with her hands behind her back. She had found she generated more command presence when she stood, the obvious center of attention.

"Shall I scan for life-forms?" asked Harry Kim, currently manning Tuvok's station while the Vulcan joined Torres in engineering.

The captain almost said yes from force of habit, but she

caught herself. "No! Let's leave the searchlight turned off, shall we, Mr. Kim?"

He looked perplexed for a moment; then he nodded. "Passive only, Captain: here's what we can see from this distance."

The tiny image of a bright dot of light appeared on the forward viewer. "Full magnification," said Janeway, but Kim was already magnifying the image.

The dot exploded into a disk that nearly filled the viewer. The image wavered, giving the captain a headache; they were so far out still that not even *Voyager*'s image-enhancing computers could fully compensate for the slight vibration of the ship.

Janeway saw a peculiar grid design against the star's image. She squinted, just about to say something when Tom Paris asked first.

"What are those lines? Is that an interference pattern in the buffer?"

"I'll check," said Kim. He worked diligently, then shook his head. "No, Lieutenant; those lines are in the original image."

"But what are they?" wondered the captain.

The image was crisscrossed by thousands of great circles, forming a faintly fuzzy mesh around the star.

"We'll have to get closer, Captain," said Kim. "I can't get any better resolution."

"Computer," said Janeway, "open a comm link to engineering and maintain it. Mr. Tuvok, can you get a better focus on the image down there?"

"Negative, Captain; you're seeing our enhanced image already."

"Are those lines natural or an artifact?"

"Unknown, Captain. But if they are artificial, then we are dealing with a civilization that is far advanced over our own . . . at least in the field of astronometric architecture."

Janeway caught herself fiddling with her hair; she lowered her hands and carefully placed them behind her back again. "Ahead two-thirds impulse. If you detect any sensor sweeps, Mr. Kim, tell me."

They approached carefully but detected no scanning. The turbolift doors slid open and Neelix entered, followed by Kes.

"Neelix, are you familiar with this star system?"

Neelix stared at the screen. "What are those funny lines across the star? Is your video equipment malfunctioning?"

"Well, that answers that question," said Chakotay quietly.

"No, the lines are actually there, Neelix. We were hoping you could tell us what they were—and where we were."

Neelix shook his head. "I've never been here before in my life."

"Without being able to make a sensor sweep," said Kim, "I can't tell if this star system is inhabited or not. There's no coherent electromagnetic radiation, but that might just mean they use fiberoptics, tightbeam transmissions that don't leak, or channeled subspace broadcast. There are no ships that I can detect . . . and I still don't pick up the shuttlecraft's distress call."

Well, did it repair itself and fly away? Or did someone find the beacon and turn it off? The latter possibility disturbed the captain far more than the former.

"Tuvok," said Janeway, "I want you and Torres to make a complete, passive scan of the area for an ion trail that a shuttlecraft would leave behind. If it came through recently enough, maybe we can track it to wherever it landed. Take us in a little closer, Paris."

The *Voyager* closed inside the orbit of the only planet; Paris abruptly declared, "I don't believe it. It's impossible!"

It was a reasonable reaction. What had looked like an optical illusion from the cometary halo was in fact a wire-mesh sphere or cage that surrounded the sun at a radius of seventy million kilometers, or approximately four light-minutes.

The cage comprised millions of cables, each thicker than a Starfleet shuttlecraft, crossing in an elaborate pattern of X's and stars. The "holes" were hundreds of kilometers wide . . . and even they were strung with smaller filament that passed beyond the limits of resolution without an active scan. Janeway was willing to bet a hundred bars of latinum that *those* gaps were strug with even finer filament, as well.

She scowled, still perplexed. "What *is* it? A protective field? Some kind of shielding?"

A soft female voice spoke up from near the turbolift. It was Kes. "Um . . . Captain? Is it possible it's an energy-collection grid?"

Everyone turned to stare at the Ocampan. "Energy collection?" demanded Paris. "From the *sun?*"

"Yes, Tom. It just occurred to me because it looks like a huge-sized version of the energy-collection grid that the Caretaker used to transmit energy to us, before he—died."

"I suppose it is theoretically possible," said Janeway, "but why would anybody want to?" *Why not just power the planet with clean fusion or dilithium crystals? Why not—*

As if reading Janeway's mind, Tuvok answered through the comm link. "We have found water to be comparatively scarce in the Delta Quadrant; perhaps the planet's supply was too precious to use for hydrogen fusion, and perhaps they never discovered dilithium."

"But are they still here?" asked the captain. "If so, why haven't they detected us and made contact?"

Nobody had a good answer to her question, so she asked an easier one. "B'Elanna, have you found any ion trails yet?"

"Yes, Captain," answered the engineer. "I tracked one recent trail, and Tuvok's laid it into the navigational computer."

"Engage, Mr. Paris. Full impulse. Let's find the ship and survivor quickly and get a safe distance." *Maybe we can continue our investigation after we talk to the pilot,* she decided.

The trail followed a hyperbolic arc, indicating that the shuttlecraft had very little power and was not fighting the natural orbit much. Every so often, the trail bent sharply where the pilot suddenly burned the engines at 105-percent rated power to lurch into a graceless turn.

"This guy was either drunk or half-asleep when he plotted this course," griped Paris.

"Or unconscious," added Kim.

The ion trail led away from the single, large planet toward a moon locked into perpetual, stationary orbit: at the L-4 position, sixty degrees ahead of the planet in the same orbit, the three bodies—moon, planet, sun—formed a stable triangle, never varying with respect to each other. From any one body, the other two were always at the same position in the sky.

The moon was small and not very massive; gravity at the surface was about one-eighth that of Earth. Janeway stared suspiciously at it on the viewer; the entire surface appeared to be sheathed in metal of some sort, as if the aliens had armored the moon, for some bizarre reason.

"I don't like this," said Janeway. "Somebody built a chicken coop around the sun and armor plating around the moon; so *where are they?* Why haven't we already been met by a whole fleet of ships?" *I would almost prefer being shot at to being ignored,* she thought. *Well, almost.*

"I don't like this one bit, Captain," said Neelix. "There's something creepy about this system. And I don't like the fact that I've never even heard of this huge cage."

"Should you have?"

Neelix looked pained. "Captain, it's the sort of thing that people talk about from one end of the quadrant to the other . . . the entire sun as an energy generator! Certainly a seasoned traveler such as myself should know of it. It's fantastic, astonishing—but completely unknown."

"Either nobody's found it before," concluded Chakotay, "or else nobody who ever found it returned to tell the tale."

"Now, that's a gruesome thought," said Neelix. Janeway noticed that the Talaxian moved closer to Kes, probably unconsciously.

Paris followed the ion trail more closely than he seemed to be following the conversation. "Captain, I think I figured out what he's steering toward: a moon or tiny planet orbiting about the same distance as the planet, at the L-four stable-body point."

Captain Janeway hesitated, then made a decision. "Ensign Kim, go ahead and scan the moon—active scanning, I mean. I think we're safer figuring out who all is here than remaining rigidly silent. Shields up."

Kim smiled. "Aye, *aye,* Captain!" He quickly passed the scanners across the planetoid that the ion trail pointed at; when that provoked no apparent response, he scanned them more thoroughly.

"Captain! It's artificial."

"The moon? The entire moon?"

Kim nodded. "Well, it's small; but it's constructed out of an alloy of titanium, nickel, copper, and some ceramic I can't analyze through the scanners."

"Do you see a shuttlecraft or wreckage?" Captain Janeway was starting to worry that they might have bitten off more than they could chew.

"Not from this angle. It might be on the other side of the planetoid; we'd have to get closer."

"Captain," said Tuvok's voice, "I conducted my own scan after Mr. Kim's. You may be interested in the results."

"Enlighten me."

"I have scanned the debris of between fifteen and seventeen other planets besides the large, intact one we see; one of the destroyed planets was a gas giant, the others were small, rocky, and very far from the sun."

"Were they destroyed by some natural phenomenon? Or were they mined to death?"

"All precious minerals have been removed from the debris, leaving only carboniferous husks. Since there is no known natural force that could do that, I suggest the most likely scenario is that the single, large planet is or was inhabited, and they mined their other planets to produce the satellite and the energy-collection grid."

Janeway picked at the most important hole in their analysis. "That's the big question, Tuvok: is . . . or *was?*"

"They have not hailed us, sir; and we are rather obviously in their space."

"Mr. Paris; take us to the moon. I want to find that shuttlecraft, rescue the pilot, and get out of here."

Paris turned half around in his chair. "We're not going to investigate? A grid built entirely around a sun, and we're just going to walk away?"

Good question, Janeway asked herself; *are we just going to walk away? This is still a mission of exploration!*

She stepped close behind Paris, aware that others—Chakotay, Kim, even Neelix—were waiting to hear her response—a certain, very specific tone of response.

"After we get the pilot," declared Janeway, "we will debrief him if possible . . . then we definitely will send an away team to investigate. This is certainly a strange, new world to explore."

Paris turned back, satisfied. "Aye, Captain."

They approached the moon at half-impulse; but as soon as the *Voyager* closed to 363,000 kilometers from the artificial planetoid, the entire solar system exploded into a frenzy of activity.

"Captain," said Ensign Kim, "the moon just changed its alebedo significantly; I think protective shutters opened along the entire surface. Captain, we're being scanned!"

"From the moon?"

"No, Captain; the *planet* is scanning us."

"And hailing us," said Cadet Chell; the chubby, blue Bolian was manning communications while Tuvok was in engineering. Chell was progressing nicely under the Vulcan's merciless tutelage.

"Are we in a position to scan the rest of the moon?" demanded Janeway.

"Just barely," said Kim, checking his instrument graphic.

"Then all stop, Mr. Paris. I guess we just rang their doorbell . . . let's see who answers. Yellow alert. Ensign Kim, continue the scan."

"I already have, Captain. There is no shuttlecraft or wreckage that I can find. It might be under the surface."

"Captain," said Chell, "the planet is still hailing us . . . should we answer?"

Chakotay put his hand on Janeway's arm and spoke quietly, for her ears alone. "They might already have destroyed one Federation ship. Perhaps it would be better . . . ?" He nodded his head toward Neelix.

Janeway gave the cook a come-hither gesture.

"What, *me?* You want *me* to answer?" Neelix was astonished.

"Unless you don't want to get involved."

"No, no! I was just flabbergasted. Of *course* I should be the one to answer; you need somebody who's able to negotiate with these unknown aliens. After all, I've made first contact at least a hundred times!"

Eager for the chance, the crested Talaxian hurried to the command chair. Kes started to say something, then clamped her mouth shut.

Janeway smiled; she had noticed that Neelix didn't say how many were *successful* contacts. "Computer, tight visual on Mr. Neelix; do not show the rest of the bridge. Mr. Chell, open a channel at the same frequency they hailed us."

Janeway waited until the Bolian said "channel open"; then she silently pointed at Neelix, like a holoplay director saying *You're on*.

Neelix straightened his tunic in the Snappy Standard Starfleet Stretch, just as it was taught in the Academy course on Uniform Wear and Maintenance. Janeway was impressed; Neelix must have been watching her closely.

"This is, ah, Captain Neelix of the . . . the Maufansian ship *Songbird*. Um . . . good morning?"

"Why have you entered our territory?" politely demanded a voice that identified neither itself nor the planetary system. No visual appeared on the viewer; audio only.

"The, ah, *Songbird* is a merchant vessel bound for ah . . . Talaxia. We . . ."

"Distress call," whispered Janeway, almost too faintly for Neelix to hear; the computer would automatically scrub any noise softer than a certain threshold, screening out background noise from transmission.

"We heard a distress call and came to investigate." Neelix smoothly incorporated the suggestion into his spiel; Janeway was impressed with how effortlessly and believably the cook spun his tale.

"There is no distress call," said the voice.

"Well, there *was* a distress call," insisted Neelix.

"It was an inconsequential matter, already handled. You may leave."

Janeway bristled; she hated being patted on the head and told to go home.

Neelix considered for a long moment before answering—
possibly getting his temper under control. Again, Janeway
couldn't help but admire her negotiator's sang froid.

"Um . . . if you don't mind my asking, what was the
problem and how did you handle it? Just as a lesson for my
own insignificant self, of course."

"The call was made in error. You may leave. Unless"—
the voice got noticibly perkier—"you're curious to learn
about the true faith."

Chakotay and Janeway looked at each other. Janeway
shrugged and nodded to Neelix, who caught the gesture out
of the corner of his eye.

"We, ah, we're just a trading vessel; but we always
appreciate an opportunity to learn about new cultures we've
not met before." Suddenly Neelix smiled. "My trade ambassador, Cap—ah, Vice-President Janeway—and I would
be delighted to learn all about your culture and the true
faith."

The voice over the audio comm link sounded downright
triumphant. "Please pilot your ship to the following coordinates," it said. The aliens transmitted the necessary data.
"Do you understand the coordinate system?"

"We'll manage," said Neelix, a bit stiffly. *"Captain* Neelix
out."

"We're off," confirmed Chell.

Janeway glared at Neelix as she returned to her command
chair. "Vice-president? Trade ambassador?"

"It was the best I could come up with at the moment!
Could you do better?"

She shook her head. Neelix had neatly trapped her: now
she *had to* allow him onto the away team; anything less
might be seen by the aliens as an insult!

*The little Talaxian gets his chance to buckle yet another
swash.*

Tuvok spoke up through the comm link from the engineering deck. "Captain, I suggest I go with the two of you. It
may be beneficial to minimize the number of humans on the
mission. The injured pilot is a human."

"The away team will consist of Mr. Tuvok, Neelix, and

myself. Let's rendezvous in the hangar bay in twenty minutes."

"And may I suggest," continued the Vulcan, "that we *not* use a shuttlecraft?"

"Mr. Tuvok, if the aliens don't know about transporter technology, why should we alert them?"

"Captain, they may not know about transporters; but they definitely know what a Federation shuttlecraft looks like. They may not appreciate a visit from the owners of the ship they may just have destroyed."

"Point taken, Mr. Tuvok. We'll meet you in transporter room two. Mr. Kim, beam us down about a half-kilometer away from the coordinates they gave us; we'll walk into the area." *And give us a chance to acclimate,* she thought.

"We'll maintain a transporter lock," suggested Chakotay.

"Well, you're going to have a lot of company," said Ensign Kim. "I've just completed a full scan of the planet. There are twenty-seven *billion* dominant life-forms on the planet—of hundreds of different species."

"Twenty-seven *billion?*"

"Yes, sir. Billion, with a *b.*"

"Ready to transport as soon as you get down to the transporter room, Madam Vice-President," said Paris.

Ignoring the gibe, Janeway rose to her feet. "Departing in twenty minutes. Ensign Kim . . . I'd still like to get a look at that artificial moon. Maybe we can find out what happened to the wreckage and the pilot."

"Yes, Captain."

"You and Paris take a shuttlecraft across as soon as we leave and scan the entire surface. Report whatever you find back to Commander Chakotay and Lieutenant Torres."

"Aye, Captain."

"*Captain* Neelix, you're with me."

Kes sucked in a breath and caught Neelix by the arm as he headed for the turbolift. He gallantly detached her hand and chivalrously raised it to his lips. "Have no fear," he said; "nothing will happen to the captain and Tuvok, not with me there to protect them!"

Janeway rolled her eyes as the turbolift doors slammed shut on his reassurances . . . probably not quite what Kes wanted to hear.

Janeway raised her eyebrows. "Twenty-seven billion. Either these people live like ants, or they've got one hell of a tourist season."

CHAPTER
3

TOURIST SEASON INDEED, THOUGHT CAPTAIN JANEWAY, standing in the transporter room with Neelix; Tuvok entered, carrying a tricorder and three phasers.

"The inhabitants have thoroughly utilized their remaining planet," observed the Vulcan in a voice approaching awe—as closely as it was possible for a Vulcan voice to approach anything. "Their life-form readings are evenly dispersed from the surface to a depth of twenty kilometers. There are no uninhabited patches . . . no deserts, no oceans."

"Hear that, Neelix?" said Janeway. "No deserts." She was thinking of the Kazon-infested surface of Kes's planet, where they first had met Neelix, Scourge of the Delta Quadrant.

"No dessert," said the cook. He stood frozen, staring at the transporter pads and looking puzzled, as if not quite sure why he had so neatly maneuvered into coming.

"Neelix," said the captain, "why do you let your mouth run away with your common sense? This is a dangerous mission; why did you force us to bring you along?"

All doubt vanished in an instant from his face.

"Captain—I predict that before we're ready to return, you and Tuvok both will thank me for coming along!"

Janeway sighed. Talking sense to a swashbuckling Talaxian was tougher than frightening a Vulcan.

With a gigantic smile, Neelix pushed past Janeway and Tuvok, leading them onto the pad.

As the transporter chief began the dematerialization, Janeway could only ask herself, *How did I manage to end up on my way to meet twenty-seven billion potentially hostile aliens?*

Correction, she thought; *we're the aliens. And we know what most races think about alien invaders.*

The *Voyager* faded around them while Janeway held her breath.

"Chakotay to Paris," said the commander. "Launch now." From the bridge, Commander Chakotay watched the shuttlecraft swiftly depart. Tom Paris and Harry Kim were on their way toward the artificial moon to try to solve the mystery.

"Blow lots of impulse power," ordered Commander Chakotay to the sometimes edgy Ensign Mariah Henley, who had the helm. "Spray a contrail all over the system. There is a good chance the aliens will miss the shuttlecraft in the fireworks."

Henley smiled. It was an old Maquis trick; Chakotay had done it many times, but this was the first time Henley had gotten to be the "Roman candle."

Janeway, Tuvok, and Neelix materialized in a dark but crowded plaza on the planet . . . or more precisely, *in* it. Planetary air suddenly surrounded them, causing Janeway's ears to stuff up momentarily. She pinched her nose and blew, and her ears popped. *High pressure,* she thought.

She noticed an overwhelming, extraordinary odor of *rot,* ten times worse than a Florida swamp in August. For a moment, Janeway's eyes widened; then she gritted her teeth and forced herself to breathe through her nose, trying desperately to get used to the stench.

A second later and they felt the heat wave. The temperature was a balmy forty-six degrees at 105-percent humidity . . . possibly higher, since the "air" was not quite the same oxygen-nitrogen mixture she was used to; fortunately, the oxygen content was somewhat higher than Earth-normal.

Twenty-seven billion bodies all crammed together, she thought miserably. *Join Starfleet; see the universe!* Tuvok, standing next to the captain, was unaffected, of course; he probably appreciated the warmth, much closer to the temperature on Vulcan.

They had materialized inside a building so huge that at first Janeway thought they were outside on the nightside. Staring up, however, she could just barely see a dark metal ceiling—iron, perhaps—arching overhead. Smaller buildings sat within the larger building, much like ordinary buildings on a city street. But the winding paths between the buildings, unlike streets, avoided any possibility of a right angle.

Everywhere she looked, she saw metal . . . rusty metal, dark and dank, looking almost as if every surface were coated with dried blood. Janeway shuddered in spite of herself; the alien planet was like every human nightmare stitched together in a surreal quilt. The effect was not comic, despite the cartoonish overkill.

They were surrounded by an extraordinary horde of beings hustling along a complex traffic pattern. They were various shapes and sizes, and many were not even bipedal; but all wore loose clothing that hid their limbs and mummy-like facial wraps that covered their features. Looking up, the captain saw a roof that looked like hot iron, very uninviting.

"I suggest we find a lane and begin moving with the traffic flow," said Tuvok; "we are attracting some attention."

Janeway slid immediately into a queue that was going approximately the right direction. She noticed that the people kept their heads down; if two happened to meet by chance, they both made a big ritual of looking down and away to the left. She whispered her observation to Tuvok and Neelix.

"Possibly a series of rituals to symbolize some element of privacy," said the Vulcan, clearly fascinated by the culture. "I do not know yet whether it is religious or merely traditional."

Janeway wished she had something to wrap around her face; it would be very convenient, spoiling any chance that the alien interlocutor would spot her for a human. Nobody noticed their strange clothing and unwrapped faces; or at least, no one was rude enough to point it out.

The plaza's darkness was no aberration. Following as straight a line as they could toward the rendezvous coordinates, the away team cut from one queue to another, flowing down long, dank corridors of blackness like the dead lining up for hell. Everything was gloomy. The only windows were slits high in the walls, letting in some dim light that gave just enough illumination for them to avoid actually tripping over the monklike figures in front of them.

An occasional glowtube supplemented the window slits. *If these guys were transported to Jorba during the Dead of Night celebration,* thought Janeway, *they'd feel right at home.*

The air was hot and very wet; Janeway's throat began to ache as the caustic moisture scored her throat. "The whole planet is an oven," muttered Neelix behind her. "I could bake pies in here!"

"That is an exaggeration, Mr. Neelix; the temperature is only forty-six point one degrees, quite a comfortable temperature on my planet."

"I'm not *from* your planet, Tuvok! And I think it's absurdly hot."

Janeway tried to follow a basic direction, working from her tricorder; but the disorienting, twisting streets made it difficult to keep on course. She saw more of the alien planet than she really wanted to; the captain felt sudden claustrophobia, as if the iron buildings were falling over on her, the mobs pushing around her too tightly for her to breathe.

Janeway glanced at the tricorder. The coordinates were only fifty meters distant; looking in the proper direction, she saw a figure lurking in the darkness of a monstrous doorway, too far away for her to make out any more details about the figure other than "tall and heavy." The doorway was the "mouth" of a huge, skull-like design. Janeway felt a premonitory shiver, strange in such heat.

"I think we're about to meet our missionary," she announced. "Neelix, you should be first to speak."

"Thank you, Captain; I accept the honor."

"For reasons of protocol only," she explained, smiling. "After all, you're the *captain;* they'll expect to meet you first."

Janeway stood behind Neelix, out of direct line of sight. She preferred to wait until "Captain" Neelix summoned her and Tuvok before stepping out, so as not to startle the aliens into attacking in an excess of xenophobic self-defense. There was the distinct possibility, she told herself, that they already had attacked the previous representative of the Federation.

"Greetings on all five points of the pentagram," said a strange voice; the Universal Translator gave their host's voice an odd, rumbling twang, like a moose from Texas.

"Greetings, magnificent being. I am Captain Neelix, master of the *Songbird* trading vessel. I come to discuss trade possibilities and, uh, learn about the true faith."

"Abandon false hope, all ye who enter here, and find strength in the Returning."

"Oh—thanks awfully."

Janeway softly cleared her throat, quickly regretting her action; not only did it hurt, somehow it made the odor stronger.

"May I introduce my trade negotiators?" asked Neelix smoothly. "This is Kathryn Janeway, a—a Veermaan from the planet Verminius; and this is Tuvok, a Vulcan from the planet, ah, Vulcan."

"Greetings on all five points of the pentagram," boomed the host. On cue, Janeway stepped close—and halted in horrified amazement.

She stared straight into the face of Satan.

Easy, girl—he's just . . . he's just a . . . Janeway recoiled in horror, actually falling back a couple of steps before she got hold of her emotions and forced her feet to stop moving.

What is it—what is *it?* She forced herself to stare the

creature in the face. The face wasn't a devil's mask. It didn't have the normal, physical characteristics she associated with the devil; and if it had, so what? Did not Vulcans and Romulans have just such features, except for the missing horns?

But the alien's face, while angular and roughly triangular, held something altogether sinister, something wild and bestial. It was sculpted from every imaginable sign of evil, every conceivable sin, every foulness or violation ever practiced by Man upon Man stitched together.

The mouth was too small, just the *wrong* size; the eyes were narrow; the cheekbones high, but cruelly high. The thin lips held such promise of torture and murder that Janeway's heart suddenly shifted into warp speed.

Its lips parted to suck in a breath, and the inside of its mouth was covered with writhing worms. Ripples flickered across its skin, vermin infesting its flesh! They crawled across the hideous face, and the captain felt her knees weaken.

She had never experienced such a reaction. Every specific or particular about the alien's face could be rationalized and accepted—*in theory*.

But the universe contains not theories but concrete actualities: and the actuality of the alien face was a nightmare of half-buried, demented, squirming little childhood fears, night terrors, seizures and suffering, flickering malevolence, befouled, spoiled beauty.

It—the thing could not possibly be dignified with a sex—it bore the Mark of the Beast.

When Kathryn Janeway was a little girl, her mother had read her that Kipling story. Rationally, even at so young an age, Kathryn had thought it absurd that the horses would detect some horrific evil lurking beneath what should have been a normal man's skin; nevertheless, it had terrified her.

Now she understood why. But she did not understand her sudden feeling of uneasy familiarity; *she had seen these monsters before,* somewhere . . . pictures, at least. But where, *where?*

A minute had passed while Neelix casually chatted of nothing with the alien, and Janeway finally got her respirations and heart rate barely under control. She turned to look at Tuvok instead and saw a sight she had never imagined to see in a hundred years: Tuvok the Vulcan was absolutely frozen with fear.

All the fears of a moment before, the fears Janeway thought she had overcome, jolted through her body like a monstrous static discharge. Tuvok was *frightened?* Tuvok was terrified!

The captain had never even imagined a Vulcan could feel such powerful emotions. She knew they "felt" the same emotions as everyone else but simply suppressed and ignored them . . . a talent they had to learn as children, for they were of course not born that way. But the thought had never crossed her mind that some emotions were simply too powerful to suppress, even for a Vulcan.

But how could a mere alien cause such a savage disruption in Vulcan neurophysiology? *Unless Tuvok remembers them too,* thought the captain, *and remembers not just the image, but whatever horror they brought with them.* Janeway shook suddenly with vague loathing; why had she thought that, the "horror" they brought?

Janeway was pulled back against her will to stare at the alien, which she dimly heard introduce itself as Navdaq, and she understood how.

She heard little but the slush of blood in her own ears and felt faint from an explosively high blood pressure. But her reaction was nothing compared to Tuvok's, for the Vulcan left finger-sized indentations in the rusted, iron doorframe.

Navdaq, to be polite, turned its gaze to include her every now and again. Janeway died a little with every glance, the look of the basilisk turning her to stone.

Neelix turned to the captain, his mouth moving animatedly. He stopped. He moved his mouth again, but Janeway could hear nothing but her own pulse. He scowled, confused by her incomprehension.

Words filtered through, though she still saw Neelix only in peripheral vision, staring pop-eyed at the demon. "Assistant . . . long journey . . . exhausted." He was making excuses for her, thank God, saving her from having to talk to Navdaq and allow it to steal her soul in addition to flattening it where it sat.

Demon? Oh my Lord, where did I get THAT from? She felt herself shrink second by second, cringing in embarrassment that she could not stop herself from staring in horror at the—the demon. Trapped in a nightmare where her will was not her own, Janeway knew her torment was nothing compared to Tuvok's hell of humiliation. A Vulcan who couldn't control his own emotional response!

Then at last, the *thing* turned its face away and stalked into the black horror of a corridor, followed by Neelix. Janeway felt her mortification finally relent to nothing more than a deep, red flush spreading across her body, mercifully hidden by perpetual, artificial night and a uniform. She could follow, albeit numbly, like a robot; she followed. She could walk; she hurried after the pair.

Tuvok forced his legs into a staggering step. He could think of nothing but the black terrors from a Vulcan night so long before bright logic touched his life that he could not even rationalize his fear. His hands shook with emotion so great, only a Vulcan could experience it: this Navdaq creature, this—this *Fury!*—had thrown Tuvok back to the age of the First Ones, a Vulcan from the time before the immortal Surak brought order, logic, order, reason, and order to his disorderly race.

Tuvok's hands shook with palsy, and he fought a wild urge to cover his eyes and run into the blackness, left or right, anywhere to escape *it.*

There is no fear! he desperately told himself. *There is no fear, no monster, no demon, no god, no devil, no angel, no past, no future; now is always now; a race is just a race; a Vulcan is logic and order; emotion is the enemy! Eliminate the enemy!*

Tuvok nearly sprinted after his captain, and a tiny moan forced its way past the paper doors of his useless, laughable self-control. A Vulcan! He should be banished to Romulus with the rest of the bloodtasters.

Choking down a sudden spurt of vomit, almost as terrified of permanently disgracing himself—pride, another emotion—as he was of *it*, Tuvok squinted his eyes and listened only, unfocusing his gaze and allowing himself to see only enough of the passageway to avoid actually bumping into walls.

Neelix spoke to the *thing*. The Talaxian cook and guide seemed utterly unaffected, oblivious of *its* hideous presence. "I am very pleased to meet your Autocrat, great Navdaq. What? No, a preliminary survey. Yes, to find out what you need that I might be able to supply. Well, no, heh, I haven't heard of the true faith; but I'm sure I will find it fascinating and enlightening."

"We missed your ship," said the interlocutor. "How did you slip through our orbital sensors?"

"We, ah, parked it a ways away," extemporized Neelix, squirming nervously. "Um, we didn't want to interfere with your port traffic."

The interlocutor did not respond, but Tuvok got the distinct impression he was not persuaded.

Janeway stumbled as she walked on wobbly knees behind her supposed "captain," and she realized she was trying to follow with her eyes firmly shut; anything to avoid having to see even the back of Navdaq. *This is insane,* she argued; *it— he is just an alien life-form, nothing more! I've seen dozens, races whose facial appearances should turn my stomach. . . .*

The Viidians, sick with the phage, their faces literally falling apart in clumps; the wormlike Knipa of Barnard II, whose flesh cracks and splits before your eyes, oozing rivulets of black oil that they suck up through vacuum appendages.

Let's be objective about this, Janeway told herself sternly; *Navdaq has nothing in its face or flesh to even begin to compare to these horrors, and I face them without a twinge!* Yet she still sweated, perspiration dripping down her forehead and into her eyes.

Slowly, the fear began to ebb. Perhaps her adrenal glands were running out of juice, she reasoned; her panic faded, and even though her heart still pounded when she looked directly at Navdaq, she could look without gagging.

* * *

The Vulcan Tuvok felt his captain start to relax slightly; her quotient of fear and revulsion appeared to ebb.

But Tuvok found no such comfort. An invisible fist continued to punch him in the stomach every time he caught sight of *it*, and nothing he did or told himself to do made the slightest difference. Tuvok knew deep in his core, so deep it never could be rooted out, that this was a monster that had come to pass horrible judgment upon the Vulcan race. Tuvok knew the Fury would tear into his fleshy meat and strip him to the bone, soon, very soon. His mind couldn't say no to his endocrine system.

Then without warning, Navdaq stopped and whirled to face them. Tuvok barely kept his feet; Janeway sagged against a bulkhead, face whitening again.

Captain Janeway could neither close her eyes nor turn away as the alien seemed to grow; it leaned forward, suddenly inspired by the breath of Mars, Bringer of War and Destruction. Its face exploded into a prismatic display of emotions bottled for more years than the alien had lived. "You are about to embark upon a spiritual journey," prophesied Navdaq; "thousands of years of devotion, preparation, and countless sacrifices, culminating in the final crusade against the most diabolical beings in the galaxy. And the righteous shall win; and you shall join us, an armored fist from behind the back. You shall come; you shall *come!*"

Janeway turned her face to the bulkhead, feeling a tear upon her cheek. She had been chosen by the Fallen One, and her soul was damned to hell!

CHAPTER 4

TIME, AND RATIONALIZATION, FINALLY DROVE AWAY CAPTAIN Janeway's entirely unreasonable fear. She still felt a weird, irrational revulsion for Navdaq whenever she looked at it; and she began to wonder whether somehow, there had been ancient contact between its people and early protohumans, contact that was decidedly horrific for the humans. Psychologically—perhaps genetically—all the features of Navdaq's race were implanted into the human neurophysiology as the synecdoche of hatred and loathing.

As crazy as the theory sounded, it resonated so *right* that she couldn't shake it.

Just as a baby that has never fallen will still scream hysterically when placed upon a tall glass table, Janeway reacted to the screams of her ancestors—even though she, personally, had nothing against Navdaq.

The strangest corollary was that Tuvok reacted even more strongly than she did; evidently some Vulcans had some sort of genetic memory of Navdaq's people, a memory that dated to a time before the great philosopher Surak taught them the path of pure logic.

Still, however, Janeway could not shake the feeling that *she had seen these aliens* somewhere before . . . not just in her "DNA memory," but in the real world—in the past, long ago, back in—

No, that's ridiculous. She had been about to think she had seen them when she was a cadet at the Academy. But that was. . . . Janeway pursed her lips, pondering; bits and pieces, they started to return. She decided not to force the memory; it would come—she was sure it would eventually come back to her.

Tuvok seemed to have gotten his emotions nearly under control; only Janeway or some other close friend, perhaps Chakotay, could have seen the Titanic struggle that still roiled just below his skin.

Neelix was unaffected; to him, Navdaq must be a member of just one more alien race, interesting and unique, as were they all. Janeway felt a surge of utterly irrational hatred of the Talaxian. *That's insane!* she railed at herself. *Thank goodness at least one of us three is still rational.* But the bile would not dissipate, a remnant of her barely controlled fear.

Navdaq led them through long, dank, creepy halls, "caverns measureless to man," as Coleridge might describe it. Or in the words of Radolph Na, a twenty-second-century poet that Janeway was just beginning to read,

> *Cold cupped hands*
> *Squeeze*
> *Squirt like Paq seeds into deep night. . . .*

Everything she saw, wherever it led them, was a living nightmare; Janeway reacted so strongly to it all that she started to berate herself for being so easily manipulated. If Navdaq were to move to the Alpha Quadrant, it could make a fortune designing a haunted-house holodeck program!

It talked incessantly, and after a time, Janeway was actually able to listen without flinching or cringing at the voice.

* * *

Neelix followed Navdaq smartly, trying to pick out the one or two useful spices of information from the rambling, bland pudding of religious catechism.

"Captain" Neelix noticed that Janeway and Tuvok appeared to have contracted some extraordinary phobia; they were struck dumb! The Talaxian felt anxious about them, wishing Kes had come along; she had the most remarkable talent for getting right inside a person and soothing the real cause of his distress, whether he knew what it was or not.

"What was that distress call about?" asked Neelix, rising to the necessity. If the captain and the Vulcan were so oddly incapacitated, it was Neelix's clear duty to find out where the missing human was.

Navdaq twitched in some satisfaction. "One of the *Unclean* invaded our temporary home, doubtless a scout for the filth who are its masters, they who envy and fear the Holy even in exile . . . and rightly so! For when the righteous finally move, the hosts shall rout the *Unclean* and destroy the last representative of the vermin that infest our true home!"

"Ah, well thank goodness for that! But tell me . . . what was that distress call about? An ion trail led through your system and to that artificial moon of yours . . . I, um, happened to notice when I was waiting for a representative of the Autocrat to contact me."

"Think nothing of it. The *Unclean* launched a treacherous attack and destroyed a very important tool; but they are mindless beasts, for the crusade shall proceed unimpeded. We have captured the *Unclean* alive and hold it for interrogation."

Neelix forcibly suppressed a triumphant whoop; the Starfleet pilot was alive! Alive, and *held*. Neelix smiled in relief. His boast back on the transporter pad had surely come true . . . in triplicate!

Tuvok was a hollow shell of a Vulcan . . . but he had finally managed to lock outside, for the moment, all the distasteful, dangerous emotions he had felt. He forced himself to Observe and Report; his captain would eventually need any intelligence he could gather.

Navdaq has never once mentioned beaming, noted Tuvok; *he wondered where our ship was docked.* It was a simplistic observation: no race they had yet encountered in the Delta Quadrant, except for the Caretaker, had transporter technology. But it was cold, rational, logical. It was Tuvok's first logical act since seeing Navdaq.

Everywhere Tuvok looked, he saw mechanical locks on doors . . . either external padlock-type devices, or integral card-key slots built into doors. *They have no shields,* he thought—without emotion.

The heat revived the Vulcan; it reminded him of home. He could not see very well in the darkness that Navdaq and those of his race evidently preferred; possibly the aliens saw by means of infrared? But Tuvok's ears were much sharper than a human's, and he had followed the conversation ever since he began to regain control of his long-suppressed emotions.

With control came a shred of memory: true, rational memory from his own experience. It was during his first assignment under Captain Sulu; something happened . . . a war, a fight with another ship. Tuvok read about it in the message traffic but paid it little mind until he saw the single image included in the subspace broadcast; the image evoked such revulsion in the young Vulcan that he quickly minimized the icon and stored it in the archives, never opening the file again.

Could these creatures be the same aliens who fought against Captain James Kirk and the *U.S.S. Enterprise?* Tuvok firmly pushed the thought from his mind; it held no practical value, just a distraction from the very real and immediate problems faced by his current assignment, *Voyager* and its crew.

Though they encountered no one along the route they followed, a very circuitous route, perhaps deliberately avoiding contact, Tuvok could hear movement and breathing behind virtually every door they passed. The planet was immeasurably crowded, many times the population of

Vulcan or even Earth in significantly less space: the planet had a diameter only sixty percent that of Earth, which meant it had a surface area only thirty-six percent of Earth's.

The aliens accomplished the improbable by stacking their population some twenty kilometers deep, and Tuvok heard large crowds of people noisily walking across metallic catwalks beneath the floor and above his head.

The time has come, thought the Vulcan, *to drive the last traces of emotion from my mind. I must confront my fear and destroy it.* Calming himself by meditating upon the IDIC, the symbolic heart of Surak's philosophy, *Infinite Diversity in Infinite Combinations,* Tuvok lengthened his stride and approached Navdaq's back.

"Sir," said the Vulcan—his voice sounded like metal grating on stone—"you have alluded to an ancient history when the Unclean drove you away from your home."

Navdaq stopped and slowly began to turn. Tuvok caught himself starting to rush the question to spit it out before seeing the Face again; he deliberately slowed and waited until he could look directly at it. "Will you elaborate?"

The Vulcan actually felt physically ill, as if he had eaten a spoiled *Tolik* fruit. He had to force his breathing and forcibly stop his hands from lurching forward of their own will to gouge thumbs into Navdaq's eyes and tear the alien's throat out.

I am not a strand of imprinted DNA, Tuvok told himself; *I am a Vulcan. I am in control.*

Navdaq considered him; it did not recognize Tuvok, either by memory or genetically. *Of course not; we were the victims. They must have enslaved and terrorized us; it is no mystery that Vulcans and humans imprinted the aliens' faces with terror and utter despair, and the aliens did not imprint us at all.*

"You shall hear the truth," said Navdaq, "and you shall understand."

It shifted its gaze upward and pressed its hands together like claws with long, sharp nails that slid out of its fingers. Tuvok was on the verge of yanking the captain away, lest the alien forget himself in hypnogogic reverie; but Captain Janeway herself backed hastily away from the suddenly lethal claws.

"A hundred thousand years or more ago, we ruled heaven. It was given unto us, and we took what was offered. Some speculate we may have come from another corner of the galaxy and only settled heaven when the Dark Ones invited us in. I offer no opinion; be it known we had been allowed inside, and we jealously guarded our blessing.

"We treated the subject races with compassion; we forbade the wanton killing of slaves and allowed them to grow and prosper within the limits ordained by their condition."

Tuvok glanced at the captain; she was not visibly reacting to the tale. *She can be as unemotional as I have ever seen a human,* he noted with some satisfaction.

Janeway presented an unemotional front, but it was only because her body seemed finally to have run out of adrenaline. The capacity for fear burned itself out. She felt sick revulsion, but that was easier to contain.

Navdaq was casually talking about its race having enslaved other beings for tens of thousands of years before somebody or something drove them away. She felt an irrational impulse to strangle Navdaq, as if she were somehow the substitute for the enslaved races and it symbolized the conquerers.

"Then came the *Unclean* to disrupt the natural, ordained order," said Navdaq, a dark tone of disharmony creeping into its voice. "They did covet heaven and came from a far place to cast out the Holy unlawfully. We are told the tragic battle lasted thousands of years; in the end, we were driven through the great gate, the longest wormhole that has existed in this galaxy, and brought to this place."

Navdaq's face lowered. "Then came our shame, for the elder son of D'Mass, D'Vass, rebelled against the holy quest: his brother Bin Mass fought without surcease eleven days and eleven nights; then he lay down next to his brother, and they slept hand in hand—only to arise and fight for eleven more days and nights. D'Vass was exiled with some of his rebels, and the rest of us are descended from the loyal hosts of Bin Mass."

"If you were in heaven," asked Janeway, surprising herself with her own unemotional voice, "how could the Unclean cast you out? Weren't you—protected?"

"The *Unclean* made alliance with the subject races, who envied the Holy their place in the order. And the subject races laid down their tools and their yokes, and laid *themselves* down, and refused to fight.

"We sent the Terrors, and still they refused. We sent the Terrors louder and louder, brighter than ever we had before, letting them see the true horror that disorder brings; but still they refused, and they fell into madness and tore each other apart in their fright. They fought and killed . . . but not for us; they killed for fear, and for the madness."

We SENT the terrors . . . Beneath her own disgust, Janeway felt a small lump of worry begin to grow.

Shortly before the Caretaker yanked *Voyager* millions of light-years across the galaxy to strand her in the Delta Quadrant, Captain Janeway, sporting a brand-new fourth pip on her collar, heard about a discovery in the Alpha Quadrant: a helmet that could project telepathic images over long distances.

Suppose Navdaq's people had similar toys . . . but instead of projecting communication, what if they had relentlessly projected mind-numbing fear and terror to sap the will of their *subject races,* their slaves?

It was a chilling thought. *The fear I felt upon first seeing Navdaq could only have been a dim, distant echo of the terror they could "send" if they used their projection device.*

If the aliens chose to *send their terrors,* they could probably enslave Janeway herself and her entire crew.

There was only one ray of hope. If Navdaq was telling the truth—assuming he knew the truth—then at least once before, the *subject races* had managed to pull off a strike at a critical moment . . . and maintain it despite the fear projector.

It worked; the aliens were defeated. But the effects of the projector on maximum drove many of them violently insane with fear.

Was it a fair trade-off? she wondered.

"For centuries," continued Navdaq, "we have planned our counterattack."

"You still intend to return to heaven?" asked Tuvok. Janeway jumped; they were the first words her Vulcan friend had spoken for many long minutes, ever since he first forced out the question about the early history of heaven. Tuvok's voice was clipped and strained; probably nobody but Janeway or another Vulcan would have noticed. *Maybe he's going to be all right after all. . . .*

"We were punished for our laxity, our complacency in power. We were meant to learn vigilance and focus; we were meant to learn that the *Unclean* cannot be allowed to remain in the Holy, not as conquerers, not even as slaves. And we have learned well our lessons. Yes, we shall return to heaven . . . and you come at a great moment, for the hour is at hand. We shall return to heaven, whence we were cast out, and cleanse it of all *Unclean!*

"Heaven was meant for the Holy—and heaven shall be cleansed of all *but* the Holy . . . this we say, and this we say! Now come, my guests; you have come on the eve of the momentous war of righteousness, and I cannot think that is mere accident. Let us go unto the Autocrat, and he shall listen to your tale and scry why you truly are here."

Navdaq turned about and strode into the creeping darkness, and Janeway and Tuvok had no option but to run to catch up.

Lieutenant Tom Paris and Ensign Harry Kim cautiously approached the artificial moon in the shuttlecraft, alert for any more robotic alarm systems—or defense systems. Kim licked his lips nervously; his engineer's mind conjured up all sorts of nasty possibilities for technoalarms, land mines, and booby traps.

Ever since the *Voyager* approached close enough to ring bells, the moon had sent a continuous data stream to the small planet; Kim monitored the data, looking for anomalies and discontinuities.

"It's repeating the same packets over and over," he announced; "it hasn't changed since we've gotten closer."

"Has the modulation changed? The frequency, anything that could convey more information?"

"No, Tom. It's absolutely identical to what it was just after we first triggered it."

Paris considered for a moment, then shrugged. "Harry, I think we've just got a beeping rack-alarm here. The only thing we have to worry about is the owner eventually coming back to shut it off."

"A beeping what?"

"Oh, that's right . . . where you come from, there is no crime. But at the Federation Penal Settlement in New Zealand, where I was hanging out with my buddies before Janeway hired me, we quickly learned that the most common method of intimidation was to burglarize someone's room while he was on work detail or at chow."

"Burglarize? People actually *broke into* your own, private room? You mean"—he glanced pointedly at Paris—"the way you broke into *mine?*"

Paris laughed, a short, ugly sound. "You did lead a sheltered life, didn't you? Yeah, Harry, they actually broke into my space. They went through my things. They left them just slightly moved . . . enough so I'd wonder if anyone had been there, not quite enough to know for sure."

Harry shook his head, savagely poking a button to change the scan range. He had read about burglary in history classes; but he could not imagine what it must feel like to have a stranger, a *criminal,* rummage through his most personal possessions. *Maybe they would even steal my clarinet,* he thought; the image made the hair on the back of his neck stand straight up.

"So one guy, Hasty Kent, made rack-alarms," Paris continued, "and the rest of us bought them. We paid him in synthehol, or homemade alcohol, if someone smuggled some in. We didn't have any latinum, usually. Huh, now that I think about it, maybe Kent was the one burglarizing the spaces, just so he could sell more alarms."

"What's that got to do with the data stream, Tom?"

"Hasty Kent didn't want to bother making the alarms very sophisticated; so he just made them start ringing when the space was violated and keep ringing until someone came and shut them off.

"So naturally, the burglars quickly figured out that if they set off lots and lots of alarms all the time, people would get tired of coming back to check . . . and they could burglarize a space while the alarm was going, and no one would ever know."

Harry thought for a minute. "Let's poke our nose in, shall we, Tom?"

"I thought you'd never ask."

Paris took manual control of the shuttle and dove toward the moon, while Kim scanned for weapons power-ups or any changes in the data stream. They looped around the back side, and Harry whistled.

"Here we go! Take a look at this, Tom." He put the scan on the forward viewer.

They saw the remains of an extraordinarily huge dish antenna, easily a hundred kilometers high and seventy kilometers in radius. It had been destroyed by a fist from heaven, an object punching out of the stars at a velocity somewhere between 0.1 and 0.7 light speed—something very like a starship shuttlecraft.

"The ion trail leads right into the impact crater," said Paris. "Harry, I think we've found where the distress signal emanated from. The only question is . . ."

"Where the heck *is* it?" Harry Kim completed.

There was no wreckage from a Starfleet shuttlecraft, not a scrap. And there was no life-form reading.

"Somebody's already done some tidying up," deduced Ensign Kim. "They've been here, seen the damage, swept up the wreckage, and removed the pilot to a hospital."

"Or more likely a prison cell."

Kim looked at his shipmate. "You think they would put someone in prison for this? It was an accident."

"Oh yes," said Paris; "I think people would put other people in prison for just about anything. If they were angry enough."

My friend, thought Kim, *you're a hell of a nice guy and a great pilot . . . but you have a dark, cynical side that scares the hell out of me sometimes.*

As they continued their orbit around the moon, Paris had to adjust the impulse engines to keep them on course; the moon's gravity was so low that true orbital velocity would be an interminable crawl. "Hey, Kim, here's another antenna. This one's an innie, not an outie."

They passed over a huge, perfectly circular indentation with a dish at the bottom five times the size of the one that had been destroyed. On impulse, Kim turned his sensors around and scanned in the direction the antenna pointed.

"This is interesting," he said. "The moon's rotational orientation is set so that this antenna always faces the sun."

"The grid—Harry, Kes was right . . . that *must be* an energy-collection grid around the sun, and this is where the energy beams to. *Holy—!*"

Tom Paris yanked the controls up and to the left; at exactly the same instant, the red-alert klaxon automatically sounded.

The shuttle veered violently to the side; Harry Kim grabbed his console to avoid being flung out of his chair. He stared wildly at all of his instruments, trying to figure out what Paris saw that made him swerve so suddenly.

"That would have been a hell of a spectacular death, Kim," said the pilot in question with a grin. "I suddenly realized that if the grid was beaming that much energy to the moon, we'd better not get between it and the collection dish with our shields down!"

Shaking, Kim adjusted his scanner. "There's energy all around this thing. I didn't think to look for microwaves; it seems so . . . primitive. Sorry, Tom; I should have been paying more attention. I almost got us killed."

Paris nodded, which Kim took as acceptance of his apology. "Now," said the lieutenant, "what's on the inside of this puppy?"

Kim shook his head. "I can't scan through the hull, Tom."

"Shields?"

"No. There are no shields anywhere I've detected in this

system. But the hull of the moon is made of some super-dense material that our scans can't penetrate."

"Don't tell me that we can't beam through it either."

Kim considered a moment. "All right, Tom; I won't tell you."

"But we can't?"

"I wasn't the one who told you that. But you're right."

"Figures. So how do we get in? We can't go down the energy-collection shaft; too much microwave radiation."

"Well . . ." Kim ran over shield-configuration equations in his head while he fiddled aimlessly with the controls. He suddenly realized he was "keying" the console as if it were a clarinet, playing "The Slionimski Variations."

Paris waited, then said, *"Yes?"*

"Maybe we can go down that shaft," said Kim, "and right through the collection antenna. I *think* I can adjust our own shields to give us a couple of minutes of protection."

"Think?"

"Hey, this is Starfleet, Tom: risk is our business!"

Paris gave him a look; pretending not to notice, Kim continued. "It won't be good for us; we'll probably get some pretty serious sunburns."

"The doctor can fix us up later. Let's do it!"

"And if you mess up the piloting, there won't be anything left to cure."

Paris raised his brows. *"Moi?* Look, you got a needle? I can take this baby right through the eye while hanging an elbow out the window." He winked.

"All right then, modifying shields now—just a minute—all right, Tom, we're ready."

Lieutenant Paris nosed the shuttlecraft over into a dive toward the gaping hole. Kim gritted his teeth, seeing his life flash before his eyes; it didn't hold his interest. "Tom," he said, just before they passed the lip of the hole, "you know if we make a smoking crater, I will never speak to you again."

Paris snorted. "Don't tempt me!"

CHAPTER
5

THE SHAFT WAS STRAIGHT, DRIVING DIRECTLY TOWARD THE center of the moon for more than a hundred kilometers. Paris kept the shuttle steady in the center, trying not to think about the walls closing in around him, about the radiation—about how they were going to get back out again without taking a lethal cumulative dose.

The first eight kilometers were nothing but shielding, the unreasonably dense material that Paris dubbed "baloneyum" when Kim informed him that chemically, it could not exist. "If you say it can't exist," said Paris, "maybe I should test your theory by ramming the wall." Kim didn't respond, not surprisingly. Tom Paris reacted to tension by incessant joking; Kim tended to clam up.

The shaft started to narrow, and even Paris ceased harassing his crewmate, concentrating on the piloting job.

"Paris," said Kim, interrupting a long silence, "you've got to pick up the pace; we're starting to get some serious leakage through the shields. If we're not out of direct view of the microwave beam in the next four minutes . . ."

"Yeah, yeah; got it. Hang on, here we go."

Paris tapped the throttle, pushing to twenty-five kilometers per minute; it would have been a snail's pace in free space, where sublight velocities were measured in kilometers per *second*.

But the space was decidedly unfree; they drove through a narrow shaft, dodging spars and pieces of equipment, guy lines, and the walls of the tunnel itself, being buffeted by the microbursts of energy "wake turbulence" that their own ship stirred up and threw ahead of them at half light speed. Ensign Kim gripped the sides of his seat, and even Paris felt his stomach clench as they careered wildly from one side of the shaft to the other.

Easy, easy! he warned himself; fried or shredded wasn't much of a career choice.

"My mother makes the greatest kimchee," Kim said; the nonsequitur helped break the tension . . . slightly.

"Does she? So when are you going to invite me over for a Korean feast?"

"Soon as we get back. Um, glass noodles—chap che, bibimba, maybe some barbecue . . . she makes wonderful, traditional side dishes."

"Gosh. All my mom ever made was meat loaf."

"Really? I love meat loaf."

A spar suddenly loomed in front of them. Reacting at warp speed, Paris swerved to avoid it; suddenly the shuttle slid out of control!

The ship rolled, inertial stabilizers straining to keep up; for an instant, Paris actually felt zero-g, and his stomach lurched.

"Yak!" he shouted, yanking the shuttlecraft back in the other direction.

Tom Paris fought the irrational but almost irresistible impulse to squeeze his eyes shut. "Watch it!" bellowed Kim. Ahead of them bulked a dense web of gold-colored wires strung across the outer perimeter of the shaft.

Grimly, Paris bent the shuttlecraft back into the center in a move that the manual insisted could not be done with the ship in question. He rotated the shuttle impossibly fast, and the ship just barely slipped through the small resonance gap in the center of the array, neatly clipping off a dozen strands of wire on both left and right.

"So," Kim said weakly, "when are you going to invite me over for a meat-loaf feast?"

"I'll cook it for you myself back on the ship, if we can tie up Neelix and use his kitchen."

"Cook it? You?"

"Man learns many things in the Maquis, especially when replicators are hit-or-miss. Hang on, Kim, here comes the antenna."

"Getting hot in here, isn't it?"

Paris wiped the sweat out of his eyes. He glanced at the temperature gauge: 52.2 degrees. They were roasting alive! "Actually, I feel kind of a chill. Did we bring my jacket along?"

Paris tapped the throttle high, then higher yet. He had adjusted the throttle scale way, way downward; at the normal range, a small tap like the one he had just given would have accelerated them to a quarter light speed. The shuttle would have drilled a neat, shuttlecraft-sized hole all the way through the moon, coming out the other end a shuttlecraft-sized ball of ionized plasma.

As they closed, Paris saw to his dismay that the antenna was not just a simple dish he could edge around. Instead, they would first encounter an inner ring, the energy-focusing mechanism, that was only *thirty meters* in diameter—followed in mere seconds by an outer dish.

Millions of threads of strong filament connected the inner ring to the shaft wall, keeping it in place like the muscles of the human eye keep the corona facing the right way. The shuttle could not simply bypass the inner ring; they would have to thread it, diving straight into microwave hell.

Paris did not need Harry Kim to tell him that in between the inner ring and the dish itself, the electromagnetic radiation would rip through the shuttlecraft's shields like a hot knife through butter, cooking the two of them in moments. Their only hope was to maintain thirty kilometers per minute all the way through.

That meant that the only way to thread the inner ring and then clear the outside rim of the dish was to perform a patented maneuver that Paris had invented flying Gawk-hoppers as a kid: the Swoop of Death.

He clenched his teeth, but smiled coolly for Kim's benefit. The kid was all right, but he really was not prepared to die, not yet; best not tell him the maneuver they were about to perform had only a thirty-three-percent chance of success.

Hell, I'M not prepared to die just yet! Alas, Paris could not lie to himself; he had attempted the Swoop of Death only six times in his life—and successfully completed it twice.

Of course, never before had the name been quite so literal. As a kid, he dove around purely holographic barriers; and if he missed and blew through one—well hell, then his buddy won that day's bet.

The inner ring loomed. Through it, Paris could actually *see* the energy, as the intensity of the microwaves produced so much heat, such intensity of infrared echos, that they actually registered on the human eye.

The Swoop of Death required exceeding the design limitations of the inertial dampers by a huge margin. Twice. "Hold on, Harry," said Paris softly. "You like zero-g inversions?"

"No, I *hate—*"

The shuttle shot through the inner ring, into the electromagnetic maelstrom. *Now or never!* flickered across Paris's cerebrum.

He grabbed the attitude slideswitch and pulled it all the way back, pitching the nose up toward a ninety-degree angle from their direction of motion.

For a fraction of a second, the inertial dampers held out manfully, throwing off the force-load as free heat; then, with a loud click, they gave up the ghost.

A fist weighing 9,600 newtons crushed down on Paris . . . twelve times the normal force of gravity; he gasped under the strain—*Can't black out—can't lose consciousness!*

Tom Paris's world turned dull gray as he closed in on unconsciousness; under heavy-g, with blood pouring out of the brain and down toward the buttocks and abdomen, the retinal cones are the first to go, and the subject loses color vision.

Then Paris's world turned into a weird tunnel as he lost peripheral vision as well.

He strained and grunted, drastically raising his blood pressure to force the heavy, sluggish blood higher; if the brain blood pressure sank too low, he would pass out and be unable to execute Phase II of the Swoop of Death . . . and they would pound into the shaft wall at nearly half a kilometer per second.

There might be some debris left for the *Voyager* to find.

Three, two, one, NOW! Just as they attained level flight, the g-forces dropped off, and the beleaguered dampers finally kicked on-line again, Paris viciously spun the shuttle-craft rightward, rolling it 180 degrees, exactly upside down from its previous orientation.

It was a necessary part of the Swoop of Death; no human could survive twelve g's straight *up* without losing consciousness; Paris had to switch "down" and "up" to avoid making a smoking hole in the shaft hull.

Then he again yanked back, pitching the nose "up" toward ninety degrees. If he pulled it off, they would be headed in the same direction they had started—but jogged a kilometer sideways. And with a reverse up-down orientation.

They would clear the antenna . . . *if* Paris pulled it off.

As soon as he began Phase II, Paris realized instinctively that he had blown the timing. He had pulled too late. They were not going to clear the shaft wall.

Color, which had just begun to flicker back, disappeared again; Lieutenant Paris's vision tunneled down, and he once again strained against the horrific acceleration that crushed him into his seat.

Wow. We're going to die. Sorry, Kim; been a slice.

Oh, what the hell . . . If they were going to go out, decided Paris, they might as well go out spectacularly.

He jammed the attitude control all the way back, pulling the shuttlecraft so hard that not only were the inertial dampers exceeded, so were the structural design limitations of the shuttlecraft hull itself.

The g-meter climbed; Paris's tunnel vision narrowed and narrowed until he skated on the merest, monomolecular thread of consciousness.

From somewhere he heard a distant thud. He blinked. Without knowing quite why, or whether he had actually cleared the rim of the dish or simply hallucinated seeing it fly past, he willed his lead-filled arm to creep forward, pushing the attitude control and killing the acceleration.

Slowly, the g-meter dropped; the crushing gravity lessened. Then the inertial dampers finally caught up with the maneuvering, kicking on-line again with an annoyed whine.

The computer spoke, but it sounded like a dream, far away; it warned him that he was making maneuvers that exceeded his shuttle's tolerances.

"Thanks," he gasped through a throat parched and burned; he realized he had jumped from one hell to another: the interior temperature was *sixty degrees.*

Another instant in between the two antennas and their lungs would have been cooked beyond the ability of the EMH program to fix.

Maybe Neelix had a recipe for parboiled pilot and Korean barbecue.

Kim! Paris quickly killed the shuttlecraft's forward velocity—they were past the antenna, and the shields could block the small bit of microwave leakage indefinitely; no more rush. He turned to his friend and crewmate.

Kim was unconscious. Paris put his ear to the ensign's mouth; to his great relief, he heard the faint stirring of breath. Placing his hand on Kim's chest, Paris felt it rise and fall at the limits of perception.

Then Ensign Kim suddenly wheezed and groaned, rolling his head gently from side to side.

Paris fell back into his command chair, feeling his own blood pressure drop slowly, slowly back to normal. He was so exhausted, fighting both the acceleration and the unbearable heat, that he could not move.

He forced his eyes open after a few seconds; the temperature had dropped to normal. He glanced at the g-meter.

They had pegged it at fourteen g's . . . a new record for Tom Paris, and without a combat suit!

He lay back in the chair, waiting patiently for Harry Kim to wake up.

* * *

Ensign Kim blinked back to some semblance of consciousness in a white room filled with white noise. He was surrounded by some sort of instrument panel.

He decided he really should know what the instruments were for; for that matter, he really should know who he was.

He remembered nothing—not even his name. *Easy . . . steady—I'm thinking, so I'm alive. Something happened to me . . . if I can just figure out . . .*

A name floated back—Kim; Harry Kim, that was who he was! *Ensign* Harry Kim, of the *U.S.S. Voyager.* But he was not on the *Voyager,* was he?

No. He was on a shuttlecraft, the shuttle with—Tom Paris!

Kim started to turn to Tom, to ask him the stupid question "Did we make it," when the pain struck.

Kim's eyes flew wide open as a white-hot needle slid through his skull, an astounding shear of agony that lasted—a second, perhaps two. Then it was gone, leaving only a dull ache, and he blinked back to full consciousness.

He stopped himself before asking the obvious. "Uh . . . scanning . . . Tom, the hull here is much thinner."

"Thin enough to beam through?"

"Yes. Yes, I think it is; and there's a livable enviro inside the hull. No life-forms."

"What are we waiting for, Harry?"

Kim set the computer to monitor and warn them of any approaching ship or anybody beaming across, as unlikely as the latter was; then he and Paris equipped themselves with phasers, tricorders, and exploration packs and beamed inside the artificial moon.

They materialized in a long corridor that stretched forward and back as far as they could see before dropping out of sight owing to the moon's curvature.

The corridor's "walls" were actually massed pipes and cables, bundles of fiberoptics and power conduits. There was no catwalk; they had to stand directly on the bottom fiber bundle.

There was also no artificial gravity, and they were nearer the moon's core than not. Kim jumped at the sudden feeling of near-weightlessness . . . a serious mistake, as he bounded into the air, squawking and flapping his arms. He banged his head on a conduit, rebounding back toward the bottom; Paris caught Kim's trouser leg and reeled him in.

Rubbing his head, Kim worked his tricoder and announced, "From fifteen g's to less than a twentieth g. My bones are going to ache worse than my sunburn when we get back."

Paris gave an experimental hop forward, traveling a long distance but having to ward off the overhead with his hand. The pair required several minutes of practice before they caught the pattern of long, shallow jumps; thereafter, they moved far more quickly than they ever could have on a planet.

Kim kept up a long-range scan, finally finding a cross-corridor; they turned and followed it for a few kilometers before running across a deep, wide chasm . . . a circular pit in the deck.

"You want to go for it, Tom?" Kim indicated the hole.

Paris leaned over to stare, holding his light as far down as he could and stepping up the brightness to maximum. "I can't see a bottom, and the sides are smooth as glass. No ladder. You know, if a thirty-meter fall can kill you in normal gravity, then a six-hundred-meter fall can kill you here. Maybe we should think about this."

Kim monkeyed with his tricorder. "Huh. You know, I've always wanted to do this, ever since I saw those animated holoplays as a kid."

"Do what?"

Kim pulled a thermal blanket from his pack. "Tom, in this low gravity, I think we really can do it!"

"Do *what,* dammit?"

Kim grinned. "Use a blanket as a parachute."

"Cute. So how do we get back up?"

Kim rummaged in his kit. The packs were generally stowed in shuttlecraft storage bins for use by away teams exploring new planets; they contained everything an explorer could possibly need, including plenty of provisions, water blastules, binoculars, tricorder, blankets and tents, inflatable rafts—and mountaineering equipment; lots of it.

The ensign removed a coil of incredibly thin rope; an attached tag read **1000 M**.

They tied off the rope to a very solid-looking, shielded bundle of fiberoptics, then tied the other end to one another, leaving ten meters of separation between the two of them. Then they stepped to the rim of the pit.

"Harry, I take back everything I ever said about you in the mess hall. Are you *sure* this is going to work? I'm a little nervous about just jumping off a cliff."

"Don't you trust me?"

"No."

"Well, how about my calculations?"

Tom Paris considered. "All right, them I trust. Geronimo!"

"Who?"

"Ask Chakotay," said Paris mysteriously. They each took hold of two corners of the gigantic blanket and stepped over the edge.

The two Starfleet officers wafted gently down the airshaft like oak leaves lazily dropping from the tree in October. Kim discovered that he could steer after a fashion by tugging on the corner in the direction he wanted to go; he kept them in the center of the shaft, away from the sides.

They dropped for a long, long time. Kim estimated their rate of descent holding steady at somewhere between 1.5 and 2.0 meters per second . . . which meant it would take anywhere from eight to eleven minutes to reach full extension.

It took just about nine by the chronometer in the pack; he was pleased at his close estimate.

The shaft suddenly opened up into a vast, gaping room, easily two kilometers in diameter; at the same moment, the rope above Kim suddenly became taut, jerking them to an ignominious halt a kilometer down from the top, yet still half a kilometer at least above the deck. They dangled like fish on a fishing line, high above the most complex, gigantic machine Kim had ever seen.

With no idea what he was looking at, Kim aimed his tricorder and began to scan the room.

CHAPTER

6

"ALL RIGHT. WE'VE SEEN IT. NOW, WHAT IS IT?"

Kim did not answer right away; he continued imaging as much of the machine as he could. *Whatever it is,* he thought, *it's the biggest whatever I've ever seen!*

"It's something to do with a huge amount of energy," he replied at last. "Those power conduits are more than a hundred times as large as the conduits on the *Voyager,* and there are hundreds of them. The grid is obviously throwing some significant fraction of the sun's radiant energy at this moon, maybe five or ten percent . . . but what the hell are they doing with it, Tom?"

"Wish I knew. But we'd better find out; it could be a weapon, and if we're going to try to extract that pilot—"

"Shh!" Kim waved his hand at Paris, indicating *Shut up, the walls might have ears.*

"Aw, hell, nobody's listening; if they were, we'd be in custody already."

"We can't take that chance!"

"I think I'd know if we were about to be captured."

"Why? You missed it when you were a Maquis."

Paris closed his mouth and frowned at Harry Kim. On

Tom Paris's first mission as a Maquis, he had been captured by Starfleet, ending up in a penal facility in New Zealand . . . whence Captain Janeway had recruited him.

"Well," said Paris stiffly, "unless we're going to unhook and drop down to the deck, possibly never to get back out again, we'd better climb back up."

"We, ah, could break out another rope and tie it off. But I guess there's no point; if we can't figure this thing out from up here, I don't think we'll understand it by getting up close and personal." He did not add that at the moment, he hadn't a clue.

"I think we have enough to take back to the ship. We'd better start putting some pieces together, or when the captain gets back, she'll be mighty pissed."

Climbing up one kilometer was almost as easy as dropping had been. A typical, adult, human male weighs anywhere from 730 to 950 Newtons; but on the alien moon, Kim and Paris each weighed no more than thirty-five Newtons.

Kim gave the rope a vigorous tug, easily giving himself a velocity of three meters per second. This lasted six seconds, during which he covered nine meters.

They rested after every eleven tugs . . . about every hundred meters. Kim coiled up the rope during the rest stops.

Counting resting time, they made it to the lip of the pit again in just under forty-five minutes. Ensign Kim was surprised at how tired his arms were, considering he had never lifted more than the weight of a Starfleet field pack in the entire journey. Of course, he had lifted that pack more than a hundred times. Paris took it in stride; if his arms ached, he did not let on.

They backtracked their trail, Kim following the heat trail with his tricorder—directly into a solid bulkhead. He pulled up short, staring at the obstacle. "Tom, correct me if I'm wrong, but . . ."

"You're not wrong, Harry. That wasn't there an hour ago."

"Didn't we come right through here?"

"You've got the bloodhound. But I sure think we did."

Harry Kim rotated in place and scanned 360 degrees

around. "There's a parallel bulkhead about a meter to the left that goes past this block. If we can somehow get to it, maybe we can get close enough for beam-out."

They returned toward the pit, but it had disappeared. Instead, the corridor they walked along veered abruptly right, then right again, debouching into the parallel corridor they sought.

"The *walls* are moving!"

"No, really? Maybe we're hallucinating."

"Cute, Paris; I just think it's . . ."

"Weird?"

"Unnecessarily complex."

Kim stared at the solid-looking walls. Far in the distance, they heard a scrape as other bulkheads presumably went wandering. "It's almost like . . ."

"Like?"

"Nah, it's silly."

"Come on, Harry, what were you going to say?"

"Like the entire moon is a gigantic logic board, with synapses opening and closing."

Kim adjusted the tricorder and rescanned. "The electrical impulses are following patterns remarkably like, you know, neurons. Some sort of planetwide neural net—or series of nets, actually; I think the walls are connecting and severing the connections between networks.

"The next evolutionary phase," he continued, "is a neural net assembled from millions of smaller neural nets. Like a fractal: each small part is a fuzzy model of the whole thing."

"Harry? Let's get the hell out of here."

They dodged through the maze; once, Lieutenant Paris almost got caught when a bulkhead suddenly came marching toward him. Kim yanked him out of the way at the last moment, and the wall brushed past, implacable, while Kim's heart raced at his friend's close call.

At last, they got close enough to contact the onboard shuttlecraft computer and request beam-out. Kim sighed with relief as he felt in his gut the familiar tingling of the transporter beam.

Back on the shuttle, they paused to figure a strategy. Paris was worried. "Look, Kim, I don't want to go through the Swoop of Death again. We made it once; let's not push our luck. I need more time to do a smooth, sideways transition."

"Tom, it's microwave soup in between those lenses! There's no way we can hang around for more than three or four seconds without our shields being ripped to shreds."

"So?"

"So we wouldn't have anything left for the rest of the shaft out of here."

"So?"

"So—" Kim scowled; he tapped gently on the computer console. "Well, maybe we wouldn't be too badly burned if we turned around and backed out of the shaft. There's more physical plating on the aft end of the shuttlecraft."

"Just give me twenty seconds between the lenses, and I'll back us out of here so fast you'll leave your eyeballs on the forward viewer."

Kim tore open a panel and set to work, desperately wishing he had gone for the doctorate in engineering instead of opting for command school. *I could have been a brilliant starship designer,* he swore to himself.

Twenty minutes later, he cleared his throat. "I can give you eighteen seconds."

"You're on. Strap up and let's get the hell out of here."

Paris slapped Kim's seat, and the ensign hustled to his spot.

Paris turned the ship around before creeping around the dish antenna, not wanting to waste time turning around under radiation bombardment. He skillfully backed up and over the dish, through the central focus like a thread through a needle's eye, then backward along the long, deep shaft toward the surface.

Kim felt sicker and sicker as they progressed, his temperature climbing way past body-normal. His skin turned so irritated and tender, he could hardly keep his mind on his task: watching the ultraviolet count to make sure they did not blind themselves. That, even the grumpy, holographic doctor might not be able to fix.

"Better hurry, Paris," he said almost inaudibly when they were three-quarters of the way out. Paris did not waste attention responding.

Kim found himself blinking rapidly, watching sweat pour down the face of Tom Paris. Paris's skin was so fair, his face turned command-red and began to peel. Kim turned away; he did not want to see it.

Just as the ensign was starting to see small, dancing bugs all over the ship, electromagnetic stimulation of the retina—a bad sign—they burst out of the shaft into the cool blackness of space. Kim was giddy, swaying in his seat; he grimly clung to consciousness as if it were a clarinet that someone was trying to yank from his hand. The universe swam; he dimly wondered how Paris could point the shuttle at the *Voyager* when Kim couldn't even point at the moon they had just left.

But Tom Paris pointed the shuttlecraft, activated the distress beacon on a tight beam to the ship, and engaged . . . all before slumping over in his seat.

"Emer—emergency—medical—beam-out," gasped Kim to the comm link. "Tractor—shuttlecraft. . . ." The young ensign lost the battle as last, loyally following his friend into the Land of Nod.

Paris woke on the doctor's operating table. For a moment, he panicked; he had dreamed that all his skin charred off, and he was dancing in agony, his muscles and organs simply exposed to the knifey open air.

But the illusory doctor was playing a simple skin stimulator back and forth across his face and hands.

"Oh. You're awake. I suppose it was inevitable."

"Hello to you too, Dr. Schweitzer."

The doctor raised his eyebrows. "I ceased using that name a long time ago, Mr. Paris. I hope you were just being sarcastic, and you haven't suffered a loss of memory."

"Pure, unadulterated sarcasm."

"It figures. I'm programmed to ignore such maldirected attacks."

"Oh, don't be so humorless, Doctor; I can see right through you."

"Is my imaging system malfunctioning again? Oh . . . another joke. Har de har har. I don't suppose it would do any good to tell you to stay off your feet for a couple of days?"

"Not a chance, Doc."

"I didn't think so. You and Mr. Kim deserve each other." The hologram snorted. "Kes, give these two the usual advice, which they will ignore, and a temperature monitor."

Kim sat up on the next table, blinking groggily. "Gentlemen," said the doctor, "you will call me if your temperature sensors register a fever?"

"You bet," said Paris. Ensign Kim nodded; *probably doesn't even know what the hologram just said,* thought Paris.

"Good. Sickbay to Chakotay: Commander, Paris and Kim are ready for the debriefing."

"Understood, Doctor," came Chakotay's calm tones. "If they will join me in the ready room? And doctor—I'd like Kes to be present, as well."

"Why not? After all, certainly I can't have any need for her . . . I'm just a hologram, after all. Holograms don't have needs."

Paris rolled his eyes. Just what he wanted to hear: a grand holo-opera with the woman he—but the woman he could never—

Kes sighed, putting her hand on the doctor's arm. "It's all right; I'll come right back. I do want to finish the test . . . it was really challenging this time."

"It was? I mean, you really were challenged?"

"Oh, it was brutal! I'll be right back, Doctor."

"Yes . . . yes, of course you will."

There is no fear. There is no pain. There is no emotion . . . let it fade and disappear. Pure logic; logic fills your brain. Thought is symbol, and logic gives you complete power over all symbols.

The meditation helped, but Lieutenant Tuvok still found himself caught in the grip of illogical emotion, the DNA memory of a hundred thousand years ago perturbing his endocrine system, triggering the release of Vulcan vidrenalase, which affects Vulcans as adrenaline affects humans. Tuvok trembled; he could not control the fine motor skills. It was the best he could do to maintain a veneer of logic and rationality across a sea of barbaric feelings and impulses.

He stumbled along behind the Fury, behind the captain and Neelix, through the warm, moist tunnel. Even in his nightmare state, he could not help but notice that it was like a return up the birth canal; but rather than fascinating him, as it should have, the image filled Tuvok with the unaccustomed *emotions* of loathing and disgust.

Like the impulse to kill the interlocutor, Navdaq, and every other demon on the planet, all twenty-seven billion of them. It was worse than the *pon farr*—at least the mating madness was carefully channeled by ritual. Tuvok had no ritual to deal with the primitive emotions that these creatures stirred in him. Only his meditation.

Tuvok was not bothered by the darkness of the corridor, nor by what the captain considered disturbing architecture: angles that did not quite meet at ninety degrees but looked as thought they ought to, tricks of perspective that made walls or ceilings seem closer or farther than they were, or strange tilts that threw off a human's sense of balance, which was tied so completely into visual cuing.

But he was far more disturbed by the sudden intrusion of a long-forgotten cavern in the Vulcan mind, the genetic memory of defeat and slavery so complete and remote it left no trace in the historical record, which was thought to have stretched back farther in time than the conquest.

Evidently not, thought Tuvok, clutching at the logical train of thought; *apparently, there are significant gaps in the historical record. I must write a report for the* Vulcan Journal of Archeology and Prehistory. Then he shuddered.

In our innermost beings, we are not very different from Romulans after all, he thought. With bitterness—another emotion; they came thick and fast now.

In fact, Tuvok realized they would never stop . . . not until he forced himself to confront the Fury. Gritting his teeth against the terrors, Tuvok increased his stride until he stood but an arm's length behind Navdaq; then with a quick move, before he could disgrace his race further by losing his nerve, Tuvok reached out and caught Navdaq by the shoulder, spinning the creature around to face him.

Tuvok looked directly into Navdaq's face—and felt an abyss open inside him deep enough to swallow both hearts.

I know you! he thought, unable to keep excitement and emotion out of even his thoughts. *You are Ok'San, the Overlord!*

Ok'San was the most despised of all Vulcan demons, for she was the mother of all the rest. The mythology was so ancient that it was consciously known only to a few scholars; even Tuvok knew only dimly of the stories, and only because of his interest in Vulcan history.

But all Vulcans knew Ok'San, but preferred not to think about her, for she represented *loss of control* and *loss of reason.* There was little else that a sane Vulcan dared not consider apart from the loss of everything it meant to be a Vulcan: logic, control, order, and reason.

In demonic mythology, Ok'San crept through the windows at night, the hot, dry Vulcan night, and crouched on the chests of her "chosen" dreamers: poets, composers, authors, philosophers, scientists, political analysts . . . the very people whose creativity was slowly knitting together the barbaric strands of early Vulcan society into a vision of a logical tomorrow, who groped for shreds of civilization in the horror of Vulcan's yesterday.

She crouched on a dreamer's chest, leaned over his writhing body, and pressed her lips against his. She spat into his mouth, and the spittle rolled down his throat and filled his hearts with the *Fury of Vulcan.*

The Fury of Vulcan manifested as a berserker rage that flooded the victim and drove him to paroxysms of horrific violence that defied the descriptive power of logic.

Tuvok had tried to contemplate what must pass through a Vulcan's mind to drive him to kill his own family with a blunt stick, striking their heads hard enough to crush bone and muscle and still have force enough to destroy the brain. In one of the few instances of the Fury of Vulcan to be well recorded by the testimony of many witnesses, a Vulcan hunter-warrior named Torkas of the Vehm, perhaps eighty thousand years ago, grabbed up a leaf-bladed Vulcan Toth spear and set out after the entire population of his village. He managed to kill ninety-seven and wound an additional fourteen, six critically, before he was killed.

Tuvok had always believed Ok'San was the personification of the violent, nearly sadistic rage that filled the hearts of Vulcans before Surak. The Fury of Vulcan always seemed like a disease of the nervous system; yet it was curious that there were no recorded instances of the Fury within historical times . . . not a one.

Diseases do not die out; and it was unlikely in the extreme that primitive Vulcans, who had neither logic nor medical science, could have destroyed the virus that caused the Fury.

It was an enigma, until now.

CHAPTER

7

THIS IS THE FURY, THOUGHT TUVOK, STARING INTO THE FACE OF Ok'San . . . albeit a male aspect of Ok'San. *I am the Fury— and everyone within my grasp is in grave danger.*

The rage was so barely under his control that Tuvok did not even hear Navdaq ask a question, presumably a variation on "What do you want?"

Trembling still, Tuvok forced himself to speak: "Sir— your features—they are—fascinating—yet others do not all—all share. Are—are—are you all one?"

Navdaq smiled, ratcheting up the emotional response another notch inside the Vulcan: the interlocutor's smile began to trigger even more genetic memories of the horrors of the occupation.

"The Holy are many, but they are one. They have come from many planets, but so many years back it disappears into the haze of memory, even for them; they joined in heaven as the only rightful heirs of the divine."

"But you still—maintain the separateness . . . ."

"The divinity of the Holy manifests as many points of a many-pointed star; but the pentagram describes the five great classes of being. I myself am of the family Sanoktisan-daruval, of the second great class. My divine ancestors ruled as kings under the Autocrat. The Holy, though one, are yet separate species and cannot mix together, cannot dilute the separateness of the points."

Ruled as kings . . .

There was not a shadow of a doubt in Tuvok's ravaged mind; the Sanoktisandaruval were the Ok'San, and they had ruled over Vulcan.

Perhaps they were benevolent kings under their own, internal standard. But tiny crumbs of ancient memory broke loose from the abyss and floated to the surface, where Tuvok could stare at them.

A smoldering furnace—perhaps a fusion power plant remembered by ancients who had no reference beyond a wood cookfire . . . a lake of fire, or radioactivity, or even liquid helium; slaves writhing in agony, suffering the torments of the damned—or perhaps struck repeatedly by the terror-projection machines . . . mountain-sized demons filling the field of view—holographic projections to convey orders quickly to a large group of slaves?

I am a slave of the household of Javastaras. I rise from a fitful three hours of dreamless sleep in which waking dreams torment me. I am compelled forward to crawl on my stomach alongside six other slaves before the hell-princess Meliflones, whom Javastaras wishes to conjoin. She is pleased, laughing and clapping her hands in childish joy.

But we are forgotten as Javastaras and Meliflones court, and I crouch on my knees, afraid to move lest I call attention to myself.

It was Tuvok's first conscious genetic memory.

More frozen images: trapped and bound in a tiny room while demons ripped and tore at the flesh. Doctors, surely, giving inoculations or engaging in medical procedures, perhaps without anesthetic. Many-tentacled monsters screaming and thrashing their limbs . . . pumps, hydraulics, electrical cables? A threshing machine?

But the genetic memories that were not simply miscon-structions were the pain, the terror, the physical abuse and overwork to the point of death, and most especially the invasion of the most private corners of a Vulcan mind, for there dwelt the Terror and the Fury—and there the Furies touched most deeply.

I am a young girl now, performing in the drama. And they make me stand frozen while a young boy approaches jerkily, anguish on his face but blood on his hands . . . .

For Tuvok suddenly remembered the slave torcs, metallic collars worn around the throat that melded into the mind, controlling the slave's every action, every word, every *thought*. They became no longer Vulcans but animals, beasts of the field, bowing and capering and doing their masters' will instead of their own. Tuvok "remembered" the shows, the degrading fantasies in which Vulcan slaves played the role of mythological beings, talking animals, children, even rocks and other scenery. Dramas of torment and humiliation in which one captive was forced to murder another, the limbs of each controlled by his slave torc.

I am an old man. I am tired. I hurt, but I cannot stop. I work incessantly; I am possessed. The demons wish me dead. I feel a pain in my lower heart, and perhaps they will get their wish after all. I haven't the strength to fight anymore, so I am useless. They discard the useless.

To genetically "remember" such specific incidents in such detail must mean, Tuvok reasoned, that they had occurred again and again, over a period of tens of thousands of years. And the worst memory of all was the utter helplessness . . . they could never even free themselves; they had to wait for the Unclean, whoever they were, to arrive and drive out the Furies for their own reasons.

It was a bitter truth to vomit up; but now that he had dragged it from the black abyss of the Vulcan unconscious into the light, where reason and logic could analyze it, the emotional charge of the memories began to fade.

It happened in the blink of an eye, though it felt like a hundred years to Tuvok. But Navdaq turned away, the conversation over, and resumed its trek to the Autocrat, leading Janeway, Neelix, and Tuvok himself while the Vulcan began finally to come to peace inside himself, suppressing the powerful emotions behind the mask of logic and restoring his natural equilibrium.

The gods had arrived, to drive away the Furies and demons.

The "gods" were hideous! Enormous, bloated, black wasps, horrors of fiber woven with metal—Tuvok caught only glimpses of writing mouths sucking the life-energy out of entire ships, *in deep space.* The gods did not need boats to sail the celestial waters; they crawled the vasty deep naked and horrible, bodies puffing out with internal pressures, mandibles and hundred of multifaceted eyes causing Vulcan slaves to fall face to the ground and sometimes even die of terror.

The Ok'San turned their terrors on the wasp-gods; the weapon had no effect on insectoid, soul-feeding horrors. In fear and fury, the Ok'San turned on their own slaves, throwing them into combat against the gods; the slaves died by the tens of thousands, split and eaten live before their paralyzed fellow slaves.

The Ok'San fell back, beaten for the first time, frightened and astonished at these beings over whom they had no power! And the Furies fled, enraged but impotent, helpless—but vowing to return and reclaim *what was owed.* But as Tuvok watched them leave, logic help him, he cowered . . . he was *afraid* that the Furies were leaving; he wanted them back!

Shame burned in his face at the racial memory, another powerful, unaccustomed emotion. Tuvok bowed his head in retroactive shame and humiliation.

Thenceforth, history fell back into the rhythm that Tuvok had studied. The wasp-gods, the Unclean, were uninterested in the Vulcan ex-slaves. There was no economically viable reason to maintain slavery in any spacefaring culture; the only reason was arrogance, the sheer joy of oppression itself. The Unclean had no motivation or interest; they saw the Furies as a threat . . . they removed the threat.

And the Vulcans, suddenly granted freedom, their fondest wish, fell to warring among themselves, for they could no longer contemplate life without the overseer's whip. They mistook custom for natural law and sought to perpetuate the vile institution of slavery.

Savage wars erupted, acts of bloodthirsty vengeance and

preemptive barbarity became commonplace. And from the chaos of "the war of all against all," as the human philosopher Hobbes had described, rose the cleansing logic and system of Surak, resurrecting Vulcan high culture on the operating table of reason.

Slowly, Tuvok began to remember who he was and, more important, *where* he was. He blinked back to the present in a dank, dungeonlike hole—the antechamber of the Autocrat. Navdaq was gone; they awaited its return.

Another stupid, useless meeting, thought B'Elanna Torres; *another chance to find out that I'm unnecessary on this ship; a supernumerary, a third engine pod, a white elephant.*

Ensign Kim cleared his throat. He and Paris had been trying, with limited success, to describe the vast machinery they had seen inside the moon.

Commander Chakotay, Lieutenant B'Elanna Torres, and Kes turned toward the young ensign. "You have something to add?" asked the commander, command duty officer in Captain Janeway's absence. B'Elanna tried not to let her annoyance show. If she could change just one thing about Harry, she would make him bolder about offering his own opinion. Half the time, it seemed he allowed Paris to speak his lines for him, as if he weren't even present.

"Actually, a suggestion, sir. Can we adjourn and go down to the holodeck? I could feed the dataclip from the holocam into the computer and simulate the machinery."

"Yeah," said Torres, a little too quickly; she was overanxious to please—and knew it. "I second! Let me get a look at it. I promise I can figure it out."

Torres was uncomfortably aware that she had contributed very little to the discussion so far; actually, Paris's description had not been particularly helpful, but she did not want to say that. It sounded too much like an excuse.

Chakotay shifted the debriefing. Ten minutes later, they stood on an invisible platform, hovering half a mile above the gigantic machine . . . exactly the position from which Kim had used the tricorder.

B'Elanna stared down between her boots; she tried to get

an overall impression of the *flow* of the system as a whole before getting a close-up. The entire apparatus was too large to comprehend any other way.

"Power obviously comes in through those conduits in the southwest quadrant. Computer: superimpose bearings over the image. There—the conduits at one-zero-seven and one-zero-eight. That's the power supply."

She paced back and forth, absently rubbing her Klingon brow ridge . . . an unconscious habit of discomfort. She noticed and stopped herself.

She held her hand out, palm down, tracing the probable movement of power from the input into the guts of the machine. "Subspace channeling gear . . . some kind of compression device—really huge, 10^{20}, 10^{25} watts. Imaging gear—never mind, just for aiming, I think. Commander? They're right on the knife edge of transporter technology, but they go off in some funny direction. I can't tell exactly what it is. But I don't think we're going to like it."

"Why not?"

"I think when you put the whole thing together—and I have no idea if it's operable yet—you somehow have the power to reach out and crush something. Maybe even through subspace."

"Something?"

"I don't know . . . a ship, a planet, empty space, a sun. Something—and crush it really hard, I mean; hard enough maybe to turn a sun into a neutron star, or even a black hole, if it starts out big enough."

"Are you sure?"

B'Elanna Torres flushed . . . an alien reaction for a Klingon; it came purely from her human half. But both sides understood doubt and embarrassment. *He thinks I'm crazy,* she thought. *He doesn't trust me anymore.*

Or am I just paranoid now? She licked her lips nervously, uncertain what to say or do next. She felt a terrible pressure to *do something,* anything! Say anything. Something, for Kahless's sake!

"Chakotay," said Kes, "I think B'Elanna's right. I recognize some of this technology . . . it's similar to the way the

Caretaker taught us to build our energy-distribution centers."

Chakotay nodded. "If an engineer and a technician agree, then that is good enough for me. Ensign Kim?"

Kim shrugged; he didn't know enough engineering to offer an opinion. Nobody asked Paris.

"Let's review what we know," said the first officer. "The aliens have built an energy-collection grid around their sun; it captures perhaps ten percent of the sun's radiant energy, but beams it via microwaves to this artificial moon. The moon contains a giant apparatus—or more likely many such devices—that takes this enormous energy and converts it into a beam that can project a crushing force, possibly through subspace, powerful enough to turn a star into a neutron star. Is that a fair statement?"

"Put that way," said Torres, "it scares the hell out of me." She tried to imagine what anyone would want with such a collection of dangerous toys.

Chakotay nodded. "Scares the hell out of me too. We also know the aliens have captured a crashed shuttlecraft and possibly a still living pilot . . . and currently, they have Captain Janeway and Lieutenant Tuvok as guests."

Chakotay stood silent, thinking. B'Elanna could almost read his thoughts by watching his expression . . . he glanced at the empty space they unconsciously reserved where Janeway would have stood; glanced down at the huge machine a half-kilometer below their feet; fingered his comm badge.

At last he spoke. "I believe we should request the captain's immediate return and tell her what we saw; I don't like this picture."

"Aye, aye, sir," said Ensign Kim. "Request permission to return to the bridge."

"Does anybody have anything else to say?" asked the commander. No one spoke. B'Elanna especially didn't speak; all she had to say was *I agree* . . . and Chakotay didn't need a yes-person. "Then the meeting is adjourned. Kim, return to the bridge and contact Captain Janeway. Paris, stand by for an emergency beam-out, just in case. Torres, you monitor the moon; tell me if there is any sudden power surge . . . I want to know if they power up their weapon. Dismissed."

The rest of the senior crew scurried off about their tasks, but Torres remained behind with Chakotay, staring down at the huge machine . . . the huge weapon.

"Chakotay? Why would anyone want to crush a planet through subspace?"

"Let's hope that's all they can do," said the commander. "I'm afraid . . ." He did not elaborate his fear, and this time she couldn't read his thoughts; eventually, B'Elanna decided to give him some space to work it out.

"Captain," said Tuvok hoarsely. Janeway and Neelix each grabbed one of his arms and sat him down on an iron bench. The bench was decorated with skulls and spider-webs. *My God,* thought Captain Janeway, *he's just passed through the dark night of the soul!*

"Tuvok, don't try to speak just yet," said the captain; "you've had a very bad reaction to—"

"Captain," he whispered, "I am well aware of my reaction. I am perfectly all right now; I have controlled the outbreak."

"Maybe we should contact Commander Chakotay . . . the doctor should look you over."

"I assure you, I have regained full control of myself. It is an effort, but there will be no future outbreaks of emotion. Captain, I must warn you about something, who these Furies actually are."

"Furies?" Janeway sat back, surprised by how *right* the name sounded. At once, her vague memory clicked into place. She had learned about the Furies—could they be the same Furies?—in her second-year Academy class in military history. A previous captain of the *Enterprise* had encountered hideous beings some six or seven decades earlier in Federation space; they almost destroyed his ship—they almost overran the quadrant!

At the time, she found the tale of marginal interest; she was worried about a term paper on rotating Okudagrams, and the adventure was just one of an improbable number of similar stories attributed to that ship and that captain.

Captain Kirk had not been stretching the truth; the similarities were too great. But if James Kirk discovered any special clues or insights into the nature of the Furies, that information did not remain in her faded memory of an Academy lecture. If the Furies were more than just monstrous-looking aliens, Janeway and Tuvok would have to "remember" for themselves, staring back along their own DNA histories.

She stared around the antechamber in which Navdaq had deposited them. The room was not quite round; the walls were not quite perpendicular; the room was an iron stew-pot, indifferently formed by a careless ironmonger. A bench tilted against one side, and Janeway and Tuvok sat upon it, recovering their self-control; but Neelix paced anxiously in front of the bench, keyed like an animal that smelled danger. His yellow cheek-streaks looked like burnt umber in the faint, red glow from the walls.

Janeway considered the Furies, wondering what Tuvok might remember; Vulcans had been civilized far longer than humans; there might be records.

"Well . . . I know they used to live somewhere else and hold other races as slaves. They used a fear projector, some kind of device to project terror into their slaves to prevent a revolt. But I don't know *how* I know all that. It's as if . . . "

"Oh right," said the Talaxian, more peeved than usual; "like you were there!"

"Yes," said the Vulcan. "As if I were there."

Tuvok closed his eyes. Calmly, unemotionally, he recounted the hell he had journeyed through for the past thirty minutes . . . and the memories it had raked up. Janeway listened with rapt attention, astonished and a little chilled by how close it struck to her own vision.

"We did encounter these Furies once before in recorded history," concluded the Vulcan.

Janeway nodded. "Yes, I remember: the original *Enterprise* fought them to a standstill some decades past. I read about it in Military History 120 or 140."

Tuvok raised an eyebrow. "Indeed. I read about it in the message traffic at the time."

The captain stared. "Tuvok, that long ago?"

"Indeed, I confess I did not pay sufficient attention at the time to benefit us now."

Janeway strained to remember everything she had heard or read about the Furies in years past; the intelligence amounted to a very little pile after all. "But why bother to come to Federation space?" She turned her hands up. "What's wrong with all this? Why isn't this enough for them?"

"Captain," concluded Tuvok, rational as any Vulcan, "I believe that heaven, as Navdaq calls it, was in the Alpha Quadrant. And the subject races included Vulcans . . . and doubtless your own."

"You mean—but we were never . . . ." She pressed her lips together; it would indeed explain much about her own reaction, the unexpected and irrational fear and disgust she felt on first seeing Navdaq.

A hundred thousand years ago, humans might have had no reason to feel such horror at these Furies—early men might think them gods or demons, but they saw gods and demons everywhere!

Yet *something* had made the entire human race, and even the savage, violent Vulcan race, simply give up and allow themselves to be enslaved for tens of thousands of years, if Tuvok's racial memory was accurate; all so long before history began that there was no record . . . except in the DNA.

And then she recalled, with a chill, Navdaq's words: *We shall return to heaven, whence we were cast out, and cleanse it of all Unclean . . . . Heaven shall be cleansed of all but the Furies.*

She stood, blocking Neelix's path; he almost ran into her before noticing and stopping.

Janeway felt a sense of unreality. She had no illusions. Biologically, humans of today were not that different from humans of a hundred thousand years ago.

If it worked then, it would work now.

The hour is at hand . . . .

"Captain, did Navdaq describe the Unclean? I confess

there were many minutes when I heard nothing of what was said."

"I wasn't listening very well myself," admitted Janeway ruefully. She and Tuvok sat quietly for a moment until Neelix broke the silence by clearing his throat.

"Well, I was listening the whole time . . . and it did paint a reasonably complete picture of what it called the Unclean. It described them as a cross between a virus and a machine."

Janeway shook her head. "That's no race I'm aware of in the Alpha Quadrant, at least not in the Federation or the Klingon, Cardassian, or Romulan Empires."

"Yet we encounter new races every day," said Tuvok. "We may yet meet with their remnants in a few years. They may not be able to help us against the Furies, however; they have clearly degenerated far enough over the millennia to lose control over 'heaven' after once defeating Navdaq's people."

"Tuvok, I get the queasy feeling that we're the thin, red line." She glanced at the iron-red walls that gave no heat; unconsciously, she stepped away.

"I am unfamiliar with that reference, Captain."

"British Army, five hundred years ago. We, my friend, are the first defense of the entire Alpha Quadrant against this terrible invasion . . . assuming they're serious."

"I don't think Navdaq is lying," said Neelix. "He seems quite sincere and passionate."

"Then we are in trouble, Tuvok. It's one ship against twenty-seven billion invaders. Been practicing with that phaser?" She smiled, taking the edge off the cut.

"Your point is taken, Captain."

Neelix interrupted. "Why always look at the dark side? You should count your blessings that you found out in time. We can overwhelm them and stop the invasion!"

Janeway glowered at Neelix. Just what she needed: more swashes to be buckled! "Next question: why all the nightmare architecture, the darkness, the moist, rotting air?"

Tuvok, fully himself again in Navdaq's absence, extracted his tricorder and scanned the local area. "I detect a great many microorganisms in the atmosphere, far more than on Earth or Vulcan."

"You mean germs?" worried Neelix. "Are we inoculated against them? I don't want to come down with some bizarre, alien disease."

"It is not likely, Mr. Neelix, that alien microbes would even recognize any of the three of us as food. In fact, I believe these microorganisms are closer to plankton than to viruses or bacteria: simple, single-celled plantlike organisms with no capability of reprogramming a cell's DNA."

"Plankton?" Janeway thought for a moment. "Tuvok, is it possible that Navdaq and the other Furies are filter-feeders?"

"I believe that is a very likely scenario. The horns and tendrils on the heads of most of the races we have seen so far, and the wormlike cilia in Navdaq's mouth, may well be organs that suck in moist air and filter out the microorganisms for nourishment."

"And the darkness and musty smell simply encourage the fungi and plankton to grow," she mused. "I wonder . . . the remote ancestors of both humans and Vulcans used to dwell in holes in the ground, tens of millions of years ago. Yet now we associate being underground with death and damnation. When did we first begin doing so?

"Could the Furies have given us that fear, too?"

They fell silent, and fifteen minutes passed. There was still no sign of either Navdaq or the Autocrat. Janeway almost touched her commbadge to ask Chakotay what was happening on the *Voyager;* but she suddenly felt reluctant to announce that the brooch on her chest was a communications device—just in case they were being observed.

After a while, Janeway opened another line of inquiry; in fact, she had decided to initiate as many logical speculations as possible to keep her Vulcan lieutenant firmly grounded in his natural element.

"Tuvok, why is Navdaq being so open with us, with the very people the Furies once enslaved?"

"If I had to speculate, I would conclude that he does not see us as the enemy. After all, we are here, not there; we are in the Delta Quadrant, and the Unclean are in the Alpha Quadrant."

"I'm getting a bit worried, Tuvok. Navdaq has been gone a long time, leaving us alone in this giant saucepan. I think we're being deliberately delayed . . . and maybe our cover is blown after all."

"Blown? Do you mean they've figured out who you are?" Neelix began to glance suspiciously into every dark, dank corner, as if expecting a horde of Navdaqs to pop out with pitchforks.

Almost as if in response, a crack as bright-red as fire opened in the iron wall immediately opposite them; slowly, an oilwood door began to creak open.

Beyond it, they saw only the red glow of more "hot" iron.

"I believe the doctor will see us now," muttered Janeway.

CHAPTER

8

I NEVER UNDERSTAND WHAT SHE'S TALKING ABOUT, THOUGHT AN annoyed Neelix as they rose and slipped through the door. The red walls were not particularly hotter than the rest of the planet; they were noticibly brighter. Neelix wondered whether such comparatively bright light bothered the Furies; was the corridor intended to put local suppliants off their game, make them nervous before meeting their Autocrat? It had the opposite effect on the Talaxian, tired of the black gloom.

The glowing-iron corridor wound around a series of bends that were perfect right angles; the floor remained on the same level; the ceiling lowered, then in a trick of suddenness exploded up and out of sight. The glow grew steadily brighter until even Neelix had to squint against it, a glow like metal heated to the searing temperature. The walls, ceiling, and floor were all of a color, so that the *Voyager*'s guide had a hard time telling exactly where one ended and the other began—the corners were lost in the glare. He could not see how far the corridor extended, and *that* disturbed him.

I'd better be ready to defend the crew, he thought, casually brushing the phaser on his belt. Then belatedly: *I'd better not die down here, or Kes will kill me.* Somehow, the Fury planet brought up the most morbid thoughts.

Not being able to really see when the corridor turned, the away team several times piled up against the wall, thankful that it was not as hot as it looked.

Then they turned and saw a black spot in the distance, the only disharmony of color since leaving the antechamber. It was a door, a simple dungeon door of some local oily wood. A mechanical lever—mechanical!—jutted from the bottom. Neelix boldly squatted down to yank on it.

The door flew open with a bang, wrenching itself from the startled scout, who yelled and lunged backward, flaring his arms to shield his companions from whatever was coming through the door—nothing, as it turned out.

Inside was a room so bright it hurt all three pairs of eyes, bright and hellish white: a combination to strike terror in the guts of a local, used to musty darkness as they were. Neelix did not need the captain's tricorder to know the air was dry and sterile, devoid of comforting plankton-food and yet another blow to the self-confidence of a Fury.

A huge figure sat in black silhouette at the far end of the room. The Autocrat's face and flesh were obscured by the difference in light; but his bulk was unmistakable. Seated, he towered even over Tuvok, while his shoulders were as wide as he was tall. His neck and arms articulated in the wrong places, and Neelix's stomach turned slowly.

There was something dreadful about the Autocrat. He slowly rose and fell, groaning up to full extension and slithering down against the desk.

As Neelix's eyes adjusted, he began to scope the room. Again, it was badly fitted, walls meeting at strange angles, alien geometry that made Neelix dizzy. The light was so intense, it hurt even Neelix's eyes. A gigantic, U-shaped desk and riveted-iron chair occupied one entire side of the room; there were no other chairs, and the three supplicants had to stand before the Autocrat like accused criminals. Beyond the Autocrat, or behind the away team, Neelix could see little because of the intense lighting.

The voice was the dry rattle of bones down a chimney, a

serpent's sound, the voice of a deadly Thrack Gourd-Shaker lizard. "So. You. Have come. For trade deal."

Neelix answered earnestly, pretending to be unaffected by the sights and sounds. "Quite so, O great . . . potentate. I am Captain Neelix of the merchant vessel *Sunbird*. I—"

Janeway, standing to Neelix's side, shifted slightly as if by accident and trod upon his foot.

"Ow! Of the merchant vessel *Songbird*, and these are my assistants. Lowly, unimportant assistants. The clumsy one on the left is Vice-President Janeway, while on the right is—"

"But what. Have you. For our interest?"

"Ah, why, we can probably find in, er, storage any item from the vast reaches of the Delta Quadrant you desire . . . the fabled Britelflowers of Dazan Two, whose merest odor fills the heart with intense longing for the object of one's affections—that is, if you have need of such an item here. A necklace made of the teeth of the Drugga Bear, the most beautiful, symmetrical carboniferous crystal teeth you've ever . . . no? Well, surely no person of discriminating taste could pass up an opportunity to buy Distak 'nk'Arat lava-water, the most intense intoxicant in the quadrant, and no lingering aftereffect! A special price, half the going rate . . . special introductory offer for new customers only."

The Autocrat began to make a peculiar noise that sounded like the death-gurgle of an animal dying of pain and thirst. *He's laughing at me,* thought Neelix in a flush of anger.

"We have no."

"Well, if you don't have—"

"Need for such. Items of frivolity. What have. You for. Our holy quest?"

"You—mean weapons? Navigational charts?"

The Autocrat rattled at a much higher frequency. "Arifacts! Have no. Need for tools. Can make ourselves. What can you. Offer of. Spiritual nature?"

Neelix opened his mouth for a moment, then shut it. He repeated the action, then a third time. *Honesty!* he told himself. *Why not give it a whirl? When all else fails . . .* "I'm sorry," he admitted, "I have no idea what you're talking about."

Abruptly, *Navdaq's* voice spoke from behind the Autocrat. Neelix had missed the huge Fury in the glare. "He means, you tendrilless coward, that all that the Furies really need is the *courage* to face the Unclean; the *purity* to gain heaven; the *loyalty* to obey without pause; the *cruelty* to war without mercy against whoever wishes to keep us from our destiny! But we find such values in short supply aboard the *Songbird*. Or was it the *Sunbird?* We've lost track."

Uh-oh. "Sir, you impugn my motives and my character!"

The Autocrat "laughed" again, sending a chill down Neelix's spine. "Yes! Yes yes. You understand! It is good."

The captain's commbadge beeped; Neelix jumped, startled by the sound. "Captain," said Chakotay's voice, "we've detected a fleet of ships lifting from the planet at constant bearing, decreasing distance. Prepare for emergency beamout."

"Chakotay, get the ship out of—!" shouted Janeway. From nowhere, from behind, a hand with suckers and squirming, wormlike digits wrapped around her mouth, cutting off the rest of her command and her breath. Quick as Nick, Navdaq stood before her; he ripped the badge from her uniform, tearing a strip of cloth and exposing her undertunic. He flung the badge across the room, while more Furies did the same to the commbadges worn by Neelix and Tuvok.

Neelix held his breath, desperately hoping the *Voyager* had gotten a lock before the reference point headed south. But he felt no welcome uneasiness of dematerialization.

"Your emergency weapon beam will do you no good, no good. *Unclean,* and ally of the *Unclean* who destroyed our projection antenna! You are nothing before the rage of the Furies. You will live to see your filth cleansed from heaven. And you, traitor to your own, friend of *Unclean*—" Navdaq turned his fury upon Neelix, who was doing his best to maintain dignity and doing a remarkable job. "You made your impious way along the right-angle path, and so shall you share now their fate. Favored, take them below."

Neelix struggled uselessly for a few moments while the

"favored" gripped his wrists in a grasp of steel to push him directly toward a painfully bright wall. The wall contained a loophole, invisible in the glare, and the guard propelled him through.

He stole a glance at Janeway and Tuvok; they were docile, allowing themselves to be gently shepherded—brawling was hardly an option, outnumbered as they were—by two of twelve massive creatures, hexapedal, a rim of what must be vision organs around their heads protected by alien visors.

Damn! Damn my instincts—and why didn't I LISTEN to them? He had no answer; it was a humiliating position for an interstellar explorer of Neelix's repute.

Neelix relaxed and went where they pushed him. They made progress into an immediate corridor as dank and dungeonesque as would warm the feeding-tendrils of any self-respecting Fury. When Neelix's eyes adjusted to the midnight dark, he saw that the favored had removed their visors, revealing six eye-orbs: two in front, two in back, one each on the side. Their limbs were articulated so that there was neither front nor back; they could move or act in either direction with equal facility.

Once in thieves' blackness, the favored dropped to four of their limbs and began to gallop, forcing their bipedal prisoners to sprint to stay ahead and avoid being knocked down and trampled. The favored steered them through hall after hall, down a spiral staircase on which Neelix tripped and fell hard on one wrist, then across a courtyard full of gaze-averting natives.

The Talaxian caught a quick glimpse of metal-grate floors and oilwood walls, of high, iron ceilings and buildings that rattled like fiery furnaces. But he could not track the route, for they were dragged too quickly.

Any thought of escape was thwarted by the breakneck speed of the hunt and the single, unyielding hand that closed around both of Neelix's wrists. No one so much as glanced up; the prisoners were stampeded through the ruly crowd, then under a skull-bedecked archway to a pit.

The favored yanked them all to a stop. Janeway and Tuvok were out of breath, but Neelix was destroyed! His heart pounded like the Autocrat's laugh, and he could not catch his breath. *I'm too old for this nonsense!* he bemoaned, not for the first, tenth, or last time. The one problem with swashbuckling as a profession was the tremendous demand placed upon the physical body.

Neelix's eyes were screwed shut, his mouth wide open sucking in the acrid, burning stench with its minute trace of oxygen, a mere contamination (so it tasted to Neelix) of an otherwise caustic gas.

The favored conversed, Neelix guessed, in extremely high-frequency, highly compressed data packets. The much-ballyhooed Starfleet Universal Translator did nothing, could not even detect that the occasional squeak they made to each other was an unreasonably speeded-up monologue; when two or more squeaked in unison, they were probably interleaving a conversation faster than the ear—or Neelix's ear, in any case—could follow. After the conference, the mob set off again, somewhat slower.

Down, down, down they continued, through dungeon and cavern tilted alarmingly, throwing off Neelix's balance, wrapped by walls of indifferent, disordered joining that seemed not quite right to the eye. Now they began to pass barred cells, and Neelix's sides ached, his lungs a searing agony. There was no oxygen at all! He was going to pass out from the exertion.

But he staggered on, driving himself forward more by pride than fear: Neelix would not be the one who collapsed; he would not shame the captain and Lieutenant Tuvok.

The favored wrenched the away team to a halt, nearly pulling Neelix's arm out of its socket. He kept his feet, though his knees buckled. He leaned over at the waist and focused his mind on one breath, then another.

He turned his head to the side, still seeing stars. Janeway's face was pale in dim lamplight, her eyes unfocused; she was having no little trouble of her own. But Tuvok remained unperturbed; his eyes were half-lidded, face impassive, Vulcan chest rising and falling in slow rhythm. *He comes from a hot, dry planet,* Neelix reassured himself, *none too different from this, save for the humidity.* He still felt a hard lump of resentment.

One of the favored skittered forward and extracted a

ridiculous key, a *physical key* from some sort of pocket somewhere—Neelix could not see where. It inserted the flat card into a slot and the cell door slid noiselessly open.

The favored did not move. When Tuvok began to move toward the cell, his favored let him go. Janeway began to join him, but she hesitated a moment at the cell door; a limb struck her back with brutal force, smashing her to the ground at Tuvok's feet. The Vulcan helped her up.

Neelix stepped briskly into the cell with the other two. The guard pulled tight the door; with a rush of wind, the favored departed along the corridor in the same direction they had been traveling.

Neelix let out a breath, sucked in another greedy lungful. "I was afraid"—he gasped—"they would slap me—in my own cell—out of respect for—my local status."

The beginning of a stately, old, human poem by Samuel Taylor Coleridge kept running through Captain Janeway's head; she couldn't stop it:

> *In Xanadu did Kubla Khan*
> *A stately pleasure-dome decree:*
> *Where Alph, the sacred river, ran*
> *Through caverns measureless to man*
> *Down to a sunless sea.*

Janeway began to prowl the cage while Neelix caught his breath. She was annoyed more than anything else by the spectacularly bad timing of Chakotay's communication, forcing her to reveal to the Autocrat what the pendants were. If the damned Furies had just held their horses a few minutes longer and attacked the *Voyager* after the away team was slapped in chokey, the favored might never have guessed that the pins were devices.

Without communicators, they had no prayer of being beamed out, even if the ship was still in orbit . . . which she doubted. Chakotay would obey his order to protect the *Voyager*, which meant getting the hell out of orbit, considering the odds they faced.

She felt the bars; metallic, very hard, the alloy not one she was familiar with at first glace, though she would need a tricorder to tell for certain. Tuvok joined her, and the Vulcan cautiously pushed his hand between the bars as far as he could, up to his forearm.

"Captain," he said, "I do not believe there is any force shield on this cage."

"You mean all that's standing between us and freedom are a few lousy steel bars?" Janeway shook her head, staring in amazement up and down the corridor at the long rows of similar cages in the cell block. The cells faced each other with no privacy; even the lump that must be the toilet was placed in the middle of the room, in full view of the rest of the cages—not to mention the other prisoners that would be held in the cell itself, which was obviously designed for four inmates. It was barbaric . . . unless the Furies did not have even the concept of actual privacy, which made a certain amount of sense; presumably, if a Fury prisoner used the facilities, the rest would avert their eyes, as they did when passing in the "streets" (which were actually underground corridors).

"The bars are not exactly steel; but your point is, in essence, correct."

Janeway sighed. "This is such a strange quadrant. They have warp drive, directed energy weapons, subspace communication—but no shields, replicators, or holodecks; and they seem to have room here for a few hundred prisoners in this block alone, and who knows how many other blocks there are? I always thought our different pieces of technology would go hand in hand . . . and all would go together with freedom."

"Evidently, our society is more a fortuitous accident than we like to believe," said the Vulcan.

"But what the Furies *don't* have is so easily deduced from what they *do* have!" She paused, considering; on the other hand, the Federation had no idea how to make an artificial wormhole. They couldn't bring people back by cloning them from the dead body. They couldn't just use the transporter to disassemble an injured or sick person and reassemble him without the medical problem. Neither could they make a deflector shield they could beam through, create a tractor beam powerful enough to bend a phaser beam, fly ships as fast as subspace communications—and for that matter, they hadn't even managed to move beyond the need for a huge fleet of starships to protect them from marauders and looters.

How long before they developed powers like the Organians? Evidently, forever.

"The view back is always sharper than the view ahead," quoted Neelix. He sounded annoyed; he didn't seem to appreciate being reminded that in some ways, his quadrant was backward compared to the Alpha Quadrant.

"Maybe so," said Janeway, not wishing to offend. "But the important point is how we get out of this cell. As a famous poet once remarked, 'Stone walls do not a prison make, Nor iron bars a cage.'"

Tuvok, still methodically testing each bar, absently muttered, "I believe you will find that the author is Richard Lovelace, and the poem is *Lucasta*, 'To Althea: From Prison,' 1649."

"I'll take your word for it."

"Well," said Neelix, "*these* walls and *these* bars look an awful lot like a cage to me."

"Damn; I wish we still had communicators. It would be easy for the *Voyager* simply to beam us out. We *have* to figure a way to stop the invasion!"

Neelix looked surprised. "You don't have a communicator?"

"Neelix . . . you saw Navdaq take them, along with our phasers and tricorders, anything we could use as a weapon or communications device."

Neelix looked incredulously at the captain. "Are you trying to tell me that, as useful as those things are, you don't carry *spare* communicators?"

"No, why should we?"

"In case someone takes it away from you!"

Janeway felt her face begin to flush; she didn't like to think of herself as unprepared—but Neelix had a point. "Great idea, Mr. Neelix—'the view back is always sharper than the view ahead.' Did *you* happen to bring a spare communicator?"

Neelix looked pained and offended . . . his natural expression, when he was not looking officious and self-important. "I most certainly did!"

Pained, offended, officious, self-important, touchy, jealous over Kes, and a highly *idiosyncratic* cook—he was all those things, thought Janeway; but he was also right more often than he was wrong—and he'd gotten them out of a number of scrapes—and he was a tiger in combat—and it looked like Neelix had once again been the prescient one. *What would we do without him?* she thought, highly irritated that she had to think it once again.

The short, chubby Talaxian sat on the edge of one of the bunks in the cell and pulled off one boot; a commbadge slid out onto the floor, tinkling loudly.

Janeway's flush deepened. She envied Tuvok, who could suppress any feelings of being unprepared. "In fact, I brought two," added Neelix, removing his other boot.

"I, ah, don't suppose you brought a spare—"

Neelix pulled free the second boot, and a second commbadge fell out. A phaser followed, and Janeway bit off the end of her question.

Wordlessly, Neelix picked up the phaser and both commbadges and handed them to Janeway, who handed one of the badges to Tuvok. The cook-guide-adventurer-equipment-storage-locker frowned. "I can't imagine why it's not standard Starfleet procedure to issue each crewman a half-dozen of the little things . . . or better yet, with your extraordinary medical technique, why don't you simply have communicators surgically implanted?"

Janeway had no good answer; Tuvok merely raised one eyebrow, the standard Vulcan expression meaning anything from *Did I just hear you correctly?* to *I think we all just learned a lesson here,* depending on context. Janeway gave Neelix a smile that was actually closer to a wolf baring her teeth. "Good thinking, Mr. Neelix. I'll enter a commendation for you when we return to the ship."

A good captain had to know when to yield gracefully and cut her losses.

She tapped the commbadge. "Janeway to Chakotay . . . Janeway to *Voyager,* emergency away-team beam-out, these coordinates. . . ."

Nothing happened; there was no response.

She exhaled through clenched teeth. "Either there's a communications shield, or else Chakotay took the ship far enough away that they can't hear us."

"The Furies have not shown any propensity for constructing shields. I suggest that the ship has problems of its own and is either maintaining a communications blackout or is out of range."

"All right," she said, "stand back from the bars. Let's get out of here under our own steam." Captain Janeway aimed the phaser at the non-iron bars that a very effective cage made.

Neelix backpedaled, turning his face and covering his eyes, in case the Federation weapon decided to bounce. Just before the captain fired, however, Neelix heard voices approaching.

"Wait!" he whispered urgently.

Janeway paused, staring curiously. "What? Why are we waiting?"

Oh, why can't humans hear anything! fumed the Talaxian. Tuvok the Vulcan suddenly cocked his larger, pointed ear. "I believe I hear Furies approaching."

"You do? Oh, wait; now I hear them too." Evidently, Captain Janeway didn't hear the sudden note of tension in Tuvok's voice; Neelix heard it clearly. The Vulcan did not react outwardly, but he was still strangely affected by these aliens.

The team waited until the Furies ambled past, staring curiously at the human, the Vulcan, and the Talaxian. *Tourists!* snorted Neelix to himself. Irritatingly, the last one lingered, peering at them from under its hood and cloak. A strange odor permeated the cell; the Fury had been dunked in some sort of perfume or cologne.

But Tuvok relaxed, surprising Neelix. Of course, this batch of Furies included many races, but not the race to which Navdaq belonged. *That must be the one that enslaved his homeworld,* Neelix realized.

By the time the last, dawdling sightseer finally decided it had seen enough and moved on, Neelix's sensitive ears picked up *another* pair of Furies coming the opposite direction along the cell block.

Captain Janeway waited, frustrated, while again the Fury spectators stared at the most fascinating creatures they had ever seen in their lives—actual Unclean from heaven! Neelix began to notice various odors: *Maybe they tell one another apart by scent, not by visual image? Or is that how they distinguish rank or position?* It made sense in a low-light situation; the powerful smell was quite identifiable, even for citizens who offered a form of privacy by averting their eyes from any passing strangers.

Two more sets of sightseers simply insisted upon finding occasion to stroll down to the dungeon and check on the prisoners . . . something which must have been a terrific violation of etiquette—unless the rule was that the Unclean have no rights and so cannot be offended or insulted. "Captain" Neelix had never been considered a patient man, even among his fellow Talaxians, nor a sociable man who enjoyed large mobs of people. He'd spent most of his life in space. He especially didn't like being the object of a mob of gawkers. More than once, he wished he had kept the phaser, instead of generously and loyally giving it to his captain, so he could . . . *Well, it wouldn't be a smart move,* he consoled himself.

Captain Janeway herself looked ready to chew her way through the bars with bare teeth by the time the fourth batch of tourists finally rolled on down the corridor, leaving them alone. "All right, let's do it quickly, men—before a whole guided tour shuttlebus comes driving down the cell block . . . stand back!"

The captain pointed the phaser at the nearest set of bars and followed Neelix's lead, covering her eyes against the possibility of the unshielded metal shattering under the energy impact. She pressed the button, firing a thin beam at the most powerful setting.

The bar glowed dullish red at the point of contact but was not otherwise affected. She ceased firing, and the glow faded immediately.

Tuvok put his hand near the bar, then touched it. "I do not believe the phaser fire affected it, Captain," he announced unnecessarily. "Perhaps if we had a high-powered cutting phaser."

Neelix stared in surprise. "Don't you carry a spare high-powered cutting phaser? It seems like a remarkably useful tool." It was cold, he knew; but he couldn't resist; he managed a sober expression, as if he were serious.

"Mr. Neelix," said the captain, "unless you have one tucked under your shirt, would you please shut up?"

CHAPTER

9

NEELIX ALMOST REACHED OUT AND TOUCHED THE BARS IN HIS astonishment; the Federation phaser had done nothing, they weren't even glowing! But he refrained, just in case.

"Tuvok—explain!" said the captain, seemingly as startled as the Talaxian.

Never put all your faith in technology, Neelix thought; *it's what I've always said—trust people, not playthings.*

Lieutenant Tuvok leaned close to the metal tubes, fingering them so gently that for a wild moment, Neelix wondered whether he was mind-melding with them—*excuse me, Mr. Bar, but why weren't you phasered out of existence?*

"Captain, I cannot say for certain without a detailed analysis, but this metal has some of the same properties as the metal that Mr. Kim scanned on the artificial moon. I suspect the Furies use this as an all-purpose shielding material—which does imply that they have the capability of scanning, else there would be no reason to shield against it—and in any event, no ability to do so."

"Can we cut it?"

Neelix stared at the bars, as thick around as his forearm and dark as *thrat* blood. *Cut it? With what, a pocketknife?*

He said nothing, only sat on one of the beds; it was uncomfortably hard and had no blanket.

"I do not believe so," answered Tuvok; "not with the materials we have at hand. I do not now believe a cutting phaser would work, even if we had one."

"Captain," said Neelix, "I'm sorry for that jest about the—"

"Bend it? Freeze it? Break it?"

"We have no means of freezing the metal," continued the Vulcan, "but if we did, it might become brittle enough to shatter. As far as bending, the tensile strength required for construction of the artificial moon is approximately . . ."

Tuvok half-closed his eyes, apparently making warp-speed estimates using rules of thumb and constant engineering coefficients. "Three point one times that of steel. The metal may be stronger than that, but probably not much stronger, as that would render shaping difficult."

Neelix stared at the lock, a boxlike device colored so black it was almost blue. If there was a weak spot, that was it.

"But can we bend it? Even a little?"

"Captain, Lieutenant, maybe we should look at the—"

"Not with the tools we have available, I'm afraid."

The captain hestitated for a moment, listening for more guards; still quiet. "Captain," began Neelix again; but she held up a hand. Then she turned the phaser on the wall for a few moments.

Fuming, he let her make another futile gesture. The wall was even less affected than the bars; it did not even glow. "Damn," she muttered.

Janeway tried to push her arm between the bars; she had better luck than Tuvok, getting just past her elbow to her biceps; but there she stuck. In fact, she retrieved her arm back through the bars only by bracing with her foot and pushing.

"I can't get much of my arm through; but that's all right—I haven't a clue what I'm reaching for, anyway."

Neelix leaned back onto the bed, searching for the proper way to talk the two Starfleeters out of brute force and into an approach that depended upon some finesse. He sat up and stared through the bars at the cell directly opposite, studying the locking mechanism as best he could, remotely. *How do you open a lock? Well, how about with a key?*

"Captain," said Neelix, "why not just wait for the next troop of Furies to wander by, stun them with the phaser, and take their key-cards?"

Janeway paused for a moment, looking slightly embarrassed. "What if they're wearing some of that metal as phaserproof armor?"

Immediately, Neelix saw the problems with his first-draft idea. Flushing, he started to withdraw it; but before he could, Tuvok administered the coup de grâce: "There is also the problem, Mr. Neelix, that the guards may not have the appropriate key-card. They may fall out of reach. They may return fire and wound or kill one of us. For a number of reasons, we must reject the naive approach of violence."

"I'm sorry," said Neelix, his feelings wounded. "I was just trying to help." *Great help! You've just undone weeks of effort getting these people to start taking you seriously!*

"Captain," said Tuvok, "I believe that the weak point of the cell is the locking mechanism itself. We cannot affect the bars or the walls, but the lock might perhaps be activated by means of a tool other than that which was intended for the purpose."

"You mean we might be able to pick it," said Neelix quickly. Too quickly; in fact, he had just been about to make the suggestion himself, but the Vulcan beat him to it.

"I believe that is the vernacular, Mr. Neelix."

"With what?" asked Janeway.

"I have not yet thought of a suitable alternative."

Janeway crouched to stare at the annoying box at eye level. "Tiny, little electrical thing, isn't it? Almost cute. I'd like to fire a photon torpedo . . . into its keyhole."

"How about the phaser?" gingerly suggested Neelix. "Can you shoot it into the lock and short it out?"

"Wait—" said Neelix, this time answering his own second-draft idea. "You'd probably just fuse the locking mechanism so it would be impossible to open."

Janeway and Tuvok continued to nag each other, but

Neelix tuned them both out. He stared around the room . . . something, *something* tickled the back of his brain, something they could use. Something—not phasoelectric; more primitive. Something . . .

I demand a brilliant idea . . . I want a light panel to go off in my head! He lay back on the slab the Furies called a bed, staring up at the ceiling.

The bright ceiling.

The bright, illuminated light panel in the—

"I see the light!" shouted Neelix, jumping up. The captain and Tuvok stared at him curiously. "Can't you see it? Look, the light!" Neelix pointed triumphantly at the light panel.

"The light?" asked Janeway, looking up. The light was bright by Fury standards, illuminating the cell to approximately two hundred lux, or half the light of a reasonably well lit room on the *Voyager.*

"That's your energy source!" announced the Talaxian. "Use that to blow the lock."

Janeway nodded slowly, obviously impressed for once by Neelix's suggestion. *Hah, take that!* he beamed.

"How many watts, do you think?" she asked Tuvok.

"I cannot begin to estimate. I do not believe much would be needed to overload the locking mechanism."

"Only one problem." Neelix stood on the bed to stare up at the tube. "How do we get the electrical current from *here* to over *there?*"

The distance to cover was approximately four and a half meters from the light to the cell door; but it might as well have been four kilometers . . . not even Captain Kathryn the Great could carry electricity in a bucket.

She fingered her hair; Neelix noticed that she did it unconsciously in times of stress. A ghastly thought was beginning to gel in his mind.

"Can we pop the light-panel cover and see whether we can even get at the electrical connection?"

Neelix went and stood directly underneath the ceiling-mounted light panel, supporting it; Tuvok began working the end closest to the bars, while Janeway stood on the bed to try to wriggle her nails under the opposite end.

After much rocking back and forth—interrupted once by another group of curious, staring Furies—the away team managed to work the cover down low enough that they could peer inside.

They saw an intricate swirl of light tubes, almost like a small intestine, irregular in shape and connected at one end by a four-pronged plug and socket.

"Looks like an old excited-gas system," the captain mused; "I haven't seen such a museum piece since—well, since the last time I visited the Hieronymous Museum of Irreproducible Technology on Urbania. If we shatter the tube, we might be able to connect directly to the leads."

"With what?" asked Neelix, his aching arms souring his mood. "Our fingers?"

Captain Janeway frowned. "Now, that's the best suggestion you've made all day, Mr. Neelix."

"What do you mean? I only wanted to know what . . ." His voice trailed off, and the spikes on his ears spread wide. He felt his face flush bright orange. "Oh, no! Oh, no you don't! You are *not* going to get me to stick my fingers in a light socket just to see what happens!"

"I wouldn't dream of it, Neelix."

"Well, thank goodness for small favors."

"Tuvok is going to stick his fingers in the light-tube socket, and you're going to hold Tuvok's other hand while he does it."

"What!"

"And I'll hold your hand."

"Captain, listen to me closely—you're overworked. I'm not one of your Federation doctors—I'm a real person—but I prescribe a long rest, a cup of my very best Dyzelian coffee, and —"

"Very intriguing, Captain," said the Vulcan, unperturbed by Janeway's wild, harebrained scheme, "but how do you propose to complete the circuit with the lock?"

Janeway played with her hair again, but to a purpose, this time. "With this," she said, extracting one of the pins that held her hair in its severe bun.

Tuvok raised his eyebrow. "I believe the hairpin is

indeed the traditional tool for extralegal operation of a locking mechanism."

Neelix sighed; he hadn't meant to be so loud, but both the captain and Tuvok turned toward him. "You're determined to do this, aren't you?" asked Neelix peevishly. *She's going to get herself killed!* he thought, but said nothing. He certainly was no stranger to being determined to do something dangerous and foolhardy.

"Neelix," said the captain, "there is no other way to get out of this cell . . . and it's more than just our lives at stake; we have to think about—"

"Yes, yes, I know, Captain." Neelix drew himself up to his full height, staring her directly in the collarbone. "I once had a planet too. Remember?"

"I'm sorry, Neelix. I didn't mean to condescend."

He shrugged. "It's a human thing; I understand. But Captain, if you're *really determined* to electrocute us all trying to blow the lock . . . then I absolutely insist that *I* be the one to stick his fingers in the light socket."

Instantly, a small voice inside Neelix's head screamed *Are you insane? You'll die!* Oddly, it sounded like Kes's voice. Janeway didn't know what to say; Lieutenant Tuvok merely raised one eyebrow—a Vulcan thing.

Now, why in free space did I volunteer to do that? Neelix wondered. But the answer was clear: Talaxians understood duty, and Neelix especially understood risking his life in a good cause. The Furies had nothing to do with the destruction of his homeworld . . . *But they might as well have,* he realized; they were tyrants and slavers—how different were they really from those who all but destroyed his home?

But how could he convince Janeway? "Captain," he began. For a moment, he floundered; then his natural glibness asserted itself. "We Talaxians have a—special resistance to electricity. It doesn't injure us the way it does you humans, or Vulcans."

"You have not mentioned this before," pointed out the stubborn Tuvok.

Neelix snorted. "You've never asked me to stick my fingers in a light socket before!"

Even Tuvok had to concede the situation had not come

up previously. But Janeway still looked dubious. "Are you sure? A special resistance?"

"Special resistance to electricity," repeated Neelix, sticking to his yarn. Rule Number One when lying, he had been taught: Don't change stories in midstream!

"I hope Mr. Neelix is not being literal," said the Vulcan. "We need a current flow, not resistance." Several moments passed before Neelix wondered if this was a droll sort of Vulcan pseudo-joke; but by then, the Talaxian was too nervous to ask.

The captain took off her slightly torn uniform jacket, pushing her bare arm as far through the bars as she possibly could; when it stuck just past the elbow, she compressed her biceps with her other hand and pushed even farther.

"Um, Tuvok," asked Neelix, "isn't the current going to short at the bars?"

"No," said the lieutenant firmly. "The metal does not conduct electricity at all . . . it is too dense. It is not properly even a metal. If it did, the phaser would have disrupted the electrochemical bonds and vaporized the bars."

Janeway gritted her teeth; probably the pressure was cutting off the blood flow in her brachial artery. *It's going to tingle a damn sight worse,* sighed Neelix.

She still could not quite reach the lock with her hairpin. "Tuvok," she called, wincing against the pain, "I need your help. You've got to get my arm farther through the bars."

"It is a dangerous maneuver," said the Vulcan; "you may get your arm so wedged in that we cannot extract it. If the circulation is cut off long enough, serious damage may occur."

"If we wait here for the Furies to execute us, serious death may occur."

"You have a point." Tuvok put a hand on either side of Janeway's muscle and began to squeeze. He got her arm just far enough through the bars that she could hold the hairpin between her middle and ring fingers and insert it into the card slot.

"Quick! Neelix, do it now—my hand's going numb—I'm going to drop the pin!"

Swallowing hard, Neelix grabbed Tuvok, who seized Janeway's groping hand. The Talaxian swallowed hard, his heart pounding at triple speed. *Am I really going to do this?* His own hand trembled; he moved quickly before she could see. *This is for you, Kes,* he swore to himself; he didn't believe his own lie, but it worked anyway.

Neelix reached up and shattered the tube and closed his eyes tight, then licked his fingers and pressed them firmly against the pair of leads.

Ice hands clutched both sides of his body and dug their spirit fingers into his flesh. Exquisite ecstasy flashed through him, burning away the mortal corruption, the cobwebs that accumulated around a person's life. He convulsed as a jolt of high-voltage electricity ripped through his body. He could not let go! His hand crushed that of Tuvok, who crushed the captain's hand in turn.

Neelix heard a loud crackle and smelled roasting meat; but with the current disrupting every nerve and neuron in his body, he could not even think about any damage it was doing, let alone worry about it.

Then as suddenly as the surge began, it ended. Blinking his eyes back into focus, Neelix noticed two things simultaneously: he lay on the floor all the way across the cage from the light panel . . . and *the cell door was slightly ajar.*

The lock was fried.

Alas, so too was Captain Janeway's arm, nearly so. "Tuvok—I don't want to open the door until we can start running, in case there are guards. But I've got a problem. . . ."

Tuvok and Neelix quickly moved to her side; past the bars, her arm was bone white. "Captain, can you move the arm?" asked the Talaxian.

She tried; her hand twitched slightly, but all she felt was pins and needles. "Maybe the nerve is pinched," she gasped.

Tuvok tried to compress her arm to extract it as he had wedged it in; but the only result was a stifled scream from the captain. The arm was stuck solid.

"Neelix," requested the Vulcan, "would you happen to have any sort of lubricant? Oil, or soap, perhaps?"

Neelix shook his head sadly. "Captain, I'm terribly, terribly sorry . . . I do usually carry machine oil, but today I was using it in the kitchen."

"Not, I hope, in your latest culinary offering, Mr. Neelix." It did seem that Tuvok was on a roll, perhaps trying to distract Janeway; but Neelix glared him down.

Janeway smiled wanly at the attempt; but she was in too much pain to be distracted.

"Certainly not!" said the sometime-cook. "I was oiling a sticky—"

"Captain, I believe your brachioradial and pronator muscles are in spasm, and they have contracted so tightly they are now wider than the gap between the bars. If we had a muscle relaxant, we could probably extract your arm without difficulty."

"Do you—want to try—borrowing one—from the guards?"

"Your joke may in fact be worth exploring. If we make sufficient commotion that the guards hear and come to investigate, they may be able to administer medical aid."

"Or else they may just cut her arm off in retaliation," snapped Neelix, exasperated with these Starfleeters who never could seem to think their way out of problems. "Tuvok, they don't even think of us as people . . . we're animals to them—*dangerous* animals! We can't rely on them to help the captain."

"I fear you may be correct, Mr. Neelix."

"We've got to get her arm out—*we've* got to get it out, because we can't count on anyone else. And I, for one, will not leave unless she leaves with us."

"No one is suggesting abandoning Captain Janeway. But we need some means of relaxing her muscles, or we shall all remain here until the guards come and notice the open door. Then the question becomes moot."

"Well, can't she just relax it? Meditate, or something?"

Janeway tried to calm herself; she breathed deeply. But the pain interfered with her ability to concentrate. After a few seconds, she gave up, her arm throbbing rhythmically with every blocked beat of her pulse.

"Can't—concentrate. . . ."

At once, the odd idea struck Neelix. Why not stun her? After all, they had a phaser, didn't they? Stunning relaxed the entire body.

While Tuvok futilely tugged on the bars, the arm, the bars and arm in combination, Neelix strolled over and picked up the nearly forgotten phaser lying on one of the beds. He started to explain his idea, but Tuvok was busy tugging and Janeway was busy agonizing. *You know, maybe it's best they don't know until after I do it. . . .*

Neelix studied the phaser. The power setting looked relatively straightforward, though in the past it had usually been handed to him preset by whoever led the away team. He thumbed it all the way over to one side. "Stand back," he said to Tuvok, barely giving the Vulcan time to get clear before he pointed it at Captain Janeway, and pressed the contact. The beam lashed out, glowing orangeish in the red light of the Fury world, and Janeway grunted loudly; the noise faded into an extended sigh. Rubbery legs collapsed slowly, bringing her to her knees.

The swelling ebbed. She relaxed and fell into a trance, nearly unconscious. Every part of her became liquid, supple, soft. Smooth.

Slippery.

Neelix and Tuvok gently worked her injured arm backward; it stuck, he pushed . . . suddenly, she fell back onto her rump, dizzy and confused, blinking back to conscious awareness. As if waking from a particularly vigorous, muscular dream, she rubbed her arm, her face a mask of confusion, as though wondering where she was.

Then full awareness returned.

"Neelix—you *shot* me!"

"Yes, Captain," said the Talaxian, nervously smoothing his hair back. "You don't mind much, do you?"

"Good thinking."

Neelix smirked, aware that he had not just recovered lost territory, he had forged ahead in his plan to prove to the Starfleeters that he was as good a swashbuckler as he often claimed. "Tuvok," said Janeway, "let's get the hell out of here. I think I hear more 'tourists' coming!"

Tuvok and Neelix helped Janeway to her feet and dragged

her behind them. She was having trouble making her legs move swiftly enough. "Wait," she whispered, just as they stepped into the corridor.

Stooping, she forced her recovering arm to reach forward; numb fingers picked up the hairpin. She had to do it by sight; it was obvious that she still could not feel a thing.

"Let 'em wonder," she explained, as they ran away from the approaching footsteps into the comforting gloom.

CHAPTER

10

COMMANDER CHAKOTAY WANTED TO PACE BACK AND FORTH across the bridge. He wanted to run to every duty station and take personal charge. He wanted to scream and shake his fist and pitch somebody down the turbolift shaft. He sat calmly in the command chair, doing nothing but casually crossing his legs, not allowing the young crew to see any emotion but calm certainty.

The captain and Tuvok were down on the planet; Paris and Kim were back in the infirmary, arguing with the emergency holographic medical program about his prescription of "rest and recuperation." On the bridge were Chakotay, a single officer to handle all science, and engineering, and ops—B'Elanna Torres—and three crewmen: Dalby, Chell, and Jarron. Torres had been remarkably silent, saying nothing except in answer to a direct question.

The *Voyager* played "hunters and buffalo" with now *six* alien ships, a veritable battle fleet; the *Voyager* kept dodging from one bearing to another, sliding around the planet, trying to keep the ships in line, so only the lead ship could shoot . . . easily deflected by the shields. But if Chakotay gave the wrong order or the helm officer responded too slugishly, the aliens could open fire with four or five ships; then the *Voyager* could be crippled or killed.

The situation taxed Chakotay's renowned inner calm to the limit.

"Turn right, bearing zero-two-zero degrees, mark forty . . . back up, bearing one-eight-zero, one-quarter impulse . . . good. Hold this position; let's see if they're going to fire again."

The alien ships paused; they too were tired of the game. They had begun to realize that the *Voyager* was more maneuverable and faster than their own ships. So far, they had utterly failed to box her in.

But there were some close calls: once, Chakotay had ordered the helm to turn starboard, then port too quickly, luffing the ship; while it wallowed in its own impulse wake, three alien ships had locked on and fired their directed-energy weapons from the port side slightly below.

Dalby's quick thinking saved them. Without orders, he engaged a course of 000 mark 90—straight up. The shots missed by a few hundred meters.

"Good initiative, Crewman Dalby," said Chakotay laconically; inwardly, he was kicking himself in the rear for screwing the turn . . . he had been thinking of his smaller Maquis ship.

"Gentlemen," said the commander, "it is good to remain at large with hull integrity intact; but we can't dodge their disruptor shots forever. We must find an end to this duel, but an end that allows us to close within transporter range of the planet to extract the away team."

"Perhaps we should fight them, sir," suggested Dalby from the helm. Fortunately, Chell had the weapons . . . Dalby's impetuousness had been good, as when he dodged the phaser blasts; but this was something else.

"No, we can't fight them, Crewman," said the commander; "they still have the captain. And may I remind you they also hold Lieutenant Tuvok and Neelix?"

Dalby grunted in resignation. Recently, Dalby, Chell, Jarron, and Henley—all former Maquis—had developed a solid working relationship with the Vulcan, who trained them in a mini-Academy course.

"Couldn't we just go out of the solar system?" suggested Chell.

"And abandon Captain Janeway?"

"No no! I mean we could shift into warp and whip around the system, coming back from the opposite side of the sun and hide there."

Chakotay answered immediately. "Chell, think about it a moment. The aliens have impulse power; they have warp. They would simply follow us the whole way."

At once, Chakotay realized to his astonishment that the impossible had occurred: *the Starfleet ship had an entirely Maquis bridge crew!* The commander smiled; *my wildest dream come true—we've finally "stolen" a Federation starship right out from under them . . . and we can't do anything with her!*

He heard a faint cough, paid it no mind. It repeated, followed by a voice so meek and uncertain that at first, Chakotay could not even tell where it came from. Then Jarron, the Bajoran, repeated himself. "Sir . . . if we were— I mean if they thought we were destroyed, they wouldn't— you know, follow . . . never mind. I'm sorry."

"Keep talking, Jarron."

"Well, if—I mean, if they thought we were destroyed, you know."

"Do you have anything in mind?"

"Well—if we dropped debris, or something?"

Chakotay shook his head. "Not enough; they would board us to investigate."

"I'm sorry."

"Don't apologize, you're on the right track. Anyone else have any follow-up?"

Dead silence. Dalby stared at the screen, watching the immobile alien ships in case they decided to attack again. Chell stared in anguished astonishment at the commander, his normal expression. And Jarron, who had shot his only arrow, returned to his navigation console and tried to cringe inside himself.

Suddenly feeling the expectance of speech from behind him, Chakotay turned. B'Elanna Torres opened her mouth, starting to make a suggestion, then closed it again. When she had repeated the maneuver twice more, Chakotay asked, "Do you have any sort of idea, B'Elanna?"

"I, ah, don't mean to butt in, but it occurs to me . . ." She faded out.

"Go on," said the commander, still aware that Torres' confidence had taken a severe nose-dive.

"If they—" Torres's Klingon side suddenly seemed to assume control, disgusted at the human side's indecisiveness. "Commander," she snarled Klingon-style, "if they thought we had burned up in the sun, they wouldn't bother looking for us."

"Let me see if I've got this straight. You propose to take us into the *sun?*"

"We have shields," explained B'Elanna; "they don't. Our shields might protect us from the intense heat and pressure; their ships would be crushed. They'll think we destroyed ourselves because our mission was a failure."

"You seem to understand them well, B'Elanna."

"They're a lot like my people. Half of my people."

"You said the shields *might* protect us. I don't like the sound of that *might.*"

B'Elanna was silent for several seconds. When she spoke, she sounded somewhat more human than Klingon. "This isn't good. I just did a simulation, and it shows us being crushed and incinerated in forty-two point six seconds."

"The shields give out?"

"Yes, Commander."

"Well . . . can we increase power to the shields?"

"I calculated for max shield power."

"But did you calculate including every bit of power on the ship, including engines, backup battery, replicators, the holodeck, and life-support? Everything but the Doctor . . . I suspect we'll need him."

"No, I didn't! Wait just a moment." She added a belated, distracted "sir" while recalibrating. "Amazing . . . Commander, the new calculation shows us surviving for almost a hundred and fifty seconds."

"Two and a half minutes," mused Chakotay, "can be a very long time indeed. Start making the necessary modifications, Torres." She turned away. "And Torres—good initiative."

"Commander!" cried Chell, stricken. "The aliens have powered up their weapons again—they're going to shoot!"

"Are the shields still at full strength, Mr. Chell?"

"Yes, sir."

"And they're still bottled up in a line? Then let's wait to see what they're going to do. I have a good notion . . . there's a tactic I've been expecting them to try for an hour now, but so far they have disappointed me."

A new voice spoke from the turbolift; Lieutenant Paris had just entered the bridge. "Would you possibly mean . . . the *starburst* maneuver?"

"You're familiar with it?"

"I have a nodding acquaintance." Paris winked, but Chakotay did not understand the reference.

"Do you want to take the helm?"

Dalby looked sour, his face flushing. He still was not used to being a junior member of the crew, after having lived the exciting life of a Maquis helmsman.

Paris noticed Dalby's reaction—and was impressed that the normally irrepressible motormouth said nothing. "Nah, I think I'll just watch, come up to speed. Change in watch in fifteen minutes; I'll wait."

"Thank you, Mr. Paris. Mr. Dalby, let me know the moment you have confirmed a starburst maneuver."

"Commander, what's a starburst maneuver?"

"You'll know it when you see it," said Paris cryptically.

"—They're moving, sir." Dalby watched for a second. "Oh! I see what you mean—starburst maneuver, sir!"

The alien ships each took off in a separate direction, exploding like a fireworks rocket in a cone surrounding the *Voyager*. In a moment, every ship had a clear shot; all six immediately opened fire on the sitting-duck Starfleet ship.

"Mr. Dalby, flank speed, bearing zero-zero-zero mark zero."

The *Voyager* shot straight forward, toward the core of the starburst . . . the one spot where there were no ships. "Now if we're incredibly lucky—or they're incredibly stupid . . ." Chakotay allowed himself a small smile of expectation.

"I don't believe it!" muttered Lieutenant Torres. She stared at her scanner. "Sir, you're not going to believe this."

"Try me."

"But their guns are following us. They're going to hit—correction, they *have* hit one of their own ships. Two of their own ships—three!"

Chakotay turned to look at Paris, who was unsuccessfully trying to stifle a laugh behind his hand.

Chell finally recovered his wits to make a report. "Sir . . . as we passed between them, all but one of the ships continued to fire, even when their own fleet was in the line of fire."

"Running the gauntlet," muttered Paris, still breaking up.

"One alien ship destroyed," reported B'Elanna Torres, "two others damaged, one seriously."

"Not bad for still not having fired a shot," said Chakotay soberly. He had tremendous empathy for Tom Paris; were it not for Chakotay's own tremendous self-control, he would be holding his sides and laughing like a hyena.

"Commander," said Torres—she did not appear to be on the verge of laughter . . . *more's the pity,* thought Chakotay—"I've completed the modifications to the shield power grid. I can send full power to the shields on your order."

After a moment, when Chakotay remained lost in thought, B'Elanna asked, "Sir? I said I've completed—"

"I heard you, Lieutenant." *Do I have the guts to do it?* he asked himself. Chakotay shrugged, feeling his heart begin to race just at the thought; but he had no choice . . . he had to get the Furies off his tail, and that meant they had to think the *Voyager* was dead meat, *glop* on a stick.

"B'Elanna," he said after a moment, "how long would it take you to reconfigure the shields to metaphasic?"

"About two minutes; but why would I want to . . . Chakotay! You *can't* be thinking of—"

He nodded, lips pressed together either in a grim smile or an amused grimace. "Directly into the sun," he confirmed. "Do you think they'll follow?"

Nobody responded; Chakotay took the first step along the trail.

"Jarron, open a channel to the alien flagship, assuming it isn't one of the damaged ones."

"It's damaged but not seriously," mumbled Jarron; Chakotay had to strain to hear him. "Channel open."

Chakotay leapt to his feet, turning himself beet-red and screaming so violently that spittle flew from his mouth. *"We will* never *be captured alive! We won't spend even an* hour *in your torture chambers! We'd rather die like* men *than live like* animals! Songbird *out!"*

Jarron was so startled, he almost forgot to kill the transmission. As soon as the red light went dark, Commander Chakotay sat back down in the command chair, perfectly calmly, and wiped his mouth with his hand.

"Mr. Dalby, lay in a course directly for the sun, full impulse, and engage immediately."

It took the entire crew several seconds to recover from their astonishment and perform their tasks. Chakotay frowned; he could not help thinking that a Starfleet crew would probably have responded three times as efficiently.

He did not like his inevitable conclusion that there really was a qualitative difference between a crew trained by Starfleet and a Maquis crew. He made a mental note to speak to Captain Janeway about expanding Tuvok's mini-Academy to include the senior officers . . . including himself.

They certainly had plenty of time, even for the full, four-year Academy course.

The sun suddenly surged forward, growing in size until it filled the viewer. The smaller, individual strands of the grid began to come into focus, silhouettes against the filtered yet still painfully bright image of the star.

"Ah—Commander?" Torres seemed a bit nervous. "Shall I transfer power to the shields?"

"Time to contact with the sun's corona, Mr. Dalby?"

"How far out? The corona extends from—"

"It's a G2 star. Let's say the photosphere, about a million kilometers from the center. Should be about six thousand degrees at that point."

"Seven minutes, fifty seconds, sir."

"Chakotay—six thousand is hot enough to boil the hull of the *Voyager.*"

"Can the shields as they currently are protect us?"

"For a few seconds!"

"Chill the ship as cold as you can make it, Mr. Torres, before you transfer environmental power to the shields. It's going to get mighty hot in here while we're in there; let's get a head start on the heat exchange."

Lieutenant Torres, at least, responded instantly. Within less than a minute, Chakotay began to feel distinctly cold as the cryogenic unit whined into action.

"Pursuing," announced Jarron, so loudly that at first Chakotay did not recognize the boy.

"Are they firing, Mr. Chell?"

"No. Wait—yes! No, I don't thin . . . yes, definitely yes."

"Mr. Chell!"

"My mistake. Yes, Commander, they're definitely firing."

"You can't commit suicide," declared Paris, dryly speaking as the alien fleet captain. "We have to execute you!"

"Reinforce the aft shields, Mr. Torres."

"Aft?" she demanded, incredulous. "But the sun is directly ahead of us!"

"And the hostiles are directly behind us."

"Would you rather be fried or shot?" inquired Lieutenant Paris.

"Reinforce aft shields, Lieutenant Torres. Don't even think about firing, Mr. Chell. Find something constructive to do, Mr. Paris."

The cryos began to strain against the heat of the sun, now only partially shielded. The *Voyager* closed to within 0.25 astronomical units from the sun.

Some of the crew paradoxically began to shiver violently; the internal temperature was down to -15° centigrade. A voice cut through the cacophony on the bridge.

"This is the emergency medical holographic program . . . what the devil is going on up there? I have crew members all over the ship collapsing from the cold. . . . Oh, I see. I have just scanned the computer log. We will all be dead in a matter of moments."

"Not now, Doctor—please."

"My, but you people lead exciting lives. Emergency medical holographic program out."

"Jarron!" called Chakotay, a little too loudly. "Alert me when we're approaching the collector."

"We're . . . we're approaching it now, Commander. Aren't we?"

"Don't ask me, *tell* me!" *Come on, he doesn't respond well to being shouted at.* "Jarron, tell me when we're within twenty seconds."

"Aye, sir. We're within twenty seconds now, sir."

"Mr. Dalby," said Chakotay, getting his voice under control, "how wide are the strands at the widest point?" Seeing the sun loom so large, Chakotay unconsciously reached up and wiped his brow, despite the chilly bridge temperature.

"Commander, we've got plenty of room—eight or ten meters on each side if we hit it just right."

Eight meters! Chakotay ordered Paris to take control of the helm . . . either Paris would come through, or they would all die.

The grid rushed toward them. This close, Chakotay could see that it was not, in fact, a uniform color, but a prismatic spray of the entire visible spectrum, as if the strands functioned like tiny light prisms, scattering the sunlight in every direction. *Probably captures each frequency separately,* he thought . . . while not forgetting to admire the sheer, overwhelming beauty of it. His father had always taught him never to lose the hawk in its feathers.

Swallowing hard, seeing the inappropriately called "strands" loom larger and larger—they were in fact monstrous cables nearly ten meters in diameter—Chakotay silently commended his soul to the Sky Spirit, but asked if perhaps he might be allowed just a little more life.

The gap loomed—they were off course! Dalby made a strangled noise in the back of his throat and tapped frantically. The *Voyager* jerked gracelessly, barreled into the web . . . and burst through! Chakotay heard the faintest ping as they passed.

"Well," said a white-faced Paris a few moments later, "I guess I overestimated slightly." He grinned sheepishly, but Chakotay had more important details to be concerned about.

"Coming up on the photosphere," said Paris, sounding preternaturally calm. "Thirty-five seconds." Under the stress of the moment, he had passed beyond emotional reaction to pure action—*an admirable quality for a future Starfleet officer,* noted Chakotay for his internal record.

"Torres!" barked the commander. "You have thirty seconds to tell me that you've finished adapting to metaphasic shielding."

"I'll have it ready in twenty!" she snapped from down in engineering.

"Then, Mr. Torres, prepare to re-norm shield concentration and feed the extra power on my mark. Twenty seconds. Ten seconds . . . five, four, three, two, one, mark."

"Metaphasic shielding is on-line, and functioning nor—"

"Sir," interrupted Paris, "entering photosphere in . . . five, four, three, two, one, mark."

"Helm, full reverse! Don't pop out the other side of the sun! B'Elanna, pump full warp-engine power into the shields, and let's call upon our ancestors to help us wait them out."

The impulse engines strained backward, their whine rising so loud that everyone, Chakotay included, had to cup his hands over his ears. Again, they overloaded the inertial stabilizers, subjecting the entire ship to the instantaneous equivalent of more than fifteen times the force of gravity straight forward—for a tenth of a second.

Chakotay felt like he had been kicked by a mule. He rocketed forward into Chell, who sprawled across the console. Within a couple of microseconds, however, the rebuilt stablizers compensated, reducing the forward acceleration to a mere four g's.

After four seconds, even that cut off as the ship almost literally screeched to a halt.

Dazed, Chakotay noticed that Paris *had* found something

constructive to do: he had sat down with his back against the forward bulkhead next to the turbolift.

Chakotay floundered, dizzy and stunned; but Paris was up the second the gravity returned to normal—fortunately, for the entire rest of the bridge crew lay unconscious.

CHAPTER

11

PARIS WORKED THE CONTROLS. THEY WERE VERY SLUGGISH . . unsurprising, considering that the *Voyager* sat in the middle of a G2 star.

It was all Paris could do to maintain position; convection currents inside the sun buffeted the ship fiercely, threatening to tear it to shreds long before the heat and radiation fried them, were it not for the supercharged shields.

He could hardly complain. In his single (required) astrophysics class at the Academy, Paris had learned that without such currents, it would take *tens of billions of years* for the very first photon to random-walk its way from the steller core, where it was produced by hydrogen fusion, to the surface.

In other words, without convection currents to bring the photons up like gas bubbles in water, the surface of every star in the entire universe would still be black as ink and cold as the depths of interstellar space.

"I don't care," he snarled aloud; "they're damned inconvenient right now!"

Fighting the bucking bronco of a ship, Tom Paris backed

away from the opposite side surface to a point about a third of the way toward the stellar core; closer, he dared not go— the core temperature was several million degrees, and he was not sure even B'Elanna's modified shields would guard against that much energy.

He almost made the mistake of a lifetime. He almost snapped on the sensors.

He stopped with his hand just touching the panel, shaking with suddenly awakened fear. Turning them on would have been like flipping on searchlights. The aliens would immediately know.

Instead, he activated passive sensors only. He would have to hope to pick up random, subspace fluctuations from the aliens' warp cores. "Computer, begin record, all readings."

Certainly it was absurd even to check for ion trails; he was sitting in the biggest ball of ionized plasma for billions of kilometers!

Spotting the alien ships was like sitting inside an antimatter reaction chamber, trying to detect someone using a communicator outside.

The hull temperature steadily climbed, despite the shields. It reached three hundred thousand degrees, and still no one else had awakened.

As Torres materialized on the surgical table, the doctor swiftly moved to her; without the chief engineer, the ship might never make it out of the sun intact.

He injected a cortical stimulant, then gently slapped her face. She groaned but did not respond.

Oh, well, thought the doctor; *she is a part Klingon, after all.*

Winding up, he slapped her across the jawline.

Torres bellowed like an angry bull and vaulted to her feet in a defensive posture. She swayed, then fell to one knee, clutching her head in agony.

"The pain will pass quickly," said the doctor; a useless piece of advice, since it would have already passed before he finished the sentence. The pain was caused by the sudden return of bloodflow to the cranial arteries after they had been drained by high acceleration.

"We're in the middle of the sun," explained the doctor quickly.

"What? Already? But we had a couple of minutes to—"

"Microamnesia. Goodbye."

Without another word, he beamed B'Elanna Torres directly to engineering.

As soon as B'Elanna Torres faded in, her brain thoroughly muddled from two sudden and complete changes of perspective, her commbadge started beeping insistently. "Paris to Torres! Are you there? Repeat, are you all right?"

"Am I *where?*" she replied crossly. "I'm in engineering . . . I think. Where am I *supposed* to be?"

"That'll do. Quick!" demanded the thoroughly annoying Thomas Paris. "Without using the fire-control sensors, tell me if there are any ships left outside the photosphere . . . we've got to get the hell out of this hell, or we're going to melt like butter!"

She turned to the sensor-array control apparatus, so dizzy she had to grab a bulkhead to keep from falling to the deck. She powered up VLAs two and seven, looking nine to three and three to nine, respectively—the full hemisphere forward and the full hemisphere aft.

She studied the blips, starting to sweat heavily in the extremely hot, dry air. "Yeah. Two ships. Both aft of us. Wait . . . a third ship just passing bearing two seven zero. It's rounding the sun, checking to see if we came out the other side."

"Damn. I was hoping they would just go home."

"How long have we been in here?"

"Two minutes, fifteen seconds."

"Damn—Paris, ships or no ships, we've got to get out of here *now.*"

"No way, Torres. We've got to give your trick time to work. The shields are holding out better than expected. They're still at seventy-two percent."

"They *are?*" She checked the power-decay curve and overlaid the projection. "You idiot! That's three percent *below* the projection!"

"How long do we have?"

"According to my model, the shields will fail suddenly and rather spectacularly in about ten seconds."

"How long will the hull hold out after that?"

"About ten seconds."

"Don't touch the controls."

Torres held on, counting silently to herself. She had reached five when suddenly she said, "Paris! They're leaving orbit, heading back to the planet!"

"Can they still see the back side of the sun?"

"Yes . . . but wait for it—wait for it—Shields just failed. Lasted two extra seconds. Well, lover, been nice knowing you. Goodbye."

"Can they still see—damn, I can't touch the controls they're so hot! No time, no—"

Paris punched the button, she thought; the *Voyager* lurched forward, ripping through the flesh of the sun and just clearing the corona as the hull temperature hit two hundred thousand degrees.

B'Elanna stared at the internal temperature gauge in mounting horror as it hit two hundred degrees—but it lasted only a couple of seconds.

Over the next hour, the ship slowly returned to normal operations. Chakotay and the rest of the bridge crew recovered, the hull cooled, the shields returned to normal, and the cryogenic units cooled the interior of the ship to a manageable thirty degrees . . . uncomfortably hot, but not catastrophic. B'Elanna returned to the bridge, taking the longer, scenic route by turbolift this time.

The aliens were nowhere to be sensed. They had swallowed the con without demur.

Paris parked the ship a couple of million kilometers off the surface of the sun, on the opposite side from the planet. He matched velocities with the alien planet, using the impulse engines to maintain his altitude above the sun—for of course, the *Voyager* was moving too slowly to hold an actual orbit at that point.

Captain Janeway clenched and released her fist, pins and needles dancing up and down her arm, as she, Tuvok, and Neelix skittered down the cellblock hallway, seeing neither prisoners—not the shuttlecraft pilot—nor more guards. The escape was not long being discovered, however; the lights began to flicker, growing nearly bright enough for a human for a fraction of a second then dropping to their normal gloom. Since the bright light probably hurt the Furies' eyes, Janeway deduced it was the equivalent of a red alert.

At first, the captain insisted upon stopping and looking sharply into each cell on left and right; after a minute, she merely glanced to either side. "Neelix," she said at last, hearing the wild hunt of pursuit not overly far behind them.

"Captain?"

"You look in the left cells, I'll check the right. Tuvok, keep an eye behind us . . . we've got to find the pilot and get the hell out of here!"

They ran full speed, hoping they would not turn a corner and smash into a favored. The cells in their section were all empty; evidently, the Furies had no intention of allowing different batches of Unclean to mingle.

Each cell was a replicator-quality copy of their own: six by five meters, two bunks along walls and even floors that did not quite meet at right angles. As Janeway ran, she frequently stumbled when the floor went funny.

Dammit, there's a limit to Lovecraftian geometry! she insisted to herself. Evidently, the Furies disagreed.

The away team bolted down a long corridor, counting eighty-four cells, including their own. At its end was a locked door.

Janeway stopped at the lock; she heard a shout of triumph behind her. "Tuvok—got any bright ideas for picking *this* lock? It's mechanical, for goodness' sake!"

"Yes, Captain. May I?"

Janeway stepped aside. Tuvok stepped back, raised his foot, and kicked the door just above the handle. The jamb splintered with a noise like Baba Yaga gnashing her iron teeth and the door sagged inward. Tuvok shouldered it open and the away team ducked through as the guards fired a badly aimed shot.

A large, five-sided room; a door directly opposite. "I've got this one!" shouted Neelix.

He barreled toward the door with a shoulder lead; just as he reached it, it dilated, four pieces pulling back from the center. Neelix sailed through without a sound, until they heard a muffled thump.

Janeway and Tuvok glanced at each other, and the captain grinned. Tuvok merely raised one eyebrow, meaning . . . Before Janeway could fill in the meaning, they head a scuffle from the room Neelix had just entered so dramatically.

Rushing to the door, which opened as politely as before, Janeway saw her cook writhing on the floor with a horrific, slithering serpent with stubby legs and muscular arms. She jumped through the doorway, reaching for her phaser.

Before she could get off a shot, however, Neelix twitched in a way she could not follow, and the snake-man stiffened and slid to the floor. Neelix stood over him triumphantly.

"Captain," said Tuvok, "may I point out we have only scant seconds before the guards enter this room, and they are armed far better than—"

Without comment, Janeway raised the phaser and fired a full-power blast at a small box jutting from the wall next to the door. "Now we've got all night," she predicted.

Moments later, they heard a terrific pair of thumps as the point and second-point of the guard squad ran full-tilt into the unexpectedly inoperative door. They began to pound, shouting dire threats about immortal souls, bright lights, and parting the Unclean on a square.

"May I suggest the window?"

"Not much choice, Tuvok. Can you see out? Is there anybody waiting for us?"

Tuvok stood on tiptoe, peering out the dark, volcanic obsidian. "I cannot see very clearly, but I do not see any witnesses," he said.

Tuvok used his elbow, tapping tentatively on the black glass, then winding up for a full-strength strike. The glass cracked; two more blows and it finally shattered.

Janeway used the phaser butt to break off the sharp points sticking into the window space. "Hoist me up," she said.

In the courtyard, the captain looked up, hoping to see sky; outside, they might possibly be able to contact the *Voyager*.

Alas, she saw overhead only the same grayish metal that neither phasers nor sensors were able to penetrate. "Don't these guys ever want to look at their own sun?"

"To crowd twenty-seven billion sapient life-forms onto this planet," said Tuvok, "one must assume a certain uninterest in outdoor scenery."

"Hm. To each his own, but I sure wouldn't want to live here."

They prowled the perimeter of the courtyard; the wall was iron, rusted in many parts, and it enclosed a large series of rounded, stone artifacts. "Are these . . . burial sites?" guessed Janeway.

"Without a tricorder—"

"You can't tell where the bodies are buried. I know, I know, Mr. Tuvok. I'm amazed at how much cuing we took from our captors . . . virtually everything associated with them now scares humans to death."

"There are many ancient Vulcan symbols of bad fortune and terror as well, Captain."

"Great!" interrupted Neelix. "Now, if you two amateur anthropologists are finished comparing historical notes, can we get back to the escape plan?"

The courtyard bent around an L shape, then stretched on for more than two kilometers. Past the bend, the yard was full to overflowing with ghastly Furies, wandering purposefully with faces down and eyes averted.

"I think we'd better get lost in the crowd," suggested the captain.

They approached. "Captain," said Neelix quietly, "maybe we had better liberate three hooded robes? We don't exactly look like Furies."

She shook her head. "We don't dare get into a fight now; we're no way prepared to attack a body of them. We'll just have to trust our luck and the pseudo-privacy of the Furies. Maybe they won't look up and see us, or won't know who we are if they do."

Breathing deeply to calm herself, she slowly advanced along the courtyard until they joined the crowd, melting into a train of aliens—two snake-men, a shambling, red-eyed *thing,* and one Fury who looked like Navdaq's species. The crowd pressed in on either side, crushing the away team by sheer weight of numbers.

"Take my shirt," Janeway called softly over her shoulder. Neelix caught on at once, grabbing her undertunic. She caught Tuvok's jacket ahead of her.

The crowd surged around them, ebbing and flowing; its movements were best described using the language of fluid flow. Were it not for the tight grip they held to each other, they would have been separated for certain.

"Captain!" shouted Neelix in Janeway's ear, startling her. "Look over there."

She followed his finger. Ahead and to the right was a group of six Furies of yet a different species: skins so wrinkled they looked like rhinoceri, pink in color, covered in dense, bristly hair, and with unshod feet that looked remarkably like hooves from a distance. They showed a series of tails running up their spines.

But the most remarkable thing about them was how they were dressed: they wore Starfleet uniforms.

Wait, thought Janeway, *not exactly* . . . . But she saw a mixture of yellow and red shirts and black pants and ankle-boots. True, some of the jackets were both yellow and red; still, they looked extremely similar to the away team's clothing. The captain, science officer, and cook clawed their way through the wall of flesh to the group, falling in step behind them, heads bowed, looking neither left nor right.

All this while, they had walked alongside a building so massive, they had not even recognized it for what it was. The ceiling even bent up, rising toward infinity. How far down from the surface were they? As soon as they cleared the building, Janeway glanced to the side from the corner of her eye and saw what could only be computer terminals . . . dozens of them lining the building's other face like public subspace communicators.

In a second, Janeway yanked on Tuvok's shirt and tugged him in the direction of the terminals; Neelix followed, of course.

"If these connect to a central guard database," she said,

"I might be able to get into the system and find out exactly where the shuttle pilot is being held."

She stood in front of a terminal about halfway back, hoping not to attract attention.

Janeway chewed her lip, tapping the flat screen here and there, getting a feel for the system.

"Can you get in, Captain?" asked Tuvok.

"If I can't," she muttered, "then I guess I'll never make chief engineer." She winked at her Vulcan friend and began to work in earnest.

CHAPTER

12

TUVOK AND NEELIX STOOD ON EITHER SIDE OF THE FRANTICALLY tapping Captain Janeway, keeping watch.

The Fury computer system used a sophisticated, one-way keycode security encryption. Poking around the edges, Janeway determined that it wanted a seven-hundred-character password.

"Well, no possible way to guess that," she muttered.

"Captain?"

"Nothing, Tuvok. It looks like we're sunk." She scowled; this was silly—to be stopped by a mere schoolboy encryption scheme! Janeway pulled the commbadge out of her pouch to make another futile attempt to contact the ship.

"Wait—belay that. I think I know how to . . ."

She faded out, staring at the commbadge.

"Yes." Smiling cryptically, she placed the badge on the terminal. The badges had a simple, artificially intelligent dataclip in them that detected an open-communications command, such as *Janeway to Commander Chakotay*. The The clip was simplistic, a moron compared to the ship's computer.

But it was still a computer, and it was the best they had.

"Commbadge," said the captain, "identify your model and year."

She jumped as a voice, the *computer's* voice, popped out of the badge. "I am a Starfleet general-issue Tang Bioelectrics Model 74-A communications badge manufactured at Rivendell Prime in 2362."

Neelix stared. "I never knew you could do that."

"I never thought of trying before." She licked her lips. "Commbadge, locate a receiver circuit in the terminal unit you're sitting on. Signal when you have done so."

After a silent second, the commbadge beeped.

"Transmit the following commands through the Universal Translator to the receiver circuit. Activate prisoner manifest." She watched the screen; after a moment, it went blank, then displayed a screenful of unfamiliar but clearly not encrypted characters.

"Fascinating," said Tuvok. "She has bypassed the entire encryption system by jumping over it, as it were, and communicating directly with the brain of the terminal."

"Um . . . I'll take your word for it."

"I never told you I was half-Ferengi, did I?" said Janeway with a wink. "Command: Display schematic of prison cells; highlight cell containing the Unclean captured on the moon."

An architectural drawing of a series of huge, roughly rectangular buildings (none was quite right-regular) appeared; one of the buildings then displayed a schematic of the cells. The building expanded until it filled the viewer, and a cell at the inner end glowed blue.

"Command: Show location of this terminal in relation to the highlighted cell."

A dot appeared on the side of the very building they wanted. All three stared at the wall they faced, then back toward the front they had seen. "Show all entrances to the building." She studied, memorizing the map. The nearest entrance was on the back side of the huge cell block.

Janeway paused; the next command was the big one. "Command: Unlock the door to the cell in which the Unclean is kept."

The terminal hesitated, then flashed a legend in the Fury's language, or one of them. Then the entire terminal went blank.

"Unauthorized access or command," guessed Tuvok. "Captain, I strongly suggest we remove ourselves from this location before the nearest guards arrive."

Resisting the urge to bolt, they slowly continued down the side yard toward the back.

The back of the building looked exactly like the front: featureless, the angles all wrong, dark and chilling, even in the heat of the Fury planet. But in the center was a ghastly, leaning, leering doorway that beckoned like an open mouth.

Janeway approached, ready to find a door that was open, locked with an electronic or mechanical lock, or ready to dilate as soon as she got close enough. She held her phaser ready.

In fact, the door was none of the above. It was closed and locked with a peculiar contraption that she only dimly recognized as a centuries-old *padlock*. The padlock actually dangled from an eyelet in the handle.

"Amazing," she said, shaking her head. The mix of modern and stone-age on the Fury planet was beginning to get under her skin.

The padlock was made out of the same indestructible material they were unable to cut through earlier. Janeway paused, temporarily defeated. Then she smiled, set her phaser on high, and proceeded to cut a Janeway-sized hole in the door itself—the door was made of mere steel-bound wood, an oily, warped wood. For once, the Fury peculiarities worked in the away team's favor.

She left the last centimeter of the top attached; when the edges had cooled—Neelix remembered himself this time— the three of them peeled back the flap with some difficulty. The flap did not drop or make any great noise; they ducked underneath into the building.

The layout was similar to their own cellblock: a door leading to the cells dilated as they approached; long corridors marched into the distance, all of them lined with metal-barred cages, each with its corresponding key-card lock. The away team kept close to the sides, in shadows deeper even than the normal gloom of the Fury world; it was a good thing, for when they rounded the corner that led to the block containing the pilot's cell, according to the database, Tuvok saw a strike team of guards checking out the cell.

He silently waved the captain and Neelix back. Around the corner, Tuvok whispered. "They must have responded to the attempted unlock command, Captain. The guards must realize some unauthorized person accessed the database. They will not leave the prisoner now."

Janeway nodded. "I agree. We've run out of options."

"You mean we're just going to let him rot in there?"

"Certainly not, Neelix. We've run out of *peaceful* options. I'm getting damned sick and tired of being poked, stared at, and imprisoned—me and the rest of you, including the pilot. I think this has passed far beyond the Prime Directive territory and deep into the realm of self-defense."

"I concur, Captain. These aliens are conspiring to launch an invasion of the Federation, and as such they are outside the domain of any treaty or law . . . including General Order Number One."

"It's time we showed them what Starfleet officers can do. Mr. Tuvok—you take the right flank. Neelix, you're on the left to prevent anyone from escaping for reinforcements. I'll take the middle two. Neelix, make believe Tuvok is your enemy; you look more like you could be a weird species of Fury. Ready?"

They rounded the corner, easily; Janeway lay on her stomach in the shadow, while Neelix and Tuvok walked deliberately toward the cell. The guards had closed the door, leaving a lump in a vaguely recognizable, burned and shredded Starfleet uniform; now the Furies surrounded the cell, seven strong. As soon as they caught sight of the pair approaching, they leveled their weapons.

Tuvok put his hands in the air, while Neelix pushed him none too gently in the small of the back. "Get along there, you!"

The confused guards backed up, still leveling their weapons but unsure what was happening and who they should believe. Capain Janeway kept as still as a corpse . . . she presumed the Furies could see in the dark; she counted on their vision being based around movement, as was human and Vulcan vision. If she stayed still enough, she might not attract any notice.

"Holy ones," said Neelix, "I have captured one of the prisoners. Ah . . . should I hand him over to you?"

The guards stared back and forth between Neelix and Tuvok. Almost certainly, the former was violating numerous social cues and unspoken protocols—the away team had had no time to study the society to be able to successfully blend.

While the guards puzzled out that paradox, they allowed the pair to close within arm's length. "Sirs," said Tuvok, his hands still in the air, "I wish to make a complete confession." He lowered his hands onto the necks of the two of guards on the right and used the Vulcan neck-pinch . . . it worked as well on Furies as it did on most other races.

As soon as they started to sag, before the others had a chance to react, Janeway opened fire from her position on the floor, steadying her aim for the long-distance shot by planting her elbow and using her hand as a tripod. She stunned two before they could fire a shot.

Two of the remaining three bolted toward her in the confusion. Tuvok turned and gave one of them a solid push as he stumbled past; the guard sprawled full length on the ground face-first, grunting in pain. She tried another phaser blast at the one who still approached, but this time he was ready; the guard ducked under the shot and connected with Janeway at her midsection, pounding the air out of her. The pair went down in a tangle of bodies.

But Janeway was a captain in Starfleet, and she had received hundreds of hours of armed and unarmed combat training. The guard was too big for her to handle by herself—but she was *not* by herself. After a few seconds, she managed to get the heel of her palm against the Fury's chin and press his head back a little bit.

It was enough. Tuvok stepped over the guard on the ground, who still struggled to get up, and pinched Janeway's assailant into the Land of Nod. The captain rolled to the side, getting a clear shot around Tuvok, and stunned the sixth guard just as he got to his knees. He fell heavily to the ground once more.

Kathryn Janeway blinked, then suddenly remembered the last guard: when numbers five and six had bolted *toward* her, the seventh turned tail and made a laser-line for the opposite door. Suddenly realizing the danger, Janeway leapt to her feet and tried to get off a shot; but Tuvok was in the way, and the guard was far, far out of her reach.

A yellow blur flashed across her field of vision: Neelix charged after the last guard, leaping onto his back just before the Fury reached a lever-style switch. The cook tackled the guard centimeters away from the alarm switch.

"Did we get them? Is that all of them?" Janeway quickly checked each of the seven, making sure he was unconscious. Then she returned to the cell, accompanied by Tuvok. "All right, got any good ideas about opening the lock from the *outside?*"

"Not at the moment," said the Vulcan. "The light panels in this hallway are mounted high enough that I doubt we could reach them."

The captain was in the process of removing her hairpin as a preliminary step when Neelix gently coughed. "Um, Captain—maybe I'm being dense, but can't you just use this?"

He handed her the key-card that had been carried by the guard he coldcocked.

Flushing slightly, Janeway inserted the card in the slot; nothing happened. She removed it, and the cell unlocked and hinged open with a noise like a rusty wheel rolling along cobblestones. They entered and discovered what once had been a man, a human Starfleet officer. He wore command red, but they could hardly tell, for most of the fabric was burned beyond recognition, probably in the fiery crash of the shuttlecraft. His commbadge was missing; whether it fell off or he removed it was unknown. He once had been a tall man; now he was stooped. He once had boasted bright, red hair; now, only a few, discolored wisps remained, and the rest was gray and frayed. Ugly brown spots and blotches covered his skin; they might once have been freckles, now grown monstrous under tortures that must have involved ultraviolet radiation. His eyes were vacant and stared far out over the horizon. The man's skin was pallid where it wasn't spotty, with bloodred cracks marbling the surface.

Tuvok carefully felt his carotid artery pulse and declared him alive. He bled from a dozen serious lacerations, and his shoulder was dislocated. He had a crushed wrist and fractured ribs—this much determined by a cursory examination of his swollen joints and chest. But whether he would live or die, whether indeed his brain was functioning somewhere under the trauma, pain, and incoherence, only the doctor could tell. The man was not talking; he stared at the away team with no shock of recognition or relief and did not respond to their urgently whispered questions. His pupils were dilated and reacted sluggishly and unevenly to light.

Janeway hesitated only a moment. "Gentlemen, we have to get this patient to the ship; he is our top priority. Besides, I'm fresh out of ideas for stopping the invasion . . . but maybe if we can figure out where he came from, how he got all the way out here, maybe we'll have a clue how to get back ourselves and warn the Federation."

"Or perhaps," added Tuvok, "we can covertly accompany the Furies when they invade and take that opportunity to issue our warning. I believe our best chance to return to the Alpha Quadrant is at hand."

"Either way, we have to return to the ship—which means we have to find the surface of the planet somehow . . . or at least coordinates we can beam from."

"How about the place we beamed to in the first place?" asked Neelix.

"Can you find it again?"

"I—can't say for certain, but I think I can. I can try."

"That's more than Tuvok or I could do; we were in no condition to note the route."

Tuvok grabbed the lieutenant around his waist and hauled him to his feet. Miraculously, he stuck there, swaying a bit; but his eyes still stared into nothingness. Janeway gave the man an experimental push, and he staggered forward a couple of steps, then stopped. By a combination of pushing and turning, they got him moving; the captain supported him with her shoulder to speed things up.

Janeway led them back through the dilating door to the plaza; then Neelix took over. They tried to get into the Fury mode of walking, keeping their heads down, eyes averted, really getting into subsuming their individual identities in the crusade of the group to recover a particular piece of real estate at the expense of their entire multicultural existence, if necessary.

After all, what could possibly outweigh the chance to storm heaven? That is what Janeway told herself, and evidently it worked, for they were neither stopped nor questioned while Neelix led them down one blind alley and along another false trail. Each time, he added "—but *now* I know where we're going!" and the Starfleet officers patiently followed, each supporting one of their new companion's arms. He felt clammy to the touch.

At last, Neelix insisted, "Wait, this time I *really* know where we are . . ." and that time, he was right. He led them around another pair of corners, across a courtyard that Tuvok agreed looked familiar, down some more passages where Neelix agreed the geometry was loathsome, to a square that even Janeway admitted was the original beam-in spot. They returned to the approximate location they had entered, and the captain touched Neelix's secret comm-badge. "Janeway to *Voyager*—Chakotay, are you out there?"

The voice crackled with static, but it was unmistakably her executive officer. "Captain! We have been trying—"

"Four to beam out right now, Mr. Chakotay—lock in on the communications signal."

"Yes, Captain, it'll be a little tricky, but we'll get you out."

Janeway turned back to Tuvok and Neelix. "All right, we've got the ship; now all we have to do, gentlemen, is survive until she gets here."

"That may not be as easy as it sounds," declared Tuvok. He pointed at the guards, including the feared favored, boiling out of the building they just left and out of two others just like it. "We might possibly escape detection by remaining within this crowd," suggested the Vulcan.

The captain of the guards made a peculiar pinging noise that might have been the equivalent of a human's whistling for attention. The guards gathered around—except for the favored, who inched close enough to hear but remained proudly aloof from the ordinary guards. The guard captain spoke animatedly, his oddly articulated limbs gesturing in impossible directions. Then he whipped out a bulky, box-like item. *Now what?* thought the captain; she didn't appreciate new rules introduced into the game in such a late round.

"It could be a Fury tricorder," guessed Neelix.

"New plan: We take our so-far unrescued prisoner and get as far away from here as possible. I'll leave the commbadge carrier signal operating, so as soon as Chakotay gets close enough, he can lock on."

Janeway took one arm of the prisoner around her neck, and Tuvok took the other; they hurried as fast as they could, with Neelix dashing forward a few meters, then dashing back, looking remarkably doglike. "Get behind a building," Janeway suggested; "maybe their own tricorders are no better at poking through it than ours."

"We will have gained little," said Tuvok; "they can still follow our life signs."

"Yes, but they'll have to *follow* us then . . . they can't head straight toward us. We can lead them in circles."

"The idea is not without merit."

Janeway shifted to their rear, poking her nose around the corner to watch the guards' progress. Temporarily safe, at least until they had to move on to the next building, thirty meters away, Janeway looked up at the ceiling high overhead and tried to mentally *will* the *Voyager* to materialize right that instant and beam them out.

Neelix joined her, watching the guards.

Tuvok began trying to revive the shuttlecraft pilot; they would make much better time if he could be induced to move under his own power. But none of the standard means of bringing an unconscious human about worked; although the man was semiaware—he groaned and occasionally rolled his head from side to side and attempted to wrap his arms protectively around his head—the Vulcan could not get him fully awake, not even enough to move his legs or balance on his own without swaying like a sapling in a wind.

"Uh-oh," said Neelix, "they've figured it out . . . they're casting for us—wait, they're going the wrong way!"

Janeway held her breath as the guards, the favored in front, crowded around the door they had just exited, weapons out; then the biggest favored rolled forward like an armored fighting vehicle, gathered speed, and burst through the cut-out hole, firing his disruptor-like weapon as he went. His bulk ripped off the flap that Janeway had left; the others followed him through, and there were a few moments of confusion while they determined that they had followed the scent in the wrong direction—a fifty-fifty chance in that sort of tracking operation.

Janeway spoke up: "Now's our chance—Tuvok, let's move quickly before they figure it out!"

Neelix and Tuvok again picked up the pilot and followed Janeway around the building. "Captain," said Tuvok, panting, his voice nevertheless cutting through the noise, "can you cross and recross our own trail several times? It might serve to confuse our pursuers further."

Keeping a wary eye on the door—the Furies had left a guard, of course—they dodged into the courtyard again, slipping from one line of pedestrians to another. Janeway could feel the Furies' confusion and resentment at being jostled, probably a severe breach of politeness; but she jumped from one conga line to another, slowly enough that Neelix and Lieutenant Tuvok could follow, and worked her way back to a spot she remembered traversing. She walked their own trail for a few meters, then cut to the left; she zigged in the other direction, into the mob again, followed it around a circuitous route, then zagged back across the previous path at right angles.

Then she got nervous. The guard outside the building leaned through the hole and talked to someone just on the other side; then he looked around as if searching for them. "Neelix—move it, quick! Behind the next building over there!"

Just as Janeway feared, the guard reached through the

hole and took the tricorder from its previous owner; then he idly scanned the area.

He froze suddenly, then pointed directly at the fleeing away team. Janeway and crew bolted for cover, but it was too late; they were spotted. The guard produced his own version of the pinging noise, and his cohorts leapt back out through the hole.

The guard captain was the third one back through, and he made the smart tactical decision not to wait until he had regrouped. He pointed directly toward them and shouted something loudly enough that the away team's Universal Translators picked it up: "Give chase to the Unclean, for if they escape, we shall all be excommunicated!"

That is a potent threat indeed, thought Janeway, *when all of society is ordered around the Great Holy Crusade.* To a Fury, being excommunicated probably meant losing all reason for living. Suicide might follow quickly, if they were a race capable of such self-immolation.

She thought this as she ran as fast as she could, carrying her burden, expecting with every step the harsh blow of an energy weapon in the back. Or worse, the terror projector. *What hell would that be?* she wondered frantically.

Tuvok gave only the tiniest portion of his consciousness to willing his legs to move; running away from the Furies was something he literally could do in his sleep, so deeply was his fear of them ingrained in the wilder parts of his psyche. He passed his left hand around the pilot's back and up to touch his left temple, then pressed his right hand to the pilot's other temple. The Vulcan tried to find and extract the tiny ball of consciousness he hoped existed somewhere inside the wall of pain, the fleshy prison. Tuvok was trying a Vulcan mind-meld on the run, something that had never before occurred to him.

Here and beyond, Tuvok caught fleeting images of horrific memories—an alien ship, an attack; battle scenes, the dying, explosions and confusion—panic, the shock of being hit—the pilot lay in sickbay, he was in pain, he was trying to protect a friend . . . another Starfleet officer . . .

Tuvok almost drew back out of the man's mind; he was

well aware of the essential, ultimate invasion of privacy the mind-meld required . . . and clearly, the man had suffered severe trauma . . . but it was not so clear whether the Vulcan should continue or back out of the man's thoughts.

He hesitated only a moment; then Tuvok recalled the central tenet of the Vulcan philosophy, a saying attributed to Surak himself: The needs of the many outweigh the needs of the few . . . or the one.

But would the pilot himself agree? Would Captain Janeway? Humans were not Vulcans, and they had a peculiar love-hate relationship with such obvious, logical, utilitarian philosophy.

In the end, Tuvok decided that the decision was his own, and he had no problem with it. The away team needed rescuing; the Federation needed saving; and both required the pilot to become at least somewhat conscious. The man's own need not to have his most private thoughts violated must take second place in importance.

Tuvok again entered the pilot's mind, forcing himself deeper and deeper, trying to find the lowest portion of the brain. Along the way, he saw many more images, horrors etched in the man's brain—the man . . . a name floated past, and Tuvok grabbed it.

The man was Lieutenant Redbay.

Then, just behind the name, Tuvok found what he was looking for: he found the reptile center, the site that controlled such simple activities as walking, balancing, running. *Open,* thought Tuvok, trying to restart the segment; *let me in . . . I am a friend. Your life is in danger; you must revive and begin running.*

Then Tuvok was surrounded and attacked by the mind's I, the "Redbay" of Redbay's mind. *Invader! Assassin! Murderer! Get out get out get OUT of my head, get out, get—*

Do not be afraid of me; I have come to help. You are in danger; you must begin moving immediately.

—devils hurling terror before them like lightbeam tearing through the ship invading invading! in mortal danger must take the shuttlecraft through the wormhole before . . .

Tuvok was fascinated; a wormhole? What wormhole?

Could they return through it and warn the Federation of the impending attack . . . an attack about which they knew no operational details?

But perhaps Redbay knew. Tuvok pressed harder. *Sir, you must return to consciousness, whether you are to fight me or the ones who did this to you. Follow my voice; follow me. . . .*

Tuvok backed slowly away; the "Redbay" grabbed hold, trying to wrestle Tuvok's consciousness to the metaphorical floor—but the Vulcan was the stronger; and slowly, inexorably, Redbay was pulled out of his self-built prison . . . a prison that might have saved him from total madness.

The only logical conclusion was that Redbay had been exposed to the Furies' terror-projection device.

The pilot groaned again; but it was a groan with more purpose than his previous ones. Janeway felt him straighten under her arm; when he stood, he was taller than she, of course, which made her suddenly a burden, not a support. She hastily let go, simply helping him to balance on his hind legs.

Neelix had been watching the three of them, transfixed; then he turned back and started squawking: "Run! Run away—*they're here!*"

The away team bolted, and astonishingly enough, so did the shuttlecraft pilot. He staggered after them under his own impulse power. The quartet ran across the courtyard, under the iron "sky," pursued by those guards who had made it back out—which did not include any of the favored, fortunately, else the *Voyager* team would have been trampled in seconds. *The favored are evidently swift of foot but not of mind,* thought the captain.

But the other guards were fast enough, motivated, and unencumbered by a still-woozy comrade. They gained and steadily closed the gap, reaching for Neelix, who brought up the rear.

At last, Neelix dug in his heels and whirled to face the angels of death, straight-arming the first one. The rest came for him with a roar.

They whirled their facial tentacles in rage; they screamed and leapt at him like wild animals; but they leapt at an empty patch of air as Janeway, Tuvok, Neelix faded into noncorporeality in front of the Furies' snakelike snouts.

Janeway discorporated and disappeared, leaving a confused, enraged, and terrified mob of cops in her dust . . . cops who would soon face their own, even more terrifying commanders with a story of failure quite unlikely to be believed.

Captain Janeway almost—*almost*—felt sorry for them as she rematerialized on the *Voyager* transporter pad.

CHAPTER

13

"AM I DEAD?"

Kes waited anxiously in the transporter room, standing first on one foot then the other, while the away team took about nine years, an entire Ocampan lifetime, to materialize. The stranger, an emaciated human who looked like a ghost, sparkled into view with that horrible question on his lips: "Am I dead?"

After Kes embraced Neelix, she propelled the stranger—Redbay, according to Tuvok—straight to sickbay, while everyone else headed bridgeward.

In sickbay, Kes watched, concerned, while the Doctor checked Redbay quickly and determined that there was nothing physically wrong with him aside from a few broken bones, deep lacerations, bruises, and general ill treatment.

Kes desperately wished she knew if Neelix were safe; but she remained with the doctor. Redbay suffered from a deep psychological wound that would be difficult to cure while still on a starship . . . perhaps impossible, as soon as the young lieutenant recovered sufficiently to realize their dire predicament. He had lost quite a lot of weight and had clearly been tortured physically and psychologically. The man looked like a walking corpse. His color was bad, bone-white, and he did not lose the long-distance stare.

"Am I dead?"

"No," said Kes; "you're aboard a Starfleet starship." *Lost in space, forever, never to return. You may as well be dead,* she did not add.

The doctor took up the conversation.

"You have some severe injuries which I will now heal, if you'll stop squirming long enough to let me do so. You may feel some discomfort and stiffness for a few days, especially in the wrist. Try not to use it as much as usual. In fact, try not to use it at all."

"This is the *U.S.S. Voyager,*" said Kes, "but you're still in the Delta Quadrant. My name is Kes, and this is the doctor. The captain's name is Janeway; she's the one who rescued you with the Vulcan. Neelix, the other one who rescued you—not the Vulcan, the *third* one—is my . . . a Talaxian native.

"Kes is my assistant," the doctor explained.

Kes watched Redbay carefully; in fact, she had struck up the conversation, hoping to jar his mind away from his morbid hallucinations.

"Is this hell? Am I in hell now?"

Kes sighed and began telling Redbay all about the *Voyager* and how it came to be in the Delta Quadrant. *I'll entertain him all night, if I have to,* she decided bleakly, concerned about the patient's frame of mind.

Janeway slid into the command chair as if she had merely stepped out to eat a quick meal; the ordeal behind her, she wanted her ship back in hand. "Mr. Chakotay, what's happening? Pursuit?"

"Glad to have you aboard, Captain. We worried we had lost you for a time. Mr. Paris?"

"Nothing yet . . . I plotted a course that stayed well away from the aliens' moon; that's how they caught us last time."

"Where are we now?"

Kim answered. "We shot around the sun, beamed you up

on the fly, and now we're right back where we started: on the opposite side of the sun from the planet; except now we're far enough out for a real orbit."

Janeway nodded. "Continue correcting course to keep from being seen.

"Did you miss me?" The voice sounded from the turbo-lift.

"Welcome back, Neelix," said Kim. "Of course We missed you . . . especially around dinnertime. Lieutenant Paris drew the black marble and had to cook."

"Mr. Neelix," said the captain, "you performed with exemplary courage, as did Mr. Tuvok, under difficult conditions. I will make an entry to that effect in the log. But right now, we have a serious problem. Senior officers to my ready room; I have to tell you what we discovered. Activate—I mean, Janeway to the doctor."

"Yes, Captain."

"Doctor, how is Lieutenant Redbay?"

The doctor frowned on the viewer, putting his finger on his chin in an eerily human gesture. "Physically? I've done my usual brilliant job. But he still has some lingering psychological problems. Kes is talking to him now—I think he'll be able to leave sickbay in a short while."

"Kes!" shouted Neelix. "Can you hear me? Are you there?"

The Ocampan moved into the frame. "Neelix, I was so frightened when we couldn't find the away team. I thought you might have been captured."

"We were! We had to break out—the captain used her hairpin to pick the—"

"But are you all right? Can you come down here?"

"I'm sorry, Kes," said Janeway, "but I need Neelix up here for right now. He's fine. I'll send him down as soon as I can. Janeway out."

Chakotay was staring at her. "What did you pick with your *hairpin?* This I have to hear."

"In good time, Commander. Senior officers in the ready room. Mr. Kim, contact Torres and and get her up here."

* * *

Chakotay sat back and listened to his captain. He was surprised how relieved he was to have her aboard again. *A few months ago, I would cheerfully have left her behind,* he realized.

"That is as much as we could glean of the Furies' plans. They may represent the biggest threat the Federation has ever faced . . . perhaps even greater than the Borg.

"When they invaded the Alpha Quadrant one hundred years ago, a *single ship* fought the Constitution-class starship *Enterprise* and a Klingon fleet to the death. If today, they chose to send a dozen ships, or a few hundred or *thousand,* how could we possibly respond?

"My words might be inadequate to convey the dire situation we face; but if you had been there with us, if you had *seen them* and felt the mindless, paralyzing terror they induce, even without their terror-projection weapon, I wouldn't need to explain anything."

Tuvok spoke into the well of alarmed silence. "The captain has been deliberately vague about my own reaction to the Furies. She wishes to spare my feelings, for my emotional reaction disgraced my logical heritage. But I have no feelings to be hurt; and if it will help make the rest of you understand the gravity of the threat, I will accept whatever opprobrium my reaction deserves."

Pausing a moment, Tuvok told Chakotay, Kim, Paris, and Torres exactly what he had felt, sparing no raging emotion, no disgraceful, illogical reaction.

When he finished, the commander was stunned. Without even having seen the Furies, he began to understand.

"There are twenty-seven billion—well, *demons* on that planet," said Janeway. "If we allow them to invade our quadrant with even a significant fraction of that figure, we will face an enemy greater in sheer numbers than any we have ever faced since before the Federation was the Federation, and before the human race was really human. And then there are the projected terrors; thank heaven we didn't have to face those. But if they do invade, we will."

"We failed to effectively resist conquest the last time," added Tuvok; "although we are closer to them technologically, the Furies could overwhelm us with sheer numbers."

Chakotay frowned. Fatalism did not sit well in his craw. "It's not just our technology that has changed. We're older now, as a people; we're more sophisticated. We are civilized, and we have met many new and some would even say horrific life-forms. Wilson's Worms on Dalmat Seven; the Viidians, even the Vulcans look a little like human demons."

Janeway shook her head. "When a human encounters a Fury, he is no longer older, more sophisticated, civilized, or even human anymore. He is once more what he was in the past: a terrified slave driven to obedience by irresistible fear."

The ready-room door slid open, and a picture of walking death loomed in the doorway. Chakotay almost winced at the vision: flesh sunk to the bone so it appeared a living skull, skin pallid as death, clammy and dry, sliding across the joints and muscles like a poorly upholstered chair trod upon to reach a high place . . . the man in the doorway did not so much fill his Starfleet lieutenant's uniform as offer it a wire frame on which to hang. Redbay—who else would it be?—listed to the side, like an ocean ship taking on water just before sinking beneath the waves.

He lurched into the room, arms outstretched, and Chakotay impulsively jerked to his feet though the lieutenant had only grabbed for the table to steady himself on legs too weak to support even his emaciated weight. He had crashed only a few weeks earlier, judging from the distress beacon; but it might as well have been years in a prison camp undergoing the punishments of the damned.

Kes accompanied the young ancient into the ready room. She caught him by the arm, levering him gently into a chair; then she sat beside him and put his hand in hers but did not attempt any more emotional greeting. *They are very private souls,* thought the commander.

"I have seen hell," croaked Redbay, and no one in the room dared contradict the audacious statement. Even Tuvok simply folded his hands and let the words hover overhead.

"You're still alive," said Kes, reassuring the young man.

"No one should see hell," insisted Redbay, "and survive."

"But you have survived," said the captain; "and you must help the rest of us survive. You know what the Furies intend? I see you do. Then you'll help us now."

Redbay closed his eyes—then quickly opened them again, evidently seeing more to fear in the blackness than in the light. He turned expectantly to Janeway, who began the inquiry.

"Yes. Well, we know the what. What do we know about the how? B'Elanna?"

B'Elanna Torres cleared her throat. Lieutenant Carey and I have continued to analyze the tricorder recordings that Ensign Kim made of the machinery inside the moon, and there is no question what it is: the moon is set up to receive a single burst of energy so catastrophic that it will destroy the moon microseconds after it begins to be absorbed."

She tapped on the console, causing a three-dimensional, holoprojected schematic of the machinery to materialize above the conference table and rotate slowly. Chakotay stared curiously, but it meant little to him; it was a big, bulky machine.

"The system Kim and Paris saw was built to channel a massive amount of energy. . . . The moon will be bombarded by a burst of energy; it has to be a burst—the circuits wouldn't last longer than fifteen milliseconds. But that hardly matters, because within a hundred milliseconds, the moon's surface will first liquefy, then a quarter of a second later boil away into ionized gas."

Paris shook his head, confused. "If the whole system breaks down in a quarter of a second—"

"Nowhere near that long," corrected Lieutenant Torres; "only one-point-five *hundredths* of a second, really, before the circuits fry."

"All right, one-point-five *hundredths* of a second—what could it possibly do in that length of time?"

"It projects energy, Paris. Enough to cause a subspace rift and probably enough to puncture through many folds of the fabric, whatever you want to call it, of the universe. It creates something very much like an artificial wormhole."

B'Elanna Torres paused. Chakotay silently pondered the hard-to-miss implication: The Furies planned to send an awful lot of them *somewhere,* and mighty fast, too.

CHAPTER
14

"I DON'T REALLY UNDERSTAND IT," CONTINUED B'ELANNA; SHE felt annoyed at not understanding. But worse, she had to wonder if she would understand, if she had stuck it out at the Academy.

"You really need a subspace physicist here. But while the heavy-particle radiation, the actual guts of the exploding star, crawls toward the moon at only about a twentieth of light speed, say thirteen thousand kilometers per second, the first burst of massless, energetic neutrinos crosses the gap at light speed itself. They strike the neutrino collectors, here." Torres caused a series of thirty-eight gigantic coils of some thin wire, like metallic spiderwebs, to glow blue on the red, floating schematic.

"In the first three hundred nanoseconds, the neutrinos are converted to Bela-Smith-Ng subspace pumped-wave energy, the same stuff we use to send a subspace message— except every particle raised fifteen or sixteen 'orbits,' or levels of energy. Theoretically impossible, of course . . . according to *Federation* science." She smiled, pure Maquis satisfaction.

"In the next fourteen hundred nanoseconds, this Bela-energy is run a few million times around a circular coil, here." She illuminated a different section of the diagram; but she could see Kim and Paris staring blankly, trying to absorb the gist, at least.

"What does that do?" asked the ensign, more to himself than Torres. B'Elanna almost put her hand on Kim's arm; he had always said he would have gone to EDO School to become an engineer if he hadn't gotten the *Voyager* billet. *He's upset that he doesn't see it immediately,* she realized; for a moment, B'Elanna felt very close to Kim, sharing the bond of imagined inadequacy.

B'Elanna Torres answered quickly. "Edvard Bela, who lived on a colony now at the core of Maquis resistance to the Cardassian-inspired treaty, thought that if Bela-energy were forced into a circular path—and I've never seen anyone even attempt it before, but that's what the Furies are doing—it would created a subspace tunnel of such intensity that it would explode along its only available expansion points . . . forward and back."

Janeway gasped. "They really *are* building a wormhole!" she exclaimed.

"You're way ahead of me; but yes, that's the conclusion Carey and I came to."

The captain continued so quickly, even B'Elanna had a hard time following. "They've built a device to focus some monstrous burst of energy into the creation of an artificial wormhole, which they're going to project. Calculations probably would show its other end pointing to the Alpha Quadrant . . . then they'll send their ships through. Have to be fast, though; they've already burned up, what, two milliseconds? And they only have fifteen, say ten for safety's sake? Eight milliseconds . . . they're not going to send their ships through the wormhole. They're going to create the wormhole *around the ships!* So the first warning sign would be when they mass their fleet in one spot. B'Elanna, what's the beam spread? What kind of radius would we have to look for? And where in the universe do they expect to get a burst like that? To vaporize that whole moon, you must have calculated them using an astronomical amount of energy. There's no way they can . . ."

She paused, scowling. Lieutenant Torres opened her mouth; but before she could speak, Tuvok drew the obvious conclusion: "There is only one source for an energy burst that large," he said. "The Furies are planning to trigger their own sun to go supernova."

In the stunned silence around the conference table, B'Elanna Torres could have dropped a molecule and made everyone jump at the crash.

Redbay smiled, but the gesture turned into a grimace of loathing. B'Elanna tried not to look at him; he frightened her.

"Yes," admitted the chief engineer. "They're going to blow up their sun. We—passed through the sun a while ago." Torres glanced at Commander Chakotay, who had said not a word. As Torres expected, Janeway stared at her executive officer in astonishment.

"You took *my* ship into the *sun?*"

Chakotay inclined his head for a moment, and the captain sat back, frowning but saying nothing more.

Torres continued, feeling embarrassed, as if she had betrayed a confidence. "And Paris thought to conduct a full scan of the immediate environment . . . passive only, so we wouldn't alert the Fury pursuers that we were still alive. I've been going over the data since, and I discovered that the core is already in an advanced state of collapse: there are hardly any bosons to speak of and nowhere near enough heat to sustain the fusion reaction . . . but the neutrino count is through the roof. And yes, I know the sun isn't anywhere near big enough to collapse on its own—or anywhere near as hot as a supernova, which can generate core temperatures of six hundred million degrees."

"A Bela-Neutron device," declared Tuvok.

"Of course. Another conceptual breakthrough by Professor Bela . . . the devices, millions of them, absorb heavy particles like hydrogen and helium nuclei and reemit neutrinos plus electrons and positrons. Neutrinos don't interact with anything except neutrino collectors, so most of the sun's energy is pumped away uselessly . . ."

"Leaving not enough energy to hold the sun's diameter apart against the crushing pull of gravity," completed

Janeway, "and the star collapses like a popped soap bubble."

"An overly poetic metaphor," said Tuvok, "but essentially accurate."

"And when it collapses," concluded B'Elanna, *"boom."*

Paris's mouth had opened wider and wider during the explanation. He might have barely passed the minimum physics credits at the Academy, but he could add two and three. "Damn, talk about burning your bridges behind you!"

Tuvok raised his eyebrows. "Mr. Paris brings up an interesting question: Once the Furies create the wormhole to transport their fleet, collapsing their own star into a supernova, what is their plan for the rest of their population? By my rough estimate, this star is large enough that a supernova would extend its radius far past the inhabited planet. Every life-form on the surface of the planet would be incinerated. There would be no survivors."

B'Elanna nodded grimly. "We wondered about that, too. The sun goes supernova, and seven and a half minutes later, the neutrinos and photons strike the moon. In a total of four milliseconds, the wormhole is projected to a target point. Eleven milliseconds after that, the circuits fry, and the wormhole begins wobbling, collapsing in maybe seven or eight seconds.

"But the moon is the same distance from the sun as the planet, in the L-four position. The moon *can't* eclipse the sun. No matter what, their planet will be vaporized, or at least biologically cleansed, by the same blast."

"Of course, the Furies live deep underground," mused Tuvok. "They might survive."

"But they'd have essentially no sun! Captain, I never answered your other question about the radius of the wormhole. That's because we can't. Nobody has any experience with this sort of pumped-wave subspace energy—it doesn't exist as far as Federation science is concerned! So it could be anything from a few meters to a few thousand kilometers . . . neither Carey nor I can narrow it any further than that."

Janeway sat at the head of the table, cupping her chin in her hand. "We didn't see any evidence of a huge fleet of ships while we were on the planet. Of course, we were pretty confined, to say the least."

Ensign Kim spoke up. "Sir, we saw nothing from orbit. I can have the computer review the records, looking for areas of the planet we never got to see; we weren't in orbit long before we were attacked."

"Do that, Mr. Kim."

Chakotay's turn. "Captain, I don't think you'll find any battle fleet, or escape fleet, for that matter."

B'Elanna listened intently; she knew that tone . . . Chakotay had just had, or was on the verge of having, an insight, a satori.

"Why do you say that?"

"I don't know. But I have a feeling that we're shooting into an empty tree. Call it a hint from my spirit guide; but there is an aspect of this we're all missing . . . including myself."

"What do you mean?" asked the captain.

"I don't know yet, Captain." Chakotay considered a moment, then shook his head. "We're missing something. But I don't think we'll find any battle fleets, and I don't think they have any intention of letting any of their people die in the supernova."

"Commander Chakotay," asked Tuvok, "I did not detect any noticible compassion or concern in either Navdaq or the Autocrat for the Fury population."

"I don't mean they're too nice to let them die, Mr. Tuvok; I don't believe they're willing to sacrifice even a single soldier who might aid their cause. It would be wasteful and inefficient . . . and I think that's how they would look at it."

Redbay giggled slightly. Disconcerted, B'Elanna turned to him; but the lieutenant had nothing to say.

"Well, the commander was right about one thing," said Kim, looking up from the screen. "The computer has just reviewed the entire planetary scan and found nothing that could possibly be a fleet of ships."

Paris added his own two strips of latinum. "There wasn't

anything on the moon that looked like a launch bay or docking port. I don't think they even think about fleets of ships."

Kim continued. "There's no ship activity around the planet, no traffic between the planet and the moon, and nothing else in the solar system."

"Lieutenant Torres," said Chakotay, "are there any nearby stars with habitable planets we passed on the way here?"

"Yes sir. Two stars, one with two habitable planets, the other with four."

"Any life-form readings?"

"None that we detected, Commander."

Chakotay looked at Janeway. The captain smiled. "So we've determined the Furies aren't very sociable and aren't interested in colonization, trade, or contact with other beings. This doesn't explain why they don't have a battle fleet on the eve of an invasion."

"Captain," said Torres, "those ships that tried to corner us . . . they were sluggish and completely inexperienced at space combat. But why didn't they shoot their terror-projection beam at us? That's the question that worries me."

Lieutenant Redbay's giggles had become more and more frequent and distracting; now he broke into loud, stentorian laughter. B'Elanna slid away from him, as did everybody at the table except Chakotay and Tuvok.

It was the crazy-man laugh of a person who no longer cared what anybody thinks of him or his sanity. Redbay lurched to his feet, yanking his arm away from Kes's restraining grip.

"A *fleet?* You wanted a *fleet?* Oh, they gave us a fleet, all right—a nice, big, fat, rosy fleet, fit for any invasion!

"And you want the terror lights? Oh, yes, indeed, they did have those, indeed indeed . . . just tell me more about the *Furies* and the fleets they don't have and the terror beams they can't project! *I'm all ears!*"

Redbay danced around a bit, pacing left and right, only a step or two. Kes rose to pull him down again, but Neelix snatched her back out of reach. *Good man,* thought B'Elanna; *no telling what Redbay might do next.*

Redbay remained nonviolent, however; he started walking energetically around the table, hugging himself, glazed eyes overlooking a starscape both alien and terrifying that only he could see. "They came out of the black; we didn't see them, but at first we thought only that they were another race, and we were explorers! But no, they came—they didn't come to explore but to conquer . . . us! Conquer us. Conquer us."

"Go on," said Janeway; Tuvok glanced at her with a questioning raise of his brow, but she shook her head.

Redbay told his tale. He told of the meeting with the Furies, the negotiation, Captain Jean Luc Picard's futile attempt to find a settlement.

Janeway's mouth twitched; it had all happened shortly after the *Voyager* was grabbed by the Caretaker and propelled through an artificial wormhole into the Delta Quadrant. Had she known of the encounter by the newest *Enterprise,* she would have put two and two together and realized the Furies were ready to go Viking again at the drop of a proverbial terror-beam.

B'Elanna squirmed, unsettled indeed to learn how intransigent and monomaniacal their enemy really was, how bloody-minded, and how he would fight to the last soldier, the final ship—to the end without a thought for treaty or compromise!

Redbay sank at last into his seat, but he was not finished. Holding his face in his hands, his voice quiet and shaking, Redbay whispered of the terror projector and how it tore at the mind, leaving it bleeding and raw and wide open to virtually any command or demand that would *make the horror stop.*

"You don't fight. You don't fight. You fall down and do what they say and anything they say is your heart's desire, anything to stop the fear that sucks you out of yourself, and you'd cut your own throat or sell your captain as a slave if they would just turn it *off!* Turn it off, turn it off, *turn it OFF!"*

Kes touched Redbay's arm; the lieutenant began to cry softly. He did not care who watched. B'Elanna sat very still, uncomfortably wondering what tearing of the mind would be necessary to make B'Elanna Torres fall to broken pieces of madness like this man. She did not like the answer.

No one else vented his fear; no one but Redbay had the guts—and he had nothing left to lose.

We're Starfleet, all of us, she thought, noticing all of their responses to a sobbing lieutenant, some uncomfortable, some sympathetic. She smiled behind steepled hands, knowing she was no different: like the rest of the crew, if the Furies projected their terrors at Lieutenant Torres, she would fall obediently to the ground and give them anything, even her Klingon honor, to make them stop. It was purely biological.

"Lieutenant Redbay," said the captain, her voice firm and in control, but gentle, "we have to know how they will come. If you destroyed their fleet—if destroying the antenna destroyed their power source—then where is the new fleet? Where will the attack come from? We can't find any other fleet of ships."

Redbay did not move. He spoke to the table. "Don't you know yet? Don't you know, know how they're coming yet? They're coming, and fear rides alongside."

"But *how* are they coming Lieutenant? Do they have another fleet around another star system? Is the fleet already in the Alpha Quadrant still operable? Mr. Redbay, *we have to know.*"

Redbay remained silent, face still in his hands. But Janeway decided the time had come for the man to begin returning to himself, to his duty.

"Look at me," she said. When he did not move, she repeated herself: *"Look* at me, Mr. Redbay, when I'm talking to you."

Her command tone shook him enough that he sat back slowly and stared wonderingly at her, like a spoiled child slapped for the first time in his life. B'Elanna was impressed.

"Talk to me," Janeway continued. "In words. Tell me how the Furies are going to invade the Alpha Quadrant. Tell me now; I have to know."

"They're—they're invading."

"How are they invading, Lieutenant Redbay?"

"Invading . . ."

"How are they invading?"

"They—create a wormhole—artificial wormhole, and . . ."

"We already know they create an artificial wormhole, Lieutenant. Report: *Where is the Fury fleet?*"

Redbay had held himself rigidly erect, staring at the captain. Now he deflated, slumping forward, more relaxed in defeat than he had been since his rescue.

"There is no fleet," he softly said. "The wormhole is . . . is for them."

"For them how? How will they invade?"

"For them. For the planet."

B'Elanna froze momentarily; then she heard her own pulse beating in her temples. *For the planet?*

"The wormhole—is for the planet."

"Captain," said Torres, "that's it! That's the missing piece Commander Chakotay was talking about—they're going to send their *entire planet* through the artificial wormhole!"

"With all twenty-seven billion aboard?" demanded Tom Paris.

"Yes!"

"But . . ." Neelix looked confused; he was having a hard time with the concept. "But even if they did, how would they move? They don't have enough ships!"

Redbay stroked the table, the smooth texture of replicated oak. "The . . . planet."

Chakotay leaned forward. "Redbay, the entire planet is a ship?"

Redbay reluctantly nodded; he gripped his hands together, fighting the residual compulsion to serve his masters in any way they desired—and not to reveal their secrets to the Unclean.

Janeway stood, towering over the table by command presence alone. "I knew we had a problem. But I was not aware of the full extent of the danger.

"With this new intelligence, I now realize we have no idea at all how to stop the invasion of an entire armed planet of twenty-seven billion soldiers. We haven't a clue how to stop their jumping to Federation space and launching the most terrible war we have ever faced.

"The war will be a holy crusade, and it can end one of only two ways: either the Federation, the Klingon and Cardassian Empires, and all the nonaligned races will end up enslaved to these demons . . . or else we will have to kill them, every last one of them, down to the last Fury. Twenty-seven billion self-defense homicides on our consciences.

"Both these alternatives are unacceptable. You will come up with another option, fast. There is nothing more to say here; dismissed."

Grimly, the entire staff except Tuvok rose to return to their duty stations; B'Elanna wondered how they could possibly obey their captain's last command. Lieutenant Tuvok stayed behind in the ready room.

Lieutenant Redbay stayed as well. Janeway understood. *They have a bond,* she thought.

She followed the rest of the crew out of the ready room, leaving the Vulcan and the dead man alone.

CHAPTER
15

"THEY MUST HAVE PLANNED THIS INVASION FOR CENTURIES," muttered B'Elanna Torres. She sat backward in a chair in engineering, resting her chin on the back and staring at part of the schematics of the moon. *Centuries!* The thought frightened her human half—and awed her Klingon side.

"You think so?" asked Captain Janeway from behind Torres. The chief engineer jumped; she had thought she was alone on the deck.

"Captain! I didn't hear you come in."

"You said they've been planning this for centuries. How do you know?"

B'Elanna said nothing for a moment; then the Klingon forced out the information deduced by the human. "Because of the mathematics of it," she said; "twenty-seven billion Furies, figure a thousand—no, *ten* thousand in a ship, they would need a fleet of two-point-seven million ships."

"That's a hell of a fleet."

"That's a ridiculous fleet! Compared to that, the entire Federation has only a handful of starships, and none of them can carry anywhere near ten thousand people. The

Federation, Klingon and Cardassian Empires, and everybody else in the quadrant have combined fewer than fifty thousand ships of any type, maybe a total carrying capacity of twelve-point-five million people if we pack them like Klingon fish."

"So you figure the Furies were planning on sending their entire planet all along."

Was Janeway making fun? *No, she's not the type.* "Right. I mean, yes, Captain. This isn't a desperation maneuver; it's what they always intended to do. The other invasions were just attempts to establish a beachhead."

"And it would have taken more than a century to build all this technology?"

"Captain, they had to develop it from scratch. If they'd had the ability to send their planet through a hundred years ago, they would have. They were planning this decades years ago, when they met the first *Enterprise,* and they must have planned it for decades before that." B'Elanna stared at the warp core, watching it pulse red, fade, pulse. The regularity comforted her in the face of timeless, implacable enmity—"vast, cool, and unsympathetic" stuck in her mind from somewhere.

"I wish we could plan that far ahead," said Janeway. "So what do we do about it? What's my third option, Torres?"

B'Elanna ground her teeth. She had thought for a couple of hours; at least, still stumped, she had finally hooked up with Lieutenant Carey, Maquis cleverness combined with Starfleet thoroughness.

Together, they had come up with one possibility—but it was impossible. Carey was back in his quarters racking out; Torres could not sleep herself, so she was left to bear the torch herself.

"Well, Carey and I have only a vague thought. Frankly, I can't see how we would implement it." Pulse, fade. Bright red, and the control console behind her was cold, hard.

"It is?"

"Destroy the moon. Blow it up somehow. No power—no wormhole."

Janeway absently toyed with her hair, distracted. The

captain's eyes flicked across the instrument readouts behind B'Elanna; *she never stops, not even for a second,* thought the engineer. B'Elanna felt the rough fabric of the chair against her chin; she felt an old dream stir, the dream of command and four pips on her collar. If only—

"All right, that sounds promising," said the captain; "how do we do it? Can we penetrate the hull with our phasers?"

"Nope."

"Photon torpedoes? How about if we rammed it, even if that meant taking out the *Voyager* itself?"

Ouch. "No, and no. We could try taking the shuttlecraft in again, but all the important guts of the system are deep inside, where we can't go."

Janeway closed her eyes; when she opened them, she stared right through B'Elanna's Klingon skull and bored into her brain. "There's another point here you haven't mentioned."

"Um . . . well, yeah." Torres started to squirm but caught herself. "If we blow up the moon . . . well, the sun still goes nova. And the planetary surface will be fried."

"I told you that wasn't necessarily acceptable."

Necessarily? "Captain, you said it wasn't acceptable at all to kill the Furies. Now you're saying *maybe?*"

Janeway pursed her lips. She frowned. "Actually, Lieutenant, I'm not saying. Not yet."

B'Elanna was careful not to exult; Janeway, like most humans, suffered from too much sympathy for her enemies. Best not to play with the inertial dampers when the ship was finally headed the right direction. The captain continued her rapid-fire questions: "How about driving a shuttlecraft up inside and transporting an armed photon torpedo onto the moon?"

B'Elanna raised her brows. "You know the shuttlecraft wouldn't be able to make it out."

"Of course not."

"No good. Transport the torpedo *where?* What are the vital links? It does no good at all to take out this circuit or that circuit; this thing has so much redundancy built into it, because it's absorbing the energy from a *supernova,* that you could take out half the circuits and it would still probably work!" *Was that really admiration in my voice?*

"So what do we do?"

Torres closed her eyes and shook her head, scraping her chin against the chair. "I don't know. And neither does Carey." She kept her eyes shut for a long moment; when she opened them, Janeway was gone without even a goodbye. For a moment, B'Elanna stared, startled. Then she shrugged and got back to work.

In her ready room, Captain Janeway repeated engineering's half-plan to Chakotay. The commander frowned. "Have you considered the moral implication?"

She waited patiently; he didn't like to be interrupted. She stood facing Chakotay.

"If we blow up the moon, Captain, then there will be no wormhole. But that will not stop the sun from going supernova."

Janeway looked her commander in the eye. "Yes, Chakotay, I thought about that."

"Kathryn, that means that . . . twenty-seven *billion* people will die as a direct result of our actions."

"It's a sobering thought, Commander."

Chakotay turned away, not meeting her eyes. "I don't believe I could kill even that many Cardassians, let alone these people with whom I have no history."

Janeway wondered, for a moment, whether she could even contemplate such a savage act. So far, she had kept the moral part of her brain sealed off in order to work on the engineering side; but she couldn't do that forever. "You do have a history with them, Chakotay; you just don't remember."

"That's the whole point, Captain; I *don't* remember. Maybe if we all were to meet them."

"No time; according to Torres, the sun will go supernova very soon, a day or two. Besides, I can't run the risk of the Furies' using their terror device on my crew and maybe forcing them to mutiny." She crossed and sat—the symbolic finality of command.

Chakotay turned to her. "You *are* the captain, Kathryn. You have to make a decision, and quickly."

She nodded, now staring at unmoving stars, the brightest pinprick shortly to go nova. "This changes everything . . . I never imagined myself *killing* people beyond my ability to count. I don't know if I can do it either, even if I decide I have to.

"All right, you have the conn again, Commander; I'm going down to work with B'Elanna on just what we could do to destroy the moon . . . just in case. Give us three hours, then convene the senior officers. I will decide then. Definitely then."

Janeway walked morosely toward engineering, hands clasped behind her back. *Sometimes,* she thought, *command is the cruelest mistress of all.*

Kathryn Janeway showed up late to a bridge-crew meeting for the very first time in her life. She entered bruskly with B'Elanna Torres twenty-two minutes after the scheduled start. The cast was a virtual rerun of the meeting nearly a day earlier, except for the absence of Lieutenant Redbay. Kes looked distracted, as if she'd rather be down in sickbay with her patient. *Or anywhere but here,* thought the captain.

"We still don't know whether we can destroy the moon," she said abruptly while sitting. B'Elanna sat beside Kim, as usual. "First, we must decide whether we *should* destroy the moon. You all know what that means."

B'Elanna Torres sounded frustrated. "Whether we *should?* How can we not? The fate of the Federation and the Empire are both at stake!"

Janeway looked across the table at Kes, who opened and closed her mouth. The Ocampan said nothing, and Neelix moved his arm to cross hers familiarly.

Chakotay spoke into the sound vacuum. "It's not as easy a decision as you make it out to be, Torres; no human— indeed, no single life-form—has ever killed on the scale we're so casually discussing. Never on any planet in the quadrant."

"We've never faced conquest and enslavement on such a huge scale, either!"

"But *do we have the right* to kill twenty-seven billion . . . even to save ourselves from being enslaved?"

Janeway frowned. The ready room seemed unnaturally dark, as if she were back on the Fury planet. *Dammit, I have to make this decision rationally—not on the basis of my own genetic horror!*

"People, people!" interjected Neelix. At the urgency in his voice, the half-heard, whispered conversations ceased. "I believe Kes has a point to offer."

"Have you considered," she said in a small voice, "that many billions of the dead will be innocent children who have nothing whatsoever to do with the feud?"

Captain Janeway began to fret; she had her own opinion on the subject—a critic might say her own agenda—but she was not a Cardassian captain and could not simply impose her will on such a terrible issue. Definitely not if she were a "majority of one."

But Chakotay and especially Kes were beginning to have an impact on everyone's mood. Janeway turned to Tuvok, but the Vulcan maintained an enigmatic silence, arms folded.

Neelix lovingly put his arm around his beloved's shoulders. "I agree with Kes. How can you even contemplate killing twenty-seven billion people? I can't even imagine such murder on my conscience, no matter what the provocation!"

Tom Paris offered his thoughts, sounding far more sympathetic and reasonable than the captain would have expected of him. "I understand what Kes and Commander Chakotay are saying. It's a horrific thing to think about, killing more people than have ever lived on Earth. But . . ."

He paused; real pain flickered across his face, memories of Maquis friends he had seen killed in his first and only raid. A friend he might have helped kill—somewhere else. *Bad decisions, an overactive conscience,* thought the captain.

Paris continued. "But as huge as the number of Fury dead would be, it's still smaller than the number they would enslave and eventually murder—if not their physical bodies, at least their spirits. The sympathy shouldn't be all so one-sided, that's all I'm saying."

Good words; Janeway nodded and turned to Ensign Kim, one member of the discussion who hadn't yet discussed anything. "We're contemplating a deed, Mr. Kim, that will either save the soul of every person of every race in the Alpha Quadrant, or will be the most staggering act of genocide ever committed in the galaxy, at least that we know of. You must have an opinion, Ensign."

Kim took a deep breath. "My people have a, uh, long history dealing with this sort of thing, on both sides. I've always wondered whether I would risk my life to escape from slavery. I think I would. I'd be scared, but I could overcome that fear, because I'm an intelligent being."

He paused. Janeway nodded again, encouraging him to continue.

"But what if my fear was artificially magnified so enormously that I biologically *could not* overcome it? That's so much more horrible than—I know this sounds weird—mere slavery or mere murder that I think . . . I think *anything* we do to stop it is right."

"Lieutenant Torres," said the captain. "I want to hear from you, too."

"Kim spoke for me," she snarled.

She's in full Klingon mode, thought Janeway. Now the tone was making her uncomfortable in the other direction—all thought of the innocent victims they might be about to kill vanished in the passion of resisting the oppressor. "I want you to speak for yourself."

"Fine. Captain, I am so terrified of these Furies, I can hardly think straight, like an engineer . . . I saw that moon, saw the power they're so casually tossing around. Sir, they may not have transporters and shields, but they're centuries ahead of us in power manipulation."

Janeway sat back, surprised; B'Elanna's anger came from her human engineer side, not her Klingon warrior side!

She continued. "Not to mention creating and exploiting artificial wormholes, which we don't have even the faintest idea how to do! Captain, what the hell makes us think we even *can* beat these guys and destroy their moon? I think it's more likely to be another Narendra Three. We'll die valiantly; big deal. They'll still jump through and enslave us all."

"Activate EMH program," said Janeway.

"Please state the nature of the emergency," said the doctor, appearing on the screen in the middle of the table. He looked around in surprise. "Again? Are these conferences to become a regular feature?"

Paris could not contain himself. "You're kidding! The fate of the human race depends on the opinion of a *hologram?*

Janeway was angry, and she let Paris have it with all phaser banks. "You've had your say, Mr. Paris. Now be quiet, unless you wish to be stripped of your rank and confined in the brig for the next six months."

"Captain, I apologize. Why bother asking? The hologram is programmed to be a doctor; we already know which way it will vote."

"This is not a vote, Mr. Paris; I will make the final decision."

She returned attention to the screen. "There is an emergency, Doctor, and I need your advice." Crisply, she outlined the two possibilities. "I must have the input of every senior staff member, and that includes my chief medical officer—even a holographic one."

The doctor's face softened; he actually looked touched. Not for the first time, Janeway wondered whether a hologram generated by biologically based circuitry might not very well qualify for consciousness, an actual life-form.

"I'm grateful you asked me. Surprised, but grateful. My position is clear: Destroy the moon."

"What?" demanded Kes. The rest of the crew except Tuvok registered astonishment; even the normally implacable Chakotay's mouth parted in surprise.

"I take it you disagree with me, Kes," said the doctor. "I know why . . . your people live only nine years, and forgive me for being somewhat brusque—it's my programming— but you were virtual pets of the Caretaker. You don't have a realistic idea of what it means to be a free person . . . and responsible for yourself."

Chakotay spoke sardonically. "And you do understand being a free person?"

"Yes. I think I do. I know what I want, and I understand that gap between my want and the physical reality. I don't know if I'm a person . . . I *feel* like one, but maybe that's just more programming.

"But I know what just such a small change as—as giving me the power to turn myself on and off has done for me. I know how I would feel if you took that away from me tomorrow."

Janeway followed the exchange avidly. Certainly, no one would ever say all sides hadn't been considered.

"But you're a doctor!" cried Kes. "How can you say . . . whatever happened to the Hippocratic oath you taught me? Above all else, first do no harm. You're talking about murder!"

"No, Kes. I'm talking about *triage.*"

"Triage?" She fell silent, stumped.

Janeway smiled; she understood at last . . . and understood how to articulate and justify her decision. Triage was a concept as well known to commanders as to doctors.

"Sometimes," the doctor explained, "sometimes we have to let one person die so that others can live. Like in ancient human wars, where there weren't enough doctors or operating tables to save all the soldiers . . . so the ones whose medical care would take hours were allowed to die so that instead, the doctors could save three or four other people with different injuries."

"You're not letting them die. You're killing them!"

"No!" insisted Kim, evidently finding the elusive point he had sought many minutes before. "We didn't start the sun going supernova; that was the Furies themselves. They wanted the energy—they set the collapse in motion. All we're doing is stopping them from *using* that collapse to invade the Alpha Quadrant!"

"It's the same thing. You're not just stopping the invasion. You're stopping them from escaping their sun going supernova . . . and they'll all die, each one of them."

"First, do no harm," said the doctor quietly. "Can we

even measure how much harm is done by slavery and the living hell of the terror projector?"

Janeway turned to Tuvok; still, the lieutenant and her closest confidant said nothing. She shook her head, angry and confused. "I said this wasn't a vote. Too bad: for the action, we have Paris, Kim, Torres, and the doctor; against, we have Neelix, Kes, and Chakotay . . . we would have a majority and a decision." She glanced at Tuvok. "With one abstention.

"But the decision is ultimately my responsibility, and I will be the one to make it. Alone. I wanted your input; but I'm not simply going to count noses. I'm going back to my quarters and make my decision."

"We don't have much time," said B'Elanna quietly.

"I know how much time we have," said the captain, a bit too harshly. "Thank you for reminding me; I'll make my decision quickly."

Janeway turned and exited. She passed through the bridge to her quarters, sat behind her desk, behind the unreviewed stack of reports, duty rosters, petty complaints, projections, and performance evaluations, and rubbed her throbbing temples. *They'll call me Bloody Kate the Executioner,* she thought. She was under no delusion that they could ever fully explain the tale of what happened here, not once they finally made it back to the Federation. And she had no doubt they would find a way back before seventy years had passed.

Or perhaps this is it, she suddenly realized. She opened her eyes, astonished no one had even mentioned it.

They were looking at a system to project an entire planet all the way to the Alpha Quadrant in one jump!

Maybe the *Voyager* could just . . . piggyback?

And then what? This small ship's crew were not going to be able to stop twenty-seven billion! They would be killed, and the invasion would proceed apace.

Unless . . . was there a way to stop the Furies from passing through the wormhole, yet slip through themselves?

It was a thought. It wanted exploring . . . soon. But not immediately: her immediate concern, as Torres had pointed out, was to decide within just a few minutes whether they were going to destroy the moon, dooming the Furies, including the children, to fiery cremation, or maybe try to send a subspace message of warning through the same wormhole, letting the Federation know—that it was about to be overwhelmed and destroyed, and all its citizens, and the Klingons, Romulans, and Cardassians, would henceforth be slaves to demons from hell.

Her door chimed. She felt suddenly nervous without any good reason to be. If there were an emergency, Chakotay would have called her on the comm link. But who else would disturb her at this moment, and why?

The door chimed again. "Enter," snapped Captain Kathryn Janeway, in command of herself again after a momentary self-mutiny.

CHAPTER
16

TUVOK ENTERED, HANDS BEHIND HIS BACK. HE WAITED PO-
litely; Janeway waited impatiently; both waited for somebody to say something. *Vulcans have the greater patience,* he
thought serenely.

The captain cracked first. Of course. "All right, spill it."

"You are using the idiom meaning to reveal one's information."

"When a Vulcan gets pedantic about human expressions,
it means he has something to say, and he's uncertain how to
say it."

Tuvok stalled, trying mentally to articulate what he had
to say in a way that a human could understand it. "An
astute observation about my race. What I have to say may
seem peculiar, coming from a Vulcan. But there are some
things worse than dying, and the Furies promise just such
things."

"Living in slavery?"

"No, Captain; that is not worse than dying. A normal
slave may dream about being free someday, and may even
plot an escape. Ensign Kim has a cogent point here. He
drew a distinction between merely being held against one's

will by threat of death, and having one's mind biologically altered to make one less than a person, an animal."

"Go on."

Did she not yet understand the special threat the Furies represented to a Vulcan? "For the Furies to return to Vulcan and make my people again what they once were, before Surak, would be far worse than merely destroying us en masse. We would be alive; but we would no longer be Vulcan. And worse—we would have the memory of what once was and never could be again."

"All right. Point taken. It doesn't make the decision any easier."

"I did not expect it would. I did not come here to explain Ensign Kim."

"You came to . . . ?"

"To remind you of your duty. Captain, you took an oath when you joined Starfleet, as did we all. You swore to uphold, among other things, the ideals of the United Federation of Planets; to defend it against all enemies, external and internal; to guard the freedom of its citizens."

"The people who wrote that oath never contemplated killing twenty-seven billion life-forms, including billions of innocent children, to carry out that oath."

Tuvok nodded; he turned to contemplate a new sculpture from Aton-77 the captain had replicated; it must have cost her many days of replicator credits.

"Nevertheless, the oath was written, and you freely offered, in the words of another great document, your life, your fortune, and your sacred honor. You cannot turn your back on that oath now. Not even in the face of killing billions of innocent children."

Janeway abruptly slammed her hands down on the desk, angry and frustrated . . . more human emotions getting in the way of rationality. Tuvok did not turn around; he did not want to see her like that.

"Mr. Tuvok! Do you imagine I don't remember that oath?"

"No. I know that you do. I do not believe you are taking it seriously enough."

"An oath! What's more important, the words, or the *ideals* the words were intended to protect?"

Tuvok said nothing, but he turned around. He had never seen Captain Janeway so racked by self-doubt, so tortured by indecision. He wished he had a magic answer that would make her see what she had to do; but that was irrational.

"The reason we don't go around wiping out races we think are evil, Mr. Tuvok, is not because we're such goody-goodies that we can't imagine fighting and killing. We've fought almost everyone in the damned Alpha Quadrant, at one time or another. It's because *we're not gods.* We don't know what would happen if we started on some great jihad to destroy evil . . . we could end up destroying ourselves!"

"That is a risk we sometimes must be prepared to assume."

Janeway sat slowly, leaning back in her chair and staring up at the overhead. "And if we have to destroy the village in order to save it, was it really worth saving in the first place?"

"If it was worth creating, it is worth preserving. Even at the cost of billions of innocent lives—if that is the only way."

"Tuvok, do you hear what you're *saying?*"

"I am in full possession of my faculties. You do not wish to do this because you do not want the guilt. But your clear duty requires you to take this guilt upon your head. That is the price you must pay—we all must pay—for the freedom we have enjoyed."

"Tuvok, you remember, via your DNA, horrors so traumatic you cannot even contemplate them. I reacted with terror as well . . . but I didn't remember anything in particular about that time. Maybe only the Ok'San were as bad as you recall; maybe only Vulcan suffered like that."

"Perhaps. The suggestion is illogical and unsupported, but possible." He leaned close to the sculpture. *Water,* it was called: a straight column of thin graphite with a hairline blue crack.

"And in any case," continued the captain, "it was thousands of years ago! Who's to say the Furies haven't changed some? Navdaq didn't seem to represent ultimate evil, even if he did throw us in jail. He might just be a petty tyrant. The galaxy is full of them."

Oddly, the sculpture, *Water,* soothed his eyes. "He might. But the evidence we do have indicates that the Furies conquered the Alpha Quadrant once before, were driven off by aliens who no longer exist, and are now planning to return."

"But we don't *know* that they're really going to attack us . . . I agree, it's likely, but not certain."

"If we cannot state for certain they will rule as demons, so to speak, we also cannot say they will not . . . and the odds favor repetition." Tuvok turned his full Vulcan attention to Captain Janeway. "Duty dictates that we cannot take that chance."

Janeway said nothing; Tuvok forbore pressing his case— he saw that she was deep in thought, and she might well be arguing the case better than he could.

She leaned back in her chair, massaging her temples. "Perhaps the doctor could alleviate that pain," suggested Tuvok, more to remind her that he was still there than to tell her anything she did not already know.

"I don't want him to. It's my pain, and I'm going to keep it."

What a peculiar thing to say . . . but so stubbornly human. "If the Furies conquer our quadrant, you will not have even that freedom."

She opened her eyes. "I've decided we're going to destroy the moon. But it's not because of any of your arguments."

"Indeed?"

"It's the argument you didn't make that decided me . . . this vessel, the *Voyager,* is the first and last defense on this side of the wormhole. We're alone—and we're either a projection of Starfleet into the Delta Quadrant, or else we're nothing but just one more ship caught far, far from home.

"And sometimes, my friend . . ." Janeway paused; she stared to the side, as if her mind had wandered from the point. Tuvok refrained from interrupting; *she is listening to a voice humans have, a voice beyond reason, that nevertheless speaks truly to them.* It was that voice the Vulcan hoped someday to understand, to explain, to map.

"Sometimes, my friend, survival takes precedence over everything," she concluded. "I hate it like hell—but sometimes, you just have to shoot the SOB and rationalize it all later." She looked directly at Tuvok with a penetrating stare.

"Tuvok, I asked myself, if not us, who? If not now, when? It sounds terribly trite, I know. But that's how trite things get that way . . . by being true." She touched her comm-badge. "Janeway to Commander Chakotay."

"Chakotay," responded the commander's voice from everywhere and nowhere.

"Tell the senior crew we're doing it."

"I am not surprised. Have you figured out how?"

She rose and stared at *Water,* frowning. She turned the blue crack toward the wall, ruining the composition, for the sculpture had a jagged red line along the backside. "No; I'll get back to you. Have Torres and Carey meet me in engineering in five minutes. Janeway out."

"Thank you, Captain," said Tuvok.

"I didn't do it for you, Tuvok."

"Thank you for that, too."

The Vulcan waited until Janeway realized he was done. Then she dismissed him, contemplatively. He ghosted out in silence, thankful he never had to stoop to the argument by which she finally persuaded herself.

Captain Janeway rose and headed for the engineering deck. They had a scant few minutes to design a bomb powerful enough to destroy an entire artificial moon, and she had no idea at all how to proceed.

But Carey and Torres were not in engineering. Janeway waited for a moment, then asked the computer to locate the errant pair. "Lieutenant Torres and Lieutenant Carey are in holodeck two," said the impersonal voice.

Janeway's curiosity—what could they be doing on the holodeck?—was satisfied the moment she entered. Carey had set up a scale model of the moon, using all the data they had gathered. Far away, barely visible on the scale, was a representation of the Fury planet.

The sun was represented by a sharp, bright star far in the

distance. The two engineers eerily floated in the empty reaches, like gods.

"Captain!" cried Torres, sounding ecstatic and worried at the same time. "Commander Chakotay just told us of your decision."

"The decision is made. Now tell me how we're going to do it."

Carey frowned; this was one of his fortes. "We're here, behind the sun," he announced. A tiny dot flickered red and green, so far away it was hard to see. "Here's the first scenario we considered."

The dot broke orbit, swooped around the sun, and dove toward the moon. As it approached, the moon began to flash red, like an angry red-alert indicator.

"We checked the records and figured out the distance at which the moon alerts the Furies," said Carey in a quick aside.

The *Voyager* continued to close as an intercept fleet launched from the planet. *Voyager* barely had time to launch a single spread of photon torpedoes and fire phasers at the moon on the first pass before it was engaged by six Fury ships. The captain frowned.

The *Voyager* ignored the gnatlike ships, firing another spread . . . but then *Voyager* turned bright white, hurting Janeway's dark-adapted eyes. *What the hell—?*

"Terror projector," said Carey. "The end."

"That reminds me—I never did hear Chakotay's theory why they didn't shoot the *Voyager* with the unholy terrors when you fought them. He seemed about to tell us when Redbay interrupted."

"In my opinion, Captain, they had no idea at first where we were from . . . and the ships they sent up simply didn't have terror projectors installed."

Torres spoke up. "We had to make an educated guess when they would fire their projectors. Now that they know where we're from, we figure they'll equip their ships with the devices."

"The range, spread, and speed of transmission are unknown," added Carey.

"When the ship flares," concluded B'Elanna, "it means we've been hit by the projector and we're—slaves of hell."

"But what about the moon?" asked the captain. She stared at the holographic projection; it looked remarkably intact.

"Well," said Carey, "that's what we found. According to the computer, even hitting the external hull with thirteen photon torpedoes and several direct phaser blasts would not penetrate the armor plating, which ranges between three-point-two and four kilometers thick."

"Between three and four *kilometers?*" Janeway was daunted; for a moment, she stepped back, despairing of being able to do a thing against the Furies.

"It was built to withstand the energy of a supernova for several seconds, for heaven's sake."

Janeway sighed. "All right, let's see some other scenarios."

Voyager loped closer to the moon, and the alarm bell went off. Ships uplifted from the planet surface, while *Voyager* expelled an experimental photon torpedo, flying as a "remotely piloted vehicle."

The ship was quickly sprayed with the terror-projection weapon, driving the crew to a madness of fear . . . but the photon torpedo escaped, racing into the long shaft that Kim and Paris had found!

Closer and closer it drove to the antenna . . . a Fury ship gave chase, flying down the same shaft; it fired round after round, using a special, wide-spread, disruptor-like weapon that would not significantly damage the antenna if it missed the torpedo.

The torpedo was never meant to sustain repeated damage. It was not a ship. It exploded harmlessly, the contained antimatter expanding outward to explosively interact with the shaft walls, "scraping" off a few centimeters of ablative material that would have burned away in milliseconds anyway when the sun went supernova.

The mission failed—and the Furies completed their jump.

Voyager loped toward the moon. Again, as the swarm of Fury ships leapt upward, Janeway launched a photon-torpedo RPV; but this time, the torpedo had been fitted with a single-use shield system.

It dropped down the shaft, heading toward rendezvous with the radiation-collection antenna . . . the Fury ship followed, frantically firing at the torpedo—but this time, the shots were absorbed by the shield.

The probe closed on the antenna as *Voyager* flared white and vanished in an explosion of mind-shredding horror. Closer, the Fury ship accelerated to ramming speed and—

Voyager loped toward the moon.

The RPV was faster this time and equipped with auto-tracking phasers pointing backward.

The Fury ship accelerated to ramming speed . . . but as it closed, the torpedo itself opened fire!

The power phaser beam held the Fury ship at bay as the photon torpedo crossed the last gap. It struck the antenna at 17,500 kilometers per second, simultaneously detonating its matter-antimatter compression bomb.

The explosion was terrible to behold. The Fury ship only added to it when it ploughed into the expanding sphere of electromagnetic radiation and blew apart itself.

The detonation was so intense, it blew a *Voyager*-sized hole in the-thirty-square-kilometer surface area of the antenna . . . destroying slightly more than 0.003 percent of its collection surface.

The mission failed.

"This isn't getting us anywhere," said Janeway, testily. "Wait—how about sending a shuttle up the shaft and transporting a photon torpedo inside the hull?"

Carey pondered for a moment, then programmed the computer.

Voyager loped toward the moon, setting off the alarm when it got close enough. Just before the Fury ships arrived, the launch-bay doors opened and a shuttle squirted out, accelerating to maximum impulse while still in the hangar.

It bolted toward the shaft, two Fury ships in hot pursuit, and sallied down the rabbit hole, aft shields guarding it from the Furies' disruptors. As the shuttlecraft neared the antenna, successfully deflecting the energy weapons, the Furies began to bathe it with the terror-projector beam.

The shuttlecraft glowed white-hot, and—

The *unmanned* shuttlecraft bolted toward the shaft, two Fury ships in hot pursuit, and sallied down the rabbit hole. As it neared the antenna, the Furies, in a last, desperate gamble, accelerated their ships to ramming speed.

But just before contact, a phaser beam lanced out of the rear of the shuttlecraft, sending one ship careering into the other. The blinding explosion would have obliterated the shuttlecraft as well, were it not for the shields already up, protecting the aft quarter.

Limping, the shuttlecraft approached and veered around the antenna, finding the "soft spot" that Paris and Kim had identified earlier, where the hull was thin enough to permit beaming.

The ship reversed thrust, braking to a quick halt. The torpedo, already strapped down on the transporter pad, was beamed aboard the moon directly to the huge room that Ensign Kim had recorded.

Within seconds, the torpedo detonated, and—

The holodeck simulation froze. Ghostly letters hung in the air, flashing over and over: EFFECT UNKNOWN, EFFECT UNKNOWN.

Captain Janeway stared at the letters floating like the voice of Fate, mocking them. For two minutes, she pondered.

"Carey, Torres," she said at last, "that's just not good enough. 'Effect unknown' is simply too vague to pin the life or death of freedom in the Alpha Quadrant on."

"We have one more scenario," said Torres.

"*She* has one more scenario," corrected Lieutenant Carey, glaring at the deck.

B'Elanna gave him a hard look. "Computer, activate simulation z-nine." She turned to Janeway. "I haven't run this one yet. Don't know what will happen."

Voyager loped toward the moon . . . but as the swarm of Fury ships tore away from their home planet on an interdiction course, the Federation starship aligned itself with the shaft—and accelerated to warp 9.9, the theoretical maximum that *Voyager* was capable of attaining. At that speed, the engines would automatically shut down in ten minutes.

It did not matter; a single minute was eternity cubed, for the ship would impact with the moon in four hundred nanoseconds.

Instantly, the simulation froze, ticking forward at a rate of ten nanoseconds per second. Janeway saw her ship jump forward jerkily as it accelerated. The initial impact with the shaft was uneventful: the ship was too wide for the shaft, but at first, it was the shaft that gave way; *Voyager* carved a pair of furrows down the rabbit hole where the saucer section impacted, like hot skates across an ice rink.

Then, over the space of a couple of frames, the edges of the ship vaporized. The energy released imploded laterally toward the center of the ship, causing the hull to buckle, then shred.

Janeway felt no emotion, though she watched a simulation of the death of everybody aboard her ship; as visceral as the thought was, it was still too surreal for her to feel it.

The ship might have shredded, but the shards were still moving in a warp field some three thousand times the speed of light. They continued forward, of course; where else could they go? Certainly nothing known in the universe could *deflect* shrapnel moving at such a speed, impossible under normal physics.

But that very point worked against them—for if nothing could deflect such hypervelocity shrapnel, *neither could anything absorb such energy* . . . and if what you want to do is create the biggest bomb ever seen, the target must *absorb* the energy. Otherwise, it just . . .

Voyager punched a *Voyager*-sized hole through the antenna, continued along the moon's axis—creating its own *Voyager*-sized and -shaped shaft—and out the other side. In one second, Janeway knew, the remains of the ship and crew would be a billion kilometers away, no further threat to the Furies or anyone else.

When *Voyager* passed through the antenna, it destroyed slightly more than 0.003 percent of the collection surface . . . about as much as had the single photon torpedo.

"I told you," said Lieutenant Carey pettishly. "I'm not afraid to die; I just knew it would be a useless, futile gesture."

The captain silently pounded her thigh in frustration. "What if we go slower? Will the antenna absorb more of the impact energy?"

B'Elanna glared at the holodeck simulation. "To force the antenna to absorb sufficient energy to blow it up," she growled at last, "we would have to approach no faster than zero-point-six times light speed . . . which is impossible: it's three times faster than full impulse, but much less than warp one."

"And warp one . . . ?"

"Is too fast. At maximum impulse, we *might* destroy a significant fraction of the antenna's surface—maybe thirty percent."

"That could be enough," mused Janeway; "it's certainly the best option I've seen so far."

"You're forgetting one little factor," said Carey from his corner. "At impulse power, we won't be able to get all the way along the shaft before the Furies come in after us . . . and as soon as we're in line of sight . . ."

"They fire the terror projector at us," finished Janeway.

"And then command us to stop, turn around, and exit the shaft. Checkmate."

"Dammit!" shouted the captain, startling everyone, most especially including herself. "You two—I want options! I want them now, or . . . or I'll transfer you both to maintenance detail. As a team!"

Furious most especially at the lack of a target for her fury, Kathryn Janeway stormed out of the holodeck toward nowhere in particular.

CHAPTER
17

AS SHE STALKED ANGRILY, BLINDLY DOWN A PASSAGEWAY, Janeway's arm was suddenly yanked, whirling her around. She snapped into a defensive posture, hands raised, ready to put the assailant on the deck with a heel-hand or a snap-kick to the kneecap.

Commander Chakotay retreated gracefully out of range.

"Are you back from the land of spirits?" he asked.

"What the hell are you talking about? What do you mean by jerking my arm like that?"

"I had to get your attention somehow."

"Why didn't you just try saying, 'Excuse me, Captain?'"

"Excuse me, Captain . . ."

Janeway felt her face flush. "Oh. Sorry; I was . . . thinking."

"That much was obvious."

"Chakotay, we're absolutely stuck here! We—Torres and Carey and I—just cannot come up with a way to destroy that moon; either we can't generate enough energy, or if we can, we can't get the machinery to absorb enough of it to fry itself."

Chakotay shrugged. "Too bad we can't unleash you on it hand-to-hand. That's an interesting style of fighting; I don't recall that from the Academy."

"Stop trying to distract me. I *like* brooding." Janeway leaned against a bulkhead, at ease in the presence of the man who once was her prey and was now her executive officer.

The commander smiled. "I like new styles of self-defense. Got a name?"

"Just something based on ancient Japanese judo; my father taught me years ago. You turn the enemy's own power against himself. Well, that's the idea, in any case; usually, I just get him off balance and rabbit-punch him." Despite Janeway's determination not to be distracted from her brooding distraction, she began to thaw.

"We should spar sometime. I would like to see what it feels like to have my own power turned against me. Say," he continued, struck by a thought, "too bad you can't use that judo stuff on the moon—turn its own power against it. Can you?"

Janeway raised her eyebrows. "You know, that's not a bad suggestion, especially coming from the engineering impaired."

"Captain!"

"Oh, you know what I mean. I can't see exactly how we can do it, but dammit, it's something to try, at least."

She turned to the bulkhead and pushed against it, almost like isometrics: she closed her eyes, letting the thoughts form their own images. She wanted the image of a great force, a tremendous force—the Fury supernova—being turned against itself to trip and fall. She felt the weight of the *Voyager* pressing all around her, but that wasn't enough of a force.

"Well," Chakotay said, "this engineering-impaired commander came up with another idea. I've been talking to Lieutenant Redbay about the terror-projector weapon."

"Does he remember anything?"

"Enough to convince me that if we could jigger the shields somehow to make them kind of wedge-shaped, like this . . ." Chakotay pressed his fingertips together and held his stiff arms and hands forward like the prow of an old-fashioned water ship. "We might be able to deflect the beam just long enough to dodge to the left or right and avoid it."

Janeway smiled. "More martial arts?"

"It's something to try, at least. Unfortunately, I haven't the faintest idea how to make the shields buckle like that." She visualized the shields, not as physical objects in Einsteinian space, which they technically weren't, but as vectors in phase space—the way they were *meant* to be visualized.

"They're designed to do just the opposite; a direct hit by a phaser or disruptor right on the seam would probably blow the shields away, and even a glancing blow would leak through and damage the ship if you monkeyed with the shield geometry."

Chakotay rubbed his chin. "Captain, the Fury disruptors were powerful, but we could probably survive a couple of direct hits. Certainly a lot better than we could survive a single hit by the terror weapon."

"I know," said Janeway, dropping her gaze. "I don't think it will matter, Chakotay, whether *Voyager* takes a few hits or a dozen. Commander, nobody gets out of here alive."

"We just need to survive long enough to destroy the moon," said Chakotay, completing Janeway's thought.

She opened her eyes and looked up at him. "Take Carey; I can't spare Torres. Besides, Carey has studied our biotech shield systems more than Torres has . . . possibly because Klingons think shields are for cowards." She smiled; Chakotay kept his face impassive.

"And take Tuvok, too. He knows the basic science better; Carey might tell you it's impossible, and it will be critical to have Tuvok backing us up."

"Thank you, Captain; and good luck."

The two parted in three different directions: Chakotay to engineering by way of Tuvok's quarters; Janeway to the bridge; and the captain's dark storm clouds back over the horizon. Having a clear goal for a change performed a miracle on her disposition.

* * *

Commander Chakotay discovered that his first obstacle was to convince *Tuvok* that the shield-wedge idea was possible; far from backing up Chakotay, the lieutenant insisted that the shields could not possibly be bent into such a strange geometry.

He stood in the Vulcan's quarters, quietly admiring the simplicity of decoration: no flashy, splashy prints on the walls or nonfunctional knickknacks cluttering up the work surfaces. Vulcans were Spartan in taste compared to most humans.

Chakotay listened patiently into the third minute of a basic science lecture before finally interrupting. "I don't want to speak before my turn," he said, "but we don't have much time, Lieutenant. I understand you believe the shield-wedge is impossible. But I don't want you to say that to Lieutenant Carey."

Tuvok frowned; he, too, stood, out of polite respect for Chakotay's rank. "Vulcans are not prone to lying."

"Then creatively avoid the truth."

"We do not dissemble."

Huh, you did a great dissembling job to me *when I was a Maquis and you were a Federation spy!* "Then don't, Mr. Tuvok; bore him to death with such a detailed analysis that he tunes out before you get to the part where you say it can't be done."

They stood staring at each other, dueling with utmost politeness; the commander wished Tuvok would sit, so they could converse without such stiff formality.

"You want me to be overly detailed and pedantic?"

"Yes."

"That, Commander, I can do with no trouble."

Chakotay bit off the smart remark that formed in his throat. He and the Vulcan left Tuvok's quarters and wandered down to the engineering deck, where they found Carey sitting slumped before the huge, curved console, B'Elanna Torres having already been summoned to the bridge. The lieutenant was tapping so diligently at a keypad, he didn't even notice their arrival until Chakotay cleared his throat, causing Carey to jump guiltily.

"No," said Chakotay patiently several minutes later, still

trying to explain to Carey, "a *wedge:* two flat planes meeting at about a forty-five-degree angle."

Carey shook his head, befuddled. "But . . . that's impossible, sir! Didn't you ask Tuvok? I'm sure he told you it can't be done." Carey gestured emphatically at the Vulcan, who did not react in any way. After a moment, Carey nervously dropped his hand.

"Tuvok?" asked Chakotay, turning to the lieutenant; Chakotay invoked his spirit guide to lead the stubborn Vulcan to back his commander. *Show time!*

Tuvok looked down at Carey as if noticing him for the first time. "Actually, Mr. Carey, the problem is not so glib or obvious as you might at first suppose."

"Isn't it? You can't make the shields bend in the middle!"

"Have you researched Admiral Anton Wilson's seminal work, 'Shield Geometry as a Function of Differentiable Manifold Dynamics'?" The Vulcan raised one eyebrow. *Beautiful!* thought Chakotay.

"Not exactly," hedged Carey; "I read the abstract. It said you can't have a shield with a discontinuous derivative . . . like a bend. Didn't it?"

"Reading the abstract is not exactly the same as reading the article itself. You depend upon the person who wrote the abstract understanding nuances and finding them important enough to discuss. I strongly advise you to read the article itself; I think you will find it illuminating—and very apropos our present difficulty." Commander Chakotay barely suppressed a smile; Tuvok was a natural at saying everything by saying nothing.

Carey nodded, his lips moving silently. "Oh, thanks, Lieutenant. I'll start reading it immediately. You really think there's something in there telling how to put a *bend* in the shields?"

"If it is not found there," declared Tuvok with finality, "it is not found anywhere."

Leaving Carey to his task, Chakotay grabbed Tuvok's arm and beetled rapidly away before the Vulcan could slip up and answer directly—and truthfully.

They paused in the passageway beyond earshot. "There, that wasn't so hard, was it?"

Tuvok frowned. "I cannot help but think I have conveyed an untruth somewhere in the exchange, though I confess I cannot find a single statement of mine that is technically false."

"Yes . . . but suppose Carey actually figures it out? Then that makes your whole part in the conversation retroactively truthful."

Tuvok raised the other eyebrow, the intragalactic Vulcan facial gesture. "I do not anticipate that the laws of physics will change to suit my present needs."

"You're too cynical," said Chakotay. "I always try to believe six impossible things before breakfast, as the Red Queen said to Alice."

"Is that reference part of the ancient lore of your people?"

"In a manner of speaking." *Yes, if "my people" includes Lewis Carroll,* thought Chakotay, amused but impassive.

"Perhaps I should return and help Lieutenant Carey," suggested the Vulcan, glancing back toward the engineering-deck door.

"Perhaps you'd better not," said Chakotay, thinking of Tuvok and his guilty conscience, which as a Vulcan he would never admit to having, but which might drive him nonetheless to confess his deception.

"As you wish, sir."

"You're more urgently needed helping B'Elanna and the captain figure out how to make the radiation collector blow itself up. I think they're on the holodeck." Tuvok left in search of his commanding officer, and Chakotay breathed a sigh of relief . . . but kept his fingers crossed. Ancient lore of his people.

Captain Janeway and Lieutenant Torres were engaged in a staring contest with a holodeck mockup of the cabling Kim and Paris had seen inside the moon; Tuvok joined them, opening a door in thin air and walking across the invisible platform on which they all stood. The mockup mocked them from half a kilometer below their feet—the distance at which Kim had recorded the scene in the first place.

Janeway was trying to get B'Elanna to hazard an estimate of what they could destroy to wreck the mechanism. "Be the ghost in the machine," urged the captain, hoping Torres could see something that so far eluded Janeway herself.

"It's just . . . this is ridiculous! Captain, we don't know what these cables do. We're just guessing!"

"Torres, guesses are all we have now." Janeway looked up to see the Vulcan impassively observing the inactivity. "Oh. Hello, Tuvok. Torres, all we need is a reasonably clear picture in our heads of the *sort* of connections to look for; we'll have to figure out the exact match on the moon itself."

"No. No way. I can't—it's impossible!"

"Commander Chakotay," announced Tuvok, "was taught to believe six impossible things before breakfast."

Janeway turned, nonplussed by the unexpected reference. "Yes," she said, "as the Red Queen said."

"But I'm not Alice, and this isn't the looking-glass!" snapped B'Elanna.

Tuvok looked perplexed. "I must make a mental note to research the original source legends; it is a powerful mythos that holds sway alike over Native American tribes, human Anglo-Saxons, and Klingons."

Janeway turned back to B'Elanna Torres, exasperated—at herself more than the engineer. "Just try! Try anything, Lieutenant."

"No, there's nothing I can . . ." B'Elanna's voice trailed off as she stared downward. "This is really weird."

"What? What's weird?"

"Captain—suddenly, it all makes sense! I can *feel* how the power flow goes . . . I can feel it! Look, that—that cable bundle is the feedback control . . . it's got to be! That tells the rest of the circuitry when a particular socket is stuffed and the energy needs to redirect itself. And . . . !"

B'Elanna fell silent, moving her hands in a complex, magical ritual that mapped the energy flow in her head.

"Kahless the Unforgettable!" muttered B'Elanna Torres. Janeway was surprised—*she almost never uses Klingon expressions.*

"What? What did you find?"

"Captain . . ." B'Elanna stared up at Janeway, mouth

open, eyes wide. "Captain, we can do it . . . we can reroute the energy flow and *blow up the whole moon!*"

"Are you sure?" Janeway held her breath; she had been disappointed once too often on this mission to leap for joy.

"Logically? No." Torres licked her lips like a starving wolf eyeing a roast. "But I can *feel* it this time. This time, I think we've got a winner."

"What is it? Tell me the plan; we'd better both know, in case something happens."

But Torres shook her head, frustrated. "That's just it, Captain. I can't tell you; it's somewhere inside here—" She indicated her skull. "—but I can't pull it out and put it into words. Yet. I'll . . . just have to do it myself."

Janeway nodded. "You lead the away team," she said. "You'll find I can take excellent direction." She started to rise to prepare for the trip; but Tuvok gently put his hand on her shoulder and quietly cleared his throat.

"Captain, I do not think your participation is a good idea."

"Why? What do you mean?"

"You are more urgently needed on the ship. Commander Chakotay is an excellent executive officer. But he simply does not know starships, and in particular *this* starship, as well as you."

"So? He also isn't a trained engineer, and I am."

"I would not suggest Commander Chakotay accompany Lieutenant Torres. She needs a first-rate pilot, a person who can fly a ship as big as the shuttlecraft through that narrow shaft with the expectation that it will arrive in one piece."

Janeway glanced at B'Elanna; the engineer turned her face back down to the holoprojection. Pulsing lights from the monstrous engine five hundred meters "below" them colored her face blue, red, then yellow; but it remained shadowed in mystery. Janeway could not tell what B'Elanna was thinking.

"I see what you're driving at, Mr. Tuvok; but I can't spare Tom Paris, not even for this mission. I need him flying *this* ship."

"I did not have Mr. Paris in mind, said Tuvok. "In fact, I was thinking of our recent guest."

"Redbay?" Both engineers turned, stunned.

"I have examined that part of his record which was transmitted to *Voyager* via routine message traffic before the Caretaker transported us to this quadrant. I am convinced that Mr. Redbay can almost certainly pilot the vessel better than any other member of this crew, including Mr. Paris."

"Don't tell Paris."

"Yes, emotional beings do not like to be reminded that there are others better than they at their chosen professions."

B'Elanna opened and shut her mouth like a fish. She muttered something unintelligible—Janeway caught only the words "basket case" and wisely chose not to hear the rest.

"Find Lieutenant Redbay," she ordered, cutting off any protest from B'Elanna. "Torres, gather what you need and return to the shuttlebay by 0430."

When they had left, Janeway stared down between her feet at the holodeck simulation of what little they knew of the moon's circuitry. Something was there . . . she could feel it, taste it—but she could not quite put it into words. Kathryn Janeway would not be satisfied until she could write an instruction set, at least in her head, for creating a feedback loop.

Neelix hovered outside the infirmary, rocking from one foot to the other, wondering how he was going to say to Kes what he needed to say without mortally offending her . . . or worse, making her *reevaluate their relationship.*

He straightened his waistcoat, smoothed his hair back, took a deep breath—repeated twice—and strode purposefully toward the door.

As the door slid open and Neelix charged through, full of the words that refused to fall into place, he crashed directly into the holographic doctor, knocking both to the ground.

"For a hologram," snapped the cook, "you sure are solid!"

The doctor made himself insubstantial and disentangled, then stood up, more crotchety than usual. "I maintain solidity when I interact with patients and equipment, of course! What did you expect, a ghost? Now what's wrong with you, aside from myopia?"

"Your what?"

"Where does it hurt!"

"Oh. Nowhere . . . I just wanted to talk to Kes." Neelix stood up; his face paled toward green, and he collapsed back down to the deck, gripping his knee and biting back a scream.

"Well," said the doctor, eyeing Neelix's agony, "I'm certainly glad you're not in any pain."

"I am now, you ninny!"

Rolling his eyes and grumping, the doctor squatted and moved his medical scanner up and down Neelix's kneecap, which the cook had cracked on the deck when he went down and the doctor landed on him. Neelix felt the tingly feeling of the bone knitting. The pain ebbed over several minutes, leaving only some residual stiffness.

Just as they finished their unexpected appointment, Kes entered and dashed across the room. "Neelix! What did you do? Are you all right? Is he all right?"

"Aside from some difficulty seeing large objects directly in his path, your friend is fine. Kes, did you finish abstracting those articles from the *Journal of the Federation Medical Association?* How did they compare with the archived abstracts?"

"Yes. They were the same. Neelix, come over here; lie down—you shouldn't be on your injured leg like that! How do you feel?"

She made such a fuss that Neelix flushed again; how could he find the words now, after all this, to tell his beloved that her deepest, most sympathetic urges were innappropriate?

How could Neelix look into his love's eyes and tell her that it was Janeway, and not Kes, who was right . . . that they simply must destroy the moon, even though it meant the deaths of twenty-seven billion souls?

And would Kes ever speak to him again when he did?

CHAPTER
18

COMMANDER CHAKOTAY AND LIEUTENANT CAREY STOOD IN A cramped, experimental laboratory just off the bionet salt-transfer monitoring equipment on the lower engineering deck. The room was Lieutenant Carey's private space, no one else allowed except by special dispensation.

"My . . ." marveled the lieutenant. "I can't believe it! It can't be done . . . but I can do it!"

Chakotay smiled, invisible behind Lieutenant Carey's back. "Can you?"

"No. But yes. But this is ridiculous . . . what *idiot* abstracted that article? Look—look at the wave function for the shield soliton."

Carey vigorously rubbed his thinning hair as he popped an incomprehensible equation onto the viewer. Chakotay stared. He could make out some of the terms: variables for the shields and tractor beams he studied when he took Space-time Engineering at the Academy; but there were six other terms in the equation he had never seen before in his life.

They probably drop out under normal shield geometry, he thought, *so they don't even teach them to us.* The only problem with Academy classes is they were ruthlessly practical: if Starfleet did not think a command-track officer cadet needed to know a large section of the engineering details of a particular system, they not only did not teach it, they did not even bother telling the cadets they were not teaching it! This left functional, efficient officers who nevertheless had gaping lacunae in their understanding of possibly critical systems . . . evidently including the standard "shield solution" of the impulse-soliton wave function.

"Here is the term," whispered Carey, pointing in excitement to one of the missing sections of the equation; his tone of voice indicated veneration, perhaps outright worship. "In the standard model, we always assume gamma of s and t must be a continuous function. But look! Professor Wilson flatly states that that assumption is not proven, either theoretically or by experiment!"

"And if you make gamma discontinuous . . . ?" Chakotay pointed at the appropriate term and tapped the viewer significantly. He actually had no idea what he was asking, but it worked to prod Carey into further thought. The engineer began writing invisible equations with his index finger, as if writing on a class stylus-screen.

"I'll be . . . scuppered. Either the shields will actually bend . . ."

"Or?"

"Or the ship rips apart like an egg in a wind tunnel."

"Really." Suddenly, Chakotay wondered whether unleashing an engineer and Coyote-tricking him into thinking an impossible problem was possible was the best idea after all. But desperate times called for desperate deeds.

"I don't *think* the ship will be destroyed; it seems more likely that the shields will bend . . . that's the least-energy solution if we allow gamma to have a line-discontinuity right at the front of the ship."

"Thank the spirits for least-energy solutions." Chakotay still understood only every third or fourth word Carey said; but he was not about to let the engineer know that.

Carey looked back at the commander with near awe. "If this is the Maquis way, it's a wonder you guys haven't taken over the Federation already. Be sure to tell Tuvok that I was wrong and he was right all along . . . it definitely *is* possible, once we suppress our 'continuity prejudice.'"

"Oh, I definitely shall tell Tuvok," said Chakotay with a mystery smile. "How long will it take to have a working shield-wedge?"

"You want me to go ahead with it?"

The commander thought for only a moment; they had no options, and he knew Janeway would agree. He rubbed his forehead, where a killer headache was forming. There was no time to go see the doctor.

He nodded. "Yes, Mr. Carey. Go ahead and do it. Can you give me a time estimate?"

"Sure, just a minute." Carey punched a few keys on his console; Chakotay had noticed that many engineers preferred to use a keyboard rather than the voice interface, for some reason. "Okay, got it."

"How long will it take?"

"What?"

"The shield conversion," snapped Chakotay.

"Huh? I just did it."

Chakotay felt a chill; he did not let it show. "You mean, the ship could have blown up just now, and we never would have known it?"

Carey looked puzzled. "But it didn't."

A ghostly finger touched the commander's heart; the pain in his head suddenly vanished in the adrenal rush. He nodded brusquely. "Good work, Lieutenant."

"Thank you, sir; it's on-line now. I'll rig a special controller for the captain's console."

"Make it for mine; she'll be rather busy when the fertilizer starts to fly." Chakotay exited the engineering lab and got all the way back to his own quarters before the shakes started.

Lieutenant B'Elanna Torres strapped a utility belt around her hips, checking the sixteen pouches to make sure she had every tool she might conceivably need to attack the moon's circuitry; and at that, she knew she would not be at her job for ten minutes before she would be wanting something she had left behind on the ship.

She mustered what little grace Klingon genetics and Maquis society had left her to utter a stiff "Good morning, Mr. Redbay" when her pilot slunk aboard, carrying nothing but a hand phaser. *Why a phaser?* she wondered with distaste. Redbay's only answer was a shrug. Torres decided that Redbay did not trust *her,* so he carried a weapon good only for antipersonnel warfare.

Torres had brought coils of fiberoptic cable, nylon climbing line, pliers, an assortment of spanners and mag-drivers, three specially programmed tricorders, each to record different types of electronic impulses . . . and no weapons.

She sat at the copilot's console of the shuttlecraft without another word, ostentatiously strapping herself into the seat. She meant it to sting, but Redbay only strapped himself in as well.

Captain Janeway stood at the hatchway of the shuttlecraft but said nothing as the door slid shut. Redbay fired up the engines, commenting only that one of the engines was running hot, and B'Elanna should keep an eye on it. Janeway stepped back out of harm's way; Redbay powered up and quickly ran through the engine-start and launch checklists. Then he picked up the ship and rotated through the bay door. As soon as they cleared *Voyager*'s shields, Redbay announced "Shields up" and flicked the switch.

Torres sat quietly, admiring his piloting skill in spite of her resolve to hate everything about him. Redbay drove directly toward the sun, veering at a comfortable distance and skimming the corona, keeping the hull temperature below ten thousand degrees but remaining in the plasma field as much as he could. They had no communications, but neither could the Furies easily see them. B'Elanna was impressed.

Then at the perfect moment, almost without thought, Redbay yanked the ship up and out of the sun's corona, aimed it toward the planet-moon system, and kicked in the warp engines. Diving straight out of the sun as they were, the odds were excellent that nobody would spot them until they approached the moon itself.

B'Elanna looked in the rear viewer; *Voyager* followed the

shuttle's trail exactly, giving the Furies but a single cross-section to spot.

At warp four, the shuttlecraft crossed the gap between sun and moon in five seconds; then Redbay cut off the warp engines, letting them drift behind the moon before shifting to impulse. B'Elanna turned on every passive sensor there was. Approximately two hundred thousand kilometers from the moon, two klaxons and a buzzer erupted with noise as the moon signaled it was being attacked and screamed for help.

No fewer than *twelve* Fury ships lifted off to intercept, and that was when *Voyager* sprang into action. The big ship pretended that it, not the shuttlecraft, had set off the alarms.

Getting interesting now, thought B'Elanna, keyed to the excitement.

Redbay began a long, slow turn to the right and pulled tighter and tighter, as the inertial dampers struggled against the high-g turn. B'Elanna Torres felt her entire body and a river of blood compressing downward as the g-meter climbed. She began to strain, forcing the blood back up her abdomen to her brain—whatever happened, she could *not* allow herself to fade to black.

Two Fury ships stayed with the shuttlecraft; the rest followed *Voyager* the opposite direction. The bogies started trying to lock weapons on the shuttle, and B'Elanna was kept busy operating the subspace countermeasures, trying to slip disruptor locks.

Janeway sat silent in her command chair. There was nothing to say. Tom Paris could pilot better without someone shouting in his ear, and Tuvok and Kim were perfectly capable of handling shields and weapons respectively by themselves. The captain followed the entire battle, keeping tabs not only on the Fury ships, the weapons and shields, and the piloting, but on crew performance, Maquis and Federation; on Commander Chakotay, who ran back and forth between the normal crew and crewmen Dalby, Jarron, Chell, and Henley, who stayed in the dead spots that were called "bullpen." Each crewman watched his normal duty station, ready to leap into the gap if someone was incapacitated.

The ship pulled hard in every direction. Paris preternaturally sensed where the Furies would head next, and he pulled exactly the right heading to keep them shooting at each other instead of *Voyager*.

Janeway's emergency inertial dampers held, but barely, responding sluggishly; the crew were yanked hard to left and right, driven forward, and pressed back into their seats at a very high g-force for fractions of a second until the jury-rigged dampers caught up. *Too bad B'Elanna's not here to see this,* thought the captain; *maybe she wouldn't feel so bad.*

Janeway began to get dizzy, and the old feeling of nausea returned with a vengeance. Paris fought it off, dodging left and right to slip the Fury weaponry. The aliens had not yet fired their terror projector . . . or had they? "Ensign Kim—can you identify every weapon fired so far?"

Kim, who looked distinctly pallid and sweaty, clutching his console, shook his head. "Negative—Captain; they've got—disruptors and old-fashioned fusion bombs, but—still some kind of beam—I'm not sure what it is, but it's causing interspace flux-ulp."

"Has it struck us?"

"One shot—brushed the neural switches—on deck thirteen—don't know if the shields—stopped it."

"Reports of damage?"

"No. No reports at all."

"They're dead silent down there?"

Kim nodded.

"Dammit . . . I think somebody down there just got a taste of Fury terrors." She squeezed her eyes shut, fighting back a tidal wave of guilt. "Activate EMH program."

"Please state the nature—"

"Deck thirteen, neural switchboard; send orderlies and security . . . tell them to be prepared to deal with probably the most horrific panic attack you've ever seen, Doctor."

"I understand, Captain," said the doctor—sadly? *Can a hologram feel sadness?* she wondered. "Team is on its way," said the doctor.

"Chakotay, how is your shield-wedge holding out?"

The commander looked down at a readout on the special screen at his side, then back up at Janeway; he crossed his fingers and held them up.

"Did the shuttlecraft escape undetected?" Janeway asked.

"Negative, Captain," said Tuvok, looking none the worse for the shaking. "Two Furies followed them toward the moon. They are evading but not returning fire."

"Don't want to attract any more attention," muttered Paris, barely audible.

"Crewman . . . Dalby? Dalby. Get us some antinauseoid from the replicator."

"Aye, sir!" Dalby shouted, sliding along the wall toward the machine and trying to avoid being sent flying across the room.

"Are you sure, sir?" asked Chell. "It didn't do much last time." He looked a much greener shade of blue; Janeway presumed that indicated the same with Bolians as did pallor with humans.

"If it helps at all, it is worth it, Mr. Chell," answered Tuvok without taking his nose from the sensor-array console.

The captain took a deep breath. The time had come. "Commence firing, Ensign Kim; let's give the—ow—the Furies something else to concentrate on for a while."

The battle was joined; *Voyager* fired her first shots in anger in yet another Delta Quadrant star system. *Cross another one off*, thought Janeway gloomily; *at this rate, the Federation will be about as welcome in this quadrant as the Borg were in ours.*

CHAPTER
19

ONCE MORE INTO THE BREACH, THOUGHT CAPTAIN JANEWAY—
she made a point not to say it; Cliché Day was tomorrow.

She dropped the *Voyager* straight "down" relative to its
orientation; the maneuver often took by surprise the young-
er spacefaring races—or in this case, races that had had
virtually no contact or conflict in space for centuries or even
millennia.

The Furies had no quarrel with anyone from the Delta
Quadrant, those of no consequence who shared their realm
of exile. They wanted only heaven. All war and conflict of
the past century had taken place there, according to Lieutenant Redbay—and no one had come back alive.

Their best fighters had been lost in the Alpha Quadrant.
The remaining forces of the Furies left behind had little
experience fighting in three dimensions with a gravitational
field to contend with—obviously, for Paris evaded attack
after attack, and the Furies often as not moved only in a
planar direction . . . and often fired when their own ships
were in the way. Janeway gave orders only when absolutely
necessary; mostly she just let her crew crew the ship.

But the Furies learned quickly; and after a few minutes,

they grouped into a coordinated unit and began to take direction from their command ship. "Now, Mr. Paris," ordered Janeway, "turn tail . . . let's see if they'll play follow-the-leader."

Voyager fired a last salvo from the forward phaser batteries; the beams lanced out, striking the unshielded ships . . . but the superdense material, a meter thick, absorbed and dissipated the blast, abating slightly.

As Paris reluctantly turned the ship around and took off at full impulse, Tuvok reported: "Captain, the Fury ships can take a lot more damage before their hulls will be dangerously abraded."

"I've got interspace fluctuations all over the board," Ensign Kim shouted. They're powering up the terror projector again!" He was frightened enough that his tone cut through his spacesickness.

"Rotating the wedge backward," announced Chakotay calmly; the announcement was hardly necessary, since the move was obvious . . . but his calm, measured voice reassured Kim and the cadets.

Janeway's eyes flicked from one to the other.

"Kim," said Lieutenant Paris, "I've given you copilot status; keep your sensors sharp, prepare for evasive maneuvers.

"But—"

"I'll pick up on it, don't worry; I won't fight your course changes."

"The Furies are powering up warp engines," announced Tuvok.

Here we go . . . ! "Jump to warp six," said Captain Janeway. "Don't let's lose them in front of us. . . . Paris, stay just ahead of them; match their velocity and add a shade."

"Aye, aye, Captain."

"Warp six—correction, warp eight," said Paris. "Nine-one, nine-three . . . damn, these guys are quick!"

"Are they—"

"Catching up still! Blast it, I can't get to nine-nine; something's wrong, we're dragging somewhere!"

The captain slapped her commbadge. "Janeway to engines. . . . Carey, what's going on? We need full power!"

The voice crackled over the comm link, full of static. "Captain, it's not the engines—it's the shield-wedge . . . it's acting just like an airbrake in an atmospheric aeroplane."

"Can you fix it?"

"I can revert to normal geometry . . . you've got your choice: a shield-wedge or warp nine point nine. Not both!" Carey sounded desperate. The captain watched the rear viewer, mouthing silent imprecations.

"We're holding at warp nine point six-six-six," shouted Paris, not turning around. "The Furies are making maybe nine point six-six-six-three; they're catching us, but *very* slowly, Captain."

"Ensign Kim," said Janeway, cutting through the chatter, "drop some torpedoes out the rear, one at a time. No juice, proximity fuses."

"Floating mines," muttered Chakotay next to her.

"Maybe it'll slow them down a bit," she explained.

Kim nodded wearily, still sick despite the antinausea drug he had taken. "Fire one . . . two . . . three."

"Yes!" exclaimed Tom Paris. "They're pulling back."

"They've figured out we can't outrun them," said the captain. "Now they're content to run us out of town." She smiled; this was exactly what she had hoped for. "We still have the whole pack, except for the two who went after Torres and Redbay?"

"Yes, Captain," said Kim. Then—"Wait . . . correction! I only count nine Fury ships!"

"Did we destroy one?" asked Commander Chakotay.

"Negative," said Tuvok; "there is no debris anywhere back along our path." He looked up from his console, impassive face unable to completely conceal the faint overtones of concern. "Captain, I'm afraid one of the pursuers has broken off and returned to the system. If he scans for ion wake, it will lead him straight to the moon."

"And he can communicate with his buddies. Paris, we're going to have to turn and fight. It's the only way to keep their minds off the moon."

"Aye, Captain!" exulted the lieutenant. *The secret Sea*

Wolf within Tom Paris burst its chains, thought Janeway grimly. She knew the feeling: she, too, wanted the fight so intensely she could taste it.

The Furies were simply too dangerous to be left alone.

"Ready, Mr. Paris—Mr. Kim, ready to slip the terror projections—cut the warp, accelerate impulse to combat velocity, *now."*

Voyager virtually halted as Chakotay shifted the shield-wedge back to the front. The Furies flashed past at warp speed, then backtracked and dropped out of warp near the *Voyager.*

"All right, people," said Janeway, "let's show them what a Federation starship can really do."

The ship suddenly lurched left, leaving them all disoriented and dizzy. Only grim-faced Kim was prepared, hunched over his console, desperately scanning for more terror projections. It was he who swerved. "Incoming," he explained, voice shaky.

Lieutenant Redbay flew the shuttlecraft tight to the moon, skimming the edges of structure. Uneasily, Lieutenant B'Elanna Torres cleared her throat: "Lieutenant, the shaft mapped by Kim and Paris is bearing—"

"I know where it is," he said softly. But he continued in the wrong direction.

It took B'Elanna another minute before she realized he had no intention of heading anywhere near the shaft while the Furies remained in hot pursuit. A second later, she was mentally kicking herself for not realizing sooner that they could not allow themselves to be trapped flying up a long, straight shaft with two enemies behind them.

I guess that's why I'm in engineering, not security, she thought.

The Furies pulled within phaser range, and Torres was occupied for some minutes trying to pop off a shot or two while Redbay did his tilted best to spin the universe out from under her feet. She *thought* she scored a pair of direct hits on the lead ship; but despite its lack of shields, it did not blow up or crash. *I must have missed,* she decided. *Great. Now I can't even shoot straight.*

She hunched over the phaser array and focused every erg of conscious will on aiming her shots by a combination of spatial visualization and Klingon "Zen." At last, she definitively *saw* one shot take the tail Fury directly amidships . . . but astonishingly, it kept on moving!

For a primitive people, without transporters or shields, they sure built tough hulls. Until that moment, B'Elanna had not really credited Tuvok's report of a material so strong and dense that phasers could not penetrate it.

But it did not matter; for if the Furies could invent such an unreasonably strong material—they still could not alter the basic laws of physics! If the substance were superdense, then that meant it was supermassive for its volume.

And that meant less-maneuverable ships, for mass becomes *inertia* when you get it moving.

"Redbay," she said tersely, "keep pulling tight turns, the tighter the better; I'm sure they outmass us."

Redbay obliged, pegging the g-meter max indicator three times, the last at a bone-crushing *twelve* times the acceleration of gravity. If Torres were not half Klingon, she realized, she would be a smear of guava jelly after some of Redbay's maneuvers.

She could not quite figure out how he himself had survived. But he seemed unaffected; bones that looked brittle and skin so blue-white it was virtually transparent came through every turn intact and unbroken.

Redbay yanked and banked the shuttlecraft, threading the tall towers that were probably comm links from one part of the moon to another, diving *under* a series of gantries in a move that almost caused B'Elanna to lose her lunch, then heading directly toward a huge block of that superdense material and rolling out left at the last moment. B'Elanna found herself clutching the sides of the seat and wishing for a combat harness, despite the inertial dampers.

The Furies struggled to follow . . . but B'Elanna was right at last: their ships were simply too massive, unwieldy, unmaneuverable; the first moment of pure joy occurred when one of the ships, trying to follow them under the gantries, simply could not pull out of its dive in time. It struck the surface, ploughing a six-kilometer-long furrow in the protective rock and vaporizing itself in the process.

But the second ship clung grimly to its task. Its pilot had to be half dead, thought Lieutenant Torres; he was pulling fifteen g's to the shuttlecraft's twelve! The Fury planet was of normal-range gravitation, slightly less than Earth, in fact; so the alien pilot must have suffered the tortures of the damned with every dive and turn.

But he stuck. Like a magnet, he stuck.

Then he began to fire a weapon that was neither disruptor nor torpedo. B'Elanna watched, mesmerized, as the pilot struggled to play the beam across their ship. She fired back automatically, without awareness—for her only conscious thought was to ponder what it would feel like to be flooded with abject, utter, belly-crawling terror.

Ahead, Redbay must have spotted a new needle eye to thread. B'Elanna saw a building and tower approaching. At first, they appeared to connect; then she saw a tiny sliver of a gap. This was the gap at which Lieutenant Redbay pointed the nose of the shuttle.

B'Elanna leaned back in her seat, baring her teeth and gripping the console, as if that would have any effect if Redbay misjudged the gap . . . and indeed, it certainly looked as though he had. The crack was never wide enough to fit the shuttlecraft!

"Lieutenant—watch out!" she hollered.

But Redbay neither stopped nor veered aside. He continued barreling toward the sliver at 105-percent impulse.

Torres forced her eyes to remain open: whatever happened, she swore she would stand before the great judge proudly, like a Klingon warrior, and never cringe.

The moment came.

The moment went. The shuttlecraft squirted through the eye after rolling sideways, a clean half-meter of space on either side.

And—B'Elanna realized with an exultant surge that the Fury ship *was not going to make it!* It was too wide; it could not clear the tower.

And it was too late for the pilot to veer around it. But not too late to open fire for one parting shot.

The terror projection sheered between the two buildings and struck them in the aft part of the shuttlecraft. The shields were never intended to stop such exquisite forms of energy.

For an instant, Redbay and B'Elanna Torres were caught in the full force of the terror-projection beam. Then the luckless Fury turned one whole side of the large building into a smoking hole.

But an instant can be an eternity.

CHAPTER
20

THE FIRST INKLING B'ELANNA TORRES HAD THAT ANYTHING WAS amiss was the overpowering and rather horrifying certainty that she was about to start crying.

The last time the Klingon had wept was when she was three years old. Her mother's explosive reaction convinced her that it was not the Klingon way.

The knowledge of what was coming, then the feel of salt water on her cheeks, gripped her heart like two giant, icy hands squeezing the life from her body. A Klingon crying! Like a baby!

But a moment later, whimpering, she realized the *true* danger . . . it was the console! It was about to short, sending hundreds of thousands of amperes through her body, frying her instantly.

With a gasp of horror, she jerked away from the death-trap, then clawed frantically with violently shaking hands at her harness, unstrapping it with terrible difficulty. She fell backward out of the chair, rolling onto her belly.

There she stuck, afraid to move forward or back, her mind virtually shut down by the paralyzing realization that the hull integrity of the shuttle had been breached, and the precious, life-giving oxygen was all squirting into dead space.

Crawling forward, whimpering like a slave, B'Elanna the Klingon felt the sharp, torn-up deckplates cutting her palms and knees, felt the diseased germs infesting her body, working their way up her veins to her heart and brain. The worms grew inside her, expelling larvae throughout her body that would grow and grow, finally eating their way out.

Terrified suddenly by the certainty that Redbay was as stricken by the weapon as was she—all her fault, for she didn't dodge that last bolt!—she tried to turn and look. But the fear was too great; she was frightened into rigid immobility, unable to see what was happening.

She could not help hearing Redbay's cries of despair, however. She did not need to turn and look; she knew they were both doomed. And the mission would fail. And all for the want of a tenpenny engineer!

The wave of horrorterror subsided. *Is that it? Is that all? It's over. That's all the stupid useless terror weapon does.*

Over? The surge of B'Elanna's adrenaline awoke a deeper fear that had only been slumbering beneath the surface, allowing the petty phobias of first contact to run dry.

The real fun had barely begun.

B'Elanna folded into a fetal position, locked her arms around her head, and screamed and screamed until she lost her wind and her voice failed. She barely saw, without comprehending, Redbay slap a button in panic before he, too, collapsed. Then a dark curtain of mindless despair shrouded her brain. And she knew nothing more.

Slowly, Lieutenant Torres came back into herself, realizing she *was* a lieutenant, even if brevetted. She had disgraced her new Starfleet, her old Maquis, herself, and her race. She still did; she lay in the dark half pressed inside a cabinet as if trying to escape the starfear by climbing back inside the womb. She still gibbered; she still sobbed, tear ducts now dry. But she had long passed the moment when mere humiliation meant anything anymore. She was alive; they had stopped the punishment. She would do what they ordered . . . *whatever they ordered.*

Unfortunately—fortunately—there was no one around to order her to do anything. She dropped her face into her arms and cried relentlessly, piteously, begging for someone to come along and give her an order she could follow to atone for her apostasy.

After five minutes of such self-abasement, B'Elanna realized how remarkably stupid her whole reaction was. Her face flushed. With still an occasional whimper, she crawled backward out of the hole. She clawed up a bulkhead to her feet, then crept along the wall to her chair.

Redbay already waited for her. He seemed hollower, colder, but no worse otherwise . . . not like big, bold B'Elanna the Klingon Warrior.

"I will re-resign my com-commission as soon as we return," she said, feeling the blood drain from her face.

"Don't be so dramatic," said the skeletal visitor.

"I disgraced myself. I am not fit to wear my uniform."

"It was an energy weapon. So now you know what I knew."

At once, Klingon pride and Maquis stubbornness stiffened B'Elanna's posture, and human rationality asserted control.

She swallowed, controlled herself. She suppressed her raging Klingon side—raging at herself, her own inadequacies—and accepted what she could not change.

"Very well. Where . . . ? Oh." Torres stared at the inside of a tunnel—presumably *the* tunnel. "How the hell did we—?"

"Autopilot," said Redbay, shrugging. "I programmed it with . . . Paris, is it? With Paris's route before we left."

"Lucky thing."

Redbay turned and stared at Lieutenant Torres. "Planning. I knew this was a possibility. I knew the devastation that terror projector caused. I maintained just long enough to engage the preset course before succumbing."

After a moment's pause, B'Elanna Torres said, almost too softly to hear, "You seem to have recovered pretty quickly."

"You were out for an additional eight minutes. I'm more used to it. I haven't as many phobic pressure-points; you've really never been frightened before—I have."

The engineer said nothing. Evidently, she was not allowed the luxury of sulking, either. So much for the simple pleasures of Starfleet life. *May as well go back to the Maquis,* she thought, not meaning it as an insult; *they were more tolerant of childish behavior.*

"We're here," responded Redbay to her unasked question, *What now?*

"I missed Paris's Swoop of Death. I was kind of looking forward to it."

"Maybe we'll survive and do it on the way out."

B'Elanna laughed, an ugly sound . . . recovery proceeded apace. Survive? What a joke. She knew as well as Redbay that their mission was pretty likely to be a one-way ticket: with the power capacity of the moon, built to receive and channel the electromagnetic energy of an exploding star, the odds were they would electro-fry themselves trying to short-circuit the works. And if they didn't, how long before the Furies sent out a massive counter force, as soon as they realized someone was monkeying with their precious machine?

"Got your . . ." She hesitated, staring dubiously at Redbay's phaser. "Got your equipment? Ready to beam over?"

"I brought a phaser."

"Good. Maybe you can shoot us a moon rat for lunch. Let's do it."

They beamed across to the same point from which Paris and Kim had begun their expedition, what seemed like three or four centuries ago. B'Elanna activated the "walkabout" program in her tricorder. She held it up in front of her right eye, looking past the tricorder and down the corridor with the other eye. The screen projected a real-time, three-dimensional model of the corridor ahead, with ghostly, glowing arrows floating spectrally ahead, pointing the path. "Follow," she said curtly, walking forward and doing her best to follow the path—though often it pointed them directly *through* gray bulkhead walls . . . logic gates that were open to Kim and Paris but had closed in the intervening time.

An hour's walk convinced her that their task was not

going to be easy . . . perhaps not even possible. No matter how hard she tried to stick to the path, she simply couldn't! When gates shuffled open or closed, they reconfigured the entire geometry of the warren, so much that they were led farther and farther astray. Finally, even the tricorder couldn't lead them back.

"All right," she muttered, "we'll have to carve our own path."

"What are we looking for?"

"The, ah, primary power switches."

"And we'll know we've found them when . . . ?"

B'Elanna Torres shrugged. "When we stop and sabotage them."

"Thank you."

"Always happy to oblige." *What a stupid question!* Torres had no more idea what they would look like than did Redbay, and he should have known that.

B'Elanna shifted away from the sarcastic. "My guess would be that they're roughly in the center of the moon. Eight hundred kilometers thataway." She pointed straight down.

"Got any suggestions? How we can travel eight hundred kilometers in the few hours we have?"

Torres slowly shook her head. "Only speculation. There *must* be some way for repair crews to get down there, isn't there? It must have broken sometime in the last few thousand years."

"Well, maybe they just transport to the proper coordinates."

She shook her head, emphatically this time. "You don't know, do you? This quadrant never discovered transporter technology, or at least no race we've encountered out here has it. Nope . . . if these Furies want to get to the center of this asteroid, they have to do it the old-fashioned way . . . a mag-lev railway or something equally primitive."

"Look for a shaft," suggested Redbay, though B'Elanna was already doing so, scanning the tricorder in a slow circle.

"This way," she said; "call it north, because it's toward one rotational pole."

Redbay nodded without expression. They set out north-
ward, tacking left and right as the movable walls required.
Lieutenant Torres swore she caught movement out of the
corner of her eye many a time on the ghost moon. It always
scuttled out of sight just before she turned and stared.

Redbay, as always, seemed utterly unaffected by the
hallucinations.

CHAPTER
21

A BEAR TURNS, CONFRONTS THE PACK OF HOWLING WOLVES THAT have pursued it—drawn after by the bear's cunning. Momentarily, Captain Janeway pressed back her head, eyes squeezed tightly shut, wondering if the forced metaphor was wishful thinking. Wondering why it so often came down to this, to a brutal fight in the cold deep. Wondering whether the bear would be pulled down this time—they don't live forever, bears.

Dangerous job. Somebody's got to do it. Be the bear.

The Furies drew back, paused before the final assault. They learned; they were people, not wolves, and they knew enough to beware the loping bearclaw swipes. Now they coordinated, and Tom Paris lost the banter that was normally so much a part of . . .

The *Voyager* rocked behind the pounding blow of a disruptor-type weapon. Janeway jerked back to present-time, leaned forward, and began conducting the battle. Her crew was good; she was good. The Furies were better than they had been. It was a hell of a fight.

Four small ships wheeled and attacked flank left, high and

low. *Voyager* had no option but to cut in the opposite direction, and this time the jaws of the trap got clever and made no effort to aim: the Fury ships to flank right simply fired spreads into the blocks along the obvious flight path.

There was no place to evade, and the Federation ship flew directly into several fusion missiles.

They rolled like an ancient cutter on the high seas, staggered and rocked by blow after blow against the shields. The shields were meant to take the force of phasers and photon torpedoes; they would not be breached by ion-powered nuclear missiles. But if the disruptors should happen to open a hole, and if a missile snuck past, detonating against the hull itself—then *Voyager* would vanish inside a spreading, white glow, "brighter than a thousand suns," hotter than the stellar core they had just passed through.

Each hammer blow shook the ship and rattled their brains, until Janeway heard a sound like ivory dice shaken inside a hollow skull . . . her own. She shouted orders that she could not hear herself—she could hear everyone else, but her internal voice was drowned out by the rattle.

Abruptly, Ensign Kim jumped up, threw himself across Paris, and in a frenzy, jabbed his thumb into the helm console. The ship lurched straight down so quickly that Janeway and doubtless the entire bridge crew (except for Tuvok) left their stomachs up on the ninety-ninth floor.

Janeway stared at the ensign, who hung his head sheepishly.

"Terror beam," he said. He sank back in his seat, watching his sensor array . . . but keeping one hand close to Paris's station.

Lieutenant Paris went back to his task of bobbing and weaving, dodging disruptors, terror beams, and big, dumb rockets. For a moment, Janeway worried that Paris might feel some resentment. With a shake of her head, she dismissed the thought.

No time, no time! She fell into the rhythm: duck and bob, bob and weave.

The shield-wedge served well to ward off the most fearsome of the Furies' weapons, the terror projector; but it weakened the structure and could not repel ordinary weapons as well. Life was a trade-off. "Shields at seventy-four percent," announced Lieutenant Tuvok, unflappable . . . but his words sent Captain Janeway into an internal frenzy she could barely conceal. She deliberately leaned back in the command chair, conscious of many eyes and many more hidden fears turning her way.

Whenever the shields began to fail, the captain's heart leaped up her throat. It was a synergetic engineering effect: the more their effectiveness sank, the more they were damaged by incoming missiles and disruptors.

Then the ship itself began to take blows, as the shields started developing "holes"—weak spots where the laminar flow was disrupted, leaving a singularity that was weaker than the surrounding shield-stuff. A shot to one of those holes shivered the timbers and rattled *Voyager*'s bones, lurching Janeway half out of her seat.

The Furies took to crossing in pairs or triplets across octants of heading. After a few minutes, Chakotay warned, "They're *herding* us back toward the planet!"

Captain Janeway saw it in the same moment: "Mr. Paris! Duck the assault and return to the previous heading . . . don't let them drive us back." While Paris complied, Janeway added more softly, "We can't let them return while B'Elanna is still back there—we must give her the time." But the ship was being pounded into flotsam and wouldn't last the time that she needed. Not unless—

Janeway spied a gap where the confusion of battle had driven the Furies too far apart. She seized the moment: "Paris, bearing zero-seven-zero, mark thirty, full impulse . . . *punch it,* mister!"

The helmsman obeyed, yanking the *Voyager* clear of the wolves. For a moment, they headed directly back toward the system. Then Paris cut obliquely and accelerated to their maximum impulse, whipping around the star. The Furies followed, but lost the order of their battle.

At last, free for the moment—a brief moment!—from the urgent necessity to dodge and cross their own trail, Janeway leapt out of her chair and attacked Kim's weapons board. It was marginally quicker to do it herself than tell him what to do, and mere seconds were all they had. She savagely programmed the board to fire shots in rapid succession, much faster than a human could aim.

When the Furies rounded the sun, the computer laid multiple spreads of photon torpedoes and spewed a lattice of maximal-strength phaser blasts . . . and *two Fury ships* were broken, shattering like anvils under a hero's sword.

"Got 'em!" shouted Kim with little dignity.

Immediately, the board flickered and died.

It started up a fraction of a second later; but a chilly fist lodged in Janeway's stomach. "What the hell was that?"

"Captain," said Tuvok, looking up from his science console, "stellar activity increased significantly, evidently some time ago; we are nine light-minutes from the sun, and electromagnetic radiation interference has just reached this part of the sector."

"Can we still see?" asked Janeway.

"With increasing difficulty, Captain."

"Mr. Kim?"

Kim opened and closed his mouth like a fish. "Losing . . . losing sensor contact, Captain. No, wait; it's back again!"

Janeway nodded. "Expect to see waves of interference with increasing frequency as the stellar core collapses by steps."

"With every collapse," continued Tuvok, "core temperatures increase until they ignite fusion of atoms at higher atomic numbers—helium, lithium, beryllium, and on up the periodic table of elements." It was unclear to whom he lectured; presumably, everyone present had taken first-year nuclear physics.

Janeway leaned forward, speaking urgently. "Mr. Kim . . . can we still operate the transporter?"

Kim shook his head. "I don't know, Captain; unfortunately, the only way to find out is to try it."

As soon as the weapons board came back on-line, Kim reactivated the captain's program and unleashed another barrage of hell upon the Furies. Evidently, the electromagnetic pulse had scrambled their sensors as well, for they foundered, drifting along Newtonian orbits while they powered up their systems again. "Like shooting drunks in a barrel," muttered the ensign, picking off first one Fury, then another by concentrated firepower.

Quickly, before the Furies could fully recover, Paris backed the ship away at full impulse speed, dropping photon torpedoes in his wake with speed-killing acceleration to park them in orbit . . . depth charges. The Furies were forced to swerve around them, throwing them into nonmatching orbits through the stellar gravity well.

Then the second electromagnetic-pulse (EMP) wave struck, and *Voyager* was deaf, dumb, and blind, every sensor kicked off-line. "Visual!" commanded Janeway; Kim quickly switched to pure video, and they could see— Janeway thanked her lucky stars they weren't traveling at warp speed at that moment; the visual distortions of pure, unfiltered video feed at warp were stomach-turning and horrifying . . . few could watch for more than a second or two.

Captain Janeway stared at the screen with eyes that were sharper, thanks to modern medical tech, than those of the ancient Greeks who had invented astronomy; she looked for parallaxing stars that would indicate the enemy ships. If they were smart . . .

If WE were smart, she thought. "Paris—shut down impulse engines; all stop! Mr. Kim, keep working on those sensors . . . passive sensing. We can't see them . . ."

"They can't see us," finished Paris, in sudden comprehension, getting it at last.

"Blind man's bluff. Wait, there's one—heading about two-eight-five, bearing—"

"I see him. Them."

"Magnify."

"Captain," said Tuvok, "without the sensors, the magnified picture will be unsteady."

Janeway was adamant; one picture was worth a thousand frets. "I want to see him . . . how badly did the pulse damage him?"

Kim touched a button, and the forward viewer replaced the starfield with a shaky, long-distance visual of a Fury ship. The ship was tumbling, and in a second, Janeway saw why: the aft end, which should have displayed three fusion engines, showed only one operating on one side. When the ship rotated again, they saw a bright white light and hot plasma escaping from one side; this unexpected "rocket" gave the Fury ship a tumbling motion.

"Containment field must have shut down," said Kim; "poor people."

"I doubt there are any people left alive to feel sorry for," said Tuvok matter-of-factly. "I would guess the radiation count aboard that ship to be—"

"Please don't," said the captain, closing her eyes. *Get used to it,* she ordered herself; *try to imagine what it will feel like to kill twenty-seven billion of them.*

She blinked; a tear rolled smoothly down her cheek, but she ignored it. It wasn't really there.

"Captain, there are two Furies left," said Lieutenant Paris; "both are negative bearing, at about two-eight-zero and zero-two-zero."

Can't be much more exact than that, she realized. "Damaged?"

"Not obviously. I think their engines are back on-line, but we haven't been tagged with fire-control sensors yet."

"Maybe they were burned out for good."

Paris turned back to his private viewer. "Maybe you're right; they're firing up and accelerating in a search pattern."

"Are we in the projected cone of search?"

Tuvok quickly punched up the same image. "Negative, Captain," said the Vulcan. "If they maintain their present systematic search, they will not locate us for another five hours."

"They're not going to wait," muttered Janeway. No one heard her, so she was spared the curse of successful prediction when, five minutes later, the Fury ships rendezvoused clumsily—by dead reckoning, the captain guessed—and headed back toward the planet.

"Mr. Kim," asked Janeway for the third time since shutdown, "how long do you estimate for the sensors to be back on-line?"

Kim shook his head. Again. "I . . . couldn't say, Captain. I'm working on it, but—the pulse fried everything!"

Janeway settled back; she began to realize how much she truly depended upon Lieutenant Torres. B'Elanna would have had the sensors back up in—no, that was unfair; Kim wasn't an engineer; he was doing the best he could. *If you really want results,* she told herself, *you'd better take over the repairs yourself. No? Too busy? Then stop whining about Kim's engineering ability!*

"Paris—follow them. Not too closely; if they start heading toward the moon, we have to stop them."

"Aye, aye."

The Furies maintained top impulse speed, evidently deciding that navigating at warp speed through a hurricane of plasma, electromagnetic radiation, and gravity pulses was not conducive to long life. After forty minutes, the two Furies and their surreptitious shadow pulled into the inner solar system. For a moment they slowed, hesitated—then altered course directly toward the artificial moon.

"Dammit!" swore Janeway in a rare loss of cool. "Paris, get ready to—"

"Captain!" shouted Ensign Kim, stricken. He pointed at the screen, and Janeway followed his finger.

A tiny sliver of white streaked away from the moon at high impulse speed. Even at this range, the sliver was perfectly familiar. It was a shuttlecraft . . . their own shuttlecraft.

The Furies accelerated to attack speed and shot after the sliver; *Voyager* took up the chase, far behind.

Janeway half stood in her chair, staring at the drama unfolding before her eyes, out of reach; she was helpless! Yet somehow, she must help.

"Almost there . . ." muttered Paris, hunched over his console. "Almost there—just a few more—"

The first Fury ship opened fire on the shuttlecraft. The second ship fired just as Paris fired a spread of torpedoes.

Voyager's shot ran directly up from behind the two ships, where the armor was weakest. Simultaneously, the powerful Fury disruptor beam sheered through the shuttlecraft, a knife through butter.

The photon torpedo caromed the Fury ship into its comrade, flying in formation next door. The resulting fireball destroyed both ships in a microsecond.

But the shuttlecraft exploded in a burn of white noise, hurling pieces of knucklebone shrapnel in all directions.

Janeway stared, numb and sick at the same time. She didn't know whether to rage or collapse in mute sorrow. "Ensign Kim," she said, "as soon as you restore communications, try to—try to contact the away team. See if there are . . . survivors."

Incredibly, all she could think was *I wonder whether they rigged the moon before they died?*

CHAPTER

22

B'ELANNA TORRES KICKED AT THE JAMMED DOOR, KICKED
again, then threw herself bodily at the obstacle. How
embarrassing! They had trekked six kilometers through a
shifting maze of passages, all alike, betimes diving sideways
to avoid Brobdingnagian columns sliding murderously
across the slotted floor of electrical connectors and fiber
sheaths—only to be frozen scant meters before the shaft by
a *locked door!*

B'Elanna exhausted herself, Klingon fury seizing control
while the human half sat back in amazement at her futile,
repetitive folly . . . unable to stop herself, able only to stare
from a height while she beat her hands bloody and finally
collapsed, gasping, in a crumpled heap on the floor.

"May I try?" asked Lieutenant Redbay, calm and
collected—comatose would be the fairer description.

"You? What can *you* do, scarecrow, if I can't even budge
the damned thing?" She realized she was whining—human
side giving vent to the frustration of the Klingon.

Redbay grunted.

He drew his phaser and blew the door out of existence.

B'Elanna stared reproachfully at the hole where the door

had been, the edges of the slide still glowing, radiating warmth. Without a word or backward glance, she rose and pushed through, followed by Redbay. There was something terribly unaesthetic about . . . She sighed, staring at the image on the tricorder.

By rights, they should already be *in the shaft;* but she saw nothing but more corridor. "It should be here," she muttered, turning in a slow circle, scanning.

"Are you sure? Dial up the scale."

"Maxed. Maybe we just have to walk forward another—awk!"

The last noise disappeared down the hole that opened suddenly at B'Elanna's feet; the floor gave way like a hollow pie crust, and she dropped twenty meters into blackness, landing on a raised track. Had they been in Earth-normal gravity, she surely would have broken a hind leg, and Redbay would have had to put her down.

"Are you killed?" he called from above, sounding not too terribly interested either way.

"No. I don't think so. Unless we both are."

A thump sounded in the darkness as Redbay leaped down beside her. Torres fumbled around, hunting for her dropped tricorder. Suddenly, the ground was illuminated by a bright light from Redbay's phasoelectric torch. *Must've been stashed in his boot,* she thought.

B'Elanna swept her tricorder in a short arc. "Power generator this way. This track is set up for magnetic levitation, and it's still powered. I think we might actually find a working subway, Redbay." They sped down the corridor, aware of passing time, and almost ran headlong into a low, flattened car with pointy edges; the exterior was blue and yellow with bright-red highlights. "I guess we know why the Furies prefer dim lighting: because if the lights were turned up, they'd all die of terminal color-clash," said Redbay.

"Ho ho." The tricorder still picked up no life-forms, but B'Elanna continued to half-see them on the peripheral edges.

Curiously, the door was manual; they had to yank it open by brute muscle—Redbay didn't want to blow it off, since they might need the airseal. Inside, the car was stuffed with seats, three different varieties, only one of which looked comfortable for humans. The "control panel" was nothing more than a blank panel with a narrow strip of hieroglyphs running along the top edge.

The interior was mostly white and mute gray, the seats molded plastic, and no seatbelt harnesses.

"How does this work?" asked Torres, touching the panel.

The car lurched forward, accelerating hard enough to hurl Redbay to the deck. B'Elanna would have joined him except she wrapped her arms around the "pilot's" seat, which had no piloting controls that she could see. The car accelerated at a rate of at least three gravities toward . . . what? The shaft *looked like* it headed into the planetary interior . . . but where? Anywhere near a power-conduit junction? Redbay struggled to his feet against the acceleration and scrambled into a crash chair designed for humanoids; but B'Elanna Torres dangled where she was, though her arms quickly began to ache from the strain.

After two minutes or so, the acceleration suddenly ceased. Torres squawked and flapped her arms in the sudden shift of "down." She fell into place in the command chair, guessing they were now traveling somewhere around three and a half kilometers per second.

The first indication she had that the car was actually sinking lower in the moon was when she begin noticing a distinct lessening of gravity. She checked with the tricorder and discovered gravity had indeed dropped from 0.2 g to nearly 0.1 g; as they neared the core, the gravity continued to diminish . . . a process that would reach the limit of zero-g at the very center, assuming it was hollow.

Many minutes passed, more than half an hour, and they were still barreling along. They said nothing to each other; they had nothing to say. Temporary crewmates did not always become fast friends.

"This might be awfully rough when we decelerate," said the skeletal pilot. B'Elanna did not respond, but she understood the problem: the human body can stand far more acceleration forward than it can backward. But moments later, the seats in the cabin, including the pilot's chair, slowly began to rotate. As soon as the seats were roughly opposite to the line of travel, the car shuddered and braked hard, just as hard as it had accelerated.

In the same length of time, two minutes, the car brought itself to a complete halt and automatically opened the cabin doors.

They were now so deep that gravitation was detectable only as a faint tug toward the floorplates—0.005 g, according to the handy tricorder, one two-hundredth of Earth's gravity. A slight movement pushed B'Elanna out of her seat and set her drifting toward the roof. Redbay was more circumspect, moving along the car and out the open door; after some fumbling around, Lieutenant Torres followed.

At the far-end platform, they tethered themselves as best they could with hands and feet, staring in silence. The platform dropped away in a kilometer-tall cliff face; the open space was so vast that the other side vanished into the blue haze of the moist air. Directly below them, the valley resembled nothing less than a monstrous dataclip packet, a power router with power conduits that must have been big enough to swallow the *Voyager,* and hundreds of thousands of kilometers of fiberoptic cable as thick as small tree trunks; a number of logic switches that B'Elanna dizzily estimated to be in the low millions; spark gaps wider than Hero's Gulch on the Klingon Homeworld; and arcing over the entire valley, forming a glittering gold dome, a godlike version of Kubla Khan's Xanadu, was an inverted, convex power-grid antenna. It was made of the same filament wire as the Faraday cage surrounding the sun. And oddly enough, though the sun grid was built to a scale unimaginably bigger than the one that spread now before them, B'Elanna Torres was more shaken by the current, smaller version. She felt her stomach contract to a tight fist, felt her breath catch in her throat: the problem with the grid surrounding the sun was that it was *too* big; it defied the mind's ability to comprehend . . . so her mind gave up and accepted it as an intellectual proposition only.

But the current grid was possible to take in all at once— perhaps the maximal size an object could be and still actually register as a single thing—unlike, say, a continent; no one walked around marveling at the size of a continent.

"Kahless's beard," she breathed, taking in the entire vista in one eyeful.

Redbay grunted. "Damn thing's big enough to scare the brass off a bald monkey," he said. "Don't tell me . . . that's the central power router, diffuser, whatever it's called. Isn't it?"

Setting herself to slowly rotate like a top, B'Elanna scanned in all directions. "There's nothing else of this magnitude anywhere in the moon," she confirmed. "This is it, Redbay."

He sighed. "I suppose there's no way to blow up the diffuser grid."

"Not unless you have about two hundred photon torpedoes in your pocket."

"Just a fallen star. No, I have no explosives; I don't even know where you would get any."

"I brought tools, not bombs. Oh well; have to leave the antenna alone. But maybe we can reroute some of those fiberoptic cables . . . well, the smaller ones, anyway." She mused for a moment, slowly drifting back to the deck after her scanning rotation. "I would bet the Furies built a thousand redundancies into the system; they couldn't know exactly how the power would flow during the supernova, and they wouldn't want to waste an erg. We can't just destroy systems; we have to set up an actual feedback loop that will channel the energy itself into an adjacent sector, frying all the circuits."

"Cut and paste."

"You got it. But how do we get down there?"

Redbay twisted sideways, placed his feet against the edge of the cliff, and launched himself out over the valley. B'Elanna gasped, then realized instantly that the gravity was so low he couldn't possibly get hurt.

Lieutenant Torres gritted her teeth; she had never before felt any twinges of acrophobia, but she was feeling it now, a huge boulder of phobic panic crushing her so she couldn't breathe. Residual from the terror beam? She thought she might be jumping at shadows for a long, long time to come. Refusing to allow a mere human to show her up, she planted herself and launched just as Redbay had, trying to mimic his trajectory as best she could.

Nevertheless, they landed a kilometer apart. Leg muscles simply weren't precise enough engines to calculate a good parabolic intercept.

Tapping her communicator, B'Elanna said, "Torres to Redbay; look toward the center of the valley . . . see that tall spike? I'd guess that was the focus collector for the antenna."

"All the power flows through there?" asked Redbay's disembodied voice.

"All the power flows through there. That's our target, Lieutenant; if we can loop those circuits around into a feedback loop, we've got a good chance to divert all the power long enough for the supernova to destroy the moon itself, and—"

"And the Furies get to sit and watch the tidal wave roll in." For the first time, B'Elanna heard real emotion in his normally grim, sardonic voice; she heard pure, malicious joy at the prospect of twenty-seven billion dead Furies.

A day ago, B'Elanna would have been appalled and sickened. But her whole life had changed since then. A day ago, B'Elanna Torres had never felt the whisper of the terror-projector needle into her brain.

Yesterday, she had not yet experienced the degrading horror, the humiliation of paralysis, the mind-numbing, marrow-freezing terror it induced.

Today, she would pull the switch herself, instantly, to fry all twenty-seven billion without a second thought.

"Head for the needle?" asked Redbay.

Torres nodded, then realized he could not see her. "Rendezvous at the needle; we don't have much time if we want to return to *Voyager*."

Redbay laughed, then signed off. *Now, what did I say that was so hysterical?* she thought angrily.

CHAPTER

23

PLANTING HER FEET, B'ELANNA TORRES LEAPED AS HIGH AS SHE could—more than sixty meters. She scrutinized the pole as it rolled past, looking for a panel, a door, an access port—a knob, anything. The antenna was smooth as glass all the way up; it was smooth as a mountain lake all the way back down.

She followed a slow spiral around the base; it was easier to move on her belly, as if she were climbing a cliff. The gravity was so close to zero that her stomach couldn't tell the difference; she was falling—a horrible feeling. She had dreaded every zero-g exercise at the Academy, and she still didn't like it.

At last she found something promising. At first, she didn't recognize the panel for what it was: it was colossal, an octagon with a diameter of eighty-four meters. She crawled the perimeter, at last finding a pair of three locks that evidently wanted a key . . . but not an electronic key; the tricorder told her there were no circuits—it was purely mechanical. The locks wanted an actual hunk of metal with teeth and notches to insert and turn!

She was staring reproachfully at the locks when Redbay finally joined her.

"Ancient locks," she said, pointing. "We need to find a—what did they call them?—a key ring."

"No we don't," said the dead-voiced lieutenant.

It took her a moment, but B'Elanna suddenly realized what he meant. She jerked away . . . a bad move under the circumstances, as Torres catapulted across the deck, landing twenty meters distant.

Redbay leveled an all-purpose lockpick and slipped it into the lock. Silently, the access hatch swung open.

Inside, they found at last the mother lode: bank upon bank of fiberoptic cables that carefully routed the electromagnetic pulse from surface, mirrors, and the giant collector into the various logic gates and circuits.

They had found the nexus where everything came together, the one piece of the system for which there were no failsafes, no redundancies, no dead-man switches to kill the power and try again. The Furies knew it would be a *one-shot deal* when the sun went supernova: there would be no second chances. Either the system would work, and they would be hurled through a brief, artificial wormhole to the Alpha Quadrant . . . or it would fail; and they would be dead, turned into ionized plasma by the stellar explosion.

But there are half a million of them! We can't make a difference!

B'Elanna had just removed one cable to read it when suddenly a horrible screech startled her. She dropped the pile of fiberoptics, and stared about wildly for the sound, nine-tenths convinced they had activated some ancient alarm system, and that soldiers were at that moment materializing out of nowhere, surrounding them. . . .

Redbay looked down at his commbadge. "Oh. That's for me."

"What the—!"

"I instructed the computer aboard the shuttlecraft to take whatever steps were necessary to lead the Furies away from us if they followed us here; that sound means they found the shuttlecraft . . . which has now left the moon."

"Left . . . *the moon?* You mean here? We're stranded here?"

"I'm afraid so, unless the shuttlecraft can outrun the Fury interceptors, which it can't."

B'Elanna stared at Redbay, who shrugged. "Torres, if they found the shuttlecraft parked just outside, how long do you think it would be until they came right here? If we can figure out that this is the Achilles' heel of the power collector, don't you think they can?"

"So that's it. We're . . . win or lose, we're not leaving."

Redbay said nothing, returning to stripping off the heavy sheathing designed to protect the cables from the electro-magnetic pulse preceding the matter stream that would tear the moon apart.

B'Elanna hesitated only for a moment; then she resumed testing every major cable to find the critical ones. All the while, she tried to summon up the Klingon warrior within, the one who would rejoice to die killing her enemies. But all she felt was numbness. B'Elanna Torres had spent so many years brutally suppressing her Klingon side that now she was unable to readily call upon it when needed.

If I get through this alive by some damned miracle, she thought, *I hereby resolve never to suppress my Klingon side again.*

Her commbadge beeped, startling her. She slapped at it, but the beep died in the middle of the second sound. "Torres. Is someone there?"

Silence; then the commbadge clicked alarmingly, a start-led beetle. Then silence again. B'Elanna frowned; it was a creepy feeling, to be buried deep within an artificial, alien moon, waiting for a supernova to destroy her—and to be called by a mysterious ghost who refused to announce himself.

After another minute, her badge beeped again. "Torres!" she snapped, hitting the metal repeatedly.

This time, she heard a staticky sine wave—a faint, ghostly voice almost seemed to overlay the white noise, as if she were listening to a conversation in another sector, thousands of light-years away, underwater.

"I don't know if you can hear me," she said, "but if this is *Voyager,* please come closer!"

B'Elanna removed her commbadge and attached it to the tricorder, boosting the gain and expanding the antenna. After another minute, the call returned . . . but this time, she actually made out most of the words.

"Janeway to Torres—[unintelligible] destroyed—do you read? Do you [unintelligible] assistance?"

"Captain! This is Torres; comm link breaking up, can't make out everything. We're fine. We need more time, more time, more time. Keep the Furies off us!"

"Torres—[garbled] shuttlecraft destroyed."

"We're fine. Redbay and Torres alive, working. What is happening? Is the ship all right?"

Suddenly the voice became clearer; the computer was beginning to compensate for the high level of electromagnetic interference put out by the collapsing star. "The ship is operational. Do you require assistance?"

"No, we're all right. We just need more time. Are we under attack?"

"We were, but we're [unintelligible]. How much time? In three minutes [unintelligible] be able to beam you back if the sun explodes."

In three minutes what? They would, or *wouldn't* be able to beam them out?

"Say again, please," said Torres, holding her breath.

"Radiation levels increasing. [Unintelligible] inoperative in three minutes. You must decide whether to [garbled]."

Well, that answers that stupid question.

"Stand by, please, Captain." B'Elanna had been cutting through one of the massive fiberoptic cables with her phaser welding-torch while she spoke; now the cable severed into two pieces. Grunting, she hefted the "hot" end up to an input cable, into which she had already bored a hole.

They were in near zero-g; but the cables were so stiff and massive, it still took all of her considerable strength to bend them into a loop. They kept wanting to spring open.

Redbay held the cable in place while Torres applied the polymer bonder and almost decided. "Captain, I . . ."

Torres stared helplessly at Redbay, who wouldn't look at

her. She didn't need to tell him what Janeway was really asking; he knew as well as she. They had no shuttlecraft, and it certainly would be too dangerous to send one from *Voyager* to pick them up after the sun went supernova.

Now that the ship had found them again, their only chance of escape was the transporter: but they would have to leave immediately, or they would lose the last window of opportunity.

B'Elanna Torres clenched her teeth, a lump rising in her throat. *Before I heard the captain,* she told herself, *I already accepted the inevitability of my own death.* Really, there was no choice to make. She had a duty that both human and Klingon could understand.

And Redbay—he lived for his revenge. He would be no problem.

"Captain—we won't be transporting out now. We have . . . there's too much to do. We'll let you know when we're finished."

"You won't [garbled] able—breaking up—[unintelligible] getting worse. This may be the last comm—[unintelligible]—chance—are you coming?"

B'Elanna finished gluing the cable and began cutting the next output. She stared down at her work. "No. Thank you, Captain. I really enjoyed serving under you . . . and I even kind of enjoyed being in one of these uniforms again. I wish—well, I wish things hadn't turned out quite as . . ."

Sometime during her speech, she became aware that the comm link had broken, and her voice trailed off into silence. There was a lot of work to do.

An hour flew past unnoticed until B'Elanna looked down at her tricorder. "Hey, it's getting pretty thick . . . uh-oh!"

"What's the problem?" asked Redbay with all the apparent enthusiasm of the man behind the complaints counter.

"Do you feel sick at all?"

"No."

"Well. You're going to."

"Radiation?"

"Not just EM; heavy particle radiation, hydrogen and helium nuclei; big, slow particles. Gamma, X-rays. It's getting dangerously high."

"You knew the job was dangerous when you took it," said Redbay comfortingly.

Torres's voice was small; she tried to make it bigger, but it trembled instead. "I just hope we survive long enough to make a difference down here." It wasn't exactly what she had been going to say, but it *was* what she should have said.

Redbay stared at their handiwork for the last ninety minutes, loops of fiberoptic cables as big around as a human leg, dangling from other cables like Christmas tinsel. He had always celebrated Christmas . . . before reporting aboard the *U.S.S. Enterprise,* the ship of his buddy Will Riker. Dead? Alive? When Redbay had driven through the wormhole, he might as well have left behind a dead world . . . for he could never hope to see any of them again.

And he was dying; every breath told him, sharp pain knifing down his lungs. He was feeling feverish, dizzy; he hadn't told B'Elanna, who seemed all right for the moment. Probably the Klingon genes. But he was sicker than he ever had been in his life.

And it would never get better; it would get worse and worse until he collapsed, entire columns of cells being crushed and collapsed by the blundering nuclear particles. A dead man; a walking, working dead man. But it didn't matter, because he was already dead. He died the day he discovered what waited for him beyond the grave. In the Furies' terror projector, Lieutenant Redbay discovered what lay beyond the curtain: *nothing.*

When he died, he knew he would cease to exist, utterly and terribly. No afterlife, nothing to live on. His despair was as great as his terror . . . and it was a rarefied terror indeed. He had screamed and crawled just as Torres had done; but it was a different thing. She was too young and hadn't seen what the Furies could do—her fears were more visceral; and when the terror projector stopped, so did the fright, after a decent interval.

But Redbay's horror was total . . . for it *never stopped.* He had looked into the eyes of tomorrow's death and seen only empty pools of endless gray. Redbay staggered under the weight of such existential agony, the certainty of pure chaos.

He stared toward his own death with a terror that mounted minute by minute, until it threatened to overwhelm even that fragile peace earned by acceptance of his own nothingness. Like he never was, never would be again; Redbay looked into the mirror and saw only the empty walls of the room, no reflection.

His hands shook as he held up another heavy cable to be polymer-glued into place. He and Torres were systematically connecting outputs to inputs, bypassing the power distributor that was supposed to channel and filter the raw energy. They were constructing the fiberoptic equivalent of a blast furnace, turning the moon's own energy collection back onto itself—where the staggering power unleashed would tear apart the tough construction of the moon and destroy the circuits that produced the giant, artificial wormhole.

That is, if they could short enough cables. *At this rate,* thought Redbay, *we should get it done—in about a year and a half. Dammit!*

He looked at B'Elanna, and suddenly he saw her as a woman, a beautiful woman; the human trapped within Redbay's shell of iron reached out for a last touch of humanity. "B'Elanna . . . would you—do you want to—be close one last time before you die?"

"No," she answered curtly.

So much for the brotherhood of humanity, he thought bitterly. Then he smiled, though she could not see; odds were he couldn't have done anything anyway, not sick as he was!

"Just a thought," he added, voice cold iron again. The brittle vulnerability was gone. He couldn't tell whether she had even hesitated before turning him down, but it didn't matter. The cables mattered; making sure twenty-seven billion Furies died by their own hand mattered. "How much longer?"

"At least forever," said B'Elanna Torres, using the same tone of voice with which she had refused him.

"Maybe we'll live that long."

Torres grunted, bending up another stiff cable.

CHAPTER
24

CAPTAIN KATHRYN JANEWAY SAT ON THE BRIDGE, STARING IN utter fascination at the viewer, where the image of the Furies' sun seemed to roil visibly. They had powered the ship up again, and again she could look directly at the sun and watch the astonishing process of collapse.

The Bela-Neutron devices—cosmic nanotechnology—were already absorbing so many hot bosons, the heavy particles like protons and neutrons, and leptons, the electronlike particles, as well as photons, units of light, that the sun was startlingly dark and cold. A human could almost stare at it directly . . . but not quite. The surface temperature remained a steady six thousand degrees, but the core, which had jumped dramatically when the sun suffered the first collapse from hydrogen-fusing to helium-fusing, was dropping again as the Bela-Neutrons gulped energetic particles and pumped out useless neutrinos.

Momentarily, the core temperature would drop cold enough no longer to be able to support helium fusion . . . and the sun had already contracted too tight to be held apart by mere hydrogen fusion. It would collapse again, causing the core temperature to rise staggeringly high . . . hot enough to begin fusing the next atomic element, lithium. Repeat as needed.

Eventually, the sun would blow itself apart in a colossal supernova. The Bela-Neutron devices would absorb a significant fraction of that energy, flinging it away uselessly; but the remainder would be more than enough to power the creation of a wormhole large enough to swallow the entire Fury planet and belch it forth into the Alpha Quadrant. The entire planet . . . twenty-seven billion warriors determined to rid heaven of all the Unclean.

Twenty-seven billion . . . and certainly some way to move the entire planet as if it were a starship, probably at warp speed. The Furies made the Borg look like pishers.

And 1.5 hundredths of a second after projecting the Fury planet through the momentary wormhole, the moon would vaporize. B'Elanna Torres would vaporize, and Redbay, too.

Or would they? A strange thought occurred to Janeway: Given the characteristics of the Bela-Neutron device, the energy that actually reached the moon might not be enough to rip the molecules apart. She shook her head; it was an impossible equation to calculate or even estimate, since no one had ever *made* a real, working Bela-Neutron device, so far as Janeway knew. But what if—what if the energy were enough to crack the moon like an egg, blowing it apart, but not enough to turn it into an ionized plasma of constituent atoms?

What if B'Elanna and Redbay were on the dark side of the tide-locked moon when it blew? Would they be flung into space to die horribly? She shuddered; far better if they were killed in the initial explosion.

Such thoughts made her morose, tempering the edge of her excitement. As a captain, Kathryn Janeway had several times ordered men, and one woman, to their deaths. But never with such certainty before. She started to feel the pain and quickly closed off the empathic section of her brain. She could not afford emotions now; she must become like Tuvok, for a few moments, at least . . . lest she try some wild, harebrained stunt to try to rescue them and lose the entire ship as well.

They're gone. They're already dead, she kept telling herself over and over. *They're already gone!*

She closed her eyes and saw B'Elanna spinning through the black, starry sky where once a planet had orbited, clawing piteously at her mouth, desperately trying to find air where there was only interstellar dust. She opened her eyes again and stared at the sun.

The ship's intercom beeped; the tense silence, as all waited for the inevitable, was broken by the doctor's voice. He sounded tense and agitated—an odd state for a hologram to be in. "Captain! Captain Janeway, I just had either a small epiphany or a ridiculous dream."

"A *dream?* Doctor, are you functioning properly?"

"I think so. Hold on a minute—yes, all systems are functioning within normal parameters."

"How did you come on-line?"

"Well . . . the truth is, nobody remembered to turn me off after I finished treating casualties from your little escapade with the Furies."

"I thought we gave you the ability to turn yourself off."

The doctor looked pensive, another neat trick. "So you did. But I . . . more and more, I find myself preferring to stay conscious. Conscious? Is that the word I want? I *feel* conscious."

Janeway felt herself getting impatient. "Doctor, is this going somewhere? What was your epiphany?"

"First, I have to ask you an engineering question: How violent will the explosion be by the time it gets to the moon?"

Janeway's eyebrows shot up toward her hairline. It was disconcerting in the extreme to have one's mind read by the emergency medical holographic program. "I've just been thinking about that very problem. I could run some simulations . . . but my gut tells me the explosion will destroy the moon—or at least the side facing the sun—but will not be powerful enough to vaporize it."

"What about the other side, the dark side? How much damage?"

"I don't know. Maybe it will remain mostly intact. Maybe my gut is wrong, and the entire moon will turn into a white, glowing plasma. Where are you going with this?" Despite her short tone, Janeway thought the doctor might well have something somewhere that would mutate a *Kobayashi Maru* exercise into something winnable, the way that James T. Kirk had reprogrammed that particular futile exercise.

"Well . . . I know it's a bit unorthodox, but it occurs to me that the human body may be a lot tougher than we generally think. I assume you know what happens when a human is suddenly subjected to a vacuum?"

"Um—explosive decompression?" It was only a difference of one atmosphere, like ascending through the water from a depth of ten meters to the surface. "Um, I think blood vessels in the lungs would rupture."

"Excellent; are you sure you don't want to join Kess as a medical student? I've run a few simulations while we spoke, and there are a lot of things that will go wrong to kill the human . . . but none of them *instantaneously*. The skin will freeze—but in empty space, it's not easy to radiate heat away, as you well know from your engineering studies. That won't happen as quickly as if the patient were dipped in liquid nitrogen, which is not as cold but transfers heat faster."

"Yes . . . yes—Doctor, are you saying that a person . . . ?"

"Blood vessels will rupture in the lungs, nose, and eyes; the patient will suffocate, but that would take longer than anything else."

"Doctor . . . what are you saying?"

The doctor paused; he was probably simply running all his simulations one more time to be sure, but it gave Janeway the impression of a man hesitating before suggesting something that might sound crazy.

"Captain, I believe the particular radiation that wreaks havoc with our transporters is the heavy neutrino flux from the Bela-Neutron devices, is it not?"

Janeway nodded, and the doctor continued.

"And after the shock wave of the supernova passes by us, the Bela-Neutron devices will be destroyed—and we'll regain functionality on our transporters."

Captain Janeway said nothing; her nod was barely perceptible.

"Then, Captain . . . if the away team is standing at the far side of the moon when the shock wave hits, and it is less severe than a normal supernova because of the Bela-Neutron devices, then they may survive the destruction. And if they do, Captain, I believe—I will stake my medical reputation that *they can survive the vacuum of space* for a few seconds, as long as ninety seconds, before they lose sufficient heat to be unresuscitatable.

"We can beam them directly to sickbay, Captain. One or both might survive."

Janeway stared, feeling a peculiar numbness touch her hands and feet. It was insane—let yourself be blown out into space, gambling that the *Voyager* can find you, lock on, and beam you aboard before you die? She had never heard of such a thing in all her years in Starfleet.

On the other hand, no one had ever seen an artificial supernova used to power an artificial wormhole, either. *The universe,* said the ancient Earth biologist J. B. S. Haldane, *is not only queerer than we suppose, but queerer than we can suppose.*

"Doctor, prepare sickbay to receive a pair of very, *very* cold crew members."

"Aye, Captain. EMH program out."

"Commander Chakotay, you have the conn."

"Yes, Captain. Where are you going to be?"

"Engineering. We *must* find a way to communicate with Torres and Redbay and tell them to get to the dark side as soon as they're able. Chakotay, monitor the sun using subspace sensors . . . when it goes nova, we'll have—what? seven minutes before the electromagnetic pulse hits, and another three hours for the shock wave of thrown-off star stuff to arrive. Keep the shields up; we'll ride out the explosion as best we can, then return and start fishing."

Janeway hopped up, more energized than she had felt in hours, and almost ran to the turbolift.

B'Elanna Torres let go the fiberoptic cable she had just epoxied and went limp. She was amazed how beat she was, even working in near zero-g . . . she was drenched with sweat, her hair plastered to her skull by the surface cohesion of salt water. She drifted on the random air currents, her feet pinioned to prevent her from drifting entirely away. She panted, eyes shut and mouth open.

Lieutenant Redbay held on to the cable, watching her; he seemed unaffected by the long, hot, sweaty work.

"Can't you even be a *little* exhausted?" she demanded angrily.

Redbay smiled, and B'Elanna shuddered. *His rage gives him all the energy he needs,* she realized.

They had done good sabotage. Scores of enormous cables now looped output directly into input, or directly into circuitry, input to input, output to output—anything that seemed likely to fry the ability of the moon to channel the energy of an exploding star into a productive, wormhole-producing beam of coherence.

She opened her eyes, unhooked her feet, and did a slow, 360-degree pirouette; and B'Elanna's heart sank, even in zero-g. It was not enough.

It was nothing! Nothing compared to the hundreds of thousands of cables still left, snaking "down" from the antenna to the power-grid circuitry beneath their feet. B'Elanna shook her head, gritting her teeth to hold back a scream of frustration, anger, and futility.

What? What do we damn well have to do? *We're not even making a dent here!*

"Do you really think this is going to stop the projector?" asked Redbay suddenly.

Torres gasped, staring at the mysterious lieutenant. Was he a psychic? Did he have one of those much-discussed human wild-talents? "Why did you ask that?"

"I followed your gaze. There are a hell of a lot of cables, aren't there? Are we making any difference?"

B'Elanna shook her head, defeated.

"Then maybe," suggested Redbay, "we should think of doing something else."

"Oh, thank you! Nice suggestion, Lieutenant . . . what do you suggest? Set the phaser on overload and blow up the moon? Spin the whole damn thing around to point into empty space? Stick a cork in the barrel of the wormhole cannon?"

Redbay smiled crookedly, like a homicidal Klingon just before going on a rampage with a *bat'leth.* "Now, *there's* an idea."

"Put a cork in it? Dammit, we don't even know where the barrel is!"

"No, the one before that."

"The phaser on overload? There's not enough power to—"

"No, no! The *middle* suggestion . . . turn the moon to point the wrong way."

"Turn the . . . ? Redbay, we can't turn the whole—"

"Look, the moon is tide-locked, right? And we all assumed that was because it needed to be pointed at the sun to collect the energy from the grid, right? But it's not just tide-locked; Torres, it's in the L-four stable-orbital position with respect to the sun and the Fury planet, isn't it?"

"I—did we ever check that? Probably . . . it's in the same orbit as the planet, about sixty degrees ahead of it. Yes, that would be the Lagrange-four stable-orbital point."

"And that means the sun, the planet, and the moon do not move with respect to each other, right?"

"That's the definition of L-four."

"Torres, don't you see it? They're not in L-four to point toward the sun . . . that's easy! It's the brightest thing in the solar system; you can't miss it.

"Torres, they're in the L-four spot *so they'll always point toward the planet.* They have to be pointed at exactly the right spot, or the wormhole won't form . . . or it will form away from the planet, and they won't pop through it or it'll take them the wrong direction—something!"

B'Elanna stood with her mouth open for a moment, mentally performing dozens of simulation calculations. "Blood of my enemies—you're right! It has to be! Redbay, do you know what this means? The slightest jar, the slightest change to the aiming mechanism, and the wormhole might miss the planet entirely!"

CHAPTER
25

"It's been a couple of hours since *Voyager* lost contact with us," said Redbay. "How long before the explosion?"

B'Elanna shrugged; she had no special knowledge. "No possible way of telling; as short as thirty minutes or as long as six hours."

"Then we'd better get moving fast, Lieutenant; we've got to find the aiming circuits soon, like yesterday, and start hooking up cables to short them out."

For nearly forty-five minutes, B'Elanna Torres scanned with her tricorder, reprogrammed the search pattern, and scanned again. Redbay alternately clenched and relaxed his hands. B'Elanna basically knew what she was looking for: a delicate mechanism surrounded by inertial and subspace navigation sensors with a direct connection to a point near the fulcrum of the eight-hundred-kilometer-long tube that was doubtless the "barrel" of the wormhole projector. The problem was that the description still produced a depressingly large number of possible "hits," which had to be sorted and evaluated by B'Elanna herself.

But she learned. When she found a potential valley site, she narrowed the focus and carefully worked up a three-dimensional picture of the location. Each was a bust, one way or another: insufficient energy to move the barrel, no line-of-sight to the planet . . . B'Elanna refined her search engine until, finally, she found a site she could not eliminate, not after ten minutes of fiddling.

"All right—I think . . . I think I might have it here. It's the best shot, anyway."

"We'd better take it," said Redbay, staring at his chronometer. "We can't afford any more time. It's this one or nothing, and we fail."

"Five kilometers, bearing, uh, thataway."

Torres in the lead, they hopped like antigravity jack-rabbits. The five kilometers flew beneath them in a few minutes, and Torres finally brought them down within a few hundred meters of the objective.

The beam-navigation chamber was not on the valley floor, but two hundred meters straight down, though *down* was a weak term this far toward the center of mass of the moon. There was no obvious access panel, and Redbay used his phaser to burn a path to the circuitry. Then, at B'Elanna's direction, he phased off thirty huge fiberoptic cables. The hand phaser was rapidly becoming the most useful tool they had brought with them, much to B'Elanna's annoyance; it was the only tool she hadn't foreseen.

They polymer-bonded one end of each cable to power-out junction boxes and pushed the other ends into the hole Redbay had carved. Then, together, the two lieutenants slid over the hole, grabbed the edge, and propelled themselves two hundred meters downward.

They worked feverishly, attaching cables to every delicate-looking circuit they could find, praying they could stick enough before the unseen sun went supernova—if it hadn't already. . . . It would be more than seven minutes, B'Elanna calculated, between supernova and the power surge striking the moon. The shock wave would be almost an afterthought, arriving a few hours later, depending on the violence of the explosion. When it did arrive, it would shred the moon like confetti.

It might already be all over. *We might be walking, talking dead people,* thought B'Elanna grimly.

Captain Kathryn Janeway—temporarily self-demoted to chief engineer—nervously wiped her hands and rearranged her hair bun, staring at the viewer on which was projected her newly devised comm-link procedure. Could she? Would she?

An hour's worth of brutal brainwork had convinced Janeway that there *was* a way to power up the communications link and punch through the radiation interference; but to do so, they would have to take the wedge-shield off-line and risk collapsing it utterly. The same modification that Carey had found to put a bend in the shield allowed Janeway to *extrude* the shield several hundred thousand kilometers in the direction of the bend.

That meant it could actually shield the comm link from the background radiation, but at a price: the shield would stretch so thin it would not function as a shield anymore. In fact, it might well stretch thin enough that the two sides touched; that would short out the circuitry, and the shield would flicker out of existence—permanently. Or at least until they repaired it—hours, maybe.

Dared she risk it?

"Lieutenant Carey, I need some input. How likely is the shield to break?"

Carey licked his lips. *He hates being put on the spot for an estimate when there's simply not enough data,* the captain thought. "That would depend on how far we extrude the shield, Captain. The farther, the—"

"I'm looking for a number, Carey; a percent chance."

Carey stared blankly. "Um, I'd give it a thirty-seven-percent chance, Captain," he said. His face flushed; he was starry-voiding, and she knew it. *I wonder where he pulled that number?*

Janeway knew it was fictitious; but she didn't care. "Thirty-seven," she said, pretending to take the number seriously. "That's not so bad. Done—prepare to extrude the shield, Mr. Carey."

Shaking, Carey nodded. "Aye, Captain." He placed his finger over the viewer, waiting for Janeway's command.

She swallowed. "Engage, Mr. Carey."

Carey touched the screen over the ProgStart label; Janeway watched the graphic in horrified fascination as the shield pulled together into a spike curve, the sides coming perilously close as the point extended for kilometer after kilometer. She watched the process, a mother cat watching her kittens; then she jabbed a forefinger and stopped the shields at just a hundred thousand kilometers' extension.

"I'm afraid to go any farther," she admitted. "Now, let's get down tight and dirty on that moon and get that comm link up!"

Lieutenant B'Elanna Torres worked in a frenzy, feeling the fool-killer creeping up behind her, his hands almost touching the back of her neck. Any minute now the sun would blow; any minute, any—

She felt driven, out of control, truly understanding Redbay for the first time since he was hauled aboard the *Voyager*. She had felt the secret terror; she knew. Never again could she calmly consider whether stopping the Furies was worth twenty-seven billion deaths. She knew.

When her commbadge beeped, Torres didn't respond. The sound seemed almost unreal. Then it beeped again, startling her out of her reverie, and she answered hurriedly.

"Torres, this is Captain Janeway. We have a brief window; I must tell you of a strange, new tactical development." So the captain began; B'Elanna found the theory wildly implausible and faintly cowardly, but she was lured by the thought of being the first Starfleet officer to take a swim in deep space without a suit and live to tell about it.

If she did live. "B'Elanna, I won't lie to you. I don't think this procedure has much of a chance for success."

"It's better than zero, which is what we have now."

"Yes."

"You'll be able to scan for our bodies?"

"I think so. Probably. Is there any way for you to get to the other side of the moon? Maybe you'd better start now."

"Actually, we have our ways. How long from when you detect the final collapse until the sun actually explodes?"

"We're not sure, Lieutenant; maybe as long as thirty minutes."

"That's all? That's pushing it . . . we might not make it to the other side. Captain, can you warn us as soon as you detect the final collapse?"

"Yes. You'll leave immediately for the other side?"

"Aye, Captain. Wait . . ." B'Elanna trailed off as she got busy gluing another fiberoptic cable into the beam-aiming system.

"We'll call you as soon as the sun collapses. Janeway out."

As soon as the captain signed off, Redbay spoke. "I thought they couldn't contact us again."

B'Elanna shrugged. They had not wasted time discussing the obvious. Evidently Janeway, with her magnificent grasp of engineering, had even figured a way around *that* problem. She returned to her new, gainful employment as a saboteur. After a moment's thoughtful gaze into the ceiling, Redbay appeared to dismiss the unexpected miracle chance for survival and get down to the serious business of stopping the invasion.

Captain Janeway ceased communications, but she kept open the comm link. Almost immediately, Ensign Kim's voice came over the ship's intercom. "Captain . . . solar flux increasing significantly. We're having some trouble with navigation; the heavy-particle stream is interfering with our sensors."

"Ensign, stay in this orbit! Don't drift away . . . this is a very fragile comm link. Is Lieutenant Paris still—"

"Aye, Captain," interrupted Kim—a rare occurrence. "Paris is preoccupied keeping the ship on—"

"Well, don't let's break his concentration. Should I come up?" Janeway held her breath, then got the answer she was looking for.

"No, Captain; I think we're all right if we just shut off the thrusters and orbit naturally. We'll be less likely to . . . *Holy*—! Captain, we're drifting!"

"Oh, no." Janeway stared as the field began to stretch,

growing narrower and narrower. "Janeway to Paris! Lieutenant, why are we moving?"

"Captain," said Paris, "we've got a stuck impulse throttle! Trying to compensate . . . The radioactive bombardment—"

"Kill the engines, now!"

"I've been trying," said Paris's professionally calm voice. "Controls are frozen . . . it's because we don't have enough shielding from the ambient solar-radiation flux."

Janeway let out an exasperated sigh. "Great! Paris, without this shield extrusion, there wouldn't be any reason to *be* here in the first place!"

"Captain," said Lieutenant Carey, "I don't want to intrude, but the extrusion is stretching dangerously thin."

Janeway stared. Carey was right. "Carey, prepare to terminate shield extrusion. Paris, get that damned engine under control! Carey, on my signal: three, two—"

Kathryn Janeway never got to zero. As she said the word *one,* at the tip of the extrusion, the two sides of the shield-wedge touched. The shield was not infinitesimally thin; it had a thickness . . . and when the total diameter shrank below twice that diameter, the opposite sides had no choice but to contact each other, like stretching a rubber balloon.

With not a bang but a whisper, all shield-intensity readings across the engineering console dropped immediately to zero. The pointers rotated all the way counterclockwise to the idle amplitude. The forward shields were dead.

They had lost their corridor; within a few hundredths of a second, they lost their comm link. Janeway stared in shock, realizing it would take hours to restore the shields; and in the meantime, if *Voyager* were facing toward the sun when it exploded, then the ship would end up slagged like the artificial moon itself.

"Paris," she said, grabbing control again, "turn the ship directly outboard the sun and *hold that position;* keep the sun aft!" That was the most important point; the aft shields would probably be sufficient to protect the ship, *if* they kept their stern pointed directly toward the sun.

Carey looked stricken. "Captain . . . should I—?"

"Start rebuilding the forward shield? Yes . . . and get that wedge into it so we can try to restore the comm link . . . move it!"

They wouldn't be able to warn Torres and Redbay. All Janeway could think was that she had promised to warn the away team, and now they weren't going to get that chance. B'Elanna and Lieutenant Redbay would have no idea the explosion was coming until the force of it struck their location, turning the moon into a floating cenotaph.

CHAPTER

26

B'ELANNA TORRES TRIED TO UNCRAMP HER FINGERS, BUT HER hand remained stubbornly clenched around a lump of fiberoptic cable. "Damn," she muttered. She strained back; the epoxy held, welding the cable end to the aiming circuit, but her abused muscles held as well, and she flapped uselessly from the cable like a flag attached by only one stanchion. "Don't just float there," she snapped, "pull me off!"

"You look so picturesque," offered the deadpan Redbay, "wafting gently in the breeze."

"You need sleep. You're hallucinating. It's a human thing; Klingons don't need—"

"*My* hand isn't locked in the On position," pointed out the expatriate lieutenant.

"Shut up! Just unhook my fingers. When the hell is that Federation going to call us? She should at least check in and let us know the comm link is still up."

Redbay stared unblinking. "If it *is* still up."

Suddenly filled with the sense of something urgent forgotten, B'Elanna slapped her commbadge. "Torres to Janeway.

245

Torres . . . Captain, do you read? Does anyone read? Great! Just peachy! It's down—it's been down for . . . for I don't know how long—the sun is probably gone supernova, and we're going to be fried in about seven minutes!"

"Torres, I think we've done about as much as we can here." Redbay gestured; all but three limp cables had been attached to various junctions and black boxes on what they hoped was the wormhole cannon aiming system.

"We're not done yet."

"If you want to live, I suggest we leave."

"We're not done yet."

Looking into B'Elanna's determined face, Redbay shrugged. *It's all the same to him,* thought the Klingon; *he died fifty thousand light-years back in the Alpha Quadrant.* Redbay pried her hand loose from the cable, and she flexed it while Redbay took over the glue job.

They took fifteen more minutes; as the hours had progressed, they became steadily faster at attaching cables to inputs, outputs, and logic switches.

"Well, Princess, can we leave orbit now?"

B'Elanna tapped at her tricorder with aching fingers. "I think there's a subway shaft heading toward the surface, opposite the sun, about six kilometers away; bearing one-one-one-one."

Taking long, slow, graceful leaps, they made the distance quickly. The shaft began some two hundred and fifty meters above their heads; evidently, the maintenance workers who serviced the valley would have used some sort of transport vehicle to get around . . . a not unreasonable guess, anyway.

But a quarter-kilometer was a long, long way to jump—even in such a low gravity. Redbay looked dubious. "That's like a jump of over a meter on Earth," he muttered, shaking his head.

"So?"

"I don't think we can make it."

"We? What do you mean *we?*"

Redbay looked at her. "Oh? How high can *you* jump?"

"I may be half human, but I'm also half Klingon. We value athletic ability. I can make it."

"If it's all the same," said Redbay with a cryptic smile, "I think I'll help you a bit. And I really have enjoyed working with you."

"Oh . . . uh, thanks." *What was he talking about?* B'Elanna shook her head; humans—Starfleet officers—were unpredictable even in the best of circumstances, let alone under pressure.

Redbay made a cradle with his hands; B'Elanna stepped into it and he launched her. She timed her leap to give her maximal push-off from his hands. B'Elanna Torres sailed into the air, closer and closer to the ladderlike rungs of the end of the subway shaft.

Her upward motion slowed and peaked . . . thirty meters below the target; slowly, like a petal in the wind, she fell back to the valley floor. They tried once more with even less effect; this time, B'Elanna got a bad push-off and rose only about fifty meters.

Redbay stared upward. "Shame you don't have three hundred meters of rope."

"Eh? I have plenty of Nylex rope."

Redbay stared at her. "More than two hundred and fifty meters?"

"Four hundred."

Shaking his head incredulously, he asked for it. "You wouldn't happen to have a grappling hook, would you?"

"A what?"

"Hm." He tightened the beam on his phaser to a fine, thin cutting blade and proceeded to cut away a hunk of some strange alloy—not the phaser-impervious metal—and shape it into the rough form of a three-pronged hook. Then he tied it off to the rope and began to cast. It took him eleven tries to finally hook the grapple through one of the ladder rungs. He tugged a few experimental times, then pronounced it fit to climb. "Torres," he asked, puzzled, "why didn't you tell me you had the rope? And *don't* say because I didn't ask."

Torres swallowed the reply she had been about to make. "I was just going to tie it off on the shaft so you could climb up."

"You were going to . . . ?" He shook his head, amazed. "I thought—only one of us was going to make it out."

"Don't be a jerk. I am human, not just Klingon."

"You are Starfleet," he said softly, "not just Maquis."

She glared, then took the rope and began to climb.

The shaft led straight up seventy meters, then debouched onto a sloping mag-lev track. No subway car waited for them. "Look for a button," B'Elanna suggested. The feeling of impending doom tightened her gut. Any moment now, the sun could—or maybe it *already had.* There would be a lag time of seven and a half minutes until the energy pulse hit them, perhaps another hundred and eighty before the heavy particle bombardment, the expanding explosion, tore the moon apart. At the core, even if they survived the initial explosion, it would take the *Voyager* too long to sort them out from all the other debris. They would die, either incinerated by the residual radiation left behind by the supernova . . . or, if the Bela-Neutron devices absorbed enough of the energy, frozen in the interstellar vacuum.

B'Elanna checked her trusty tricorder, a device she was more and more beginning to think of as her lifeline back to the light, out of the long darkness of their suicidal mission. She stared, seeing a strange reading. It took her a few moments to figure out what was rushing toward them. "Hey, Redbay—what did you press?"

"Nothing. I haven't found any—"

"The subway's on its way; we should see it in . . . hell, there it is!"

The blur in the distance raced closer, alarmingly fast; then it braked to a rough, angry halt scant meters from where the two stood, immobile with surprise. The doors popped open; quickly, before it could change its mind, Redbay and Torres launched toward the open hatch. B'Elanna missed slightly, grazing her head on the hatch rim. She struggled to a chair and pushed herself into it, using her feet against the seat ahead of her; only then did she clench her teeth and rub her injured scalp, which bled profusely. The blood drifted out and finally down, bright globules of red darkening visibly as they wafted toward the deck.

The train started with a lurch—Redbay had touched the forward panel—and B'Elanna was kicked back into her seat with an acceleration eight hundred times what they had lived in for the past seven hours.

She fell back into her seat in agony, unable to breathe, still dizzy from the blow. Her inner ears refused to orient themselves; her balance insisted she was lying on her back on a terribly dense planet, being slowly crushed to death.

At last, after two minutes, the acceleration ceased abruptly, and B'Elanna Torres could breathe again. She gasped for air while gravity slowly returned to the "bottom" of the car, increasing perceptibly with every second's travel of five kilometers, some of it upward.

"Now—comes—the long wait," she wheezed. "We going—to make it?"

Redbay did not answer. Looking across the car toward the front, B'Elanna saw that the man was sound asleep.

She debated waking him, then realized that he would have plenty of time to wake up and panic when the explosion came, the explosion that would almost certainly kill the pair of them anyway. Both would have the same chance to get a last breath before being blown into free space to die horribly.

They were virtually at the surface itself, by the tricorder's estimation, when suddenly the lights flickered. A huge, loud thud jarred B'Elanna's sensitive ears; the whole car skewed violently to one side, and she heard a loud scraping noise. It took her a second to realize that the car had lost all power . . . the electrical power was gone.

With a chill, Lieutenant Torres realized that the electro-magnetic pulse had just struck the moon. *It's all over,* she thought in near panic; *either we won or we lost . . . either the Furies jumped to the Alpha Quadrant, and when we return, we'll return to a dead, alien battlefield, or they didn't make the jump, and—*

And what? There were too many possibilities. "Redbay," she called, as the train ground slowly to a stop, friction eating away at even their terrific speed. "Redbay, wake up!"

"I'm awake," he said, bleary-voiced. "Who turned out the—"

"Start the timer, Lieutenant. The car didn't make it all

the way to the top before the pulse fried the power circuits. We've got about a hundred and eighty minutes before the explosion . . . three hours to make—looks like two point five kilometers. A little less than a kilometer per hour, straight up." It was harsh, but just barely possible in the low gravity of the moon.

"B'Elanna? It was a pleasure working with you. I'm glad we—"

"Redbay, didn't we go through all this? We're dying in battle, of a sorts, with the greatest enemy our quadrant has ever faced. Isn't that enough?"

Silence. Then Redbay responded, cynical and sardonic as ever. "Sure. My little heart is all aglow with the honor of it."

B'Elanna closed her eyes. The tricorder was programmed to give her a signal every hour, then at the final thirty minutes, ten minutes, and a big alarm the last minute before the explosion, to give her time to hyperventilate, supersaturate her tissues with oxygen, a last-ditch technique she had discussed with Redbay.

It would alert her. She could close her eyes, offer a last prayer for an honorable death to Kahless the Eternal. They started the long climb up the ladder that ran along the inside of the shaft. Three hours for two and a half kilometers—not impossible on level ground. An absurdity climbing a ladder.

She smiled; she would finally get a chance to see whether she was human or Klingon in the end.

CHAPTER

27

COME ON, URGED CAPTAIN JANEWAY SILENTLY TO HERSELF; *come up—just for a moment, just long enough to warn—*

Not for the first time, Janeway wondered why they don't teach the most important command course at the Academy: how to be in two places at the same time. She was in engineering, monkeying with the shields; she desperately needed to be on the bridge.

"Captain," said Lieutenant Tuvok from the bridge, "I must inform you that we are being bombarded by subspace chroniton particles. I believe the final, chain-reaction collapse has just begun. In approximately one and a half minutes, the star will experience full collapse and will explode into a supernova. We have about nine minutes before the radiation front arrives."

"Mr. Kim . . . ?"

"We're not at a safe distance, Captain."

"Mr. Paris, take us into the moon's shadow. If we're lucky, that's where Torres and Redbay will be anyway. I'm on my way to the bridge. Carey, keep on those shields! Damn—I wish we had sensors." Janeway cut off the rest of her complaint; the radiation levels were simply too high.

"Aye, Captain." Paris pressed an illuminated square on his viewer, and the ship changed course.

Janeway continued her frenzied work, trying with Lieutenant Carey to restore the forward shields and give them their new wedge shape, so she could extrude the shields and restore communications—or work the transporters—despite radiation interferance. But the bioneural circuitry of the *Voyager* had reacted badly to the short when the shield walls touched; in fact, if the doctor were to examine them, he would probably pronounced the cells "in anaphylactic shock," as if they were truly biological and suffering a severe allergic reaction to each other.

Now she stepped off the turbolift; ship safety had just taken precedence even over the shield operation. Chakotay rose and shifted to the his seat as Janeway sat down.

"Kept it warm for you," said the commander with a wink.

"Janeway to all ship's personnel," said the captain. She waited a beat, then spoke to the entire ship. "Attention, crew; this is Captain Janeway. As I explained, the star is just now collapsing and will momentarily become a supernova. There may be disruption of critical systems; I'm putting the ship on red alert.

"The *Voyager* will easily survive the explosion. I want all transporter manned with a double staff, immediately.

"Thank you all; it is as always a pleasure being your commanding officer. That is all."

Janeway waited a moment for the computer to realize her transmission was over. "Activate EMH program."

"Please state the nature of the emergency," said the doctor from the viewer; then he nodded. "Ah. I see you are about to engage in some dangerously theatrical maneuvers in the middle of a supernova. Do you, by any chance, expect any casualties?"

"This isn't the time for sarcasm, Doctor. Prepare sickbay for crew injuries and for the imminent arrival of Torres and Redbay."

"Aye, Captain. The ERT crash-crew is already standing by."

"Good. Now all we have to do is wait for—"

"Captain," interrupted Tuvok, "two large Fury ships off the starboard bow." His laconic voice belied the shocking intelligence.

"What? Where?" Instinctively, Janeway glanced first at her own sensor-slave display on the arm of the command chair.

"The sensors do not register them because of the radiation. They are, however, visible on the forward viewer."

Janeway looked up. The two Fury ships were nothing like the small patrol craft they had fought earlier. These were long, cigar-shaped, sporting hundreds of metallic tendrils with pods on the ends—weapons? Sensors? Fighter spacecraft? It was impossible to tell until they did something, by which time it might be too late.

"Paris—how'd they get so close?"

Lieutenant Paris squinted. "Um . . . they're not very close, Captain; by the magnification and the parallax effect, I'd say they were, oh, a couple of hundred thousand kilometers."

The bridge fell silent, everyone doing the same calculation. "Tuvok," said Janeway with quiet authority, "check my math on this: assuming Mr. Paris is correct, *how* big are those ships?"

"Mr. Paris's estimation is essentially correct," concluded the Vulcan, "and the Fury ships are approximately two hundred and eighty kilometers long, seventy kilometers in diameter, and the pylons supporting the pods extend some three hundred kilometers from the center. By the albedo and color, I suspect their hulls are made of the same dense metal we observed on the Fury planet."

"Mr. Paris, come about one-eight-zero degrees," ordered the captain without hesitation.

"Turn *around?*"

"Yes, Lieutenant. Turn and run like hell."

A bright flower bloomed at the forward end of a pod, then another at another pod; while Paris turned the ship, maintaining a video feed at the ships in the upper half of the forward viewer, Janeway watched seven more flowers bloom bloodred from seven more pods.

"Evasive maneuvers, Mr. Paris; those are weapons of

unknown strength—but probably a damn sight more deadly than the scout ships' disruptor cannons!"

The *Voyager* began an intricate, preprogrammed series of evasions—Janeway recognized the pattern as EMP 11-Delta—but the flowers kept turning to track. They moved somewhat slower than photon torpedoes, but faster than the nuclear missiles the smaller ships had occasionally fired.

"Kim," snapped Janeway, "can you get a phaser lock on the missiles?"

"Uh . . . uh . . . no, ma'am! I mean Captain! The sensors won't—"

"Mr. Kim, photon torpedoes; program them to home by visual image on the missiles. Fire as soon as you've set the program."

"Aye . . ." Kim pounded frantically at the console, muttering below the audible range.

Janeway sat in her command chair, staring at the screen, forcing herself to remain outwardly calm, confident, in command: the consummate starship captain. Inside, she was screaming in utter panic; these Fury ships dwarfed the biggest thing the Borg had ever thrown at the Federation . . . and *the Voyager had no forward shields!*

One of the missiles had already tracked too close for a safe shot by the photon torpedo; fortunately, the torpedo's own programming caused it to bypass the near missile and focus on one farther away. The torpedoes and the flower-missiles met in empty space; the explosions lit the starry sky with a flare so bright that the viewer could filter it only by whiting out the entire field of view, both ahead and behind. In the brief flash before the light flared, Janeway could actually see a shock wave spreading at about half light speed; six hammer blows struck the ship's rear shields, sending the *Voyager* skittering in a random direction, tumbling so hard the inertial dampers could not keep up, and the crew were flung against their combat harnesses.

The tumble saved them; the shock waves blew the ship out of the first missile's path, and it could not turn fast enough to track. It brushed past and continued into nowheresville, out of sight and out of mind—so Janeway thought.

"Damage report!" she shouted, trying to be heard over the residual explosions and the red-alert klaxon; "and shut that bloody noise off!"

Tuvok killed the klaxon while he rattled off a list of decks damaged by the multiple explosions.

"Captain," said Kim, his face paling as he stared at the rearview viewer. "One, two, three, four more rose-missiles launched from the second Fury ship!"

"Wonderful," snarled the captain. Then she smiled. "Mr. Paris—hard about one-eight-zero again; let's try driving right down their throats . . . see how smart their missiles really are."

Paris grinned; but it was a bloodless smile. He manhandled the ship hard about and began dancing and dodging toward the closest Fury.

"Captain," said Tuvok, cutting through the soldier's fog that had seized the bridge crew, "the missile we evaded has turned around and is closing on us again."

"Still? What's the intercept ETA?"

Tuvok closed his eyes for a moment; in a pinch, the Vulcan could calculate quicker than consulting the computer. "At the present velocity and course, it should strike us just about the time we intercept the nearest Fury ship."

Janeway leaned back; she was so awash in adrenaline—battlefield pump—that she was actually intoxicated on it. She smiled, mirroring Paris. "Gentlemen," she said slowly, "have you ever played the ancient Earth game of chicken?"

"No," said Kim.

"Of course," said Paris simultaneously. Chakotay merely sucked a breath through his teeth.

"I am not aware of such a game," added Tuvok pettishly. "How is it germane to our present difficulties, Captain?"

"Mr. Paris: dead-on toward the closest Fury ship, constant heading. Ramming speed," she added thoughtfully.

"Aye, *aye,* Captain!" Paris changed course to point directly toward the gigantic target and increased the *Voyager*'s velocity to full impulse. "Show *them* who's chicken," he mumbled.

The two ships closed at a terrific rate, and behind *Voyager,* the missile gained on them both. As they cracked the hundred-thousand-kilometer range again, a number of smaller weapons on the pylons opened fire on the Starfleet ship. Energy beams, the terror projector, and tracers flared across the gap, trying to focus on the incoming kamikaze.

"Captain," reminded Chakotay, leaning forward, chin in hand, like Rodin's *Thinker,* "we have no forward shields. One shot and we're dead."

"If *we're* flying blind, *they're* flying blind. Ensign, return fire, photons and phasers. Aim manually using the computer . . . let's see whose fire-control system is the better!"

Like two wounded duelists riding toward each other firing their flintlocks, thought Janeway, slipping into a fantasy from the era of her favorite holodeck program, *one of us ends up with a pistol-ball in his gut.*

Tuvok called the distance: "Fifty thousand . . . forty . . . thirty . . ."

Paris's hands began to tremble as they hovered over the helm console, ready to pull away. But Janeway did not give the order.

The ship loomed so large it overflowed the viewer; Paris stepped back the magnification, but within seconds, they stared at a solid wall of metal at normal view.

Lieutenant Paris aimed *Voyager* for the largest viewport—the window alone could swallow the entire Federation ship.

At ten thousand kilometers, Tuvok began ticking off each thousand: "Nine, eight, seven, six—"

Captain Janeway crossed her legs. She folded her hands neatly in her lap. She said nothing. She quickly lost all perspective: the Fury ships were as large as good-sized asteroids! Dark in color with few reference points or markings; seconds before impact, an impact that would destroy the smaller ship, Janeway hallucinated that they were dive-bombing an enormous city of the dead—or Pan-Demonium, City of All Demons in hell.

Next to her, Chakotay leaned back in his chair, gripping the sides. The computer continued firing, aiming at the weapon sites up and down the pylons. Still, the Fury fire-control computers had not been able to lock on to the onrushing starship.

Chakotay sucked in yet another huge breath, face white as porcelain. He grinned through clenched teeth, unblinking. Janeway understood perfectly; she wanted to duck and put her head under her arms—but she was "driving," in a real sense.

"Two thousand—one thousand—seven six five four—"

At one hundred fifty kilometers, Paris evidently couldn't stand the suspense. He grabbed the console in a panic, not waiting for orders, and threw the guidance control all the way right and forward.

The shriek of ripping metal—*not the hull!* begged the captain—cut through the bridge silence like needles through a drumskin. Janeway was pulled so violently against her seat that for an instant, less than a second, she blacked out. When she blinked back to consciousness, she saw nothing but the artificial moon ahead of her; in the rear view, she saw the Fury ship illuminated against a flash as bright as a stellar core.

A fraction of a second later, the shock wave from the hunting missile struck the *Voyager.*

The bright blue glow of hell surrounded the ship in all directions, matting out the stars, the missiles, the faint, twisted threads that once were Fury ships. For a brief instant, before the video feed in all directions went blank, Kathryn Janeway saw the outer skin of the moon boiling away like water on a hotplate.

The supernova's radiation front had finally arrived.

CHAPTER

28

STILL GROGGY, JANEWAY STARTED TO RECOIL BEFORE REMEM-
bering she was looking at a video—a video that had just
vanished, as the external holocams were fried by an electromagnetic pulse of many giga-ergs.

She staggered to her feet to rouse the others, but Tuvok
was already doing so. The Vulcan lieutenant appeared
unruffled, but it took the two of them to get Kim and Paris
back to consciousness; the weapons officer had struck his
head on his console when he was slammed down by one of
the explosions.

While Tuvok revived his auxiliary cadet crew members,
Janeway took command of the situation. "Kim, get that
viewer repaired."

"Captain, the exterior monitors are gone." Kim held his
hand to his head; Janeway could see blood dripping from
the slash, but she couldn't spare the ensign, not even long
enough to send him to sickbay.

"Replicate new ones and send someone EVA—in a rad
suit—to replace them . . . we've got to have our eyes! We
don't have much time. Janeway to EMH program."

"EMH here."

"Doctor, how many injuries?"

"I was already treating twenty-two casualties. I've got a lot more now, mostly minor."

"Casualty report?"

"There are no deaths among the crew, Captain. Seventy-two reported injuries so far, mostly from falling and striking body parts against panels, railings, and consoles."

"We've got a head injury up here; can you send a medtech up for Ensign Kim?"

"On her way, Captain."

"Thank you. Janeway out. Paris! How long before we can see again?"

"Uh . . . looks like engineering is estimating two hours to get the monitors back on-line."

"Two hours! We only have three total!"

"Well, that's what they're saying," responded Paris reproachfully.

"All right, get 'em hopping. Offer them time and a half."

"Offer them *what?*"

"Never mind. Old Earth reference. Sensors?"

Tuvok answered. "You will not be able to use the sensors for at least seven hours, unless you depart the immediate vicinity of the supernova. There is too much radiation of all types at every frequency."

"Great. We have to get those monitors up. Get all nonessential crew members to viewports—*filtered* viewports. When that shock wave hits, the moon will literally disintegrate. I'll want every eye on this ship watching for B'Elanna and Redbay. Report any sighting immediately to Lieutenant Tuvok for relay to the transporter teams."

The turbolift doors slid open and Kes hustled into the room, carrying a medikit. The elfin Ocampan stood over Ensign Kim and expertly repaired his split scalp. "It's nothing major," she said, loudly enough that Janeway could hear.

The captain fidgeted, waiting for Kes to make some cold point about what they had done; but Kes surprised her, saying nothing. The Ocampan finished with Kim, then tended to the rest of the cuts and bruises on the bridge. "The doctor is handling the serious cases in sickbay," she said, wiping the sweat from her eyes with the back of her hand. Her hair was matted; she looked harrowed. *She's not going to sleep very well,* thought Captain Janeway. *I wonder if any of us will.*

The last thought echoed around the caverns of Janeway's skull as she nervously felt behind her for the captain's chair, trying not to show the hollow emptiness she felt.

She sat down again. "Well, that's it, gentlemen. Whatever was going to happen, happened. Either the Fury planet disappeared . . . or it's not going to." She paused, almost afraid to ask the next question. "Well . . . ? Can anybody pick it up on visual?"

Chakotay leaned into the ship's intercom. "Attention, all crew; this is Commander Chakotay. All nonessential personnel are to report *immediately* to any *filtered* viewport on decks seven through nineteen. Do not, repeat, *DO NOT* use the viewport on the hangar deck, since it has no radiation filter.

"For right now, each crew member should look for the Fury planet. Our external sensors and monitors are inoperative . . . we're down to eyeballs, people. So look sharp; senior officer or petty officer in every viewport stateroom report to the bridge what you saw. Chakotay out." He turned to Janeway. "Well, now we sit. And wait."

"Damn, I hate this," she said quietly. "I wish there were something more we could do. I can't stand just sitting. Chakotay, you have the conn; I'm going to inspect the ship."

"Captain," said Tuvok, "I do not wish to overly alarm you, but I suggest you continue working on restoring the shield extrusion instead."

Janeway frowned. "I was going to make a damage inspection of the ship and see to the wounded in sickbay."

"Our aft shield is too flat; when the stellar material strikes us, it will act as a sail on an early sailing vessel, propelling us forward. Captain, unless you restore the wedge-shield and point the bow toward the supernova, we will be blown far off course by the particle barrage . . . perhaps into the moon itself at twelve thousand kilometers per second, sufficient energy to destroy the ship with or without a shield."

"I hadn't thought of that. Yes, the wedge would deflect the particle stream to either side and stabilize us."

"And unless you re-create the shield-extrusion formula, we will find ourselves unable to lock on to Lieutenants Torres or Redbay to beam them aboard, even should we find them."

I forgot about that too! she raged to herself. *I'm fading fast—what's the matter with me?* But outwardly, she nodded and said, "Yes, I know." The captain of a starship had a duty to appear calm and confident in front of the crew.

Commander Chakotay spoke up, interrupting his stream of commands to various departments on the *Voyager.* "If it's all right with you, Captain, I'll conduct the inspection and visit the wounded. I had a lot of practice patching up ruptures in my old Maquis ship."

Janeway smiled. "Ganging up on the captain, eh? Banishing me to engineering? Well, good luck. Kim, keep a sharp eye out for more Fury ships. And Paris—recalculate the moon's orbit assuming . . . assuming the Fury planet suddenly vanished. Just in case."

"I've finished," said Kes. Janeway jumped; she had completely forgotten about the Ocampan.

"Finished?"

Kes's hair hung in front of her eyes, muting her look—for which the captain was profoundly grateful. She did not want to meet Kes's stare, not yet. "Yes, Captain. I've finished tending the wounded. May I leave? The doctor may need me in sickbay."

"Disappear." As Kes turned to leave, Janeway added, "Oh, and Kes? If you get a chance when the time comes . . . take a look out a viewport. Might see something. Every eye counts." Janeway smiled.

Kes, standing at the turbolift doors, nodded slowly; but she said nothing, just turned and left. During her entire visit, she hadn't said a word about the Furies, the dead, the potentially inconceivable destruction.

In a way, thought the captain, *I almost wish she had.*

Janeway rose; just as she was about to enter the turbolift,

Chakotay stopped her with a word. He listened grimly, nodding occasionally, though the communication was audio only—directed so that only Commander Chakotay could hear it. He looked up as he severed the connection. "Captain," he said, his voice at once sad and sympathetic, "I've heard back now from four view stations, including two department heads."

Feeling a cold hand grab her intestines, Janeway asked the sixty-four-kilobar question: "Is the planet still there, Ex?"

Chakotay said nothing for a moment. The invisible hand squeezed hard; it was all Janeway could do not to double over from the pain . . . was it stress?

"No, Captain," said the executive officer at last. "The planet is no longer in orbit around the sun. It has . . ."—he turned his hands palm-up—" . . . vanished," he concluded.

Utter silence reigned on the bridge. Not a man or woman there did not know what that meant. All their plans, all their—

"Captain," interrupted Lieutenant Tuvok, "I have an anomalous reading."

"Yes, Mr. Tuvok?" Janeway suddenly was so weary, she could fall asleep on her feet.

"The reading is difficult to isolate because of the extreme level of electromagnetic radiation enveloping this system. But tetrion particles are singularly transparent to high-energy photons, and are produced in copious amounts in the vicinity of a wormhole.

"Using the stream output, I was able to make a reasonable estimate of the main direction the wormhole occupied.

"Captain, wherever they went, they were *not* heading toward the Alpha Quadrant."

Janeway hesitated. "They weren't? Which way were they headed? Where does the wormhole terminate?"

Tuvok checked his screen. "I cannot tell without better sensors where the wormhole terminates; but the part of it I can readily see is heading in the general direction of the Lesser Magellanic Cloud."

Janeway could not figure out what Tuvok was saying exactly; but she knew enough to relegate it to the back burner, so she could concentrate on the most important task: restoring the shield system, wedge and extrusion and all, before the wave front arrived and flung the *Voyager* millions of kilometers away.

Lieutenant B'Elanna Torres hauled herself up another hatchway, flopped over the lip, and lay on the floor, exhausted. She had never before in her life attempted to climb a kilometer straight up; even in the relatively low gravity, every muscle in her body felt as if it had been seared by red-hot iron bands. Her only satisfaction, a grim one, was that Redbay's strength of despair had long ago given out; he could only climb a few rungs up each ladder and wait for B'Elanna to help him the rest of the way up.

At first, he had suggested she leave him behind. But this was not the warrior way: a Klingon did not leave fellow warriors behind . . . and the human side of B'Elanna rebelled at the thought of letting a fellow human die, even if he was Starfleet. Killing enemies in battle—that was acceptable, even heroic! But not letting former enemies be blown to pieces in a lifeless moon.

This time, however, Redbay could not even make it to the ladder at all. He lay on the deckplates, a level below Torres, panting.

Lieutenant Torres unslung the tricorder she had stubbornly carried up meter after meter. She checked the time: two hours and twenty-eight minutes; they had exactly thirty-nine minutes until the tricorder timer read 03:07, B'Elanna's best estimate of the time from the explosion—seven and a half minutes before the mag-lev failed. It took light and other electromagnetic waves seven and a half minutes to travel from sun to moon; the expanding shell of stellar matter that would destroy the moon would take twenty-five times longer to reach the moon.

Unless, of course, it's moving faster than I expected. She had not shared that worry with Redbay; it was a silly fret . . . after all, the star stuff could just as well be moving slower. Without analyzing the supernova itself, there was no way to tell.

"Call it thirty-five minutes," she announced between gasps, "to make—half a klick. We're doing well, Redbay— come on, just a half a kilometer . . . move!"

Redbay glared up at her with the first honest emotion he had shown toward anyone but the Furies: desperation beyond words. He looked down, utterly spent.

B'Elanna climbed back down. "You *think* you're exhausted, but you're not. You can always take just one more rung, one more, one more, until you make it or you die from the effort." She dropped lightly to the deck, faking strength and breath she really didn't have. It worked; Redbay struggled pathetically to his feet. B'Elanna steered him toward the ladder, then climbed right behind him to push him forward.

They slogged the last, bitter half-kilometer, while B'Elanna deliberately did not stare at her timer. She even turned off the alarms when they began sounding faster and faster . . . it made little difference whether they hyperventilated if they were still a quarter-kilometer below the surface.

But they made slow progress. At last, they reached the surface. B'Elanna whipped her tricorder around and stared at it.

T plus fourteen. T *PLUS* fourteen . . . so much for time estimates!

"Well, Redbay, we're fourteen minutes late. Fortunately, the particle front is no prompter than we. Better start hyperventilating; it probably will strike at any—"

As darkness closed around B'Elanna Torres, she heard and felt the distant impact of a Klingon warhammer against her entire body. Then she floated in timeless discontinuity.

CHAPTER
29

For the thirtieth time since Captain Janeway and Lieutenant Carey began trying to reconstruct the forward shield, introduce the fold to make a wedge, and re-create the extrusion formula, the captain hallucinated exactly the right figures that indicated success.

For a moment, her heart rate rose to full impulse; then she checked herself. Twenty-nine previous hallucinations tempered her momentrary feeling of triumph.

But this time, the figures did not melt back into the real numbers, different enough to turn success into total failure. In fact, this time, the more she stared, the more the figures looked like a real, bona-fide solution.

"Lieutenant," she said, "check my eyes on this. What does the bioelectrical Griffin potential read?"

Carey turned his own glazed eyes onto the screen; he squinted, shook his head, then sat bolt upright. "Captain, the shield's up," he breathed, so quietly it was almost as if he were afraid to shout for fear of knocking over the fragile thing with too boisterous a shout.

"Time check."

Carey looked at his screen timer readout. "About, what, four minutes?"

"Janeway to bridge: Chakotay, the forward shield is up."

"Yes, Captain, we just noticed."

"Turn us around while—"

"We already have, Captain. Give us a wedge . . . hurry!"

Janeway smiled. "Aye, aye, Commander. *Captain* Janeway out."

The minutes ticked by as Janeway followed exactly the recipe she had used successfully to introduce the fold the last time. After a time lapse, she glanced at the ship's chronometer. Eight minutes had passed; they were already into overtime. "Let's hope it's a really slow explosion," she muttered.

"Two more sequences," hissed Carey, hands trembling as he typed the instructions.

Janeway forced herself not to watch the viewer; the wave front would come when it came, and watching would only waste more time. Carey, however, was not so circumspect. "Captain!" he said. "I can see it—*I see it coming!*"

"Thank you, Lieutenant. Now stop staring at the viewer and type!" Carefully, checking each character, Janeway typed her last command, a direct, bioneural assembler-code sequence . . . the final piece of the Carey formula: the command sequence was actually a set of construction instructions that forced the neural-net shield-control computer to conform to a discontinuous function . . . the shield bent, and bent, and suddenly *folded* neatly along the line of force-equilibrium.

"Got it," announced Janeway, smiling in triumph muted by the grim possibilities awaiting them after the wave passed them and struck the moon.

"Fifteen seconds to spare," said the captain; "hardly even a ra—"

The expanding shell of superenergetic debris, nearly ninety percent of the former sun's mass, struck the *Voyager* head-on. The ship jerked with the shock and was driven backward at 0.15 impulse speed, about 11,500 kilometers per second, the speed of the impact shell. Slapping her commbadge, the captain bellowed, "Janeway to bridge: compensate!"

If there was an answer, she didn't hear; the ship rumbled like thunder, shaking violently. Janeway had once felt a 7.9 earthquake on Sprague XI, the hedonistic paradise sometimes used for shore leave; the shaking was nothing compared to what her own ship now suffered.

In the viewer down in engineering, the stars were jagged streaks where they weren't obscured by the roiling mass of superheated plasma bursting past the *Voyager;* without the shields, the ship would not have lasted a microsecond. But Tom Paris kept it on course; the computers compensated for the buffeting, and the great part of the particles deflected off of the forward shield-wedge and broke to either side, stabilizing the ship left to right; the impulse engines took care of the relative movement up and down, and Chakotay and Paris refused to allow the ship to be driven backward.

The shaking was worse than when they were en route to the Fury star system and the gravitic stabilizers broke—was it really a thousand years ago?—and again, Janeway caught herself fighting back nausea. Lieutenant Carey lost the battle.

Then suddenly, it stopped; the bulk of the shell continued past, headed toward the moon, which it would batter apart in just a few seconds.

Captain Janeway lurched to her feet, fumbling for her badge. "Janeway," she croaked. *"To the moon,* Paris!" Then she dropped back down; nausea or no, she had to restore the shield extrusion immediately, as in yesterday.

B'Elanna floated back to consciousness, feeling nauseated, sore, and dizzy, with a head big enough for its own set of moons. Three questions lined up for attention; the first was *What the hell was I drinking?*

Then she woke fully. "Why the—the hell is there still *gravity?"* she demanded aloud. Belatedly, she allowed the third question: "And why is it pinning me to the ceiling?"

She staggered up and discovered she had no sense of balance. She fell heavily, weighing more than she would on the *Voyager*. Redbay was across the upper chamber, which was dark, lit only by light streaming in the jagged holes in the bulkheads. He lay against the floor, upside down by B'Elanna's reference, as if he were glued there.

Jagged holes? In a flash, B'Elanna Torres realized what had happened: The entire chamber had been ripped loose by the shock wave, and it spun through space, pressing the two away-team members against the perimeter by centrifugal force.

Spinning through space! By itself—and the hurricane rush past her ears indicated the air was rapidly gushing out the gashes in the metal seams, the superdense Fury metal torn apart like cardboard.

B'Elanna wasted precious moments gawking; outside the rips, the vast, black abyss of space was neither, filled with glowing gas that lit the inside of the chunk with a hellish glare.

"Redbay!" She belly-crawled along the perimeter, fighting the increased acceleration when she got into the corners, which were nearly one and a half times as far from the axis of rotation as where she had been thrown . . . which meant they dragged her down at one and a half times the gravity.

She reached the stricken lieutenant and shook him into semiconsciousness. "Red . . . bay," she gasped, becoming lightheaded in the thinning air. "Get up, get—breathe deep!—get . . . get out—find us—beam . . ." B'Elanna fell over, panting with the exertion. Already, the sound of the air was growing distant and tinny, her own voice sounding like it came from the bottom of a well. The thin air didn't carry the sound.

She summoned up some strength and slapped Redbay, rousing him fully. He stared at her, looking sick, miserable, and at last showing some real, honest fear. He had come back to himself—only to come back to a nightmare.

"Breathe!" she screamed, costing her enough oxygen that her head pounded and she almost fainted. Weakly, she pointed at the nearest rip.

Hyperventilate, she warned herself. She began to pant like an overheated dog, and Redbay noticed and imitated her. She could not watch the stars and bright mist swirl past the rips; it made her sick, and the very last thing she needed at that moment was to waste precious time and invaluable air vomiting.

The room seemed unnaturally white; her peculiar, oxygen-starved brain spat up the most useless piece of information it could find: that the low pressure and lack of oxygen was affecting the rods and cones in her retinas, washing the color from her vision.

EYES! She remembered. "Close . . . eyes," she croaked, pointing to her eyes. Redbay nodded, terrified beyond words.

Together they rose to hands and knees and crawled toward the rip, toward death and emptiness. Toward the only silly hope they had left. They panted, trying to suck down as much air as possible to prolong the agony before their brains finally suffered fatal damage due to oxygen deprivation.

Redbay balked; Torres grabbed him by the seat of the pants and hurled him out the rip. *Bones of my ancestors,* she thought sickly; *that's the first time in my life I've ever thrown someone out the airlock into deep space.* She flopped over the hole in what felt like the floor, though it looked like a bulkhead, and was hurled, tumbling, into interstellar nothingness.

B'Elanna shut her eyes tight and rolled into a tight, tight, fetal ball, wrapping her arms around her to preserve as much heat as she could. It was unnecessary; the instant she was out and unshielded, she felt searing fire across her back, her legs, and her arms. *It's a million degrees!* screamed her shocked and tortured mind. *It's the debris, it's superheated gas from—*

The shock bit deeper into B'Elanna's body and brain, and consciousness slipped deeper and deeper beneath her thick, Klingon hide.

She was—she was going—she was going to—

Kes pressed so hard against the window port, her nose began to bleed. She didn't notice Neelix, crowded right next to her and everyone else. But they were too busy staring and squinting, trying to pick out a pair of tiny figures who might lurk anywhere within the bright, expanding gas cloud, which the *Voyager* followed at an altogether indiscreet distance.

"There!" Neelix shouted, pointing at a speck.

"No," she said, "that's a piece of conduit."

"Are you *sure?*"

"Yes . . . wait! What's that over there?"

Neelix shoved against the port as if the extra millimeter might make a difference. "Yes, it could—I think I can see— yes! No!" He pulled back involuntarily, angrily swatting the transparent aluminum as if it were to blame. "No, no, no! It's just another . . ."

Ocampans had good eyes, better than human eyes. She liked to think Neelix's Talaxian eyes were better. In the far, far distance, to the left, Kes just barely made out a speck. It was at the limit of her vision. The ship was paralleling it, and it was growing no larger.

"Neelix," she breathed, suddenly faint, "I think I might have something solid."

"Where? Where?"

Keeping her eye on the dot, Kes moved behind Neelix and pointed past his face—"To the left," she whispered in his ample ear; "further . . . now up a bit—there."

Neelix stared for a moment. Then he touched his commbadge. "Neelix and Kes," he said. "We've got one."

"Coordinates," snapped the unemotional, uninflected voice of Tuvok.

"Um . . ." Neelix felt his heart race; he wasn't used to the Starfleet system. "It's a little to the left and—"

"What port are you standing at?" interrupted the annoying Vulcan.

"Um . . ."

From behind Neelix, Kes shouted, "Number UV-eighteen!"

"There is no need to increase your vocal volume," said Tuvok. "The comm link includes you as well."

On the bridge, Tuvok said, "Captain, I suggest we turn to heading one-nine-seven."

"Proceed, Mr. Paris," said Janeway. "Increase to thirty meters per second." Paris engaged the new course. "It's crunch time," continued the captain. "Mr. Kim, extrude the shield . . . but on your ensign's pips, *don't let the shield walls touch.*"

Licking her lips, Janeway touched her commbadge. "Captain to engineering. Mr. Carey—are you ready with that modified monitor?"

"No," said the acting chief engineer.

"Good. Turn it on anyway; let's see what we can see."

The forward viewer, a blank wall at the moment, flickered and displayed a few dozen diagonal lines of color. "I told you it wasn't ready," said Carey.

"Extruding the shield now," announced Kim to an unappreciative audience. Sweat rolled down his face; it was one of the most terrific responsibilities he had yet faced on his first, and probably last, ship assignment.

"Dammit, Carey, we can't see a thing!"

"Something must be loose, a connection."

"Do something—kick it!"

"Captain, it's probably in the monitor itself! That's outside . . . I'll have to go EVA and—"

"Kick the stupid interface! It's right in front of you!"

Tuvok looked puzzled. "Captain, I fail to see what good—"

The image lurched, then settled into an oddly flat picture of bright splotches of color—hot, ionized plasma gas—with here and there a star visible through the glow. The image was bizarre, disorienting; with so many of the ship's systems off-line, including the replicator, it was the best they could do. It was weak, dizzying; but they finally had eyes . . . or rather, one eye.

After a moment, she stood from her chair. "I see them! One of them; Tuvok, can you get a visual lock and send it to transporter room two?"

"Not yet, Captain," said the science officer.

"Janeway to transporter two; prepare to area-beam a humanoid directly to sickbay from coordinates that will be transmitted by Lieutenant Tuvok. Janeway to EMH program; prepare to receive a patient, Doctor."

"I have a visual lock now, Captain; transmitting to transporter room two."

"Energize when ready, transporter two."

Tense seconds passed. Janeway stared and stared; but before she could make out anything more than two arms and two legs, Tuvok announced, "It's Lieutenant Redbay." Before Tuvok finished the sentence, the speck dematerialized.

"Doctor to Janeway," said the disembodied voice of the emergency holographic medical program. "I have Lieutenant Redbay. I am initiating CPR now."

Janeway nodded, absurdly since it was a voice link. "Where is she—*where is she?*"

The universe moves by strange and bizarre turns. With all the eyes on the bridge scanning the glowing plasma cloud for B'Elanna Torres, it was Chell, of all people, who spotted her. Chell, who was only on the bridge as an observer—with no responsibility except to watch and observe.

Tom Paris yanked the helm to port without waiting for an order from Captain Janeway; she barely had time to say "Proceed, Mr. Tuvok" before the sharp-eyed Vulcan oriented the jury-rigged monitor to center Lieutenant Torres and transferred the coordinates to the transporter room.

"Energizing," said Transporter Chief Filz.

CHAPTER

30

VOYAGER MATCHED VELOCITIES WITH THE TINY, REMAINING CORE that used to be the Fury star just an hour earlier. Commander Chakotay, Lieutenant Tuvok, and Ensign Harry Kim slowly took measurements as the frenetic crew got the ship's systems back on-line after both the electromagnetic pulse and the plasma shock wave. The bridge crew measured traces of chroniton particles, neutrino flux, subspace folding effects, residual superstring twists, alpha-particle radiation levels and directions, and residual heat in the form of radio echoes.

But Captain Kathryn Janeway had a more pressing problem down in sickbay.

The doctor circled around and around Lieutenant Redbay, whose skin was burnt bright red over a disturbing pallor. Redbay's eyes were open, but the pupils did not respond. Neither did the eyelids blink; Kes, the doctor's assistant, reached across every few moments and rehydrated Redbay's eyes from an eyedropper of saline solution.

"There is as yet no brain activity from Mr. Redbay," said the doctor; "well, for either of them. But I'm more worried about Redbay. I have applied cardiac stimulators, but as yet, his body is not even producing autonomic nervous responses."

"B'Elanna is doing better?"

"Lieutenant Torres is unchanged. She is not on life-support, but we took her off six minutes after she was beamed here. She required only a few forced breaths to begin breathing on her own . . . but she, too, is still in a coma."

Janeway closed her eyes. When she opened them again, the scene had not changed. She was so tired, but it wasn't all just a dream. "Will they recover?"

The doctor shook his head. "That is up to Torres and Redbay. There is little I can do except monitor and—"

"Doctor!" interrupted Kes. "B'Elanna just went into cardiac arrest!"

The doctor raced to Lieutenant Torres and ran a fast scan with his medical tricorder. "Cortical seizure," he diagnosed. "I'm going to try to stabilize her with a cortical stimulator."

"What's happening?" demanded the captain. "Doctor, you said she was doing all right! Why is she—"

"Be quiet!" snapped the doctor.

Janeway clamped her mouth shut, then backed swiftly away. After a moment, she commanded herself to turn and leave the sickbay. It was the hardest order she had ever given or received.

She waited in the passageway, pacing back and forth. Kes and the doctor didn't need her inside distracting them; they most decidedly did *not* need her presence at that moment.

The doctor frowned. *I'm not supposed to feel anything,* he thought; *I can't feel—I'm just a hologram!* But it certainly felt as though he felt concern, worry—even fear. Evidently, the programmer, Zimmerman, did a more thorough job than anyone had imagined, least of all the doctor himself. He had experienced quite a few feelings lately.

"I stabilized her," he announced, "for the moment, at any rate. How is Mr. Redbay, Kes?"

Silence. The doctor turned to find Kes standing over Redbay's bed. The Ocampan looked stricken. "Doctor, you'd better look at this." She held up her own tricorder. "Lieutenant Redbay's neural receptivity is failing. The cortical stimulator can't maintain the electrocolloidal circulation . . . he's dying, Doctor."

The doctor stared. There was no need to check Kes's readings; he had trained her well. "I might be able to rebuild the pathways," he said.

"The operating table is prepped. Which patient should I transfer?"

The doctor looked back and forth. "This is the worst part about being a doctor, Kes," he said, voice firm. "Remember what I said about triage, during our conference? Well, here it is in all its ugliness."

Triage: deciding who would live—and who would be left to die. This case was different . . . but really the same. There was no truly *medical* reason to choose one patient over the other. The doctor scanned his entire library of writings on proper triage and found no comfort, no help. Redbay's case was the more difficult; but with the proper care, he stood a good chance of living . . . neural receptivity collapse—"cortical stiffening"—was better understood than Torres's cortical seizure.

But in reality, neither was a textclip case; because, simply put, no one had ever before been fished out of deep space without a spacesuit in the middle of an exploding supernova.

The doctor ran every computer program in his limitless—he had thought!—medical profiles; but no mere program could convincingly tell him whether to save Lieutenant Redbay or Lieutenant Torres. Of course, each program picked one of the two . . . but there were as many hits for the first as the second.

It always comes down to this, he thought, exasperated and concerned; *it always comes down to the gut feeling of the doctor. But holograms don't HAVE guts.*

There was, he concluded, no *convincing* medical method to resolve the triage dilemma; each patient had his own reasons to live, to die, to sacrifice for the other.

"Doctor?"

What do I do? What do I do? He swiveled his virtual,

holographic head back and forth, virtual mind wrestling with a very real dilemma. No amount of prior programming could help him. *You make a decision, that's what you do!*

"I'll call the captain," said Kes, reaching for her commbadge.

"No!" the doctor almost shouted, grabbing her wrist. "I'm the doctor . . . this is my responsibility." *But WHAT DO I DO?*

He turned away, covering his holographic face with unreal hands. "How can I be torn like this? I'm not even a real man!"

After a moment, Kes spoke, so quietly the doctor had to increase his receiver gain. "You're real to me, Doctor."

"Maybe that's what being real means: making decisions that can't be made by a . . . by an emergency medical holographic program."

"You have to choose. B'Elanna's cortical stimulator can't stabilize her—" Kes fell silent, allowing the doctor to speak, to choose.

"She's a member of this crew. And—and I guess she's my friend. I know her—I can't make this decision!"

"Should I call the captain?"

"No! Help me—wait for me. Trust me, I know the time! I can't help knowing; I'm a computer program."

"You're real. You're a man and a doctor. And my teacher."

"But I have no objectivity!"

"Not every decision should be objective."

At once, the doctor relaxed. His virtual shoulders slumped. He turned around with a deadpan expression. "Transfer—B'Elanna—to the surgical table, Kes. I'll—I have to—"

Without another word, the doctor crossed the distance between the tables, reached out, and removed the cortical stimulator from Lieutenant Redbay. "Med—Medical log: Lieutenant Redbay pronounced deceased." Almost angrily—a comic sight, he thought—the doctor swiftly removed the respirator and pacemaker as well, laying them on one of the other beds in intensive care.

Kes had already transferred B'Elanna to the surgical table

using the antigravs and begun fitting the neurosurgical helmet over the lieutenant. By the time the doctor approached the table, Kes had already activated the holoprobe and microscanner and focused both on the outer portion of B'Elanna's cerebral cortex.

"Prepare to terminate the cortical stimulator," said the doctor, forcing himself not to look at the convulsing Redbay . . . a man already dead, dead ever since he fought the Furies the first time; a man who didn't know he was already dead, who fought it for nearly a minute.

"Terminate the stimulator, Kes; and get ready to immobilize her with repeated shots of desoasopine. She's half Klingon, and I think she's going to fight us every step of the way."

"Captain to the bridge," said Chakotay's voice from nothingness, startling Janeway. "On my way," she said, grateful for the excuse to cut and run. She had dreaded being called in and told that B'Elanna had suffered irreparable brain damage; irrationally, Captain Janeway half convinced herself that even standing in the hallway would "jinx" her engineer's chances—but she was afraid that simply leaving, *abandoning* B'Elanna, would give the wrong impression.

"What's happening, Mr. Chakotay?" she asked as the turbolift doors slid open at the bridge.

"Nothing."

"Didn't you just call me to the bridge?"

"Yes, Captain. It's what happened an hour ago that I think you need to see."

Tuvok took up the tale. "We have spent considerable time using every means available to track the Fury wormhole. It has been, I must admit, an unsatisfactory experience. The supernova left high residual radiation levels: the sector's current temperature is still several hundred degrees, broadcast as electromagnetic radiation in the infrared and radiowave portion of the spectrum. This temperature dissipates the energy signature left behind by the wormhole."

"Give me the short version, Mr. Tuvok."

"The Furies' attempt to create an artificial wormhole

large enough to transport their entire planet was largely successful."

Janeway was silent for a long time. "Then we failed," she said at last, mastering her emotions so completely that Tuvok was impressed.

"Not exactly," said Chakotay. "I don't know what B'Elanna and Redbay did down there, but the Furies didn't jump to the Alpha Quadrant."

"Tuvok just said—"

"I said the effort was *largely* successful, Captain. They did, in fact, jump . . . *away* from the Alpha Quadrant."

Janeway looked back and forth between her senior officers. "Do we know where they jumped to?"

"No, Captain," said Chakotay. "We cannot narrow down the trail smaller than about a ninety-degree spread. They could have gone in any direction within that spread."

"All right, where *might* they have gone? Which direction?"

"They might have jumped into the Gamma Quadrant, or they might have jumped completely outside the galaxy."

"Mr. Tuvok, what are the odds that the Furies will jump anywhere near a star system?"

"I have insufficient data to make even a plausible conjecture, Captain."

She thought about a planet of twenty-seven billion condemned to wander for eternity, lost between the stars. Twenty-seven billion souls whose only crime was attempting to eradicate or enslave every living being in her home quadrant.

"They must have had some provision for supporting their population away from a star," she mused; "they were planning a blind jump into *our* quadrant, after all."

"That would be logical."

Janeway leaned her head back, closing her eyes, not caring who saw her in such a state of exhaustion. "We didn't have to kill twenty-seven billion people. That counts for something, doesn't it?"

She hadn't expected an answer; she got one anyway, from Tuvok. "It counts for much, Captain."

"Have we merely unleashed the same horror on the Gamma Quadrant?" Janeway opened her eyes; the entire rest of the bridge crew was silent, staring at her. She looked from one to the other, pausing at last on Chakotay's inscrutible face.

"I don't think so," he said. "They were utterly peaceful to everyone except the ones they called Unclean: us, in the Alpha Quadrant." The commander paused, pressing his lips together. "I think the rest of the galaxy is safe . . . unless somehow the Furies make it back to a planet in our own quadrant."

"Tuvok?" asked the captain.

"Insufficient data to estimate the odds," said the Vulcan.

Janeway shuddered. Eventually, when the dust settled, the Furies would take stock. They would not lose interest in their holy war; they would begin building the same technology all over again, as soon as they found a star to suck dry for the energy to jump across the galaxy to hurl themselves again upon what they *knew* was theirs.

All over again; it would happen all over again, and again and again, until finally—somebody *did* kill them all. Or until they succeeded.

Somebody, someday; but not Katherine Janeway, not this day. "Still . . . it's—it's quite something to think about. What we did."

"We defended ourselves!" exploded Paris.

"We defended our civilization," corrected Tuvok.

"Aren't you the ones who preach about Infinite Diversity in Infinite Combinations? They simply wanted to retake what had once been theirs."

"What they held by force and terror."

Chakotay sat back, simply observing; he allowed Paris and Tuvok to carry the point. But the captain held her own.

"Yes, a slave revolt. For thousands of years, they nursed their hatred and determination to retake heaven, which their god gave them, they believed. What will they do now? I think they'll figure out pretty quickly that they went in the opposite direction and can never get back. Then what? What violent race have we unleashed upon another part of the galaxy, driven into permanent exile? Will they set up a Fury empire in the Gamma Quadrant? Will they start enslaving the races in the Magellanic Clouds?

"I would rather we had stopped them completely and killed every last one of the twenty-seven billion. *That* guilt I could live with, or die with, as the case may be."

Chakotay spoke out. "I feel no guilt whatsoever, Captain. We did what a warrior must do. We took the best victory condition offered."

"Is your spirit guide okay with this?"

"I will find out tonight."

"Take me with you. Please."

Chakotay inclined his head in the affirmative.

"Captain," said a hesitant Ensign Kim, "I didn't want to interrupt. But I just monitored a log entry by the EMH program."

"Yes?"

"The doctor just pronounced Lieutenant Redbay dead. He thinks Lieutenant Torres is going to make it."

Janeway rose and crossed to the young ensign. She put her hand on his shoulder. "You care very much about her, don't you? I think Chell can use some watchstanding experience . . . why don't you go down to sickbay."

Kim stood without a word and hurriedly walked to the turbolift.

CHAPTER
31

TWO DAYS AFTER THE SUPERNOVA, THE RADIATION LEVEL HAD dropped substantially in the sector that once had belonged to the Furies, the first true terrorists of the galaxy. The *U.S.S. Voyager* remained in the sector; Captain Kathryn Janeway had ordered them to maintain orbit around the remnants of the Fury sun until Lieutenant B'Elanna Torres regained consciousness. Janeway wanted to know what happened, what Torres and the strange Lieutenant Redbay from the *Enterprise* had done, before the captain decided whether it was safe to leave. That meant Torres had to wake up.

Twelve hours later, B'Elanna sighed. It was a good sign but not spectacular; she had emitted sounds before. But the sigh was followed by weak sobbing, and that *was* exciting: it was the first actual emotion she had shown since she was beamed aboard.

The captain took B'Elanna's mummy-wrapped hand, while Kes gently touched the patient's brow. Tucked as she had been, the lieutenant had mostly shielded her face from the intense, searing heat. The rest of her body would take weeks to heal fully, even with the most advanced skin repligrafting techniques in the Delta Quadrant.

B'Elanna opened her eyes and began to scream. When the doctor moved to restrain her, she bit his hand hard enough to sever his thumb—had he been flesh and blood. Fortunately, B'Elanna did not break her teeth on the holographic forcefield.

They held her and talked her back for another half hour before she was coherent enough for Janeway to debrief her. Haltingly, B'Elanna Torres told of finding the aiming mechanism at the very last moment and sabotaging it.

"It's a damned good thing you thought of that," said the captain. "None of the other gremlins you pulled did a thing: the beam still fired, created the wormhole, and the planet still passed through it to . . . to anybody's guess where."

"I saved us?"

"You saved us, Lieutenant."

"Are the Furies gone?"

Janeway smiled, an oddly down-turning expression that simultaneously expressed warmth, reassurance, and deep sadness. "They're gone. They were sent into the middle of nowhere; I doubt they'll ever find their way back to our galaxy, and definitely not to the Alpha Quadrant. Not ever."

"We fished you out of the exploding supernova," said Kes. "You were really badly burned and more than fifteen bones were broken! But you're going to be all right."

"And . . . Redbay?"

Janeway answered quickly before any awkward pauses. "He didn't make it, Torres. I'm sorry."

The doctor leaned close. "You survived in part because you're half-Klingon, Lieutenant. Lieutenant Redbay was a human, and his body couldn't take the strain."

She stared at the doctor as if he'd grown a second head. She did not seem pleased. Then B'Elanna closed her eyes and tilted her head. *So once again, my face is rubbed in it,* she thought; *either I'm flying off the handle because I'm an angry young Klingon; or I survive a supernova because I have a tough Klingon hide! Can't I ever just be ME?*

But she knew the answer almost before she asked the question: she was who she was, and part of who she was was a bumpy-headed, thick-skinned, warrior-hearted Klingon. She could no longer deny it. And now it had saved her life!

Later, when the doctor had moved on to other patients, and Janeway had left, Kes returned to B'Elanna's side. Ocampan eyes met the Klingon face; Kes bit her lip and finally asked a question that had built inside her like an overinflated balloon. "You said you were hit by the Furies' terror beam . . . what was it like? That kind of fear. I've never . . ." Kes paused, admitting her grievous fault. "I've never even imagined that kind of emotion!" she blurted.

B'Elanna said nothing.

"Is it different from just being afraid? I have to know . . . I have to know there was a reason why all the races of the Alpha Quadrant would rather be slaves and give up freedom than face that weapon. It has to be something more than just being afraid of death or pain."

"I don't remember," said Lieutenant Torres. "Selective amnesia. The doctor said it might happen."

Kes lowered her brows, puzzled. "But you remember everything else!"

"I *said*," hissed Torres, "I—don't—*REMEMBER.*" Cold, defiant, Klingon eyes burned into the Ocampan face. Kes understood, and she dropped the subject.

STAR TREK®
INVASION!

A Word from Our Authors

Diane Carey is the author of eleven STAR TREK novels and novelizations—Dreadnought, Battlestations, Final Frontier, Best Destiny, The Great Starship Race, First Frontier, Ghost Ship, Descent, The Search, The Way of the Warrior, Station Rage, and INVASION! Book One: First Strike. As the only STAR TREK author who actually sails the Tall Ships, she has a unique perspective on sea captains—and on space captains as well.

Of Ships and Men

"THAT'S WHAT SETS YOU APART FROM THE REST OF US, JIM. YOU look at these alien people with nine eyes and no arms, and you see the fact that they just want a home and safety. You look at aliens in terms of how they're like us, while everybody else sees how they're different."

I'm not sure whether Dr. McCoy said this to Jim Kirk in First Strike, or I said it to him myself during a misty moment at the schooner's wheel, but I'm sure one of us did.

Star Trek as a TV show, or shall we say as fourth-wall theater, gave us a glimpse into a future we wouldn't mind living. While most science fiction of the 1960s and much of it now shows us a glum, dismal, postholocaust future where people wear rags and are reduced to ratlike behavior, STAR TREK gave us a clean, bright future with crisp military panache melded into the dynamism of individuality.

Jim Kirk was the individual who set the design, and without him there would be no STAR TREK today, but not because he was perfect or charismatic, though he was certainly the latter. Jim Kirk provided a magnetic compass for us because he was charismatic and yet deeply flawed. Yes, as classical heroic drama has always shown us, the hero's imperfections and how he handles them are the real barometers of heroism. Perfection is easy. With perfection we don't need drama to provide exemplars in life, and in fact we don't even need heroes.

But life isn't perfect. Neither are any of my captains, and I've sailed with several. As many of you know, I work as a deckhand and helmsman aboard several Tall Ships, including the tough old 125' Baltic trader topsail schooner *Alexandria* out of Alexandria, Virginia, the pilot schooner *William H. Albury* out of Man-o'-War Cay in the Bahamas, the 1883 Portuguese fisherman barkentine *Gazela* of Philadelphia, which is the oldest and largest working square-rigger on Earth, and the breathtakingly fast Baltimore clipper *Pride of Baltimore II*. I mention these ships because they are all a piece of the *Enterprise* to me. She is their legacy.

My captains range from a former Chesapeake Bay tug captain to a former CIA mercenary. Yeah, really. I've never had a female captain yet, but I've worked under many female first and second mates and bosuns, some of whom had their captain's licenses, so I also feel quite comfortable watching Captain Janeway at work. There are some people under whose command I won't go to sea—but I'd go with her.

She's not perfect either. If I ever run into a captain who seems to be perfect, I ain't signing on that ship.

Why not? Because I'm not perfect; neither are any of my shipmates, and for that matter neither are any of my ships. A "perfect" captain just couldn't function on the real sea, with a real crew and real trouble, and that means life or death to those of us who man the sheets and halyards.

My work on ships is certainly one of the reasons *STAR TREK* is so comfortable for me, though I do write in other genres and media. I seem to keep coming back to *STAR TREK* no matter how far I wander—whether my continual returns are like springtime or the flu season is a matter of personal taste, but I leave that to the readers. Surely it bears an eerie resemblance to going back out to sea—no matter how taxing, wet, crowded, hot, cold, or scary the last voyage was, I keep signing back on.

Yes, that's what I mean—it's not always fun, but it's always a challenge, and that's what fuels me. I have yet to tire of watching my captains try to sort out a gripping situation, wrestling with their own flaws and the flaws of the amalgamated crews, usually a gaggle of persons from all walks of life and any dozen given philosophies. I watch my captains trying to figure out which person has which best ability, and which duty that person just shouldn't be assigned to—and all this very often in the midst of notable danger, whether during Hurricane Andrew or piloting upstream on the swollen Mississippi.

Or trying to pull the starship out of a gravity well or to survive a battle of monumental odds. Yes, I watch my starship captains the same way. I've watched Jim Kirk for the better part of my life, and he's a bundle of extremes, both noble and petty, and even nobility can be a fault in some situations. What sets him apart is his determination to work through those faults. I never tire of examining that kind of person, and *STAR TREK* has continually given us a vehicle with which to hold that mirror up to ourselves and take a close look.

To date I've written more Jim Kirk books than any other author. I've spent more hours watching him over and over again and working with him than anyone. With so many thousands of words to write about him, I've had to examine his personality very closely and find out just what about him makes me keep watching, so I can make you keep watching.

What I discovered during the writing of *First Strike* was Jim Kirk's relentless plumbing for the commonality between people and peoples. He'd stare into alien eyes, if he could find them, and sift out the ways he and that alien were alike. That's where he'd start—from the point of familiarity. Everyone who met him—crewmates, aliens, enemies—felt instantly as if they'd known him for years. They might not like him or agree with him, but they always knew where he stood, because he would chip out that common element and work from there.

Most science fiction concentrates on the differences. Kirk and his crew had the idea that there would be, had to be, something in common even with the oddest creature, and all we had to do was find that thing, that common desire, goal, passion, no matter how small.

Jim Kirk looked at women much the same way—the ultimate alien, of course. He saw not only face or hair or figure, or how different women were from one another, but how much they were the same. He saw not females, but femininity. His attitude changed when, in the episode "Metamorphosis," he found out the Companion was female, just as it changed during "Devil in the Dark" when he found out the Horta was a mother protecting her young.

William Shatner knew that also, instinctively if not professionally. If we pay attention to the way the professional science-fiction writers wrote the original *STAR TREK* and the way Shatner played it, we discover that Jim Kirk wasn't a hound after all. He was an appreciator. He appreciated women for the poetic loveliness he saw in all of them, human or otherwise, and he appreciated aliens for the relationship that could be built out of a vacuum.

That's what set the original *STAR TREK* apart from other science fiction and sets the pace for us now—it went out of its way to show how individuals, ever separate unto ourselves, are more like than unlike. That is also what real captains have to do—bring together crewmen who may never have seen each other before, and by the time the ship leaves the dock make us all have a common goal. Usually it's something quite humble, like making the next port on schedule. Occasionally, survival itself is at stake. But sea and space are great equalizers—keep the water out, the people in, and get to the next port.

Whatever happens between is just the pub story we'll tell.

So be careful whose command you sign under. Make sure your captain has flaws and a good stout temper. Your chances of surviving are better, and you might even have a great adventure between those dockside sighs of relief.

Fair weather,

Diane Carey

Diane Carey

Kristine Kathryn Rusch and Dean Wesley Smith are the authors of the *STAR TREK* novels *The Big Game* (as Sandy Schofield), *The Escape, The Long Night, Rings of Tautee,* the novelization of *Star Trek: Klingon* and *INVASION! Book Two: The Soldiers of Fear.* They are also, respectively, the editors of *The Magazine of Fantasy and Science Fiction* and *Pulphouse Magazine.* Below, Kristine tells us a bit of what *STAR TREK* has meant to both of them over the years. That both their middle names are the first names of *Star Trek* characters is strictly coincidental.

Our
STAR TREK Memories
(Or How Can a TV Show
Be So Important?)

When my husband, Dean Wesley Smith, and I met, I was twenty-five and he was thirty-five. We lived in separate parts of the country, and we both wrote science fiction. I was an admitted *STAR TREK* fan who had never been to any of the conventions because I was too broke to attend. Dean, who never speaks of the things he likes, was a closet Trekker whose love for the series turned out to be a big surprise to his friends. The night *Star Trek: The Next Generation* premiered, I watched in my apartment, and he watched it in his, and it wasn't until the next day that I discovered he loved *STAR TREK* as much as I did.

At that point, we had been seeing each other for nearly a year.

So, when John Ordover, our editor at Pocket Books, asked us to write an essay about how *STAR TREK* had influenced us for the last book of the *INVASION!* series, we knew we immediately had a problem. Because when *STAR TREK* premiered, I was six. Dean was sixteen. I was in grade school. He was in high school. I saw two episodes during the show's entire first run (I couldn't stay up that late). He saw them all when they aired. And so on.

Dean and I run into these generational things all the time, especially concerning the sixties. While I was learning to walk, Dean was learning to duck and cover in preparation for a nuclear attack. While I was riding my bicycle after school, he was worried about being sent to Vietnam. When I experienced my first kiss, he had broken off his second engagement.

Even though we have a lot in common now, our ages prevented us from having a lot in common then.

So . . . how did *STAR TREK* influence us? Well, it influenced us differently.

Dean grew up in Boise, Idaho, then a fairly small city on the scale of things. It had an air force base and it was near several nuclear bases. It was, in nuclear parlance, a first-strike area.

During his years in grade school, Dean learned how to protect himself in a nuclear attack. Instead of fire drills, his school held duck-and-cover drills. The children hid under their desks, covered their heads, and waited for a teacher to whistle an all-clear. This, somehow, would save them from a nuclear explosion. People built bomb shelters in their backyards. And most public places had a visibly displayed yellow-and-black sign that showed where to hide if the sirens went off, warning of an attack.

By the time he was ten, it seemed clear that the world wouldn't last the decade. By the time he got into high school, that prediction came true on a personal level. Many boys his age went to Vietnam, and most never came back. High-school graduation meant, for many, the draft, and years of service in a war few believed in. Dean spent the first twenty-four years of his life thinking that (1) the world would end and/or (2) he would die in a police action so controversial Congress never voted it into war.

But this was just a backdrop. On the surface, Dean was a regular guy. I went to his high-school reunion. The folks who didn't know him well thought he was handsome (and he was; I saw pictures), smart, and shy (and he wasn't; I heard stories). He made the newspaper fairly regularly as part of the golf team, and he spent most days after school in the winter skiing at nearby Bogus Basin.

Except on Fridays. On Fridays, Dean W. Smith, handsome high-school student, stayed home.

To watch *STAR TREK*.

He watched it because it was science fiction and, unbeknownst to all but his closest friends, he was an avid science-fiction fan. But if *STAR TREK* had been bad science fiction, he might have dated on some of those Friday nights. Some of the episodes were bad, but more were good. But it wasn't the quality that held him.

It was the hope.

The hope existed in science-fiction novels. Man lived beyond 1970 in Robert Heinlein's books and Arthur C. Clarke's. But not on television. Television brought us the grim visions of Rod Serling and the *Outer Limits*. Television showed us the world ending, not thriving.

STAR TREK showed us a world in which the human race somehow survived the nightmares of the mid-twentieth century, and developed a culture that went to the stars in peace and exploration. Hope, for a generation that didn't have any.

The possibility that the world wouldn't end, that wars like Vietnam would become anathema to the human race. The idea that human beings of all races, all nationalities, and all credos, could get along.

The belief that we had a future after all.

It was that vision that kept Dean home on Fridays. And made him first in line to all the movies. And made him stay home for the premier of *Star Trek: The Next Generation* in the off-chance his new girlfriend (me) hated that *STAR TREK* stuff.

Well, the new girlfriend loved that *Star Trek* stuff. The first short story I ever wrote was *STAR TREK* fan fic about Jim Kirk coming to Superior, Wisconsin, and saving a lonely fifteen-year-old from—

Never mind. You get the idea. I was twelve at the time. Fifteen seemed awfully sophisticated back then.

STAR TREK didn't have the wider implications for me in those days. I simply loved the series. It came on every day after school (about four o'clock). My best friend, Toni, told me about the show, and we started watching it together. We even wrote a *STAR TREK* novel in Mrs. Anderson's English class (except for the week we took off to read *The Exorcist,* which we kept hidden in our English text). We were going to finish over the summer, but during the summer Toni moved away, and I was left to watch *STAR TREK* alone.

By the time I was fourteen, *STAR TREK* was cool. All my friends watched it. We all discussed it. And during those discussions, I learned to read the credits on TV shows. When my new best friend, Mindy Walgren, heard that my favorite *STAR TREK* episode was "City on the Edge of Forever," she loaned me a short-story collection by Harlan Ellison, the guy who had written that marvelous episode. Harlan's short stories led me to his essays, and his essays led me to some of the best writers working in the field at that time.

A television program opened a whole new world for me. The world of science fiction. The world of short stories. The world of essays. Television, instead of turning me away from books, led me to books. It expanded my horizons instead of limiting them.

I will be forever grateful.

I love to write *STAR TREK* novels because I like to play in the *STAR TREK* universe. I've played in it since Mrs. Anderson's English class twenty-four years ago. But I don't write the books solely because of that. I also write them for people, like me, who go from television to books. In *STAR TREK* novels, some of the best writers in the SF field get to play with SF ideas too big for the television screen. Like Jerry Oltion's planet rescue in *Twilight's End* or Peter David's wonderful spin on time travel in *Imzadi*.

Dean plays with big ideas in our *STAR TREK* novels (the commuting-through-time idea in *The Escape* was his; and so were the Jibetians in *The Long Night*). But he brings something else to our books.

He brings the hope. Because he's never forgotten how badly it's needed.

You see, sometimes ten years is a long time. When I graduated from high school, Vietnam was a name from a (seemingly) distant past. The kids in my class went to college or into the workforce. No one died (except in car wrecks). We never ducked or covered. Those yellow-and-black signs were dust-covered oddities in old buildings. We knew we'd live to see our grandchildren. We knew the world wasn't going to end.

We had hope and we didn't even realize it.

Which isn't to say *STAR TREK* became irrelevant. It didn't. But we took different things out of it. We talked about the show's racial unity. We liked the way women held positions of power. We liked the strange new worlds because we believed we'd visit them someday.

That there would be a future was a given. We simply had to decide how to live it.

How important was *STAR TREK* in creating that attitude?

Let's be real for a moment. We are talking television, after all. Television is entertainment. Entertainment is a way to kill a few hours. Nothing more.

Right?

Maybe. Maybe not.

You see, I believe we create the futures we can envision. If we can see only death and destruction ahead, then that's what's going to happen. But *STAR TREK* and science-fiction novels gave us a future, a real future, a future to envision.

It touched me at twelve. It touched Dean at sixteen.

And it touched countless others in his generation and mine. His needed the hope. Mine needed the goals.

How important is *STAR TREK*?

Important enough.

Terese Kathryn Russel

Some people require little introduction; L. A. Graf is, or are, one or more of those people. So without further ado . . .

A STAR TREK Appreciation

Captain's Log, Earthdate 012696. On a routine trip through the wormhole, the *Defiant* apparently encountered an editorial anomaly of unkown origin. As a consequence, the crew has been transported off the ship and thrown into a strange world of eerie black on white. . . .

Dr. Bashir craned a look at the monstrous column of print towering over their heads. "Does Paramount know we're here?"

"Let's hope so, Doctor." Sisko tugged at a nearby comma, making a face when it came loose in his hand and left only a poorly constructed sentence behind. "If not, *Deep Space Nine* is going to be the first Federation space station ever commanded by a Ferengi."

Kira banged her fist against one square of black text, then grunted with annoyance when even the dots on the tops of the i's failed to move. "Whatever this is, it's awfully dense."

"Looks like nine-point to me," O'Brien volunteered, from where he'd crawled underneath a paragraph to examine its basic structure.

"Dax . . ." Sisko ducked beneath a dangling participle to shoot a keen look at his science officer. "Can you identify the typeface?"

Dax nodded, stepping into the plain white border to scan one cleanly justified margin. As the results scrolled across her tricorder's little screen, she glanced up at the others with a smile. "It's all right, Benjamin—we're in a *STAR TREK* novel."

"Am I on the cover?" Bashir asked eagerly. Dax flicked the question mark at him with a sigh.

"Well, what are we doing here?" Kira wanted to know.

She stooped to catch the question mark as it tumbled past, turning it over in her hands in the hopes of finding something useful about it. "We're supposed to be back on *Deep Space Nine,* protecting Federation space from the Dominion, and the Cardassians, and the Klingons."

"Not to mention *Xena: Warrior Princess.*" Bashir ducked to avoid a rain of displaced apostrophes and commas from farther up the page. "Chief, what are you doing?"

"Scouting our surroundings," O'Brien called down from above. Scrambling for better footing on the end of a run-on sentence, he squinted at the bold title overshadowing the first few paragraphs of text. "According to this, we're in an appreciation of *STAR TREK,* written by somebody named L. A. Graf."

"L. A. Graf?" Dax maneuvered around a closing parenthesis to look up at him. "Isn't she the only Trill *STAR TREK* author?"

"Not exactly, old man." Sisko plucked a period from within the author's name and tossed it in his palm as though weighing it for a curveball pitch. "Although she is a bimodal entity, consisting of award-winning science-fiction author Julia Ecklar and university scientist Karen Rose Cercone. You're just not familiar with them because *INVASION! Book Three: Time's Enemy* is their first *STAR TREK: Deep Space Nine* novel." He lobbed the period at the edge of the page, grinning when it bounced neatly back at him. "All their previous *STAR TREK* books were about *The original series.*"

O'Brien slid off the bottom of the column with a thoughtful grunt. "So why did they decide to write about us now?"

"Because we're the best-looking crew *STAR TREK*'s ever had?" Bashir suggested with a puckish grin.

Dax bounced an apostrophe off the top of his head. "No," she countered. "They like us because they feel we've continued in the spirit of the classic *STAR TREK* series by focusing on cultural conflicts and sociological problems in addition to exciting action/adventure."

"They seem to like our nifty new starship, too," O'Brien

admitted, scrubbing his hands against the legs of his trousers to wipe off the printer's ink. "They use it a lot in their story."

"Also, L. A. Graf has always celebrated the diversity that *STAR TREK* represents." Sisko replaced the period with a respectful smile, and leaned back against the edge of a paragraph. "They highlight the fact that *STAR TREK* has depicted women and minorities in positions of responsibility since the 1960s."

"They were particularly impressed by *STAR TREK*'s courage in introducing a character of Middle Eastern descent in the early 1990s," Bashir picked up as he used a hyphen to boost himself onto the second page. "If you think about it, that was as progressive as casting a Russian as part of the *Enterprise*'s crew back in the 1960s."

Dax took the hand he offered her and stepped across to join him as she passed her tricorder over the new words piling up below them. "According to this, L. A. Graf says that their own optimistic views of the future were strongly influenced by watching *STAR TREK*. They hope that the fact that *STAR TREK* has remained so popular through the decades means that people haven't given up hope that the world can be a better place in the future."

"But that's all about a TV series." Kira took the low route through a subversive comment and came in near the bottom of the page, at the bottom line of their discussion. "How does that relate to writing novels? All this black and white is so . . . so . . ." She pawed through the words close at hand, looking for something appropriate, until Bashir suggested, "One-dimensional?"

"Precisely!"

"Well, actually, that's not true." Frowning at her in disapproval, O'Brien lifted the previous comment out of Kira's hands and fitted it neatly back into place. "Written *STAR TREK* fiction can go places the television and movies can't. There's no special-effects budget, no one-hour time limit. *STAR TREK* novels can blow up entire planets, create enormous space battles, and introduce complicated and bizarre alien societies without worrying about makeup restrictions."

"Besides . . ." Bashir crouched beside Dax to give Sisko a hand across the page break, tearing the sleeve of his uniform on the underside of a quotation. "I like having thoughts as well as actions. For example—" He planted his hands on his hips and looked around the page. "—right now, I'm thinking that Odo really should be here. L. A. Graf always gives him the funniest lines, after all."

Just then, the constable's name ran into a glossy blob and dripped down the available white space. As he recongealed into his former self, Odo remarked dryly, "I am here, Doctor. I was just blending with the native inhabitants of this place in an effort to find some means of escape." He looked smugly at the humanoids surrounding him. "Which I did."

"Did you find a secret passage?" O'Brien asked eagerly.

"Or find a phaser so we can blast our way out?" Kira threw in.

"Whatever it is," Dax sighed, closing her tricorder, "I hope it's quick. I'm getting hungry."

Bashir tossed her a grin from behind a line of dialogue. "And I'd hate to have to eat my words."

This time it was Sisko who silenced the doctor with a scowl and a brandished exclamation point. "Would you all just let the constable tell us?"

"There's no need now, Captain." Odo peered at the widening scene break beneath his feet, and the two ominous words quickly closing on them from below. "I'm afraid we're already almost there."

"Really?" Sisko followed the constable's gaze. "How will we know when we've reached it?"

"We'll know. . . . Here it comes. . . ."

THE END

L A Graf

Julia Karen Rose

Eklar Cercone

302

Dafydd ab Hugh—not a pseudonym, really!—is the author of *Star Trek: Deep Space Nine #5: Fallen Heroes* (the one where everybody dies), *Star Trek: The Next Generation #33: Balance of Power* (where there's a big auction and nobody dies), and *INVASION! Book Four: The Final Fury* (the one you've just finished reading); he also cowrote all four *Doom* books, turning the bloodthirsty computer game phenomenon into an award-winning literary event (Green Slime Award from BuboniCon for "most awful novel of 1995"). But he has a life outside media series books, you know. I mean, like, he's also written many other books, including two (2) fantasies (*Heroing* and *Warriorwards*), two SFs masquerading as fantasies (*Arthur War Lord* and *Far Beyond the Wave*), three non-SF young-adult thrillers about floods and teen serial killers (*Swept Away, Swept Away II: The Mountain,* and *Swept Away III: The Pit*) (you find them in the YA section of your bookstore), and, of course, a hard SF book with rivets, *The Pandora Point* (in press). The dude usually writes a book a week in between hanging out on GEnie, arguing with weenies.

STAR TREK: Shaken, but Not Stirred (and with a Twist)

So, it's not like thirty years ago, dude; and there's like, you know, a dozen sci-fi shows on the tube now—rilly. (Forgive him, Caesar; for he is a Southern Californian and thinks the customs and traditions of his native speech are laws of English.) There are or were paranoid detective shows about alien conspiracies, silly shows about Space Marines who can't even get a haircut, shows about humans fleeing (a) cyborgs, (b) aliens, (c) the remnants of our own evil culture; there are or were shows about alien cops, alien pops, and pets from a peculiar planet; there are or were so many time-travel shows that you haven't time to watch them; there are or were—dude, I don't have the patience, man. You know the list; you probably watched them all . . . I did—some only once.

But none invaded the American psyche as *STAR TREK* did—the sometimes campy, sometimes brilliant chronicle of Kirk and Spock and the crochety, old dude who was a doctor, not an antediluvian ark-builder. So, like, why not? Why didn't *Space: $19.99* or *Space: Behind and Between* take off and grab America by the—ah—by the lapels and shake us into submission?

I can't tell you for certain; I'm not Howard Rosenberg, and nobody pays me three hundred Gs a year (or, these days, should I like say three hundred *K?*) to tell you why TV shows are cool or suck. But one thing even I notice: of all that litany of sci-fi shows, past and present, even marching off into the distant future . . . *only one* showed us a human race driven to explore space *by our natures,* not our failures.

In *STAR TREK*, we *weren't* chased away from Earth by metallic cyborgs with red dots in the middle of their foreheads; we *weren't* blown out of orbit, riding our own moon, by the explosion of a backyard barbecue; we *didn't* get lost in the starry deep; we *weren't* invaded; we *didn't* have to take in a refugee alien population; we *didn't* stubbornly rebuild a space station that big, bad aliens had destroyed four previous times.

Earth *wasn't* destroyed to make way for a hyperspace bypass, the empire *didn't* strike back, we *didn't* become unstuck in time, and bug-eyed monsters *haven't* infiltrated the FBI. In *STAR TREK*, we set out deliberately to explore the galaxy—you know, like the whole strange new worlds, new life, and new civilizations rap, dude.

Don't misunderstand: a lot of the other sci-fi shows were cool; they didn't all suck. In fact, I enjoyed watching most of them. Well . . . let's say some of them. But only *STAR TREK* actually embedded itself into American culture, making the *Starship Enterprise* as instantly recognizable as the dude with the red cape and the big, red S (or the yellow dude with spiky hair and a skateboard). And (coincidence?) only *STAR TREK* was about humans with a future— humans needing to reach out to the stars, not because Earth was closed to us, but because it's in our natures to demand to know what's over the next mountain range, what's across the ocean, what's past the last planet in the solar system . . . we're monkey-boys, all of us, and we're driven by a mechanism so deep it must be evolutionary to monkey around with stuff we find.

I don't know why no other show has tried to tap into the potential of the human need for exploration, excitement, and (as Freeman Dyson says) "disturbing the universe." Maybe the rest of TV Land thinks that theme is already "owned" by *STAR TREK;* or worse . . . maybe the guys who produce shows where the human race is on its last legs really, honest-to-God, believe humans—let's be honest, Americans—don't even have a future . . . and don't *deserve* one.

If they really think that, then they should make depressing police procedurals or produce a gaudy talk show, with its endless parade of whining weirdos for whom America is dead. If a person has no vision or hope for the future or doesn't believe in the greatness of the human race; if a person can't see any damned good coming from science and technology; if he thinks There Are Some Things Man Was Not Meant to Know—then he has no damned business calling himself a *science-fiction* writer. Stay outta my field, you sniveling creeps!

I'll just take Kirk and Picard, Janeway and especially Sisko instead; they've read their Heinlein and Asimov— they know there's a brave new universe out there, full of such people as . . . as *STAR TREK* is made of. Remember Bob Browning: "A man's reach should exceed his grasp." Is there any other show where men and women constantly reach far out past yesterday's grasp? Not even, dude. So let's, like, you know, give *STAR TREK* credit for being—in that sense—the only *real* science-fiction show that's ever been on TV.

Thanks, team

A Word from the Editor

First of all, a hearty thanks to all our writers: Diane Carey and her writing partner and husband Greg Brodeur, who took a small notion and turned it into *INVASION!*; Dean Wesley Smith and Kristine Kathryn Rusch, who took many frantic 7:00 A.M. (Pacific Time) phone calls; Julia Ecklar and Karen Rose Cercone, otherwise known as L. A. Graf, who took their normally excellent work to a higher (and longer!) plane for this series; and Dafydd ab Hugh, for constant good humor under stress and for extraordinary professionalism.

But a project the size and complexity of *INVASION!* would be impossible without tremendous effort from a number of people whose names didn't make it to the book covers. I would like to thank Paula Block of Viacom Consumer Products for helping to develop this series, and for pulling double duty with Thom Parham in the final stages; Terry McGarry for her exemplary copyediting; Carol Greenburg and Terry Erdmann for sharp-eyed continuity editing; Kathleen Stahl, Penny Haynes, Donna O'Neill, and Joann Foster of Pocket for working the magic that makes a manuscript into a real, honest-to-God book; Keith Birdsong for a top-notch painting that made a great poster and four top-notch covers; Matt Galemmo for designing said poster and covers; Greg Cox for the great cover copy; Scott Shannon for his active support throughout this project; John Perrella for Xeroxing above and beyond the call of duty; Tyya Turner for keeping track of it all; and Kevin Ryan for saying, "Cool idea! Go for it!"

Thanks, guys!